all that we are together

ALICE KELLEN

sourcebooks
casablanca

Originally published as *Todo lo que somos juntos*, © Alice Kellen, 2019 (represented by
Editabundo for Spanish language and c/o Planeta Book & Film Rights for worldwide
translation and audiovisual rights). Translated from Spanish by A. Nathan West.

The characters and events portrayed in this book are fictitious or
are used fictitiously. Any similarity to real persons, living or dead,
is purely coincidental and not intended by the author.

All brand names and product names used in this book are trademarks,
registered trademarks, or trade names of their respective holders. Sourcebooks
is not associated with any product or vendor in this book.

Published by Sourcebooks Casablanca, an imprint of Sourcebooks
P.O. Box 4410, Naperville, Illinois 60567-4410
(630) 961-3900
sourcebooks.com

Originally published as *Todo lo que somos juntos* in 2019 in Spain
by Editorial Planeta, an imprint of Grupo Planeta.

Cataloging-in-Publication Data is on file with the Library of Congress.

Printed and bound in the United States of America.
WOZ 10 9 8 7 6 5 4 3 2 1

For Elena, Dunia, and Lorena,
Thank you for accompanying me on this voyage.

Todo el mundo lo sabe:
cuando te rompen el corazón en mil pedazos y te
agachas a recogerlos,
solo hay novecientos noventa y nueve trozos.

Chris Pueyo,
Aquí dentro siempre llueve

Everyone knows it:
When your heart gets broken into a thousand pieces
And you crouch down to pick them up,
There's only nine hundred and ninety-nine of them there.

Chris Pueyo,
Here Inside It's Always Raining

PROLOGUE

IT SCARED ME THAT THE line between hate and love was so fine, so slender that you could jump straight from one extreme to the other. And I loved him... I loved him in my solar plexus, with my eyes, my heart. My entire body reacted when he was near. But another part of me hated him. I hated him with my memories, with words never uttered, with scorn, and was incapable of opening my arms and offering him forgiveness, however much I wanted to do so. When I looked at him, I saw black, red, throbbing purple: emotions welling over. And feeling something so chaotic for him hurt me, because Axel was a part of me. He always would be. Despite everything.

November

—

(SPRING, AUSTRALIA)

1

Leah

MY EYES WERE STILL CLOSED when I felt his lips sliding down the curve of my shoulder, before they traveled further down and left a trail of kisses next to my belly button, sweet kisses, delicate, the kind that make you quiver. I smiled. Then my smile disappeared when I felt his hot breath on my ribs. Close to him. Close to the words Axel had once traced out with his fingers on my skin, that *Let it be* that I got tattooed there afterward.

I shifted, ill at ease, then opened my eyes. I put a hand on his cheek and tugged until his mouth met mine, and a feeling of calm swept over me. We took off our clothes in the silence of that still and sunny morning, a Saturday just like any other. I held him as he slid inside me. Slow. Deep. Easy. I arched my back when I needed more, one last hard, intense thrust. But that didn't give me what I needed. I wedged a hand between us and stroked myself with my fingers. We came at the same time. I was panting. He was moaning my name.

He flopped to one side, and I stayed there looking at the smooth white ceiling of his room. It wasn't long before I sat up in his bed and he grabbed my wrist.

"You're going already?" His voice was soft.

"Yeah. I've got stuff to do."

I got up and walked barefoot to the chair where I'd thrown my clothes the night before. From between the sheets, hands folded behind his head, Landon watched me getting dressed. I adjusted the thin belt of my skirt, then threw my tank top over my head. I slung the bag my brother had given me for Christmas over my shoulder and pulled my hair back in a ponytail on my way out the door.

"Hey, wait. Don't I get a kiss before you leave?"

I walked back to the bed smiling and bent over to kiss him. He tenderly stroked my cheek, then sighed with satisfaction.

"Will I see you tonight?" he asked.

"I can't; I'll be in the studio until late."

"But it's Saturday. Come on, Leah."

"Sorry. How about dinner tomorrow?"

"Okay."

"I'll call you," I said.

I walked down the stairs beneath the warm gray morning sky. I took my headphones out of my backpack, grabbed a lollipop, and stuck it in my mouth. I ran through the crosswalk just before the light turned red and cut through a park full of flowers on the way to my studio.

Well, not really my studio. Not exactly. Not totally.

I had worked hard all through college to get a scholarship that would allow me to have a little space for myself. And this was it.

When I stepped in, the scent of paint permeated everything. I dropped my junk in a plush armchair and grabbed the smock hanging on the back of the door. I was knotting it as I walked over to the painting overlooking that old attic space.

I shook as I observed the delicate outlines of the waves, the splatter of foam, and the iridescent sunlight that seemed to radiate from the canvas. I grabbed the wood handle of my palette knife and mixed colors as I went on glancing from the corner of my eye at that canvas that seemed in some eerie way to be challenging me. I picked up a brush and felt my hand shaking as my memories crashed down. There was a trembling in my stomach as I remembered the night I had to come running because I needed right then to paint that stretch of beach I knew so well, even if it had been three years since I'd set foot there...

Three years without that bit of sea, so different from all the others.

Three years in which everything had changed.

Three years without seeing him. Three years without Axel.

2

Axel

I GLIDED DOWN THE WALL of the wave beneath the faint light of dawn, then dropped into the water, closing my eyes while I sank and the sounds of the outer world turned distant. I rose upward when the lack of air got to be too much for me. I struggled to hold on to my surfboard and took a deep breath. Once, twice, over and over, and no matter how many times I inhaled, nothing filled me up inside. I stayed there, floating in the solitude of my sea, contemplating the traces of foam and speckled light shining between the waves while I asked myself when I'd ever be able to breathe again.

3

Leah

I'D BEEN WORKING NONSTOP ALL week. Sometimes I got scared when I realized what I was doing was only work; it was a need, or a mix of work and need. Painting was the motor of my life, the reason I'd been able to stay standing, strong, full of material that begged to be dredged up and expressed. I remembered the day Axel asked me how I did it, and I answered that I didn't know; I just did it. If he'd asked me that before...I wouldn't have given him the same answer. I'd have confessed that it was my escape valve. That what I didn't know how to express in words, I expressed in colors, forms, and textures. That this was mine, all mine, and mine alone, in a way nothing else in the world was.

If it hadn't been my birthday, I would have stayed in my little attic until the wee hours of the morning, the way I often did on weekends, but my friends from school were determined to throw me a party, and I couldn't refuse. I got dressed and remembered Blair calling a few hours earlier to congratulate me and let me know that her and Kevin's baby was going to be a boy. It was the best gift I could have gotten that day.

I went up to the mirror and braided my hair. It was so long now that I almost always kept it tied back. I'd been thinking over and over about cutting it, but the way it hung down reminded me of the days when I used to walk barefoot and I lived in a house far away from the rest of the world, not worrying about whether or not I needed to take care of it. In that way, too, I had changed. I dressed more discreetly. I tried to control myself when I felt some impulse taking hold, because I'd learned such stimuli didn't always take you down the right road. I was working on being more balanced, thinking before leaping, and I took time to think about consequences.

The phone rang again. My heart skipped a beat the way it always did when I saw that name on the screen. Georgia Nguyen. Axel's mother. I took a deep breath before picking up.

"Happy birthday, honey!" she exclaimed. "Twenty-three years old. I can't believe how fast time passes, it seems like just yesterday that I was holding you in my arms and walking you around the yard to try and get you to stop crying."

I sat on the edge of the bed and smiled.

"Thanks for calling. How are you?"

"We're at the gate at the airport, waiting to catch a flight." She started laughing like a girl. Apparently her husband was tickling her to try and get the phone away from her. "Don't be a pain, Daniel; I'll pass her to you now! So what I was saying, honey, is that we're in San Francisco, and in an hour our flight leaves for Punta Cana."

"That's some trip. I'm jealous!"

"I'll call you in a few days so we can talk longer without interruptions."

"No worries. Put Daniel on."

"Happy birthday, Leah!" he shouted. "You going out with friends to celebrate? If so, enjoy."

"Thanks, Daniel. I'll try."

I hung up and went on looking at the screen with nostalgia for a few seconds, thinking of all the congratulations I'd received that day...and all the ones I hadn't.

It was dumb. One of those things that catches you off guard now and then because your memories of people are so closely linked to details that seem like nothing and then turn out to be everything. Axel had always been such an important presence on my birthday, the one person I really wanted to see and celebrate that day with, the one who brought me gifts I liked and who showed up in my wishes as I was blowing out the candles when I was still just a little girl.

It felt like an eternity ago.

I looked back at my phone. I don't know what I was waiting for, but it didn't ring.

I took a deep breath, got up, and walked to the long mirror still leaning against the wall in the very same place Oliver had put it three years before, when I bought it on impulse at a shop close to my dorm.

Distracted, I toyed with the end of my braid as I stared at my reflection. "You'll be all right," I repeated to myself, more out of habit than anything else. "You will."

Night had fallen by the time I was on my way to the restaurant where I was supposed to meet everyone. I'd only taken a couple of steps when he reappeared.

"What are you doing here?" I laughed.

"I wanted to go with you." Landon handed me the rose he was holding, then gave me a slow kiss.

I looked at the flower when he pulled away, and touched the scarlet petals. I brought it to my nose to sniff while we walked.

"Tell me about your day. Did you get a lot done?"

"Yeah, I'm about to finish a painting..." I gulped as I recalled that stretch of sea that was so mine, so ours, and I shook my head. "I don't want to bore you with it. Tell me about you."

Landon described his week, how hard he was working on the capstone project for his business degree, how bad he'd wanted to see me those past three days when we hadn't managed to find an opening, how good I looked that night...

We walked slower once we caught a glimpse of the restaurant.

"I hope you like your parties without surprises," he joked, and then he turned serious. "Everyone's here. Sometimes, when you get all shut up inside yourself, locked away in that attic, I worry about you, Leah. I want you to enjoy tonight."

His words made me melt, and I hugged him tight.

I promised I would.

A smile spread across my face as I stepped over the threshold to the restaurant and saw our friends getting up from the table in the back to sing "Happy Birthday." People pinched me and kissed my cheek, and then I sat down with them. Almost everyone who was part of my life in Brisbane was there: my classmates, but especially Morgan and Lucy, the girls I met my first month in the dorm and hadn't separated from since. They were the first ones to hand me a present.

I unwrapped it carefully, without my customary impatience, picking at the tape with a fingernail and folding the paper before thanking them after seeing the drawing materials they knew I needed.

"You're the best, you shouldn't have done this…"

"Don't start crying!" Morgan shouted.

"I wasn't going to…"

"We know you," Lucy cut me off.

I laughed when I saw her face.

"Fine, no tears, just fun!" I looked over at Landon, who was grinning with satisfaction and winked at me from the other end of the table.

When the party was over, it was late and I'd drunk way too much, especially knowing my brother, Oliver, was coming to see me the next day. But I didn't care. Because under the lights of the bar where we landed for drinks, I felt good, happy, surrounded by Landon's arms and my friends' laughter. I stopped thinking about the people who weren't there, about Axel's deep voice congratulating me and the gift he'd given me that year in a parallel reality where the two of us still were, somehow, the same people who believed they'd never be apart.

It had taken time to understand it, but…life went on. Axel hadn't been my destiny, just the beginning of a stretch of the path we walked together, holding hands until he decided to take a detour.

I lay down drunk in bed, and the room seemed to spin around me. I hugged my pillow. There were times when I barely thought of Axel, hung up on my classes, the hours I passed in the attic, the times I was with Landon or the girls. But he always came back. Him. The feeling that I still had him under my skin was bothering me more and more. The memories started to glow in moments I least expected: when I saw a stranger holding his cigarette between his thumb and index finger, when I smelled tea, when I heard a certain song, saw some silly gesture…anything, really.

I remembered what I was keeping in the top drawer of my nightstand, but I resisted opening it and picking up that object purchased in a flea market not long after I got to Brisbane.

I closed my eyes tight. Everything was still spinning.

I asked myself what he was doing in that instant…

4

Axel

I TOOK ONE LAST LOOK at the gallery before leaving and going home. I walked back, because I was never in a rush. No one was waiting for me.

But that day, I was wrong.

Oliver was sitting on the steps in front of the door.

For some reason, it hit me just as hard as it had the first time I saw him there four months before. Because I wasn't expecting him, obviously, and because...fuck, because I could hardly breathe when it hit me how much I'd missed him during those years when he was away.

So just like that, Oliver showed back up in my life the same way he'd disappeared.

I was paralyzed, and it took a few seconds to convince myself he was real, but he was, and he hadn't changed a bit. He shot me a nervous glance, and when I opened the door and asked him to come in, he didn't reply; he just followed behind me. He grabbed the beer I passed him, we went out on the porch, and we smoked a cigarette in silence. I don't know how long we were there, hours maybe, or maybe just twenty minutes. I was so lost in thought that I didn't know. All I can say is when he got up, he hugged me with anger and love at the same time, then left without saying goodbye.

It happened a couple more times, him showing up at my house by surprise. I knew he'd be coming when he went to visit his sister in Brisbane; he always tried to see my family for a bit on his way. For three years, we didn't see each other. He had kept up that routine but hadn't once bothered to come say hi. Then, eventually, something or other changed his mind, and one day there he was at my door. I didn't ask why. Nor did we ever talk about Leah. We had a tacit agreement, and there was no need to discuss the ground rules. We knew them by heart. We started to be friends again. But the friendship was...different, because when you break something and put it back together, it's never perfect. You always see cracks and rough edges that weren't there before.

"I didn't know you were coming," I said the fourth time he showed up.

"Me neither." He followed me inside. "Actually, I didn't have any days off, but I was able to make a last-minute change..."

For Leah's birthday... Fuck. I closed my eyes.

"You want a beer?" I interrupted.

"Yeah. A cold one. It's burning up outside."

"Maybe it's your outfit."

I shook my head as I took another look at his dark pants and his button-down shirt. Even rolling up the sleeves gave him little relief.

"Oliver, is everything okay?" We went out on the porch.

"Yeah. What about your gallery?"

"No complaints. It's fun. Different."

Just over a year ago, I'd started working at that little gallery in Byron Bay where, ages back, I'd thought I'd exhibit my own work. One that had once held a promise. But that wasn't why I took the job; it was rather because...I couldn't find a reason to say no. I didn't have much else to do. I was bored. Sometimes the silence was all too deafening. And I thought it would do me good to pass through there now and then, without a fixed schedule.

I was right to do so. It was one of the few absolutely right decisions I'd made in recent memory. I was still illustrating, but I could now be choosier with the jobs I accepted.

The fundamental thing a gallery needs to work is a clear and well-thought-out project. I had decided to come up with one, to decide what kind of art and artists we were going to promote, and that was what kept the place running. The owner, Hans, was a businessman, and he dropped in only occasionally, letting me be free to do as I wished. And I had the constant support of Sam, who worked there full-time.

The first months were hard, but at the end, we had a more defined, uniform, and coherent catalog thanks to the links we'd cemented with our artists. I focused on finding them and convincing them to join our team, encouraging them to hold their first exhibitions in Byron Bay. After that, Sam would bring them into the fold. She was good at what gallerists call "the poetry of the job." A sweet woman with infinite patience, she was a mother of three children and could put up with any artist's oversized ego—and that was something I wasn't cut out for. Sam saw magic in watching the young promises we had bet on grow, being in regular contact with them, and, especially, visiting them at their studios.

But I had a hard time giving it my all. There was something that held me back.

"How many artists do you have on the roster now?" Oliver was watching me with curiosity while he scratched at one edge of the label on his beer.

"Me?" I raised my eyebrows. "None."

"You know what I mean."

"Sam's the one who *has* the artists. I just find them and get them to the gallery."

We stopped talking as the sun descended over the horizon. Having Oliver back in my life gave me a false sensation of normalcy. But actually, everything was different. Or maybe I was different. I'd changed a lot since our college days, when we were inseparable. He was still one of the people I treasured most, but it felt as if we'd been slowly piling up bricks until finally there was an entire wall between us. And the worst part was, even though we were talking through that wall, which had been the case even before I ever got with his sister, I was certain he was there, nodding and listening, but failing to understand. Not because he didn't want to, but because he couldn't. And I hated knowing that incomprehension was in the air between us when we talked, because it reminded me of the only person who'd ever truly seen me as I was, every layer of me, every piece: a girl who tasted like strawberries, a girl I missed so much...

5

Leah

I GOT NERVOUS WHEN PROFESSOR Martin called me after class to set up a tutoring session. While I was waiting outside, I kept chewing on the nail of my little finger. She opened the door to her office a minute after the agreed-upon time and smiled at me. That relaxed me a little. I had been studying so hard, and I was terrified that I'd made some mistake on my last exam, screwed up the class average, or somehow disappointed someone.

She returned to her seat behind her desk while I settled into the chair across from her. I bit my lip to try and keep everything in, but it was pointless.

"What did I do?" I blurted out.

I hated that part of myself. The impulsive part. The one that kept me from managing my emotions, controlling them, guiding them. That slightly dark side of me that one random night made me strip naked in front of *him* and ask him why he'd never paid attention to me. For some reason, that memory cropped up a lot.

"You didn't do anything, Leah. Or rather, you did, but something good." She opened a folder that was on the desk and took out some photos—photos of my work. "I recommended you for an exhibition that will take place in Red Hill in a month. I think you'd be the perfect candidate. You exactly fit the profile they're looking for."

"Are you serious?" I blinked to keep from crying.

"It's a big opportunity. And you deserve it."

"I, uh…I don't know what to say, Professor Martin."

"*Thanks* will do. It'll just be three pieces, but that's fine; the exhibit is going to attract all kinds of visitors. What do you say?"

"I'm so excited I could shout!"

Professor Martin started laughing. She told me the details, and I thanked her a hundred times while I stood up and grabbed my bag. When I walked outside, I looked up at the sky and took a deep breath. The wind was warm and pleasant. I thought about my parents, how proud they'd have been, how much I wished I could share this success with them… Then I dug through all the junk in the inside pocket of my bag to find my phone and look for Oliver's number. I waited impatiently until he picked up on the fifth ring.

"Are you sitting down?" I asked, excited.

"Yeah. Well, lying down. In bed. Does that work?"

"Dammit! Don't tell me you're with Bega?"

"Whatever. Spit it out."

"I got picked… I'm going to be in an exhibit…" I drew a breath. "It's just three pieces, but still…"

"Jesus, Leah." I knew my brother was thrilled as those seconds of silence passed. I heard his steps as he got out of bed and caught his breath. "You can't imagine how proud I am of you. Congratulations, pixie."

"It's all thanks to you…" I whispered.

He said it wasn't, but we both knew I was telling the truth.

When everything fell apart three years ago, I was mad at him for weeks, and would hardly speak a word to him. That was early on, before I understood it wasn't his fault. Oliver wasn't the one who'd made that fateful decision. Oliver wasn't the one who fucked it all up. Oliver didn't choose that path for me.

But I wasn't willing to see that back then. I didn't want to admit that Axel lost it whenever things got too heavy for him; that whenever complications arose, he would turn away, ignoring all the things he couldn't control; that he could never give himself fully to anyone or anything.

Maybe it was my fault for idealizing him.

Axel wasn't ideal. As he had shown me, he had his ugly side, a side you wanted to scratch and rub away. And he had his gray areas. Virtues that could turn into vices in the right circumstances. Things that were bright and clear, but that shadowed over with the passage of time: his dreams, his courage that turned to cowardice.

I shook my head and turned right around a corner.

I rang the doorbell. Landon buzzed me in.

By the time I was upstairs, he was waiting for me, leaning on the doorframe. His hair was uncombed and his sleeves rolled up. He was handsome, I thought, and I smiled before leaping at him and hugging him tight.

"Why the enthusiasm?" he asked with a laugh.

"I'm going to have three pieces in an exhibit!" I shouted.

"Damn, babe, you can't imagine how happy I am…"

I tucked my face against his neck, swallowed, and frowned at the sound of that word I hated hearing and had told him over and over never to use.

Babe... I still couldn't help hearing it in Axel's voice. With lust. With love.

I squeezed Landon tighter so I would stop thinking about anything but the good news. I kissed him on the neck and then climbed upward till I reached his soft lips. I wrapped my legs around his waist, and he closed the door. He carried me across his apartment and dropped me on the bed. I watched him standing there in front of me unbuttoning his shirt.

"Back in a sec," he said and walked to the kitchen. I heard noises, and he returned with two beers in hand. "I thought I had a bottle of champagne, but no luck. So this'll have to do."

"It's perfect." I grabbed the opener and popped the caps.

"To you." We clinked the beers audibly. "To your dreams."

"And to us," I added.

Landon looked at me gratefully before taking a sip and finally removing his shirt. He lay down beside me in bed and drew me toward him. He kissed me. He calmed me. He filled me inside. My legs got tangled with his, and I thought to myself that no one could be better.

6

Leah

I MET LANDON NOT LONG after I moved to Brisbane.

I'd agreed to go out for a while with Morgan and Lucy after having a terrible day, the kind I kept having those first few months, that confronted me with memories too difficult to bear. I got it together enough to wash my face—because my eyes were swollen from so much crying—put on a dress that had been hanging unused in the closet, and wound up in a bar with them having drinks.

At some point in the evening, we started dancing. The first song was a slow one, and I walked off, allegedly for another drink, but really what I wanted was to get away from them and be by myself. Sitting on a barstool, I watched them moving in time to the music, smiling and kissing and whispering in each other's ears.

"You paint?" a guy said.

"How do you know?" My brow furrowed.

"Your nails," he answered, sitting on the stool beside me and trying to catch the bartender's eye. He had dark brown hair, almond eyes, and a contagious smile. "What exactly do you paint?"

"I don't know. Depends," I said softly.

"Got it. You're one of those mysterious girls…"

"I'm not, I promise." I smiled. His deduction was amusing. I was actually the opposite: all too transparent. "It's just… I had a bad day."

"I hear you. Let's start over. My name's Landon Harris."

He stretched out his hand. I shook it.

"Leah Jones. A pleasure."

We talked the whole night through. I don't know what time it was when I'd finally drunk enough to decide it was a good idea to spill my heart to a complete stranger. I told him hurriedly about my parents' death, Axel, how hard the first months in Brisbane had been…everything.

Landon was one of those people who exude confidence. He listened attentively, interrupted me when necessary, and shared details of his life: how demanding his parents were, how he loved poetry, how he went climbing every chance he got.

When my friends wanted to leave, I told them I was going to stay a little longer with Landon. He said he'd walk me back to the dorm. As we wandered through the streets and our voices broke the silence of the night, I realized it had been a long time since I'd felt so calm. When we reached the door, he came close, a little insecure, planted one hand on the wall, and gave me a kiss. It was nice. Not awkward.

He pulled back and looked at me under the orange light of the streetlamps.

"You're still in love with him."

It wasn't a question, just an affirmation, and I nodded and tried not to burst into tears, because I wished it wasn't true, I wished my heart was blank and I could get to know a guy as charming as Landon.

After that day, he became one of my best friends. In the years since, I had met many other guys, and he had a couple of girlfriends who turned out to be different from what he'd expected. I stuck to one-night stands while looking for something I never found. I soon learned the difference between fucking and making love, between truly wanting someone and just lusting for them. There was a major difference, and I wasn't yet ready to handle the former.

One winter morning, I rang his doorbell, almost in tears, with my heart pounding against my ribs. Landon opened right up.

"What is it?" he asked, closing the door behind us.

Anxiety. I knew the symptoms well.

"I don't think I can feel anything, Landon. I think...I think..."

I couldn't speak. He hugged me, and I pressed my head into his chest, suppressing a sob. It was a bad time. I was terrified of being empty again, of going numb. Of giving up painting... The mere possibility made a knot form in my throat. With every day that passed, I could feel my emotions withering and found myself getting up every day just because I had to do it. Kisses from a stranger no longer satisfied me, nor did the memories I held on to when I had to paint, when I had to let them out.

"Take it easy, Leah." Landon stroked my back.

I shivered as his hand moved up and down. Then I stopped thinking and let my impulses carry me away. I breathed against his cheek, quivering from fear, noticing how good he smelled, how soft his skin was...

Our lips met as if it was natural. Landon pulled me into him, and we kissed for what seemed like an eternity, unrushed, just enjoying it. When we started taking our clothes off, I felt safe, and as we landed on the mattress in his bedroom, a sensation of comfort enveloped me. When I felt him move inside me, I felt loved. And it had been a long time since I'd felt that, so I grabbed on to him: his back, his friendship, his world, because holding him close was serenity and the calm after the storm.

A week later, my brother came to visit. We met in a simple café that made a delicious chicken sandwich. We ordered two of them plus two sodas, and I noticed him rubbing his neck and sighing.

"Is something up?" I asked, nervous.

"I think I need to tell you something."

"Spit it out. What?"

"I saw Axel."

My stomach quivered when I heard his name. I wish I could say I hadn't reacted, that I was indifferent to those four letters, I wish…

"Why are you telling me this?"

"It's the right thing to do, Leah. I don't want us to ever lie to each other. I wasn't planning to do it, but after I saw the Nguyens the other day, I just drove to his house without even thinking about it. Or no. I did think about it. Because since I got engaged to Bega, I can't stop thinking about it, about who should be my best man, and I…goddammit. They were as close to us as our own parents were, Leah."

"Let it go, Oliver. It's fine."

He looked at me with gratitude. I understood. I really did.

I knew how important Axel had been for my brother, and there was no way I would stand between them if there was still something left for them to salvage... But that didn't mean it hurt any less. It hurt throughout our meal, even though we never mentioned it again. And it hurt later as I was walking down the street. The pain only faded when I reached Landon's apartment and he took me in his arms. Safety. Free from everything else.

Since that time, we had turned into something more.

I wasn't sure what that *more* meant, and I didn't feel ready to look too deeply into it. We weren't a couple, but we weren't just friends either. Landon tried several times to get me to talk about it, but I asked him for time.

7

Axel

A LIGHT RAIN WAS FALLING when she appeared.

I snuffed out my cigarette and crouched in front of her. She was skinny, and she was struggling to breathe. I hadn't seen her for weeks. She laid on the porch, and I stroked her back gently. She whimpered, as if it hurt.

"What is it, pretty girl?"

The cat's eyes were half-closed.

I don't know how or why, but I understood her.

I understood she'd come to die with me, to spend the last minutes of her life in the shelter of my arms. My eyes stung when I thought of loneliness and how raw it can sometimes be. I sat on the ground, leaning back against one of the wooden posts, and stretched her out across my lap. I stroked her slowly, calming her, accompanying her until her breathing became less and less audible, as if she were falling asleep.

That's what I wanted to think. That her death was just a tranquil sleep.

I stayed there a while, watching it rain, staring at the dusky

sky on that warm evening. I got up when there was nothing left of the sun but glimmers. I went inside and looked in the closet with the tools until I found a small shovel.

I dug and dug, making a far deeper hole than necessary. For some reason, I couldn't stop myself until morning. I was covered in mud. I buried her there with a knot in my throat, then I filled the dirt back in.

I went back inside, got in the shower, and closed my eyes.

I put a hand on my chest.

I still couldn't breathe.

8

Axel

"YOU LOOK ROUGH," JUSTIN SAID, concerned.

"I didn't sleep much. My cat decided she'd rather die with me than do it alone."

"It's funny that the first time you call her yours is now when she's no longer here," my brother said as he dried a couple of glasses.

I sighed, finished the tea I'd ordered, and waved as I left the café. I walked to the gallery and killed time looking at the paintings on the wall and thinking about the secrets hidden behind each brushstroke, about how each painting represented thoughts, emotions, something human left behind on canvas for eternity. I asked myself why I'd never been able to do that. To make something. To paint. To leave parts of myself on the canvas.

"You're early today." Sam smiled at me.

"Let me help you." I grabbed two bags from her hands and accompanied her to her office.

Sam's cheeks were glowing. I glanced around the corner where she worked, which was full of more...*amateur* work. I smiled when I saw a new drawing she'd hung close to the others, done in crayon, of five people, with a child's irregular scrawl reading, *For the best mom in the world.*

"That one's got a future," I joked, pointing at it.

"I'd be happy if they'd just let me sleep one night for more than two seconds in a row."

"You should have thought about that before you decided not to use a rubber."

"Axel!" She threw a pen at me and laughed.

"Isn't that workplace harassment?" I raised an eyebrow.

"You're a lost cause. Let's focus. Tomorrow I'm meeting Will Higgins around ten for a studio visit. He says we might be interested in some of his new work. I hope so, because the last stuff he did..." She frowned amusingly.

"Show me the photos. I want to see."

"Wouldn't it be easier if you just came along?"

"I'll pass. Walking around a studio, looking at all those pictures, dealing with him..."

Sam groaned as she pulled back her hair.

"You're the weirdest person I've met in my life."

"Have you met a lot of people?"

"More than a few. Do you even like art, honey? Or do you hate it?"

"I still haven't decided. You want to grab lunch later?"

"Sure. Let me clear a few things off my desk."

I looked over the agenda for the upcoming months, the pieces that were coming in and going out, the upcoming fairs, the ones we'd submitted work to by artists we represented. That was the best way to promote their work—apart from Hans's numerous contacts in Europe, of course.

We headed out for a bite an hour later.

Sam had the habit of telling me in detail her three children's each and every feat. One of them, the oldest, went to the same school as my nephews, and they were masters of the art of cooking up new schemes. According to Justin, the twins had inherited the *bad genes* in the family. In other words, mine.

"So when I got home, the three of them were covered in chocolate syrup, and I put them straight in the tub, clothes and all, to save time." She brought her fork to her mouth, chewed, and turned serious. "What about you, Axel? Doesn't the idea of having children tempt you? They'd be adorable, with those little eyes of yours and that eternally furrowed brow..."

"Kids? Me?" I felt a pressure in my chest.

"I said kids, not aliens or dinosaurs."

"I think that would be more likely."

Sam had more than enough maternal instinct to go around. When she passed by me, she liked to pinch my cheek or muss my hair, and whenever I had a headache, she'd take my temperature. My headaches were becoming more and more frequent. She always carried around a huge purse packed with all things useful: towelettes, mint cough drops, Kleenex, ointment for mosquito bites...

She stirred her coffee and looked at me pensively.

"You've never been in love before, Axel?"

The question caught me by surprise. Leah flashed in my head, one of the many mental photographs I had of her. The smile that filled her whole face, her penetrating gaze, the feel of her skin on my fingers...

"Yeah. A long time ago," I grunted.

"So what happened?"

I shifted uncomfortably in my seat.

"Nothing. It just couldn't be," I replied curtly.

Sam seemed to sympathize and waited without any more questions until I got up and went to pay the check. Afterward we walked silently to the gallery, both of us focused on our respective tasks. Sam knocked at my office door later, when it was almost closing time.

"Hey. I just wanted to make sure you were okay."

"Why wouldn't I be?"

"I don't know. Anyway, I'm leaving. You need anything?"

"No. Lock the door on your way out. I'm going to stay a while longer."

"Sure." She passed by me, ran her hand through my hair as though I was one of her little boys, and kissed me on the cheek, making me grumble.

I rubbed my face, reached in my drawer, and took out the reading glasses I had started to need when I was tired to continue looking over some interesting CVs Hans had sent me. It was night-time when I left. I thought about going to my brother's, because I wasn't in the mood to have dinner alone. I liked the idea of spending time with him and Emily and the kids, away from the silence. But I changed my mind and headed home.

I made a sandwich and went onto the porch to smoke. Without music. Without any desire to read. Without stars in the cloudy sky. Without her.

I should have stopped missing her by now… I should have…

December

—

(SUMMER, AUSTRALIA)

9

Leah

"COME ON, LET ME GO with you. I want to see."

Landon's adorable gaze was pushing me, but I refused. I couldn't let him into the attic, into my studio. I didn't want to, to tell the truth. The idea of him invading my space terrified me, because that place was mine alone. Somehow, I could open my heart there; I didn't have to hide anything. And there was no one I trusted enough to let them just burst in, not even my brother.

"It would be weird," I said. "You don't get it..."

"Then explain it to me again." He smiled.

"It's just...it's too personal."

"More personal than sharing a bed with someone?"

Yeah, much more, I wanted to say, but I bit my tongue.

"That's not it, Landon. It's just very *mine*, that's all."

"And I want to be a part of everything that's yours."

I felt a slight pressure in my chest. He seemed to realize he was stressing me out and took a step back before kissing me softly.

"It's fine, sorry. Can I see you later?"

"Yeah, I'll call when I'm done."

I walked to the studio in a slight daze, not even noticing all that was around me. I climbed the old staircase two steps at a time, and when I reached the attic, a sensation of tranquility filled me. The scent of paint. The canvases staring back at me. The creak of the wood floor. I put on my smock and opened the little window, the one that always got stuck before finally lurching upward.

I looked back at that patch of sea bathed in sunlight on the canvas, thinking that maybe the picture didn't do the place justice, or not just the place, but everything it meant to me, that stretch of beach where I put myself back together piece by piece before breaking apart again. Luckily, the second time it happened was different. I wasn't torn into little pieces. I just broke in two. Quick and clean: that's what Axel did to me.

I grabbed my palette and mixed colors, taking time to pick up a brush. I inhaled deeply and painted and painted until my stomach growled and I decided to go downstairs and grab one of the chicken empanadas they made at the café on the corner. Once I was back, I sat in the armchair to eat it, staring at the painting, the colors, the way the light slipped down toward the water...

Lately, I was thinking more about Axel.

Maybe it was because I was working on something that seemed like him if you could see him from every angle. The sea. Immense. Mysterious in its depths, breathtaking, transparent where it touched the shore. The strength of the waves. Its coward-ice when it licked the sand, then retreated...

Or maybe that wasn't the only reason I was remembering him. Maybe it was the exhibit too. Because at some point, when I was fourteen, or maybe when I was nineteen and fell in love with him, I started taking it for granted that he'd be by my side when I had my first success. That the first time a painting of mine was hanging on the wall with a label next to it, I'd have Axel there, smiling, proud of me, ready to say something stupid to calm my nerves.

But now that wouldn't happen...and it hurt. Not because of what we'd lived through, not because I didn't have him as my boyfriend, but because I didn't have him at all, not as a person, not as a friend. He wouldn't be there...

I set aside what was left of the empanada when the knot in my throat made it impossible to swallow another bite. I got up, grabbed the brush with my heart pounding out of my chest, every beat hard and relentless. Instead of dipping it into the pastel blue I used for the sky, I looked for a jar of something darker.

I looked at the spongy clouds I'd painted.

An hour later, I'd covered them with a stormy sky.

10

Axel

I SAW IT, AS ALWAYS, when I entered my room.

The only picture I'd painted in recent years. The one I made with Leah while I was fucking her slowly on top of the canvas, coating her skin with color, with kisses, with words now lost to oblivion. I stared at the lines, the chaotic blotches. Then I looked up in the top of the closet and sucked in a breath. I hesitated. Just as I'd hesitated many times before. I let my routine carry me, left my bedroom, and grabbed my surfboard.

11

Axel

OLIVER WAS SITTING ON THE front stairs when I arrived just before nightfall. I waved at him, and he came inside. He opened the fridge as though nothing had ever come between us and pulled out two beers.

He looked happy—over the moon.

"Let's toast!" he said.

"Sure. What's the occasion?"

"I didn't want to tell you, but then I thought…" He rubbed the back of his neck, uncomfortable. "I thought it was the right thing to do. Leah's got an exhibition this month in Red Hill. Just three pieces. But it's a huge step; her professor recommended her. And I thought…I thought you deserved to know. Because all this is thanks to you, despite everything." He reached his hand out and clinked his beer against mine.

But I didn't move. I couldn't. I couldn't…

I stood there glaring at him. Hating him. And hating myself even more. I realized I was pissed he was telling me this, stirring up so many memories all at once. Still, it would have been even worse if he hadn't told me, and with the bitterness of knowing that, I kept quiet. What did it matter? Nothing he could have said would have made me happy, and I was struggling to pretend that nothing was wrong.

"Axel..." He looked at me hesitantly.

"When?" I murmured.

"Next week."

"You going?"

"I can't; I've got work."

"I will." It wasn't a question; it wasn't a suggestion. It was a decision. A firm one. I was going, I had to, I needed to see it with my own eyes.

Oliver set his beer down on the counter.

"You can't. You think you can just show up and ruin her day? I only wanted to tell you because I was proud and I know you helped her, dammit, even with all the rest of it... I've been thinking a lot about that lately..." He trailed off, as though he didn't know how to continue.

"I don't care what you say. I'm going."

The muscles in his jaw twitched.

"Don't fuck everything up again."

My heart was racing. "I need a smoke."

I walked out onto the porch. Oliver followed me. I lit one up and took a deep drag, trying to calm down, though I knew I was far from being able to. Those words...they destabilized me. Imagining it. Her in a gallery, standing in front of her own work...

"Why?"

I didn't expect that question.

"Because I need to..." I struggled to reason like a normal person. "Because she was my life, Oliver, and I can't not be there for a moment like that. Because..." *I still love her.* I swallowed those words. "You're right. I won't fuck her night up. I won't approach her. I'll try to keep her from seeing me."

Oliver rubbed his face and exhaled.

"Jesus, Axel. I hate this. The situation. Everything."

I bit my tongue to keep from telling him what I thought, because he was still a part of my life, even if things were different now, colder, tenser.

I stubbed out my cigarette. We looked at each other. I saw the doubt, the uncertainty in his eyes. And I imagine what he saw in mine was determination, because he eventually looked away, then took a cigarette out of the pack in my hands. I realized I'd won that battle, at least. What I didn't recognize then was that this was one of the first times I ever confronted anything head-on.

12

—

Leah

I TOOK A SIP OF the day's second linden blossom tea, but it didn't have much effect, I was still nervous as hell. The opening of my exhibit was still hours away, and all I could think about were the things that could go wrong: withering criticism, looks of indifference, tripping over my own feet and falling down in the middle of the gallery...

The phone beeped. It was a reassuring message from Blair. After hearing she hadn't felt well those first few weeks of her pregnancy, I refused to let her come. Not just her, but Justin and Emily too. They'd said they could leave the twins with a neighbor and get away for a bit, but I said there was no need. I even tried to calm down Oliver after he asked his boss for another day off. She'd already let him off for my birthday. This time she didn't give in.

I thought about my parents again... If only they were here...

I took a deep breath and went to the tiny bathroom to comb my hair. I'd gotten dressed in the afternoon, not long before putting on my makeup. I went back to the bedroom, stirred the rest of my tea, and drank it down just as someone knocked at the door.

I hugged him so hard I thought I might hurt him.

"I'm so nervous!" I raised one of my hands. "Look. I'm trembling."

Landon laughed, grabbed my hand, and spun me around.

"Don't be dramatic. You look gorgeous. Everything will go great."

"You think? I feel like I'm going to puke."

"Are you kidding, or should I hold your hair back?"

"I don't know. My stomach's upset."

I grew calm as Landon talked me down, telling me stories about silly stuff his project companion did, showing up for work in his PJs or sticking a pencil up his nose because that allegedly sparked his creativity. Before I knew it, I was cracking up and it was almost time to go. I stood up slowly and looked all around for my purse. "I'll bet I'm forgetting something important."

"You always say that, and it's never anything."

"Yeah, but..." I glanced around.

"We need to go, Leah. Come on."

I nodded, still unnerved, and I stayed that way as we took the stairs outside. The gallery wasn't far. We walked in silence, holding hands, together. I knew he'd be by my side that night. Some friends would come later, too, and Linda Martin, my professor. That calmed me down a little.

The setting was intimate. It wasn't one of the city's big galleries, but it still seemed like the best place in the world to me. It had a sloping roof, a green sign, and a garnet-colored facade.

It still wasn't open to the public, so our steps echoed loudly over the wooden floor as we advanced into the first hall, where we heard voices.

Linda was already there. She smiled at me before presenting me to the head of the gallery and other people who were working on the exhibition, including several artists.

I tried to relax and accepted the glass of wine they handed me. For the next half hour, we chatted with the others and walked through the still-empty rooms where the guests would contemplate the works hanging on the walls. When we reached the corner where mine were, I shivered. I looked for Landon's hand and squeezed it in mine.

I had talked a long time with Linda about which three pictures I should choose. It wasn't easy, because sometimes I got ideas in my head and she couldn't easily grasp their importance to me. When I looked up at my pictures hung on that wall, I felt proud of myself for the first time, even as I noticed the shaking in my knees.

The first picture was done in all dark colors. A black night. A destroyed heart. Anguish. Confusion. Fear.

The second was bittersweet, with traces of light and purpose, but other muted lines, as though the canvas were consuming itself. Nostalgia.

The third was light. But real light. With its shadows. Hope.

They didn't have individual titles. The group of three was called *Love*.

I looked at Landon out of the corner of my eye and asked myself if he understood the meaning behind them. Once, when we were still just friends, I had asked him to tell me what he saw in a print I showed him, and he was incapable of seeing between the jumble of lines. I didn't blame him; I realized it couldn't have the same meaning for anyone else that it did for me. He couldn't feel those lines the same way. Differently, sure, but still.

A few visitors started strolling in. I felt calmer as the rooms filled up and the voices rose around me. My friends arrived a little later, and Landon went with them to the next room over so I could talk a while with Professor Martin.

"Two people have already asked about them."

"Really? Who could ever want...?"

"To have something by you?" she interrupted me. "Get used to the idea."

I rubbed my hands together nervously. The gallery director's assistant walked over and started chatting up the professor. I stayed between them, not really knowing what to say or do. I didn't dare try to see how the visitors would react to looking at my work. That was terrifying.

I took a deep breath. The worst was over already.

And then I sensed him. I don't know how. On my skin. In my body. In my heart. How many heartbeats does it take to recognize someone? In my case, it was six. Two where I stood there paralyzed and the world seemed suddenly to fall silent. Three more to decide to turn around, even though it terrified me. And one...just one to look into those blue eyes that would follow me for the rest of my life.

I didn't move. I couldn't.

We fell slowly into the trap of each other's eyes.

It was vertigo. Like stumbling all at once into the void.

13

Axel

I DIDN'T MEAN TO RUN into her, but I saw her as soon as I stepped into the gallery. I was breathless. It felt as if someone had just punched me in the stomach. Leah was there, her back turned. I thought of all the times I had kissed the nape of her neck before hugging her while we were making dinner in the kitchen. Or when I took her from behind on the porch. I saw that blond hair pulled back in a tight bun, with two or three strands breaking free of the hair elastic and the hairpins holding them in place.

And then, as though she could feel me, she turned around.

She did it slowly. Very slowly. I stopped in the center of the room. Her eyes met mine. We looked at each other in silence, and I felt everything around us disappear: the voices, the people, the world. I took a step forward, almost without realizing it, as if something were pulling me toward her. Then I took another. Then another. Until she was in front of me. Leah never looked away. Her gaze was defiant, dangerous, hard.

I held my breath. I had a knot in my throat. I wanted to say something, anything, dammit, but what do you say to a person who made you feel everything just before you destroyed her heart? I couldn't find the words. All I could do was look and look as if she might disappear at any moment and I needed to retain that image of her as clearly as possible in my mind. I looked at the curve of her neck. Her trembling hands. Her lips. Those lips.

Just when I found the courage to try and speak, the woman next to her turned around and grabbed Leah tightly by the arm. "Come here, I need to introduce you to some people."

She gave me one more penetrating look before taking off for the other end of the room. I was almost thankful for the interruption... I needed to pull myself together.

"Shit." Everything had gone wrong.

I walked around on edge, checking out the pictures, trying to calm myself down. I went to the next room over. There was potential under that roof, in some pieces more than in others. I concentrated on analyzing them to keep from thinking of her, of how just a few steps separated us and I had no idea what to say to her.

I stopped dead when I saw them. I didn't need to get closer to read the name on the paper and know they were Leah's. I could have recognized them anywhere. I don't know how long I stood there analyzing those three paintings, but when I felt her next to me, I shook and drew in a long breath of air.

"*Love*." I whispered the name of the composition, and it was ironic to me that the first word I spoke to her after three long years of absence was that one. "Pain. Nostalgia. Hope."

We both kept staring at the pictures.

"You're intuitive," she whispered in a voice soft, almost like a caress.

I felt a tightness in my chest and brought my hand to my heart. I blinked. I couldn't remember crying even once in my life. Sure, I'd had feelings there, just under the skin, feelings that threatened to overflow, but I'd always managed to keep them in check. That night, though, standing in front of that love that had once been ours, I cried. One tear, in silence. Not from sorrow, but from its opposite. And I told her, in a hoarse tone, "I'm proud of you, Leah."

14

—

Leah

I CLOSED MY EYES WHEN his words penetrated me, filled me, lodged inside me. That *I'm proud of you* that I hated and loved in equal parts. I had to gather all the courage I had left to dare meet eyes with him. Axel's eyes were slightly red, and I didn't know what to say. All I could think of was that I had him there in front of me, and he didn't even seem real. His presence suffused the entire room, every corner, every wall...

"Leah, here you are. I couldn't find you."

I turned toward Landon.

I think all he needed was a quick glance to realize who was standing next to me and that I needed to get out of there, because I couldn't breathe...

He stretched his hand out; I took it. And I walked away from Axel...

I didn't look back. I didn't say goodbye. I just walked, because that was what I needed: to walk, be somewhere else. I almost held my breath until the night wind brushed across my face. When the silence outside turned dense around us, Landon hugged me. I clutched him tight. He was my safety.

"You okay?" He didn't let me go.

"Let's go home." He kissed my forehead and held my hand again.

Every step we took pushed me farther away, brought me more relief. Before we rounded the next corner, I did look back over my shoulder, and I thought I saw his silhouette in the gallery door, but then I blinked, and he wasn't there, and I told myself it was better that way.

Soon, we were back in Landon's apartment.

We got into bed, and I curled up beside him. My hand strayed under his T-shirt and I covered his lips with mine. He panted, and our tongues met in a kiss that was urgent but was also much, much more. I took off my dress and let my hair down.

"Leah…" Landon's breathing was agitated.

I leaned over and grabbed a condom from the nightstand. He whispered my name again, his lips close to mine, and grabbed my wrist before I could proceed.

"Not like this, Leah. This…"

"But I need you," I begged.

"Why?"

"Because you're the best person I know. Because when I'm with you, I feel safe, and for an eternity now, I've had the feeling I'm walking on tiptoe, scared. Because you make me feel stronger."

Landon rolled over and lay on top of me, and then I thought only of him and of the moment we were sharing: his kisses, his touch, the way we made love, always gentle, always making me feel I was precious in his eyes.

15

Axel

TIME DOESN'T HEAL ALL. TIME calms, softens, files away the hard edges, but it doesn't make them disappear. Time didn't cure me of her. Time wasn't enough to avoid my entire body reacting to her, as if it remembered every freckle on her skin, every curve my hands had grazed three years before. Time did nothing to change that. And when I had her there and I sank into those eyes the color of the sea, I realized I would never be able to forget her, because that would mean erasing myself.

16

Leah

I GOT OVER LOSING MY parents. No, it wouldn't be honest to say that. In reality, I assimilated it, accepted it, but I lost parts of myself in the process. And I acquired new ones. I opened up. I fell in love. And I got my heart broken. I left Axel's home one night at the end of spring with all those pieces of it in my hand. It was a different type of pain. A pain I gnawed at alone on the days when I used to walk through Brisbane and get lost in its streets.

One of those days, I went to the flea market by the river. It was full of stands with all kinds of goods, but only one thing caught my eye. Maybe because I still missed him then and thought I'd be able to get closer to him if I bought that object I'd later stick in the top drawer of my nightstand, hoping I'd never need it again. But that night, when longing and loneliness took hold of me, I grabbed it. I took out the shell I'd bought, put it to my ear, and listened, eyes closed, to the sound of the sea. And I heard him.

17

Leah

OVER THE NEXT FEW WEEKS, I isolated myself and focused on my own issues. For days, I didn't pick up the phone when Oliver called after finding out he knew Axel was going to the exhibition opening. He offered explanations, but I didn't buy them. Still, he was my brother, and I wound up answering, and between the fourth and fifth apology, I growled at him that it was fine, I forgave him.

I was more focused than ever on painting.

The exhibition had gone well. The reviews weren't glowing, but they weren't bad either. The experience pushed me forward. It was the thing I needed to convince me to give myself more fully to my art up in the attic, where I had started spending the night. I didn't tell anyone I was sleeping there, and I sometimes felt the urge to hit the brakes and return to normalcy, seeing Landon or hanging out with my friends.

When Linda asked me to meet her again during office hours, I wasn't so nervous. That was a mistake, maybe. Because I didn't see it coming. I just sat down in her office with an expectant smile on my face.

"I've got good news, Leah." Her eyes were sparkling.

"Don't make me beg..." I said, my voice trailing off.

She leaned back in her chair, visibly happy.

"Someone's interested in representing you."

"Me?" I blinked, amazed, trying to hold in my excitement.

I'd never imagined something like that, not even in my wildest dreams. To start with, I was just a beginner, trying out new techniques, refining my style. Plus, the art world was complicated, harsh, competitive. Not many people managed to make a living at it or find an agent.

"Yeah. He works at a gallery in Byron Bay..."

"What's his name?" I felt suddenly stifled.

"Axel Nguyen. It's an important gallery. Small, but the owner, Hans, has contacts all over Europe and collaborates with... Leah, are you okay?" I must have gone pale. She looked worried.

"I can't." I stood up. "Sorry."

"Leah, wait! Didn't you hear what I just said?"

"Yeah, but I'm not interested," I managed to say, squeezing the strap of my purse in my hand. My knees were trembling. The office seemed to close in on me.

"This is a golden opportunity. Not just for you, but for the university too. The prestige of one of our students getting representation before even graduating..."

"I'm sorry, but it just can't happen," I interrupted her, hurrying out of the office.

18

Axel

OLIVER CAME INSIDE LIKE A whirlwind. He didn't bother saying hello; he just paced back and forth in my living room, then finally looked me in the eye with his hands on his hips and his face frozen in an incensed expression.

"What the fuck have you done? How could you? First of all, you told me you wouldn't even see her. You said you wouldn't fuck up her night. Now I find out you got in touch with the university to represent her? Are you serious? Did it not even pass through your head that you should tell me?"

"I was going to. I haven't had time."

"What the fuck is up with you?" he roared.

"What's up is I'm tired of faking."

I leaned on the kitchen counter trying to stay calm, because that was the only way I could imagine having this conversation without coming to blows, and I still wasn't sure about that, because this was all too...mixed up. We were acting as if we'd already talked about Leah, but we never had, not really. Not without punching each other, anyway. That was the only time we ever tried to get any clarity about it, and it didn't turn out well.

"What are you after, Axel?"

"I can't ignore it anymore."

"Ignore what?"

"Her. Everything that happened. That it *did* happen, goddammit. I can't keep talking to you through this fucking wall between us and pretend nothing happened, that everything's the same as it used to be." I didn't realize I was almost shouting.

"What are you trying to say?" Oliver asked. I think he was actually surprised.

I ran my hand through my hair and tried to carefully weigh my words. "Why'd you come back? Why'd you just show up at my house one day?"

He was still surprised, but this time it was because of the question that had changed the course of what looked like an imminent conflict. He leaned his head toward the porch and I followed him out there. I gave him a cigarette and took another for myself. He didn't say anything for a few minutes. But I wasn't about to retreat this time.

"I'm getting married," he finally said.

"What the hell does that have to do with anything?"

Not that I wasn't happy for him, but still...

"When Bega asked me who was going to be my best man, I realized it couldn't be anyone but you, that we weren't just friends, we were family." He looked at me. "And family's forever, Axel. I couldn't stop thinking about you and me and all that happened, all that went wrong..."

I took a long drag from my cigarette. I'd been asleep for three fucking years, numb inside my routine, and now, all at once, everything had exploded, and I wanted it to, I wanted the dams to break once and for all, because I couldn't bear this indifference anymore, this monotony that held me stagnant in the present, spending my days remembering the past, the better times before the color had drained from everything.

"Damn, Oliver..."

"I was thinking about you for weeks, about everything we've been through together, and finally I decided to just come here one day. I didn't even think it over. And it was easy to just not talk about uncomfortable subjects, to just pretend nothing had happened."

"But it did happen," I whispered.

"I wanted to forget. To leave it behind."

Sure. The problem was, that wasn't what I wanted. Time hadn't cured me. I hadn't managed to forget her. Leaving Leah behind was like forgetting the best thing I'd ever known, and I couldn't. I shook my head.

"I'm sorry, Oliver. I can't..."

"You can't be my best man?" He scowled.

And I felt like a part of me shattered.

"I can't be that; I can't be your friend. Not like before."

Oliver was angry, shocked, and he exhaled loudly.

"What is your fucking deal, Axel?"

"Things just can't be the way they were before. It's not you, it's that...when I saw her..."

Fuck. I was about to say something stupid. I turned around, but he grabbed my shoulder before I could walk away.

"Wait. Tell me. I want to understand."

"When I saw her the other day...when I saw her..."

"You still love her? After all this time?"

That almost hurt more. Him thinking Leah had been a fling, him never once facing the truth: that I'd fallen in love with her, that what I felt was real. I asked myself how he must see me: cynical, impulsive, a coward.

"I'll love her for the rest of my fucking life..."

"But Axel..." He seemed confused.

"I know. I know I fucked up; I know I did things wrong, not telling you and all. I know it wasn't the right time, and I know you thought it was a passing infatuation." I was trying to decide whether to be completely sincere or cover things up. I decided on the first, maybe because everything was so screwed up, I didn't have anything to lose. "You're important to me, but she'll always mean more; she's different, and we can't be friends because she's your sister, and I thought I could deal with it, but I can't. The only thing I could think about when I saw her in the gallery was taking off her dress and dragging her off to a corner and fucking her."

"Jesus Christ, Axel!"

"That's how it is."

"Try and filter yourself!"

"I wanted to be sincere."

"For fuck's sake! She's my sister." He scratched his head and turned toward the door.

I thought he'd walk through the house and out the front door, but he didn't. He turned around and took a deep breath and looked at me.

"I don't want to lose your friendship. And you're right, I

didn't think you were serious about it, but goddamn, you're never serious about anything. And you did fuck things up, Axel; you lied to me; you went about it the wrong way…"

I grabbed on to the wooden railing.

"I know." My jaw was clenched.

Oliver lit another smoke, and so did I. I felt almost like we were doing it to keep our hands occupied because things were getting to be too much for us. A pause to light it, a pause to take a drag, a pause to blow the smoke out slowly…

"So now what?" Oliver asked.

"Now I want her to sign with me."

"That's a bad idea…"

"It's a good idea, and you know it. No one could rep her better; no one will look out for her interests like me. And believe me, someone else will sign her soon, because she's that good."

"I thought you didn't represent talent, that you were just a scout," he said, repeating words I'd told him the month before on that very same porch.

"For her, I'm willing to change. I swear to you, I'll take care of her, and I'll…"

"Don't fucking do this; don't tell me you'll take care of her," he hissed.

And I remembered this wasn't the first time I'd promised that.

"I'll try and do the best I can. She's got a future, Oliver. I know she can do great things if she has the tools to do so. And I can give them to her."

Oliver rubbed his face. He looked weary.

"I think she's going out with someone."

"No one asked that," I hissed.

He waited a moment, then asked, "You really think she can make it?"

"I don't think it; I know it. She's always had talent."

"I'll try and talk to her then, but no promises."

A few minutes later, when he was gone, I went to the kitchen, grabbed a bottle of something—I didn't even look at the label—and went outside. I took a long sip on my way to the sea, and when I reached the shore, I lay down. I took a breath and closed my eyes, or at least I tried to take a breath. If only the murmur of the ocean could have quieted my thoughts.

I had made all that happened. Just me.

I remembered the kid who was with her at the gallery, the one who hauled her out the way I would have done three years before, getting her away from danger. Some fucking irony that the person who loved her most would turn around one night and tell her she needed to meet people, live, have fun, fuck. I thought that was it. That she was like me, that she could navigate that sea of strangers and still come back to me, even if I told her not to. That sooner or later, we would have to meet again. And that when we did, we would be in the same place in our lives.

The problem was, there was an infinite distance between imagining her in bed in someone else's arms and knowing that she felt something for that someone else. A connection. A relation. Something like what we had.

The first thing stung. The second burned...

19

Leah

I WANTED TO SEE NO one. I didn't want to think. I went to class, slept, and painted. I had the feeling I was trapped in a giant snow globe and someone had shaken it and all I could do was watch the snowflakes fall around me. I walked and walked, but somehow, I kept ending up in the same street, looking into the same eyes. And no matter how much I tried to run away, when I reached the end of the road, he was always there.

20

Axel

"WE CAN'T OFFER ANYTHING ELSE? Sweeten the deal? Talk to her school?"

"Axel, why are you so fixated on signing this girl?" Sam leaned back in her chair and looked at me the way she did when she caught her boys getting into trouble. Lines crossed her forehead. "She's good, but I've never seen you show this kind of interest in anyone."

"She's…" I couldn't tell her the truth. I couldn't talk about her out loud with another person.

I'd only had a few conversations about her, with my brother, and that was at the beginning, when I still could hardly find the words to define what I felt because in truth, I didn't feel it yet.

"I've got a hunch," I said.

I got up and went back to my office. I opened the desk drawer and took a pill for my headache. Usually I try to avoid medication, but that day, I thought my brain would explode. It had been that way for a while now. Obviously, my mother had insisted I go to the doctor, and I finally gave in so she'd stop calling and bugging me about it. The diagnosis? Tension, too much alcohol, too much caffeine, emotional stress, anxiety, not enough sleep…

I made a few phone calls and spent the rest of the time staring at the photo the art gallery had sent me the week before. Those three paintings titled *Love* captured in an image that failed to contain all the things they represented. I sighed and slipped it back into a folder.

I left early that day because I was supposed to meet with Justin in the afternoon. I couldn't remember anymore the first time he showed up at my home with his kids in tow and a surfboard under his arm, ready to let me teach him something he'd always seemed to hate. It didn't matter; it was now a family ritual, and we arranged to do it regularly.

My nephews cornered me when they got there, shouting while their father tried to calm them down and keep them under control. They hadn't taken after him, not at all. They were wild and not too interested in following the rules their parents set for them.

"Can I take your board?" Max asked.

"Obviously not." I tried to laugh.

"Come on, Uncle Axel!" he shouted.

"Me too!" Connor looked at us.

"Boys, take your own boards," Justin griped. "It's time to go down to the water!"

They ran across the sand toward the shore while my brother and I continued at a more leisurely pace. I could feel him staring at me. I rolled my eyes, because I had already told him, the week before that I'd gone to see her at the gallery, and naturally, he wasn't just going to let the subject slide.

"Did she answer you about the offer?"

"If she'd said yes, I'd know, right?"

We got into the water. My nephews were a few feet away, close to some smaller waves next to the shore. I think my scowl was enough for my brother to understand I needed some time alone on my board to burn off the energy I'd accumulated and wear myself out, even if—unfortunately—that still wasn't enough to let me get any sleep. I concentrated on my body, on my posture, my balance, on hugging the walls of the waves as if nothing else existed.

When Justin got tired of doing the same thing, he came to find me. Connor and Max were already on the shore laughing at some joke only the two of them understood. I stayed there stretched out on my board next to my brother under the orange sky.

"You can't go on like this, Axel."

"What I can't do is stop being this way."

"You know I get you, but still…"

"She's going out with someone." I spat it out just like that, and the words seemed to stick in my throat, sharp, hard. "I don't know what I was expecting, but not that, dammit."

"It never crossed your mind that she might meet someone in three years?"

"Meet, yeah. Fall in love, no."

"Isn't it basically the same?"

"No, it's not even close. They're not even in the same galaxy."

My brother had married his high school girlfriend, Emily, the only girl he'd ever had feelings for. I had been with so many women I could barely remember half of them, and for me, all of them counted as *meeting someone*, and that never went anywhere.

It was nothing like what I'd experienced with Leah. Nothing. Not even the sex, because with her, it wasn't about pleasure, it was about...a need, as simple as that.

"Axel, what did you expect?" My brother was sitting on his board looking at me sternly.

"I don't know. I was hoping..." I took a deep breath, paused, tried to clarify the tangled thoughts overwhelming me. "I think a part of me always thought we would see each other again, and it would be like nothing had ever changed. That maybe we couldn't be together three years ago because of something about the moment or the situation, but now..."

Maybe I was trying to deceive myself, because all that time it had been easier to cling to that idea than admit that we might be finished forever.

"So what are you going to do?"

"No idea. Try and accept what this represents." *And die a little inside every time I see her.* "I believe in her. I have to try..."

"For her father?" Justin guessed.

"Yeah. And for me too. And for her."

"You know you're walking into a minefield, right?"

"Things with Leah never were easy."

21

Leah

"YOU CAN'T BE SERIOUS!"

"Leah…" Oliver's voice was soft.

But I didn't care how tender he wanted to be or how hard he was trying to sound delicate, all I could think of was how much he wanted me out of Axel's arms before, and I wanted to close my eyes and pound at him with closed fists. I was furious. Enraged. I'd accepted they were friends again and hadn't asked for explanations of any sort, but it wasn't my job to deal with his changes of opinion or all this volatility.

"Listen, it's a good opportunity." He sighed on the other end of the line. "I know the situation is complicated, but time's passed. You're with another guy, right? Axel represents artists, and…he's family, Leah."

"No he isn't. Not anymore." I hung up.

I hung up because I couldn't go on listening to things that weren't true, because it hurt, all of it, and because I couldn't understand Oliver. He wanted me to do well and make a name for myself, but at what price? I wasn't sure it was worth it to cross that dangerous line. Especially because I knew Axel well and there was usually a reason behind whatever he did.

I flopped down on Landon's bed and sank my face into the pillow. Since the exhibition, I'd felt unstable, without a center. Every time I remembered seeing him standing in the middle of the room looking at my work, I felt claws digging into my lungs and depriving me of air. And I couldn't bear that feeling, that weakness coming back to me, the trembling as those irritated eyes of his returned to me, his expression...

His words: *"I'm proud of you."*

I got up when I heard the lock turning. I grabbed the bags Landon had brought from the supermarket and helped him put the things away in the fridge. It was Friday, and I'd decided I'd stay there for the night: have a light dinner with him, watch a movie, fall asleep in his arms.

"This goes in the freezer."

"Ice cream!" I smiled.

I kissed him on the cheek before grabbing the carton; then I put it away along with the bags of chips and other things he handed me.

I heard my ringtone. I'd left my phone in the bedroom.

"Someone's calling you, Leah."

"I know."

"You're not going to pick up?"

"It's my brother. And I'm mad at him. So no."

"What happened this time?"

Oliver and I had more than our share of spats, the way a brother and sister do. It doesn't mean they don't love each other.

But Axel was something more than an ordinary spat: he was blunt-force trauma, a fence you could barely see past, and I wasn't ready to climb over it just because Oliver was having a sudden change of heart.

I looked at Landon, a little uncomfortable.

"He wants me to say yes..." I whispered.

"He wants *him* to represent you?" He tried to make sure this was what I meant, since I'd just mentioned it in passing a week ago, when I was at his apartment and upset after leaving Linda Martin's office with my heart in my throat.

I'd tried not to bring it up since, even though I couldn't get it out of my mind.

"Yeah. That's my brother. Mr. Consistency."

Landon leaned on the counter. "What do you think?"

"I don't think anything," I responded, putting a carton of juice into the refrigerator.

Landon bit his lip and looked at me.

"What?"

"Nothing. It's just... You should think about it."

"What? You can't be serious!"

He grabbed my wrist before I could leave the kitchen. I tried to keep a lid on things, breathe deep, and listen to him.

"Wait, Leah, babe..."

"Don't call me that," I begged.

"Sorry." Tense, he ran a hand through his hair.

We weren't used to arguing. Landon and I didn't have the usual couples' fights, we just enjoyed each other hugging on the sofa or taking walks through town.

"I didn't explain myself right. If you don't want to do it, there's nothing to talk about, okay? I know you've got your reasons. Believe me, I'm the first one to wish you'd never be in the same room with him again..." His voice cracked before he looked back at me. "But I can imagine why your brother thinks it's a major opportunity for you. Come here, give me a hug."

I held him tight and closed my eyes when I felt his chest against my cheek. I understood. If I tried hard, I could get that they were just thinking about my future, that they realized three years had passed and that was enough time to confront the demons of a past I'd left behind. It made sense. The reality was stifling, because Axel was holding out a piece of candy he knew I couldn't resist: painting, my dreams. And to get it meant stirring up feelings I'd hoped would stay buried.

Landon pulled away softly. "Let's forget about it. What do you want for dinner?"

I bit the inside of my cheek. "It would be so complicated..."

He stopped when he realized I was still talking about the thing from before. He pushed away the stray hairs that had escaped my ponytail and took a deep breath before asking a question he seemed to have been holding on to secretly for months: "Are you still in love with him?"

"No."

I wasn't, because Axel wasn't the person I'd thought I knew, because with the passage of months and years he had stripped away the layers of what I thought I'd fallen in love with: his sincerity, his way of life, his transparent gaze... And when they were all gone and I looked again, I saw there was nothing left.

Just a void. I hadn't found the boy I thought was there under all that bright, shiny wrapping.

I could tell Landon was breathing easier.

"Then what are you worried about?"

"I don't know! It'll be hard. Weird. I don't know if I can just act like nothing ever happened with him after he hurt me so bad. It's not just what happened between us while I lived there; it's everything else, all the stuff from before. We were friends, family. We were the kind of people you look at and think they'll never be apart because somehow their lives are just woven together."

I realized I was taking big steps back and forth across the kitchen, agitated, when Landon got in front of me to stop me. He bent down so we could look into each other's faces.

"And you can't get that back?"

I thought about it. Separating one part of Axel—the part of his kisses, our bodies united, the nights on the porch—from the other that had been the root of all that: our friendship, tenderness, an unconditional love that could last a whole life...

"I don't know, but the situation is..."

"Uneasy? I bet. All I want is for you to really take stock of all your options, to think it over calmly before you reach a decision." Landon kissed my forehead and draped an arm around me. "Next subject: today it's your turn to choose the movie, right?"

22

Leah

I WAS PISSED.

Pissed at the world for putting me in this situation. Pissed at Oliver for being so contradictory. Pissed at Landon for not telling me what I wanted to hear. Pissed at Linda for pushing me and making me come talk to her during office hours. Pissed at Axel for everything. And especially pissed at myself for nearly losing an opportunity, because I wasn't willing to see if I really had broken free of that part of my past, and, ironically, my dreams were leading me down a path I'd spent years trying to avoid. And I had to decide if I would chase them or let them get away.

23

Leah

DOUBTS WRAP AROUND YOU, LIKE a thick blanket you can't take off, and the longer you spend beneath it, the less you can breathe. I'd tried to throw it off, but I couldn't. When I lifted one edge, the other fell back down. When I thought I had the answer in front of me, fear loomed again and made me take a step back, and there I was again walking in a circle while all those doubts crushed me.

Then one random morning, I drew a deep breath and decided I was going to throw the whole blanket off in one go. I tried to think coldly, without getting trapped again in that tangled forest of thoughts. I got out of bed, looked out the window, and made a decision.

24

Axel

I BROUGHT THE PHONE BACK to my ear, stunned.

"She agreed?" I asked again.

"Not exactly. She wants to talk about it. It's a step."

"Oliver..." I took a breath, nervous, because a part of me had already decided her silence meant *no*, while another part of me had been struggling for weeks to keep from getting in the car and driving to the door of her dormitory and threatening not to leave until I got what I wanted. "Thanks for this."

There was tense silence on the other line.

"She gave me the address of a café for you two to meet next Monday afternoon. You got a pen and paper? Write it down."

I took down the details with the phone pressed between my shoulder and ear, wondering what had made Leah choose her brother as an intermediary. Then I thought...I thought maybe she had erased my number from her contacts. Maybe one day she was mad and pressed the button in a rage, trying to erase from her life something she'd left behind to embark on a new stage.

"Okay, Monday around five," I repeated.

"Yeah. And another thing, Axel...be delicate. I know you never are." I rolled my eyes and was thankful he couldn't see me. "Stick to painting, nothing more."

"Relax, Oliver," I said.

"It's easy to say; it's hard as fuck to actually do it."

"Leah's an adult, man. She's twenty-three years old; I think she'll be able to have a normal conversation with me in a coffee shop."

Ironically, I wasn't sure I would, since I'd barely been able to utter that phrase there in the gallery. But I wanted to ease Oliver's mind, to keep from letting this make our relationship even more awkward and tense. Sometimes, it seemed things were the same as always, but the next second, it was as if we were strangers.

I was about to hang up when he said, "Axel, one other thing."

"What?"

"Don't make me regret this."

There was a note of pleading in his words, and I wondered what he was feeling, because he seemed willing to let me meet with Leah again, but he also seemed petulant.

He said a quick goodbye, not giving me a chance to answer.

I stayed there with my phone in my hand for a moment, looking out the window as the breeze shook the trees growing around the cabin, thinking about her, about how I'd see her in a few days and wasn't too sure what to expect. And that fucked me up, the uncertainty about that girl I had watched grow up and then shared everything with: my home, my life, my heart.

What was going to happen to all that?

People come and go with time, close and open doors, walk through them, walk back out. It happens every day. Someone leaves your world, they stop taking your calls, and then what happens with all the things they can't take with them? The memories, the feelings, the moments…can they really vanish and turn to dust? Where do they go then? Maybe some people can hold on to them tighter? Maybe I was someone who'd been capable of keeping all those invisible things, and now they were in a giant suitcase filled to bursting, while she could walk down a different road without some giant burden on her back.

I walked out to the porch and lit a cigarette.

I smoked it slowly in the silence of the night. One of those memories that I always cherish shook me while the smoke faded into the darkness. The notes of a song swirled inside me, and I heard Lord Huron's "The Night We Met" again from that time when I was dancing with Leah squeezed against my body, right before I kissed her and we crossed that line that changed everything.

I closed my eyes and took a breath.

25

Axel

I DIDN'T REMEMBER EVER BEING that nervous.

The café where we met was rustic-looking, with wooden walls and shelves packed with plants and antiques serving as decorations. When I went in, Leah wasn't there yet, so I sat at a table in the back, next to a window that opened onto a not very busy street. I ordered a strong coffee, though I knew it wouldn't help calm me down, and I massaged my temples with my fingers while I stared at one of the balconies out front with its matching flowerpots, and the colored petals dangling down on stems left unpruned: yellow flowers over intense green...

Everything was art. Too bad I couldn't portray it.

I looked up when I heard the doorbell chime, and my mouth went dry. Leah walked forward slowly, her eyes staring straight into mine, exactly as I'd thought she wouldn't do. She always managed to surprise me.

So unpredictable...

I'd assumed she'd be looking away all the time, but no. She was defiant. I held my breath as she came over. She was wearing tight jeans and a plain gray T-shirt, and still, all I could think was that she was radiant in a way no other girl I'd ever seen had been. She was brilliant, she shone. I asked myself how it was possible that no one else in the café noticed the light that her skin was reflecting, the sheen of her eyes, the strength in each step she took.

I rested both hands on the table and stood up.

Leah stopped in front of me. I bent down and gave her a kiss on the cheek, or not so much a kiss; I just grazed her cheek with my lips, and she jerked away and sat down, hanging her bag on the back of the chair. I settled down across from her.

How should we start? What should I say?

I could see the tension in her narrow shoulders, and I wanted to calm her down somehow. The way I used to. Every time she had been in pain, and I was her life raft and not the person who caused her problems.

"You want something to drink?"

Leah took a moment to untangle her eyes from mine and look up at the waitress, who was holding her notepad after serving me a coffee. I contemplated the dark liquid while she ordered an apple juice, and I wished I could trade it for a shot of anything I could knock back to ease my nerves.

"So...here we are," I whispered.

"Here we are," she repeated softly.

I was an idiot. After years of not talking to her, that was the only thing I could think to say. I closed my eyes and took a deep breath to gather my courage.

"Leah, I..." I had a knot in my throat.

"The contract," she said, cutting me off. "We should talk about it."

"Right. Exactly." I paused while the waitress returned and served her juice. "I sent it to your professor."

"She didn't tell me the details."

"Why?" I looked at her, intrigued.

"I didn't want to hear about it."

"Well, that's...promising."

She didn't smile. Not even a bit. I shouldn't have expected her to. I suppressed a sigh and opened the folder I'd left on one end of the table. I slid a copy toward her and took mine. She knitted her brows as she read. She hadn't touched her juice. I tried to stop looking at her like a stupid child and concentrated on stirring my coffee.

"Is there anything you'd like to know more about?" I asked.

"Yeah, I want you to explain the whole thing to me. No surprises."

"You used to like surprises."

Her eyes drilled into mine. I'd fucked up when I said that, but I sure missed the feeling that awakened in me when I saw her face.

"Axel, don't waste my time."

"Fine. Here's what you need to know."

26

Leah

I WANTED TO GET UP and run out.

My entire body asked me to: my racing heart, my nervous stomach, my sweaty palms, and above all, my instinct. That feeling that seems to ignore reason and simply guides us when it needs to.

Axel was the same as always. His hair, just a bit longer than usual, brushing his ears; his blue eyes that called to mind the depths of the sea; his skin toasted by the sun; lips full, jaw square. I realized he'd shaved before coming; he had a few little cuts on his cheek; he was never very attentive with a razor. I saw his hand resting over the contract: masculine, with long fingers, short nails, a couple of hangnails.

It was as if I needed to memorize each detail again, all those little things you forget with the passage of time: the tiny scar over his left eyebrow that he'd gotten when he was sixteen and had hit his head on the edge of his surfboard, the eternally unbuttoned top buttons on his shirt, the curve of his lips…

"With the gallery representing you, you'll have ten pieces

minimum in our catalog. Not just the same ones: the idea is to change them out frequently. We'll be sure you attend art fairs and exhibitions. The profits are split fifty-fifty."

"I don't think that's fair."

"Sorry?" He raised an eyebrow.

"I won't take less than sixty percent."

Axel seemed surprised, but then I saw him purse his lips to keep from smiling.

"Fine. Sixty. But remember, the gallery's investing in you; we take care of transportation, which isn't nothing, plus we advise you and get your name out, among other things."

I was wringing my fingers under the table, I was trembling, but I didn't let Axel see it. A small part of me had thought he wouldn't give in so easily to my objections. Maybe if he hadn't, we would have struggled to reach an agreement, and I would feel less like a coward for not sticking to my guns.

I tried to keep calm. "You're going to handle all that?"

"Yeah."

"There's not someone else who can do it?"

He looked at me strangely. "Am I that horrible to you?"

I blinked, a bit thrown by the sound of his husky voice. *How should I respond?* Yeah, it was horrible to think of all the time we'd have to spend together; it hurt me to look at him; I missed what we had before I ever stepped foot in his house and my universe changed forever. And it made me sad to think we could never get any of that back.

"What else will you do?" I ducked the question.

"I'll evaluate your work. It's complicated, but we need to

price everything. We'll study each piece before we decide how to sell you."

"How long does the contract last?"

"Eighteen months."

"And what happens if I regret it and I want to break it?"

"Leah..." he sighed. "That won't happen. You won't regret it."

"Does it surprise you that I question your promises?"

He needed a few seconds to assimilate my words. A muscle tensed in his jaw.

"I won't fail you this time."

His voice was barely a whisper. The first thing I thought was that he seemed sincere, and I scolded myself for trusting him.

I shook my head.

"I want to negotiate the term length."

"It's a standard contract, Leah."

"Then I want a nonstandard contract."

"That's not how it works." He was getting tense.

"I'm not signing for eighteen months."

"Fuck." Axel rubbed his face, huffed, and leaned back in his chair. "Fine. A year. And I'm making an exception for you, so don't push it, Leah."

"What you were proposing was ridiculous," I said, defending myself.

And I meant it. Everyone in the field said the same. Galleries took advantage of their artists, making them sign abusive contracts just because they were so excited to see their work hanging on walls somewhere. There were agents that offered thirty percent of profits and kept seventy, or made the artist cover expenses, or just broke the terms of the contract, period.

"Give me your email, and I'll send you a copy of the modified contract," Axel said, grabbing the papers and sticking them back in the folder. "When you sign, we'll set a date for me to visit your studio."

"My studio?"

"You've got a scholarship, right?"

I nodded, but I had to set my glass down because my hand was shaking. I realized Axel hadn't taken a sip of the coffee sitting in front of him either.

"I don't want anyone else in there."

"Are you kidding?"

"Absolutely not."

"Leah, this isn't negotiable."

"Everything's negotiable," I replied.

"I need to see your work. I need to make a study of it. I need to evaluate it, price it out, catalog it. You get that, right?"

"Yeah, but…" I wanted to cry. I wanted to run.

"Leah…" Axel stretched out his hand across the table to look for mine when he saw me blinking over and over, but I pushed it away and retook control. "We'll do this a little bit at a time, okay? The first day, I'll just take a quick look. We've got time."

I nodded, because I couldn't speak, and I stood up when the attack of nerves subsided.

"I've got to go."

Axel's mouth opened, but then he must have thought twice, so he closed it again while I bent over and wrote my university email address on a napkin. Before I could turn around, he'd stood up and was grabbing my wrist. I shivered. His skin was still warm, his grip firm, resolute.

"Do you still have my number?"

"I erased it," I admitted.

He wrote it down on another napkin that I tucked in the back pocket of my jeans. I didn't tell him I knew his number by heart. I didn't tell him how many times I'd wished I could erase it just like that, by pressing a button.

I didn't look back as I left the café. I needed air. I needed to get away, to find myself.

27

Axel

I SAT DOWN ON A stool and rested a hand on my brother's shoulder, then shook him until he started to complain. I laughed as the bartender approached.

"Two rums?" I looked at Justin.

"Okay, but nothing too strong."

"We've only got one brand," the guy responded.

"Well…" Justin seemed hesitant.

"We'll take two of those, then," I cut him off.

The bartender turned around, and Justin nudged me with his elbow.

"Don't order for me!" he complained.

"That's what you get when you invite me out."

"I just wanted to know how you were." He grabbed his glass as soon as it was set down, took a sip, and grimaced. "It burns like fire!"

"Come on, show me you're actually my brother."

He smiled, shook his head, and clinked glasses with me. As we drank, he told me about the twins' latest shenanigans and other, more boring things, like how he'd installed a new lock on his bedroom door so he and Emily could be intimate without interruptions. I stopped him when he was about to start describing their last session.

"Honestly, Justin, you don't have to go into details."

Over the past few years, my brother and I had grown closer, and almost without realizing it, we'd become the kind of friends who could meet up now and again and hang out. He was still too stiff for my taste, a little prying, and bad at most of the things I liked to do, but in his defense, putting up with me after what happened with Leah was no easy task, and he was the one person who went on doing it unconditionally even after I had the worst fight of my life with my parents at the unfortunate age of thirty.

With my father, getting through it had been easier, but Mom... I wasn't sure she didn't still hold it against me somehow. For months, she'd complained that she *simply couldn't believe it* and would cry about how after the deaths of Leah and Oliver's parents, Douglas and Rose, our family was even more fragmented than before, and there would be no more family meals on Sunday or anything like that. Ironically, that was what made my parents pack their bags a few months later and leave on their first voyage. It had been a short one, an experiment, almost. But it was followed by many more, each longer than its predecessor. By now they were regular globetrotters.

"Another round," I told the bartender, raising my glass.

"You don't want to just share one?" Justin looked up, and my expression was enough for him to sigh in resignation.

"You know where our parents are?" I asked.

"In Panama, I think. They haven't called you?"

"No." I took a long sip.

"Mom says every time she tries to call you, your phone's dead. Is it really that hard to keep it charged?"

"When you get in big brother mode, that tells me you haven't drunk enough. And for your information, I've had my phone charged for several days now." I took it out of my pants pocket. "See? Magic!"

"That's a big achievement for you. What's the cause?"

"I need to stay in touch." I shrugged.

I didn't add that since the day Leah had written her number down on a napkin, I'd turned into one of those people who never puts their phone away. Why? She never called. She hadn't even answered the email I sent her with the new contract.

"You're like a fifteen-year-old boy who just met a girl," Justin said in a stern voice that jarred me when I was trying to joke around. I couldn't help laughing, because he was right, even if I'd never admit it aloud. "She hasn't answered you?"

"No. Nobody wants to call me, you know?"

"It's because you're unbearable."

I punched him on the shoulder and he moaned ridiculously and finally we cracked up laughing. And we went on laughing all night, and every time Justin was about to go, I ordered another round and convinced him to stay a while longer. I didn't want to be alone. I didn't want to go home, because when I was there I thought, and thinking made me remember, and with all that silence, I started slowly dying inside.

I looked down glumly and he nudged me.

"Cheer up! We're supposed to be celebrating you signing her." Justin's eyes were glassy and his face slack, and he'd clearly had too much to drink.

"Yeah. I guess that's something."

"She's not going to hate you forever, Axel."

That was easy to say if you didn't know Leah like I did. And I was the person who knew her best. That way she had of opening herself up and revealing everything, or the opposite, locking up and staring you down so coldly that your hair stood on end... Leah couldn't take half measures. She was emotional, impulsive, one of those people who fight tooth and nail when they really want something. Special. Not at all like me...

"Wait here, I'll be right back."

I got up and walked across the bar to the bathroom. The main room was full of people chatting and drinking under the garlands of colored lights. Chill-out music was playing in the background, same as at almost all the bars lining the beach.

When I got back, Justin wasn't there.

I rolled my eyes, grabbed my mojito, which was still sitting on the bar top, and turned around to try and find him. I waved to a few friends and helped out some tourists who seemed interested in something more than the sights of Byron Bay: I had to grab the hand of one of them to keep her from undoing the remaining buttons on my half-open shirt. As I walked away from them, I found my brother on the patio. I could see he was stumbling a bit as I came over, and talking to some young guy.

"What kind of chocolate's in them?" he asked.

I couldn't believe it. The guy was trying to sell him marijuana brownies. It was all I could do not to burst out laughing. I wrapped an arm around my brother's neck.

"Justin, that's not what you think it is."

"I've got a café, we make pastries."

The guy frowned, a little confused. "I mean if you want chocolate instead of weed, I know this dude who…"

I was surprised and did nothing while he paid for the brownie, bit into it, and chewed with his mouth open. The guy left in search of new clients, and I suppressed a smile, drinking my mojito and leaning back against one of the outdoor columns.

"It's weewy good," Justin mumbled.

"What the hell did you do when you were younger?"

"What do you mean?"

"I mean, what the hell were you doing when you were young that you never got around to trying one of these?"

It was no secret that marijuana in all its forms was widely consumed in Byron Bay. Sometimes I had the feeling my brother was living on an entirely different planet from mine. I clapped him on the back as he swallowed.

"You know, man. Going out with Emily."

I envied him briefly. If Leah and I had been the same age and met when I was sixteen, I probably wouldn't have been interested in that shit either, or in staying out till the crack of dawn. I'd have been too busy gawking at her and having sex with her every night.

"You're going to start feeling weird in a few minutes," I told him. "So, for your sake and the sake of your sex life, I'm going to call your wife and tell her you don't feel good and you're going to stay over tonight."

He ignored me and started dancing to a song with his hands raised in the air. A couple of girls played along with him as though nothing could be more amusing than watching a guy who probably ironed his underwear acting like an idiot.

I lost sight of him when I called Emily, who immediately asked me what kind of trouble I'd gotten her husband into. I ended up telling her the truth.

"Well, he could probably use a bit of fun," she replied.

"Did anyone ever tell you you're incredible?"

"Don't kiss up to me, Axel; we know each other."

"I can't help it."

We agreed it was best if the twins didn't see him like that. I went back to find him and pulled him away from the group. Justin protested, but finally gave in as I was pushing him out the door. We walked to my house on a dirt path. Justin was stumbling, shouting out whatever passed through his head, and leaning on my shoulder every time he needed to catch his breath. When we stepped into my house, he flopped inert on my sofa, and I thought of how long it had been since I'd enjoyed myself like that. Who'd have told me years ago I'd have fun partying with my brother? I went outside, lay on the wood floor of the porch, and lit a cigarette. It was almost morning, and all I could think about was how bad I wanted to see her. I contemplated the smoke undulating against the starry sky, asked myself what Leah might be doing then, and forced myself to stop when I imagined her in the arms of another guy, wrapped up in the sheets, because it hurt, it just hurt too much...

"What are you doing?"

I turned my head as Justin lay down beside me. "Nothing. Thinking. How are you?" I ask him.

"Relaxed."

I tried not to laugh. "What are you thinking about?"

"Her..."

"You used to be different."

"Yeah."

"Or maybe you were always like this, but you needed the right person to bring it out of you. But that doesn't make any sense, because she was always there, even if..."

"Don't overthink it."

We just laid there in silence for a while, until I took my phone out and looked for her number in my contacts.

"What are you doing?" Justin asked.

"I'm going to send her a message."

"What kind of message?"

"One that says if she doesn't answer and we don't meet to sign the contract, I'm going to take the liberty of surprising her one day at her dorm."

"You sure that's a good idea?"

"No, but she's not leaving me with other options."

I hit the send button and looked back up at the stars, which seemed to tremble. It wasn't the first time I felt I needed to push Leah, to tighten the screws, and I knew if I didn't, she'd run away. And that scared me so much...

I'd already been through this once, and I wasn't about to repeat the experience and let her get away again. Seeing her had made me relive everything vividly, as if the memories had remained dormant until then. I hadn't had contact with Leah for three years, and all of the sudden, the idea of not hearing from her for a week was intolerable. And there was no going back now.

28

Leah

MY PHONE BUZZED. I PUT aside my paintbrush and trembled when I saw his name on the screen. Then I read the message, the implicit threat in those words that seemed idle, but weren't.

It was a Friday night, and I was still up in the attic painting something I wouldn't know how to name, uncertain lines, an explosion of intense colors, a scream contained in a canvas. I weighed my options, because a part of me refused to allow Axel to burst into my new life, and I knew, when I signed those papers, he would be there, and there'd be nothing I could do about it.

But I also couldn't turn back now…

29

Axel

I CLIMBED THE STEPS OF the dorm two at a time and knocked on the door of her room. I waited nervously. Leah had answered my text and said we could meet in her free period between classes on Monday. Obviously, she didn't want the encounter to stretch on too long. And I agreed, because I would have said yes to whatever she asked. That's how fucked up I was.

Leah opened up, looked at me, stepped back.

I walked in and examined every corner of the room while she closed the door behind me. I'd hoped I'd see a print of her work, but the walls were empty. Her desk was full of books and art materials. I walked over to it to get a better look at a drawing sticking out of a pile of paper, but she grabbed it and pulled it away as soon as my fingers reached it.

"Don't touch anything!" she whispered.

I saw the movement in her throat, and I wanted to kiss her there, in that hollow of skin that I always felt was made to measure for my lips.

"All right. But you know, touching is one of my specialties..."

She stared daggers at me. I grinned, because I liked that better than indifference. Awakening something in her, even anger, was enough.

"I don't have much time, Axel."

"Fine."

30

Leah

I FORCED MYSELF TO SWALLOW to try and soften the knot in my throat as he sat on the bed and opened the folder. He passed me two stapled contracts.

"One for me, one for you."

"Sure. Can I look at it?"

"Of course. I'm not the one who's in a rush."

I almost rolled my eyes, but at the last minute, I stopped myself, because I knew Axel and what he was after: provoking me, knocking me off balance. I sat at the chair in front of the desk and read in silence. I only looked up when I saw him from the corner of my eye lying back on my bed. The thought that my sheets would smell like him later was more than I could stand. I tucked a strand of hair behind my ear, feeling the room shrink with every second that passed, as if Axel's mere presence caused the walls to close in, while his masculine aroma enveloped me and transported me elsewhere: to the sea, the sun, the salt breeze...

I finished turning the pages, barely able to read them, and signed the last one to keep the moment from stretching on any further.

"Done. Here." I handed him his copy.

"See? It wasn't that hard…"

The words *shut up* danced on the tip of my tongue, but I managed to swallow them down to keep him from getting what he wanted. I was pissed. What the hell did he know about difficult decisions? About all the nights I'd lain in that very same bed crying my eyes out? What did he know about feelings, about being true to them, about fighting for something no matter how hard it was?

"I need to go," I said dryly.

"To class?" he asked.

"Yeah." I locked the door behind me.

"I'll walk you there," he said.

I stopped halfway down the steps and grabbed the handrail before looking over my shoulder. He was grinning at me. I tried to ignore it.

"You can't do this."

"Why not?"

"Because I don't want you to."

I continued walking downstairs to the landing. I was happy the wind was blowing when I got outside, because before, Axel had seemed to suck up all the air and all the space around me too. I headed off, but he got in front of me, stopping me with his hands on my shoulders.

"What's the problem?"

"Axel, don't make things worse…"

Even uttering his name left a bitter taste in my mouth. *Axel.* Those four letters seemed to be pursuing me. An entire life summed up in a single person. I tried to hold it together as he leaned in.

"I know this isn't easy," he said.

"Well, don't make it harder than it is."

"Here's the thing: we're going to have to work together, and I can't fucking stand you looking at me like that, Leah. We should... I don't know, we should talk it out. Make peace. Whatever you need."

My heart sped up. *Talk it out.* No, I wasn't ready, because that would mean opening locked drawers that were full of dust, and just thinking about it terrified me. There wasn't anything concrete for us to come to terms about; it was everything, a relationship, an entire life that had crumbled to bits in an instant, and I was still stepping on shards of it I hadn't managed to pick up off the ground.

People walked back and forth on the sidewalk or crossed the street a few steps away, and yet, for the seconds we stared at each other, the world seemed to freeze.

"A truce," I managed to mumble.

Axel stepped back. I don't know if he was disappointed or relieved. Maybe it was both.

I started walking again and Axel did the same beside me. We didn't talk. Ten minutes passed, eternal and evanescent at the same time. He made me nervous, his hand so close to mine, his loud steps, his calm breathing...

"We're here." I stopped at the door to the building.

"It hasn't changed a bit." Axel observed the gardens, then lowered his eyes until they met mine. "Tell me a day when I can visit your studio."

"I still don't know..."

"Leah…"

"Maybe Friday."

"Maybe or definitely?"

I hated how he just pressured and pressured and pressured. And Axel was damn good at it. He didn't know when to let up or keep his mouth shut; he always went all in, at least when the situation didn't require him to look at himself.

"Definitely. I'm done with class at five."

"I'll be here waiting for you."

"Okay." I turned around without saying goodbye.

31

Leah

LANDON TOOK A DEEP BREATH and rubbed his chin wearily. I couldn't stand to see him like that, because he was ordinarily so bright and excitable, the type to always see the glass half-full.

I sat on the other end of the sofa.

"So, he's coming to your studio Friday," he repeated.

"Yeah. It's...it's work."

He stared down at his hands.

"Dammit, Leah, it's just..."

"I know," I interrupted. "I'm sorry."

"Maybe if you'd at least let me see it too..."

"Maybe one day I will. Later."

That wasn't an option then. If I could have, I'd have kept Axel from setting foot in my attic, and yet, for some reason, I also wasn't really bothered by his doing so. Maybe because Axel had already seen every part of me, from a thousand different angles, without any shield there to protect me. I didn't have anything to hide from him. And that showed me I had made a mistake in the past. Because when you open yourself up completely to a person, you become transparent to them. And when you give everything, then you're empty inside. I didn't want to commit that error again. While I was with Axel, I was so unaware, and I kept nothing of myself back. I didn't give him my heart piece by piece; I handed the whole thing over to him, eyes closed, without hesitation. Just the opposite of what I was doing with Landon...

It was different with him. We were taking short steps down our path, almost as if we were gripping a handrail. I didn't feel unstable the way I did with Axel, worried I'd slip or fall around every corner. I had my hands on the controls, and now I was terrified of letting them go.

"Come here." Landon hugged me.

"I'm sorry this is so complicated."

"We'll get used to it." He kissed me on the head. "I'm sure this will be a great opportunity for you. It's funny, just a few nights ago I dreamed you made it and your paintings were hanging in the best galleries in the world."

I pulled away from his chest and looked him in the eyes.

"Why are you so good to me?" I moaned.

"Because I'm your best friend."

"You're much more than that."

I hid my face in his collarbone, and I stayed there for I don't know how long, feeling the warm comfort of his neck against my cheek. Landon was a pillar, and I was walking around and around him, unable to step away, afraid of falling.

I guess a first love is always full of shortcomings and insecurities, but it's also special, magical. When you find out what it is to be in love, you feel emotions you're not ready to embrace, let alone deal with. And so you just feel: you love, you throw yourself into it. You don't hit the brakes because you haven't yet realized you're about to crash into a wall at the end of the road. But then you find out. That's the problem. And when you feel that tickle again, you remember what happened, that sudden blunt pain, and you decide to take it slower, but that has its consequences: reflection instead of impulsivity, calm instead of intensity. And you start to see gray where the colors used to be vibrant.

I helped Landon clean up the kitchen later before I left. I'd been so flustered when I left my room with Axel that morning that I hadn't even thought of taking my books for the next day in case I decided to stay over. So even though I didn't feel like being alone, I told him goodbye and walked to the dorm. I was in the mood to stroll and clear my head.

When I got in, I took a shower. I let the hot water run a long time and concentrated on that feeling, letting my muscles relax while the tension from the day vanished. I'd been distracted during class, thinking how surreal it was that Axel had walked to school with me just a few hours before like it was nothing after three years of not seeing each other.

That's how things were with him. Different. Illogical. Maybe that's why it was so hard to understand him, because we didn't think alike. I was incapable of feeling or thinking something and not shouting it to the four winds; I got carried away by my urges, by the first sign of an emotion. Not him, though. He could hold it in. He gathered up his emotions and hid them away in the closet or buried them, and then he just went on with his life.

I got out of the shower, leaving a trail of water, because I forgot to grab a towel. I dried off once I got one out of the closet and put on some comfy pajamas, then brushed my hair and left it loose so it would dry. When I looked at myself in the long mirror, I thought again about cutting it—it was getting too long.

I got into bed. Then I sensed him. Him.

My cheek on the pillow, I felt the tears filling my eyes, and I closed them so they wouldn't pour out. I took a deep breath, bringing his scent inside me... I thought of the shell I had put away, how it had helped me fall asleep so many nights during those early months, but I resisted the impulse to take it out. And I knew...I knew I'd have to get up, strip off the damned sheets, put them in the laundry bag, and fetch new ones from the dresser. Georgia had given me three different sets the year before. She was always planning ahead. *I'm sure Oliver never thinks of these things.* She was right.

But for some reason, I didn't do any of that. I stayed there swallowing my tears, smelling him next to me, and remembering how beautiful it had been to have him in my life: showing him every painting I did, inviting him to every birthday, seeing him smile slowly, our eyes meeting in the middle of a Sunday family meal...

I missed my life from before. Everything. My parents. The Nguyens. Us being a family. Waking up every morning and staring into the blue, blue sky...

32

Axel

I GOT THERE A HALF hour early, so I leaned on the wall of the university's main building and waited, looking at the interwoven clouds crossing the leaden sky. I hadn't slept all night, and my head hurt, but I was so used to both that I didn't even think to grab an aspirin before I left the house. I regretted it now, because I wanted to see everything clearly, be at a hundred percent when I entered the studio.

For the first time, I understood Sam.

I understood the sense of expectation she showed before visiting each of her artists and seeing what they'd been working on during the preceding months. She often said it was magic, like looking at an entire world contained between four walls. And there was nothing I wanted more than to see the lines and colors of Leah's world.

I saw her in the distance as she walked distractedly along a path surrounded by plants. She was wearing headphones, lost in thought, in threadbare shorts that revealed those long legs of hers that used to wrap around my waist while I sank inside her. I tried to clear those memories away, because we were so far from that moment now that it almost seemed like it had been other people instead of us.

She looked up and saw me. When she reached the wall, she took off her headphones, and I bent down to kiss her on the cheek, even though I knew it bothered her. I saw she'd been biting her nails, and her eyes were nervous.

"I promise it won't be as horrible as you think," I whispered. "I'll just take a quick look around; we don't have to do everything today."

"No. We should go ahead and get it over with."

I understood her not wanting to spend more time with me than necessary, but it burned. I put my hands in my pockets and followed her down the sidewalk. We walked in silence for a few more streets until we reached an old building. It looked like it was only three stories. Leah took her keys out and opened the door. There wasn't an elevator, so we took the stairs, and immediately I noticed the scent of paint. When we were at the top, that smell invaded everything. I took a deep breath; it brought back memories: her father Douglas, her, my forgotten dreams, a whole life concentrated in something I couldn't even see.

"Sorry, it's a bit of a mess," Leah said, picking up empty tubes and rags off the ground.

I didn't respond; I was too busy trying to take in everything around me. Leah pulled away when I stepped toward the row of paintings leaning against one wall. I don't know if it was her, the sloping roof, the wood floor, or the torrent of color all round, but that attic had me spellbound. I shivered as I looked into every corner, noticing the strength of all those works, no matter how different they were, works I assumed she'd painted at different times in her life.

"How much time do you need?"

I turned when I heard her quavering voice.

Leah had sat down in a round black chair in the corner farthest from me. She looked so defenseless that for a few seconds, I saw in her that same little girl I'd watched grow up. I smiled to put her at ease.

"It's a long process; I need to evaluate each piece individually and divide them up according to style, but like I said, I can come back another day."

"No, it's fine, I just…wanted to get an idea."

I nodded, hoping that wasn't all, because I still remembered back when she was so excited to show me everything and let me be part of her process. How far away it all was. How things change.

I spent a bit more time getting a general sense of what was there, and I had goose bumps, because for some reason this was even more intimate than if I'd undressed her there in the middle of the attic. I could see her. I could find pain in the blotches of paint, the unsaid words, the emotions in each line, the confusion, hope, courage, glimpses of time past, murmurs of what was then to come…

I held my breath and stood there in the middle of the room, my head almost touching the ceiling. In that moment of stillness, I noticed a canvas tucked into the lowest corner. And I felt inexplicably drawn to it.

"Axel, no…"

But I didn't listen to her. I couldn't; what I felt, my emotions then, were so powerful that I could take in nothing else. Entering that studio had been like a blow, and all at once I knew what Leah had been during those three years of absence, and I could embrace each instant when we hadn't been together through these traces she'd left behind...

I didn't stop till I reached the picture.

And when I picked it up to look at it, it took my breath away.

It was us...our bit of sea.

I almost burst into tears like a little boy. I knelt down on the ground and ran my hands over the sky, feeling the layers of paint, the places where she'd corrected her vision. I wanted to scratch the surface and see what lay below it, what her very first version was... Because what I had in front of my eyes was a sky of purple and blue, dark, intense. A storm. I asked myself if that was what Leah felt like when she remembered what we were, and I hated that possibility, because for me she was still a clear blue sky...the most beautiful sky in the world.

Fuck. My hands were quivering. I put the canvas aside and stood up slowly. As I turned around, I felt a pang in my stomach.

There Leah was, in the middle of the attic, staring at me while the tears slid down her cheeks, and I... Something in me broke just then. My heart seemed ready to jump out of my chest. With its every beat, I took a step forward, coming closer to her. I didn't know if she'd pull away when I touched her, whether she'd push me or just stay there motionless, but I couldn't suppress the impulse crying out to me to feel her again...

I hugged her. I hugged her so tight, I was worried I'd hurt her.

And, as always, Leah surprised me, hugging back, passing her arms behind my neck, doing none of the things I'd predicted in the second just before. I pressed my head into her shoulder, and she pushed into my chest and let a brief sob escape her while her body quaked... I wanted to melt into her. Take her pain away. I closed my eyes, feeling so much, feeling her so much. I asked myself how long I could stand being there and holding her, breathing against the skin of her neck. I didn't know a hug could be more than a kiss, more than any declaration, more than sex, more than everything. But this one was.

I stroked her hair with one hand, not letting her go.

"It's okay, babe, relax..."

"I hated you so much..." she whispered, leaning her forehead into my sternum. My knees were shaking. I took a deep breath. "Just as much as I missed you."

A warm sensation shook me. I wasn't ready to let her go, I focused on the feeling of her hair, her body's curves melding with mine as if she were reclaiming her shelter. We were a mirror. A perfect, ephemeral mirror.

When I realized that, I slowly pulled away from her. Before she could turn around or run away, I brought her back close, wiped her eyes with my thumbs, my fingers. I held her face in my hands so she would look at me.

"I want to make this easy for you, Leah. I know we've got baggage, but if you let me back into your life, I promise I'll try and make sure you don't regret it. Babe..." I moaned when she tried to look away, and stroked her cheek with the palm of my hand. "I won't ask you for anything you don't want to give me."

Her eyes gleamed with tears.

"Why now? Why did you come back?"

"Because the day Oliver told me you were going to show your work, I knew I'd die if I couldn't witness it. I had to be here, Leah. I didn't want to fuck up your night, but I had to see. Anyway, it was going to happen sooner or later, you know that."

"I shut that door," she replied.

"Maybe you didn't throw away the key, though…"

Leah went to the armchair and grabbed her bag.

"I need to go out and get some fresh air."

"I'll keep working here," I responded.

Her steps were less audible as she descended the stairs. I stayed there in the middle of Leah's world, staring at artwork that seemed to stare back at me and still feeling her skin on my fingertips.

33

Leah

I CLOSED MY EYES AFTER walking outside. Inhaled. Exhaled. Tried to stay calm, focused on feeling the air slowly enter and leave. Just as I figured, I'd needed only a few days to fall apart in front of Axel.

When we saw each other in the gallery, I was so flustered I barely registered it. A few weeks later, in the café, I managed to keep my cool, despite the tension. The day he showed up in my room, I started to crack, especially when I came back that night and realized the bed smelled like him. And then the ground shook beneath my feet when I saw him in the attic looking at everything with those curious and insightful eyes that seemed to see more than the paintings showed at first glance. I was breathless when I felt his arms surround me and his body press close to mine.

I wanted to keep it all in, the way he did, hide all I was feeling, but I couldn't. Because it was true. I'd hated him, sure. But I'd missed him too.

It was almost unnatural for these two sentiments to coexist, but in some twisted way, they did. Because I hated that last part of our story, the part where I realized Axel wasn't the guy I thought I'd known, but one with many more layers, of cowardice, of emotions never really processed. I still remembered the last words he uttered before I ran out of his house in the middle of the night. I felt like a little girl listening to my own voice in my head telling him: *"You're incapable of fighting for what you love."* And then his voice, filling everything, the porch, the morning, my heart: *"I guess that means I don't really love then."*

That Axel I wanted nothing of.

But the other one, the one who had been a friend, family, the Axel I didn't have to ask more of than he could give, because there was no need to, given the circumstances—that Axel I missed. Him and his jokes and his cheerful mood. I missed having him in my life.

The problem was that it wasn't easy to separate the two, because they blended together like two drops of paint, two different colors that blended together to form a new tone, and I wasn't sure where it belonged on the canvas.

I took a few slow turns around the block.

When I felt calmer, I retraced my steps, but instead of going back up to the attic, I walked into a café on my street and sat at one of the tables in the back. I ordered a coffee before taking out a notebook and looking over my class notes in silence.

My phone rang almost an hour later. Axel.

"Where are you?" he asked when I picked up.

"Downstairs at the café."

"I'm on my way," he said, and hung up.

Five minutes later, Axel was sitting across from me, elbow

leaned casually on the wooden table, face pensive as he decided what to order. The waitress waited, intrigued. I'd forgotten the kinds of reactions Axel could provoke if he put his mind to it.

"How's the vegetarian sandwich?"

"No complaints so far."

She smiled and he smiled back.

"One of those, then. And an iced tea. Thanks."

"You're very welcome." She winked and walked away, while I raised an eyebrow at him.

"I was actually on my way out..." I told him, though there was no need to do so, since my coffee cup was clearly empty.

"I'm still not done with the artworks."

"How long do you need?"

"Quite a bit more time, Leah. I need to organize them—you've got to help me with that—and I need to appraise them, and I'll need Sam's opinion for that. Don't worry, I've already snapped a few photos. Then we need to choose some to take to the gallery. Maybe you've got some ideas there."

"What do you mean?"

"Are there any pieces there that are special to you?"

"I guess. Listen, about before..."

"There's no need to talk about it, Leah."

I knew with Axel silences said more than words, but I needed to lay the groundwork before we went any further.

"You're really going to make this easy for me?"

His eyes looked straight through me. I shook.

"Yeah. And you?"

"Me? I always made things easy for you..."

"You're wrong there, Leah."

The waitress returned and left the sandwich and tea on the table. Axel leaned back in his chair before taking a few distracted bites, as if we hadn't been talking about us, about everything, just one minute before.

I concentrated on the grain of the table's surface.

"So...you're going out with someone," he muttered. I looked up and just nodded. "Good. I'm happy for you." He sucked in a deep breath, drank his tea down in one gulp, and stood up. "You want to leave the keys with me? I can come by your dorm later if you don't feel like waiting here."

I thought of how freeing it would be to take a walk and not have to pass through the door of the studio with Axel once more on my heels, but then I saw his expression, and something changed. I don't know what it was. Nothing special, nothing revealing. Actually, his face was almost inscrutably plain, and yet...

"No, I'll go with you," I replied.

The creaking of the steps was the only sound that accompanied us as we climbed up to the attic. This time, I stayed beside him while he took photos of each picture from different angles and organized them into three groups.

"The good thing," he said, pointing at them, "is that they're easy to differentiate. Those are darker, more visceral. The ones on the other side are brighter. And the rest...I'm not really sure how to catalog them."

In this last group was the painting with our slice of the sea, along with others, the symbolism of which wasn't even clear to me, but still, they were things I'd just wanted, even had to paint.

"What about them?" I asked.

"Nothing. I'm just not interested in them."

I blinked, surprised.

"I don't get it. You said I was good."

"Of course you are, but there's better and worse stuff, don't you think?" I could see he was trying to take it easy on me, as if my ego were made of glass, and that irritated me. "As for this one..." He grabbed the picture of the sea. "I want to buy it. Name your price."

I opened my mouth, then closed it again.

"Have you lost your mind?" I shouted.

"No. I like it. I'll hang it up in the kitchen."

"Axel, this isn't a joke."

"I'm not joking, Leah. Name your price."

There he was, the same Axel as always, the one who could knock me off-kilter with three or four words. Even if he was trying to *make things easy* for me, he would always be complicated. I tried to stay afloat, to keep from falling into the trap.

"Take it. It's free."

"Are you sure? To what do I owe the honor?"

"To me wanting you to shut up," I replied. "It's a gift. A symbol to celebrate our truce."

Axel smiled. I could see the outline of the dimple on his right cheek fleetingly before he turned around and placed the picture by the door. Then he returned to the other pieces, looking thoughtful as he walked around the room.

"We should pick five from here and five from there."

"Okay, sounds good," I said. "Any preference?"

"For sure. This one's incredible."

I felt naked as he stood there looking at a canvas of tones running from black to purple to garnet, with a girl in profile whose features could barely be distinguished among the vague lines, but who was very clearly holding a heart in her hands.

"Can I ask you a question?"

"Depends on what you want to know."

"I'm wondering about the girl in the picture." He clicked his tongue. "The heart she's holding, did she just get it back or is this the moment she tears it out of her chest?"

I bit my lip. "She's gotten it back."

Axel nodded, walked away from it, and pointed to a few others he wanted for the gallery. I wanted to take part in this, and I chose two I liked a lot. When we finished with the selection, he kept going around looking at the others from the *unclassifiable* group. For some reason, they were the ones he seemed most curious about. Seeing him there on his knees in front of them, he reminded me of a wild cat that only came close to eat before wandering away and continuing its life in solitude.

"Is the cat still showing up...?" I was about to say *at home*, as if that place were still a little bit mine.

Over his shoulder, Axel said, "She died."

"What?"

"She was old."

"Axel..."

"It was last month. She died in my arms. She didn't suffer. I buried her that same night."

I was still sitting on the wood floor with my legs crossed while he went on sizing my work up. I realized it was late when I looked at the window and saw the sky turning a dense, dark blue.

"Those paintings...why'd you paint them?"

The question caught me a bit by surprise.

"I don't know. What do you mean?"

"You must have felt something. Some reason."

"No." I shrugged. "I did them without thinking. Same as the rest. I guess the idea or the feeling just showed up, and I poured it out in the picture."

Axel nodded, but I knew my response hadn't satisfied his curiosity. I remembered that this was the thing that ate him up inside, not being able to grasp that painting was just that easy, letting yourself go, feeling, living through the brush in your hand...

I got up when I heard my phone ring.

It was Landon. I picked up.

"I'm still here," I said.

"You want to have dinner together?"

"Sure." I was about to walk outside, but I stopped when I realized the conversation wouldn't go any further. Landon said he would go for Mexican at the place a few blocks from his apartment. "Yeah, tacos, sounds great. Nachos are good too. See you later."

When I hung up, Axel walked over to the door.

"I won't keep you here any longer," he said softly.

"I wasn't trying to..." I started to protest.

"I get it. It's Friday," he cut me off.

We walked downstairs. When we got outside, the shops were

closed, and there was hardly anyone around. All you could hear was the whisper of the trees shaken by the wind and the hum of some cars in the distance.

"So now what?" I asked nervously.

It was the first time Axel looked away. His brows furrowed, and he seemed to be entirely focused on the cracks in the sidewalk and a stone he was kicking with the toe of his shoe.

"I guess one of us should say something like it would be a good idea to start from zero, but it sounds so ridiculous we should maybe just pass. So I guess we can just say goodbye, you can go eat with your boyfriend and I'll walk back to the university, grab my car, and go home."

I looked up into the dark sky.

"This is all so…uncomfortable," I said.

"I know," he answered in a low tone.

"I hate that."

"Me too."

"It's terrible. It's weird."

"It's just a question of getting used to it." He uttered these words looking down into his shirt, almost as if he was saying them to himself.

We looked at each other. Axel stepped close and hugged me again, this time less tentatively, harder, as if he wanted to memorize the moment. I wrapped my hands around his neck, and we stayed there in silence on some street in the warmth of evening. His hot breath grazed my ear.

"Have a good time, babe," he whispered, letting me go and kissing me on the cheek.

I couldn't move. I watched him walk away beneath the orange light of the streetlamps, lighting a cigarette as he did so. Then he disappeared around the corner. I needed a few seconds to process, but eventually I turned around and went in the opposite direction.

January

—

(SUMMER, AUSTRALIA)

34

Axel

IN THEORY, MY MOTHER LOVED me. In theory.

Because seeing her shoot lightning out of her eyes wasn't what I'd call an expression of love. And yet, there she was, looking at me with a face that could have made hell freeze over in three seconds. Lucky for me, Dad restrained her, resting an arm over her shoulders in what seemed to be a relaxed gesture, even if I noticed it was a little stiff.

"How could such a thing even pass through your mind? Showing up at the little thing's exhibit, just like that?" I tried not to react, but I hated the way she said "little thing" when Leah was anything but. "We go on a trip, then we come back and I find myself with this! You can't be left on your own!"

I tapped my index finger on my empty plate. "Are there any sodas in the fridge?"

"Dammit, Axel!"

Unfortunately, she followed me when I got up and left the dining room. It was a Sunday, my parents had gotten back the day before, and we'd decided to have lunch as we did in the old days. We weren't doing justice to the word *family*, that's for sure. I took a deep breath, opened the fridge, and closed it again, not finding anything interesting. My mother was there behind the door, looking at me nervously.

"Calm down," I said. "Everything was fine."

"But Leah said you're going to represent her…"

The closest airport was in Brisbane, and every time they left for a trip or came back from one, my parents would try to see her.

"Yeah. What's the problem?"

"After what you did…"

That fucking hurt. I guess the years always give you a different perspective, and what had once seemed wrong or forbidden was starting to appear in a different light. I no longer saw things the same way. And if I could have gone back in time… Let's just say the last night Leah and I saw each other would have had a very different ending. I would have kissed her, taken her in my arms, carried her to my bed to make love and talk about our plans for the future, about keeping up a long-term relationship until she was done with school. With time, Oliver would have understood, just as he did later, after he left and the years gave him some tranquility. The same would go for my family. I just needed to be firm and take risks for what I loved.

And what I loved was her, in a way almost beyond reason.

But I hadn't done any of that, so all I had was this parallel reality that would never exist because I didn't lift a finger when Leah vanished from my life. She had struggled, had come for me, to my house in the morning, had tried to convince me that what we had was worth it, had cried in front of me without hiding or even bothering to wipe away her tears, and I did...nothing. Same as always. Nothing. Stood still, not even taking a step forward. Or backward. Anchored in the middle of nowhere, holding myself back.

"I didn't do anything wrong," I replied.

"Showing up without warning!"

I grabbed her arm to keep her from rambling on forever, and she stopped.

"I didn't do anything wrong. Not even back then. Three years ago."

"Axel..." She looked at me with a mixture of tenderness and disappointment. "What happened was bad. Leah was just a girl, and she had been through a really difficult time."

I could feel my jaw tense. I took a deep breath.

"You have no idea what we experienced when she was at my house. It's easy to judge things from the outside without bothering to understand them. I...I fell in love. That's it. I never thought it would happen, but it did. And what we had was real."

I walked off. I'd never talked to my mother that way; I usually spent all my time with her joking around, grumbling, being sarcastic. After what happened, I'd never bothered explaining things to her; I'd let her yell at me, and I'd taken it all in because I thought that I deserved it.

"Axel, honey..." I let her hug me.

Justin and the twins entered the kitchen before we could keep talking, and I was grateful for it in part, because I wasn't used to the idea of saying what I felt aloud, and when I did, it felt as if I were suddenly empty inside.

I grabbed a beer out of the fridge and returned to the living room. My father was sitting next to Emily watching the sports news. He looked at me, apparently happy.

"What's up, dude? How's life?"

"Just trying to make it," I replied.

"Peace and love, son, peace and love."

I smiled. I smiled for real.

35

Axel

SAM TOOK OFF HER GLASSES while I flopped into the chair in front of her desk. I looked around as always, noticing the silly gewgaws she'd stuck in the corners, her kids' drawings, toys they'd left lying around when they came to visit, family photos...

"You got something to say?" She looked amused.

"I just wanted to make sure you'd talked to the shipping guys."

Leah and I had agreed that we'd move the paintings from her studio to the gallery the following week. Taking advantage of the end of class, she was going to come to Byron Bay for a few days to help organize the exhibition.

"I talked to them; everything's good to go."

"Excellent. So that means..."

"You owe me an explanation."

"Did your kids spike your coffee this morning?"

"Don't try to joke your way out of this," she warned me. "I want to know why you're so interested in this girl. We may not have worked together too long, but I know you well enough to see there's something special that's made you get so involved. Don't worry, Axel. I don't bite. For now."

I held back a smile. "It's her. She's the girl I talked to you about."

"The one you were in love with?"

"Yeah." I struggled to get the word out.

"You didn't tell me much of anything, Axel."

"Well, now you understand..."

"Did you really need to get weirded out for weeks just to tell me this?"

"It's not easy for me."

"I can tell. So what's the plan?"

"I just want the exhibition to be perfect."

I kept back the most important part, the fact that I was finally keeping the promise I made to Douglas that night at my house when I renounced my dreams and stuffed them away in the closet, choosing instead to commit myself to the dreams of another. I shivered when I remembered his words: *Axel, you paint or don't, and one day you'll love or you won't, because you won't know how to do things any other way.*

How fucking right he was.

"You want us to do something special?"

"I don't know." I stroked my chin. "My idea is something with a family feel."

"Family?"

"Yeah. She's from here. I want it to be cozy. For people to come and not just take a look at the pictures and go. I want them to feel like they can stay a while and talk..."

"I think I understand. Remember that exhibition where we hired the caterers? With Leah, there's not many pieces on display, but we could still do it."

"Yeah. And plus, we could bring some more pieces in just for the opening. She's got a couple that are...unclassifiable." Sam looked at me with interest. "I don't think they're right for the catalog, but we could reserve one room for them for twenty-four hours."

"You should probably talk it over with Hans. But I like the idea. It's been a while since we've had a strong exhibition, and if the girl's from here, that always brings in more people. It could be interesting."

36

Leah

FRIDA KAHLO SAID ONE TIME, "My painting carries a message of pain." The day I read that, I got more interested in the work of the real woman who was hidden beneath the growing popularity of her work. The woman who had loved, suffered, screamed. Something connected me to her. That's the magic of literature, music, painting, and any other art, the way you find yourself in something another person has created.

Sometimes we feel alone: we're individualists, and we think only we have felt that emotion that twists our soul or that idea that makes us feel so strange. Then one day, you realize that isn't true. There's an immense world out there full of people, experiences, lives. When you accept that, you realize two things: first, how much there is around you, and that makes you feel smaller, like an ant running back and forth and suddenly learning its anthill isn't the only one, there are millions and millions more. And second, you're relieved to feel understood when you encounter traces of yourself in a song, a poem, or the lines of a picture.

That's a way of not feeling alone.

I thought about this for a while as I coated the tip of one of my brushes in paint. I was working on a girl with her back turned, with long dark hair, and colored butterflies were flapping out of her mane, along with musical notes and flowers that symbolized memories. Some had wrinkled petals, others were freshly blossomed. I used impasto, thick layers of paint, mixing bands of color on the canvas, making it more real. It was important to note the angle of every stroke so the paint didn't get away from me, and I was so concentrated on what I was doing that for a long time, I didn't realize it was night.

I cleaned my brushes, gathered my things, and left.

When I got to Landon's apartment, he had already eaten and was on the couch watching a comedy series he loved.

"I left you some fish in the oven."

"Thanks, but I'm not that hungry."

I kissed him and went into the kitchen, grabbed a piece of fruit from the fridge, and ate it absentmindedly as I returned and sat down next to him. There was some kind of tension between us. We'd never felt that before. I didn't know how to deal with the situation, and I'd screwed up again because I'd promised we'd have dinner together and I still hadn't told him I was going to spend a week in Byron Bay.

"I'm really sorry, but I lost track of time."

"Don't worry about it." He shrugged.

"Landon." I left the fruit on a napkin on the table and hugged him. He didn't pull away. He wrapped his hands around my waist. "Are you mad?"

"No..." He bit his lip and exhaled. "I want this to go well,

Leah, and I get that you need to work a lot of hours to guarantee that."

"But..."

"But everything would be way simpler if our situation was clearer. We've been hanging out for months, and things are getting more complicated, and in the meantime I feel we're not going anywhere."

I pulled away, looking for some space.

I understood Landon. He'd always had stable, more or less long-term relationships. Relationships where he could call the other person his *girlfriend* and not worry about it. I'd come into his life, and what we had was very clearly more than just friendship. And there we were, in limbo, and I didn't know what to call it, but analyzing it also scared me. I loved him a lot, and the idea of losing him terrified me... I had lost too many people along the way.

"I don't know if I'm ready for this," I whimpered.

"When will you be?"

"Isn't what we have enough?"

Landon rubbed his face, stressed.

"Sometimes, yeah. Sometimes, no," he admitted.

"Tell me what worries you the most."

He looked away before answering. "You seeing what we have as somehow temporary."

"I never said that..." I protested.

"Do you think it's forever, then? Look at me, Leah."

My stomach turned. Forever? Be with Landon forever? A part of me did want that, because it would be so simple, so comfortable, like curling up under a blanket when it's cold. But the other part of me wasn't ready to decide. The other part didn't even know what it thought about all that.

"Let it go. You don't have to answer that."

Landon got up, and I followed on his heels to the bedroom we had shared so many nights those past few months. He brought his fingers to the bridge of his nose and closed his eyes. I hugged him from behind.

"I'm sorry. I love you, Landon, but the idea of deciding now whether I want to stick with someone for the rest of my life… I think we're in different stages, and I don't even know if I understand myself."

How could I explain it to him? I didn't know where to begin. The past few years had been full of changes, and it was hard for him to grasp all that I had been through. Landon had never known the girl who used to walk around Byron Bay with a permanent smile on her face before the car crash that changed everything. Nor did he know the other Leah, the one who had closed up on herself, who stopped painting and had only stayed afloat thanks to a certain stubborn someone who did everything possible to get her out of the black hole she was stuck in. But then… Well, then everything turned out wrong, and when I got to Brisbane, I was yet another version of myself.

I felt like I'd spent the past few years changing skins. Maybe that was why I wasn't sure who I was just then.

"What should we do?" he asked.

"I don't know." I was still holding him.

I'd have liked to give him the answer he was looking for, but I didn't want to lie to him. It's not that I could never imagine a distant future with him, I just hadn't made it that far. It had never passed through my mind. But that worried me.

"I need to go to Byron Bay for the exhibition. I've been meaning to tell you for days."

He pulled away, turned around, and looked at me there in the shadows.

"I get it." He kissed me on the cheek.

"Come with me," I whispered without really thinking. "I'll rent a room in a hostel. I don't know. I can introduce you to my friends, show you the place I grew up..."

"Leah, you're going to be working all day, and I've got things to do here; I can't just drop everything." He slid a lock of hair behind my ear.

"You'll come to the exhibition, though, right?"

"Yeah, for sure. I'll try to be there."

I stood on my tiptoes to give him a slow kiss that warmed up my breasts. Landon's lips were soft and firm, full of lovely promises that a part of me wanted to see fulfilled. But the problem was the other part, the one that wouldn't give in, as if it were hanging on too tight to something else...

37

—

Leah

AXEL WANTED TO OVERSEE THE entire process of packaging and transport. We started on Tuesday at the break of dawn and stayed with the workers who were wrapping the pictures and taking them down to the van. I grabbed a sheet of the bubble wrap they were using and entertained myself popping it while I sucked on a strawberry lollipop.

He came over after talking to one of the men.

"You bored?" he asked.

"No, but I don't have anything to do."

"You want to go to the café for a bite?"

"Sure." I stood up and followed him to the street.

We sat at the same table where we'd been the day I let him into the attic for the first time. We ordered a couple of sandwiches and soft drinks.

"You seem absent." Axel tilted his head.

"It's not that, it's just…it almost doesn't seem real. I feel like this is happening to someone else, and I'm just here watching it like a spectator. Don't worry about it."

"No, I think I understand. You haven't assimilated it."

We looked at each other while they served our food. I broke eye contact, picking my sandwich up and taking a bite, even though I wasn't very hungry. Axel ordered some fries, and when he asked if I wanted to share, I shook my head, because, dumb as it seemed, there was something intimate about that act, and it was still almost impossible for me even to look up, knowing he was right there in front of me. I hadn't assimilated that either.

Him, the exhibition...everything had happened all at once.

I looked at his arms bronzed by the sun. His long masculine fingers. His nails—chewed. His gestures, all of them firm.

I looked at everything, honestly. Because there was something about Axel that entrapped me, and I gave in to it, capturing the little gestures and feelings, and then letting them go and letting them *be*. He always *was* in some weird way, and I was certain an artist could create a whole series of paintings just observing him attentively for a while.

When we were done eating, Axel went once more to the studio to make sure they'd left nothing behind. It was sad to see the place so empty, without all that work that had piled up because I'd never considered actually doing anything with it.

He made sure everything was arranged in the van, and said goodbye to the driver after repeating for a third time that Sam would be waiting for him at the gallery in Byron Bay.

"You're a little obsessed, you know?" I said when we walked back to my dorm, where we had met to walk to the studio.

"I want everything to go well." He smiled.

And that smile gave me goose bumps as we walked down

the street in silence. For the first time since we'd met again, the absence of words didn't make me uncomfortable. It was a little like before, when we could spend hours with each other without saying a word.

When we reached my room, Axel grabbed my suitcase. I followed him as I ran down a list of all the things I had packed for those days in Byron Bay, because I always had the feeling I was forgetting something.

"Goddamn! What the hell's in here?" he grunted as he lifted it to the trunk of his car.

"The basics." I sat down in the passenger seat.

"The basics? Clothes, stones, and a dead body?"

I tried not to grin, chastising myself for letting the reins go so quickly. But Axel just was that charming, and I remembered then why I had missed him and forgot all the reasons I had hated him for three years.

I looked out the window while we left behind my neighborhood in Brisbane. It was a sunny summer day, and the cloudless blue sky accompanied us all the way. We were almost outside the city when he turned on the radio. The melody of *3 Rounds and a Sound* surrounded us.

"So you're going to sleep in a hostel…" he said.

"Yeah. I got a good price because the owner knows Oliver."

"You could have stayed at my brother's place." He then made a breezy gesture. "Or mine."

The speed with which I turned my head must have been a clear sign of how much that comment disturbed me. I looked him over while he drove, hands calm on the wheel, and asked myself how it was possible that Axel could just accept this situation so easily, as if all we'd lived through years back meant nothing to him. For a second, just one, I envied him. But then I simply felt pity.

Pity because Axel would never die of love for someone. And at a certain moment in my life, I had, and I knew the sensation well, and there was nothing else it could be compared to: that electrifying feeling when a person touched you, the way your heart sped up when they smiled, the way the whole world revolved around a boy who, despite his many defects, was perfect in my eyes.

I realized long before that he might not be the best thing for me or for my heart, which was crying out for relief. And so I slammed on the brakes.

But I still kept the memory with me.

I passed two people who were obviously in love on the street one day, and I knew what it was they were feeling and that Axel would never know what that was like. He would never love enough to fight for it tooth and nail, despite everything, against everything.

"Leah, are you okay? You didn't answer me."

I forced myself to look at him, hard as it was.

"I'd rather stay in the hostel, it's more comfortable."

"More comfortable for who?"

"For me," I replied curtly.

38

Axel

RESTRAINT. IT WASN'T THE FIRST time I'd been hounded by that word with her around. I had restrained myself years ago, when I started to feel something for her. I thought it was bad, that it wasn't right, that I couldn't let anything happen between us. But I failed and fell in all the way, because suppressing my primal yearnings wasn't something I was as good at as I'd have liked.

And now I was back in the same situation. Restrained. Unable to stop ruminating about how she'd put her life back together, how she had someone else, how she'd left what we had behind. It was like traveling to the past, to those forgotten feelings: having her there and dying to touch her and not being able to do it, swallowing my words, my lust, my desire.

I drove a while without saying anything, concentrating on the road. Leafy trees bordered the asphalt, and I had the strange feeling I was getting closer to her with every mile we left behind, as if we were returning home. And we were, in a way, even if just temporarily. I glanced at her. She had her head leaned back and was looking at the blurred countryside through the window.

"I remember you being more talkative."

"For real?" She raised her eyebrows.

"Except for the year you stopped talking, obvs."

"Very funny," she muttered, then turned away.

"You honestly don't have anything to tell me? You didn't do anything interesting for three years?" I kept on because, as always, I preferred her bad mood and cutting replies to her silence. Leah's silences were...dangerous.

She wrinkled her nose and looked straight ahead. "I painted, I studied, I went out."

"You're overwhelming me with all those details."

"Why don't you tell me something about you?"

"I haven't done much to speak of."

"You changed jobs, didn't you?"

"I'm still illustrating, but I'm pickier with the jobs I take. The rest of the time I'm at the gallery, though I don't have a set schedule."

"How'd you wind up there?" she asked.

"You really want to know the story?"

Leah nodded and crossed her legs. I looked away from the road a second. If she'd done that three years before, I thought, my hand would already be between her thighs, even just to hear her laugh and knock me away.

"Last year at New Year's, I drank more than I'd like to admit. I was alone. My brother, Emily, and the kids had gone to celebrate with some friends, my parents were on the opposite end of the world, and I didn't want to see anyone else, so I went to the most expensive restaurant I could think of..."

"That's sad," Leah interrupted me.

"Why?"

"You could have called Oliver."

"He still wasn't talking to me, but that's not the issue, Leah. I could have gone out with friends if I'd wanted to, but I didn't. So I had dinner by myself. And it was good. Remember when we were talking about being conscious of the moment and enjoying it? Well, that's what I did. Then I went to the boardwalk, and I ordered a couple of drinks. I didn't realize I'd drunk too much until this guy sat down and started talking to me. He told me his family lived in France, and he had spent the night alone, too, because work had kept him from going home. And guess where he worked..."

"At the gallery..." she whispered.

"Turns out he was the owner. And with all the drinks I'd had, I started running off at the mouth about how half the pieces they displayed there were mediocre, and we ended up talking about art and what they were trying to do there, and when the night was over, I had a job offer, but since I could barely stand up, I didn't take it too seriously. I left, I didn't even say bye, but then Hans showed up at my door a day later, and you can't imagine how fucking stubborn the guy is."

Leah smiled timidly. "That's typical of you."

"What, exactly?"

"That. Going out one night with nothing else in mind, getting drunk, saying something offensive to a guy you just met, and getting lucky."

"Offensive?"

"Unnecessarily sincere, let's say."

"You've lost me. Tell me what you mean."

"It doesn't matter," she said. "It's silly. Let it go."

"Would you rather people lie to you, Leah?"

"Of course not. But that sincerity…"

"Tell me! I want to know what you're thinking."

"I don't think that sincerity is real."

Leah bent forward to up the volume and put an end to the conversation, but I grabbed her wrist to stop her. She pushed me away quickly.

"You don't feel like talking anymore?"

"Did you have something else to say?"

"Let's see…" I said, turning thoughtful. "I live in the same place, I have the same phone number, and I still wear the same size clothes. Since I'm so uninteresting, why don't we talk about you? You must have done something fun these past three years."

"Axel, I'm tired…"

"That sounds like an excuse."

"It is an excuse."

I tried not to smile at her honesty. It was almost as if, after criticizing my sincerity, she was trying it on for size herself. But not thinking my sincerity was real—that burned me, because it was partly true. I hadn't always been honest, at least not when it came to Leah. I was a goddamn hypocrite sometimes. And she knew it.

I let the whole thing go and concentrated on the road with the radio blasting, thinking of how electrifying it was to know Leah was beside me again; even if a million barriers were between us, it didn't matter: having her was always better than nothing. It had been before, when I used to prefer her angry, even enraged, to absent and hushed. And it was now, when I no longer knew what was left of *us*.

She fell asleep before we arrived in Byron Bay.

I stopped in front of the hostel where she was staying. It was a two-story building with six rooms on the edge of the city, just a short walk from my house. I parked and stared at her a few seconds. Not a sound could be heard. My eyes glided over her long hair, pulled back in a ponytail, and her face, the same one I had covered in kisses years before. I felt the impulse to stretch out my hand and caress her cheek, but I stopped myself.

"Leah..." I shook her slowly. "We're here."

She blinked, confused, until she understood where she was; then she sat up and hurried out of the car. I helped her with her enormous suitcase and insisted on accompanying her to her room, because it weighed a ton. She didn't protest much, probably because she was still half asleep.

We picked up her keys and went upstairs, and I dropped the suitcase on the bed. Her room was small but clean, and the afternoon sunlight was coming through the window that opened onto the back garden.

"When will we see each other again?" I asked.

"I don't know. You tell me. Supposedly we need to get things ready for the exhibition..."

"Rest for today. I'll make sure everything's arrived okay." I stepped back toward the open door. "See you tomorrow at the gallery at ten?"

"Okay."

She seemed so uncomfortable that I didn't want to drag things on any longer, so I waved goodbye, then walked down the narrow wooden staircase.

Despite everything, when I stopped in the middle of the road to take a deep breath, I had the feeling things were suddenly coming together, as if having Leah in Byron Bay gave the city new color, and after years caked in rust, the motor of my life was starting up once again, with all the gears spinning in the same direction.

39

Leah

I TOOK SOME CLOTHES OUT of the suitcase and hung them
in the closet so they wouldn't get wrinkled. Then I remembered
I was back in Byron Bay, and no one cared whether I ironed my
clothes.

I hadn't slept well that week, so I was tired, but I ignored
the feeling and grabbed my bag and left the hostel. As I walked
through those streets I knew so well, I called Landon to tell him
I'd gotten in.

Then I wandered aimlessly. It had been so long since I was
last there that I decided to take some time for myself, without
needing to arrive anywhere special, just enjoying the walk, the
shop windows, the blue of the summer sky, the mild, agreeable
aromas coming from the cafés I had left behind. It was as if I'd
hit pause on my life. And though I thought it wouldn't happen,
I felt back at home. I'd grown up here, and now I couldn't help
but remember that this was the place where I'd started painting,
where I'd spent afternoons with Blair and my classmates, where
I'd said goodbye to Oliver in tears when he went off to college,

and he finally gave me permission to use his room when he was away. The place where I fell in love, fell apart, became the person I was right now.

When I reached the boardwalk, I stopped to look at the sea and the surfers climbing the waves. I was sad when I remembered it had been three years since I'd set foot on a surfboard. I'd missed it for months on end, when I woke up at dawn and knew Axel would be out until sunset on our stretch of sea. And now that feeling was so remote that I wasn't even sure I ever wanted to surf again.

I wound up sitting at an outside table at a café and ordering a caramel cappuccino while I enjoyed the breeze. I don't know why, but after I'd been there for a while and my coffee was cold, I grabbed my phone and called Oliver.

"What's up, pixie? Are you in Byron Bay?"

"Yeah, I'm here…"

"You doing okay?"

"I'm just out for a walk, and I keep remembering things." I blinked when I felt the tears trying to come out. I don't know why I was breaking down like that for no reason, but I felt a blend of nostalgia, sorrow, and joy at the same time, all jumbled together. "I feel weird, but I feel at home too."

"Leah, I'm so sorry I can't be there…"

"I can't stop thinking about our parents. About how lucky we were, you know?" I wiped a tear away with the back of my hand and crossed my legs under the table. "They were the best parents in the world, and I swear I still miss them every single day. I don't know if that feeling's ever going to disappear, and now that I'm here, it's like some ridiculous part of me believes that I'll round the corner and find them out shopping or laughing while Dad's whispering a joke in Mom's ear—remember how they used to do that? How they'd hide what they were saying from us?"

"Yeah." Oliver took a few seconds to respond.

"I always wanted to know what they were saying."

"Probably it wasn't appropriate for you." He started laughing and sighed in a way that almost sounded like a moan. "I miss them too, pixie. And I'm sorry I couldn't be with you these days. I tried to put in for vacation, but…"

"I know, Oliver. You shouldn't do it anyway. You shouldn't use all your days off coming to see me. It's not fair to you and it's not fair to Bega."

"Nothing's more important than seeing you, pixie."

"I'm a big girl now, Oliver."

"Not for me. Never," he joked. "I did manage to switch shifts with someone to go to the exhibition. And before you complain, Bega's coming with me. We'll stick around for a few days. I want to introduce her to the Nguyens and show her the town."

I smiled, because I loved Bega, and I was happy my brother had met the love of his life when he least expected it, at a time when he had to leave his entire world behind to take care of me and pay for my school. It was as if fate had given him back a little of that generosity. I'd had the opportunity to get to know Bega better over the two summers when I traveled to Sydney to spend a few days at my brother's place, and she was perfect for him. She was strong-willed and could come off as cold at first, but she melted every time Oliver looked at her.

"Fantastic," I said.

"We'll all be together."

"Yeah."

"How are things going with Axel?"

"They're going. I think. Off and on."

"Doesn't sound that great..."

"It's complicated, Oliver."

Talking to my brother about this was too. In fact, we'd never even done it, apart from those early days when I couldn't stop crying and trying to convince him that what Axel and I had was real. I still remembered Oliver's answer: "You don't know Axel. You don't know what he's like when he gets into a relationship, how he just shoves away all the things that stop interesting him. Has he ever told you how he stopped painting? Has he ever told you how when something gets complicated, he refuses to fight for it? He's got his black holes too."

Once he'd seen he was right, we never dug those memories up again. I don't think either of us really realized that sometimes life takes unexpected turns, and you might end up missing a friend you thought you'd never need again, or a lost love who crept back into your life almost without permission...

"Did he do something wrong?" he asked.

"No." Actually, he'd behaved incredibly well, too well for him. I was surprised he didn't ask me any uncomfortable questions, but I knew him well enough to have all my barriers up.

"If you ever have any problems..."

"I'll tell you," I said, cutting him off, and laughed.

"Cool. We'll see each other in a week then."

"Yeah. Give Bega a kiss for me."

"And you enjoy being home for me."

My brother's voice turned nostalgic just before he hung up. I stayed there on the café patio for a while looking at the gleaming sea under the last light of day and asking myself what blend of colors I'd use to recreate it and round out the shadows and details. Then I realized I didn't have a studio or paints here, or anywhere I could pour out all those things shifting inside me.

I asked myself how long I could hold it all in.

It was almost nighttime when I turned away from the beach and disappeared among the streets and memories. I checked the address on my phone before ringing the doorbell of a small white house, two stories, with a pretty garden.

She greeted me with a huge smile.

"Leah!" Blair hugged me so tight I started laughing. We hadn't seen each other in months, not since the last time she'd gone to Brisbane to run errands and we'd had lunch together. "Sorry, I'm gonna crush you." She let me go and took a step back.

I was excited when I saw her round belly.

"You're huge!" I shouted.

"Believe me, I know. I look like a spinning top."

"Don't be silly," Kevin interrupted as he came into the living room. "You're beautiful." He caressed her belly.

I smiled as I witnessed this gesture and gave him a kiss on the cheek. They were both sparkling.

"Get comfortable, because I want to know everything," Blair said.

I'd given her a quick rundown of my unexpected encounter with Axel and the exhibition in Byron Bay, but I hadn't gone into details.

"The frying pan's on the stove, so I'm going to leave you two alone." Kevin looked at me. "Will you stay for dinner?"

"I don't know; I'm tired, and…"

"She's staying," Blair said.

"I'd advise you not to contradict her, because a few months back she acquired a talent for transforming into a raging T. rex in a matter of minutes."

Blair glared at her boyfriend.

"Yeah, now that you mention it…" I agreed.

Kevin went back to the kitchen, and we stayed a while on the couch chatting about the old days. Blair told me she'd quit working a few weeks ago so she could rest, but she was hoping to get a job at the day care as soon as she could sign her child up. I lost track of time as we talked about everything and nothing. From time to time, she'd grab my hand and place it on her belly so I could feel the baby kick.

The feeling was absolutely unique, and I asked myself what it would be like to feel a life inside me. I couldn't imagine anything more intimate or profound.

"What are you thinking about?" Blair asked me.

"Nothing."

"Come on, Leah. We know each other."

I bit my lip and shook my head. "About this. How magical it is. How I'd love to experience it one day."

"You're just as intense as ever." She smiled at me. "I'm sure you will, Leah. And when it happens, the way you feel things so deeply, it'll be wonderful."

"I used to be so sure, but now…I don't really know."

"What are you talking about? What's changed?"

"You know. Me. I've changed. I don't know if I can ever love again the way a person deserves to be loved. I'd like to. I'd like to choose, the way you do when you go to a store and pick out a dress you like and take it home and that's that. But love isn't like that."

"No, it isn't," Blair said wistfully.

"If only."

I didn't add that if I were given that possibility, I'd choose Landon. I'd choose to love him crazily, passionately, the way you love a person when you can't control it or even stop to analyze the consequences. I'd choose not to be a day without him and to miss him. I'd choose him because I knew I'd be happy that way. But love is much more complex than that. And there are many ways to love. There is a kind of love that involves serenity, trust, security, friendship, and that was what I was trying to learn.

Blair looked at me a bit warily.

"Has it been complicated with Axel?"

It was almost funny she should say that. The word *complicated* was a given when you were talking about him.

"A little, at first. But I've gotten past it, and I think with time we can manage to be friends again."

"I didn't know you ever were."

"Blair..." My look was like a warning to her.

"Sorry, I know it's not my business."

"It's not that; it's just..." I bit my lip.

"I get it. I'm sure you'll be able to become friends." She didn't seem very convinced of it, though. "Anyway, you've both changed."

"Axel's changed?" I raised an eyebrow.

"We all do with time, right?"

I had my doubts. Grave doubts. Serious ones. And I thought of a question that I had put out of my mind more than once in recent weeks. I felt bad just for thinking it, for that curiosity that tugged at me as if trying to get my attention.

"Do you know if he...? All this time, I mean. Who cares. Forget I asked."

"If Axel's gone out with anyone?" Blair guessed.

Fear overtook me, the fear that my friend could see right through me, and that if she could, someone else could too. I wanted to get up and run out, run away from my memories and the idea that I was still so predictable after all this.

"Girls, dinner's ready!" Kevin chanted.

I stood up to escape Blair's searching stare. Luckily, the rest of the night was relaxed, no sore spots, nothing really significant. As always, hanging out with Kevin was pleasant, and before I knew it, I was eating dessert, licking the last bit of lemon mousse off my spoon.

It struck me, strangely, that Kevin was a bit like Landon. Both were cheerful, optimistic guys, open-armed, patient, uncomplicated, and they showed you exactly who they were. I'd lost my opportunity to enjoy what Blair had now, the comfort, the security of knowing your life isn't going to be a roller coaster with ups and downs, but instead a straight, relaxing road where you don't even need to bother buckling your seat belt.

Blair accompanied me to the door while Kevin cleared the dishes. We shared a long warm goodbye hug.

"You guys seem so happy... And you deserve it. You were right not to let Kevin get away. The way he looks at you, any girl would die for that." She smiled and wiped her thumbs across my cheeks. I hadn't realized I was crying before then. "I swear to you, sometimes I don't know what the hell's going on with me; I get so maudlin so easily, I think I've got a problem."

"Feeling things as deeply as you do should never be considered a problem."

"If that's what you say..." I laughed through my tears.

"Oh, Leah. Come here." She hugged me again.

I smiled at her and turned around. I was still fiddling with the lock on her white wooden fence when Blair broke the silence.

"Just in case: I haven't seen him with anyone all these years."

I looked back at her, swallowed, and walked away slowly toward the hostel, enjoying Byron Bay, the starry sky, the familiarity that embraced me with each step. When I got to my room, I took a shower, put on my pajamas, and lay down in bed. I dug a strawberry lollipop out of my bag and put it in my mouth before I picked up the phone.

"Did I wake you?" I asked when I heard him on the other line.

"No, I'm sitting on the couch. How's it going?"

For some reason, even though we'd spoken just a few hours before, I had the sensation that I hadn't heard his voice for days. And I didn't like that.

"Good. I had dinner with Blair and Kevin."

"How's it feel to be back?"

"Weird," I admitted. "On the one hand, I feel at home, but at the same time, I haven't been here in so long that it's like I've lost all sense of time. Have you ever experienced that? Like when you go on a trip and you don't even know what day it is or anything?"

Landon laughed. I loved the sound of his laughter. I settled deeper in bed, resting my back against the covers and pulling up the sheet.

"I think I know what you're talking about. It's normal."

"Tell me what you did today," I asked, because for some reason I didn't want to hang up right away. His voice was so comforting.

"Work. Work, work, work."

"Fun," I joked.

"Yeah. So I think I'm gonna go to bed."

"Sure. Get some sleep, Landon."

"You too, precious."

"Good night."

I left my phone on the nightstand, turned around, curled up, and closed my eyes.

40

Axel

I WAS NERVOUS WHEN I got to the gallery. Things were different that day. Waking up knowing Leah was in Byron Bay changed everything. I'd been distracted when I was surfing that morning and had fallen off my board several times, so on my way to work, I went to the café and asked Justin to serve me a strong coffee. Bad idea. Right away, my head started hurting.

"You're looking chipper," Sam joked.

"God, let it go." I rolled my eyes.

"You've got the same look my kids have on Christmas right before they open the gifts under the tree. Come here, let me fix your collar. Do you not know how to use an iron?"

"Do I need to answer that?"

"I guess I shouldn't have asked."

I didn't even have an iron; I didn't see the need for one. When on earth did mankind choose to make life more complicated by deciding wrinkles were ugly? Why couldn't the opposite be the case? I sighed while Sam arranged my shirt with exasperation and smoothed out my clothing with her hands. I smiled at her.

She was just a few years older than I, but she was acting like my mother.

"I doubt one wrinkle more or less will keep her from hating me," I said, hoping to calm her down.

"So you fucked it up bad?"

"One hundred percent. That's me. When I decide to do something, I go all in."

Sam slapped the back of my neck just as someone rang the doorbell. She hurried over to let Leah in while I waited there trying to ready myself for the impact seeing her again would cause me.

"Sorry, the gallery was open, so…"

"Don't apologize. It's a pleasure meeting you, Leah. My name's Sam. I'm guessing you've already been briefed. But in case you didn't know, I'm the general manager of the gallery."

"Really, Axel didn't tell me too much." She gave me a look that would have cowed most people, but that jarred me awake, as if I'd been suddenly roused from a long period of lethargy.

"Come on, I'll show you the space," Sam said.

"I'll come along."

Sam showed her all around the gallery and told her stories about it and how we worked with the various artists we represented. I followed behind them. Why lie—I liked the view. I barely heard what Sam was saying—Leah's body held my attention. That's why Sam's question caught me off guard.

"Sorry, what did you say?"

"The framing, Axel."

"Sure, what about it?"

Sam crossed her arms.

"We're in a hurry and you said you'd handle it. The artworks are already in the warehouse, so you can organize them today. You should try to put together two proposals, and we can decide which one is best." She looked at me with worry. "Are you okay, Axel?"

"Yeah. Headache. Same as always."

Technically, that wasn't a lie.

"Take a pill," Sam advised me. "I have a lot of work today, but if you need help, come find me. And Leah, welcome."

"Thanks."

She left us alone in one of the empty rooms, looking at each other for a few seconds that felt eternal. I forced myself to react when the moment got uncomfortable.

"Come to my office; I need to get some things."

Leah followed without complaint. She stopped on the threshold and gazed around, while I took a pill and grabbed a folder and my glasses. I put them on, and when I looked up, I felt her eyes boring into me.

"They're glasses, not a clown nose," I said.

"Sorry, it's just..." She shook her head.

"No, please, say what you're thinking." I crossed my arms and rested against the desk.

"They just don't look right on you." And she started to laugh.

Throwing me off, as always.

The first long conversation we had years ago, back when she would barely speak, was about the ears of a kangaroo in an illustration I was wrapping up. It shouldn't have surprised me, with the tension so palpable around us, that she would do something so unexpected, laughing with such vibrancy that I never wanted to take off my glasses again. I feigned indignation.

"You trying to give me a complex?"

"I doubt that's possible."

Her laughter stopped when we entered the area closed to the public, a kind of warehouse with concrete walls and floor where we kept pieces before putting them on display or after taking them down. Leah stopped upon entering to look at the works of another artist mounted on panels.

"May I?" she asked.

"Sure, go for it."

One panel had two pictures mounted on it. She pulled it out to look at it more closely. They were two portraits. She never painted those anymore. Sometimes her works contained a girl's face or the outline of a hand, but it was never anyone real.

"Who are these by?"

"Tom Wilson."

"He's good."

"Yeah, he sells."

"Are those the same thing?"

"Sales and quality? Sometimes yes, sometimes no. Not always."

"All this, your job here, it's all interesting."

I nodded while she looked at another panel.

"Why don't you ever paint faces, Leah?"

She looked back at me over her shoulder, wrinkled her nose, and went on studying Wilson's work.

"No interest. They don't say anything to me."

"You'd rather distort reality?" I smiled.

"I wouldn't say that. It's more about showing my interpretation. Isn't that how everything is? I don't think it gets any more real than that. Human beings are subjective; all of us have our own vision of each thing, each story. A different perspective."

I interiorized her words. Yes, life was like that sometimes, a succession of different ways of seeing the same thing that sometimes led to incomprehension.

"We should get to work."

Leah followed me to the other end of the warehouse and started unwrapping her pieces. I had finally decided to bring almost all her *unclassifiable* pieces.

"What now?" she asked me.

"We need to think about the work as a whole, you know? When you're placing the paintings around, you need them to show continuity, as if they were telling the visitors a story."

"A logic..."

"Exactly, because that will affect their perception of them. If we put this painting next to that one, the person who looks at it will see light and then darkness right afterward. That's saying something important. Describing a change. A happiness broken by a painful event, say. If we do the opposite, then it expresses something else: hope, overcoming. No one knows better than you what you were trying to say with each painting, and we need to create an attractive setup, one that communicates."

Leah bit her lower lip, still contemplating her work, as if she didn't really know where to begin. I made myself stop gawking at her and sat on the ground, asking her to follow suit.

"Let's start at the beginning. We've got three rooms for your exhibition." I pulled a piece of paper out of the folder I'd brought and handed it to her, a blueprint of the gallery. "In this room, the smallest one, we've only got space for three pieces, so they need to have an impact, right?"

"I hear you," she whispered.

The next hour flew by.

We still hadn't made a firm decision about the first room when Sam came in and asked if we wanted to have breakfast with her. We ended up ordering the usual at the café on the corner: coffee and toast with Vegemite. Sam talked nonstop about her husband, her kids, and the menu at the restaurant where she'd eaten the night before. The mood was casual, and she got Leah to relax.

"Speaking of menus, yesterday I got an idea for the exhibition. What if my brother took care of the food? We could ask him to do something savory."

"That would be amazing!" Leah said with a dazzling smile. "Actually, I wouldn't mind sticking with the sweet stuff, though."

"Sweets at a gallery opening?" Sam said.

"Why not? We could toast with chocolate milkshakes!" I bit my lip to keep from grinning when I saw Sam's stupefied expression as Leah got more and more riled up. "To hell with champagne. We could serve little pastries and cookies. Or even gummies!"

"I'm not sure about that," Sam said.

"Let's do it," I interrupted her.

I loved how Leah didn't want one of those snooty, refined exhibitions so many artists dream of. Not that one was better or worse, but this one was all her.

"I guess it'll be original," Sam conceded.

"Will you talk to Justin?" Leah asked.

"Yeah, I'll go see him around noon. You want to come?"

Leah shifted uncomfortably in her seat and set down her coffee. "I promised your parents I'd have lunch with them."

"So I'm like the girl at high school no one will ask to the prom. I guess I'll cry," I joked, and Sam nudged me with her elbow before getting up with the words, "I've got the check."

Leah ran a finger over the handle of her cup and looked at me. I could feel tension flowing between us, but beneath that negativity, there was a gentleness still that continued to throb in our memories.

"Sorry. I think your mom felt it would be uncomfortable and decided to avoid it."

"Sure." I couldn't take my eyes off her. "Is it for you?"

"Sometimes it is. Sometimes no."

"Always so ambiguous."

She smiled and stood up.

I wished I could plant my lips on that smile.

41

Leah

I SAID GOODBYE TO AXEL when he closed the gallery at midday, and I walked to the Nguyens'. I got the urge to listen to some music along the way and stopped to pull out my headphones. I skipped through several songs on the sidewalk until I reached those of a band I'd barely listened to those past few years. I hit play and heard the first chords of "Hey Jude."

I started strolling again to the song's rhythm.

Georgia greeted me with one of those hugs that squeeze the breath out of you. Daniel just clapped me on the back as he accompanied me to the living room. The table was set and full of food.

"You've outdone yourself. This is too much."

"I know how much you like a good roast. Sit down before it gets cold, honey." They sat with me. "There's also cheesecake for dessert."

I tried not to get too excited.

"You're gorgeous. Look how long your hair is!" Georgia poured me some water and grabbed the knife to carve the meat.

"Now we need you to tell us every last detail about the exhibition, don't we, Daniel?"

"We sure do." He smiled affably. "We knew you'd make it."

"I mean, it's really all thanks to Axel."

I don't know why I felt the need to point that out. Maybe it wasn't the right thing to do, because I noticed Georgia had to take a sip of water to get down the bite of food she was chewing. But still, it was true. Despite everything, it was Axel's doing, like so many other things. He may have made mistakes, but that didn't take away from his virtues.

Georgia was nervous as she looked at me. Her husband smiled with pride though.

"My boy's intuitive. He's got a good head for business."

"That doesn't surprise me. He seems to like it."

"We hope it lasts." Georgia sighed and twisted her paper napkin up between her fingers. "With all that happened, we…"

"What my wife's trying to say is it isn't any of our business," Daniel said, cutting her off, but she gave him an irritated look and continued.

"It is our business in a way. What I want to tell you is, I know Axel can be complicated, and what he did was wrong. But he's not a bad boy, and you know that. We don't want you to vanish again, Leah. These years have been hard on all of us."

"What he did?" I asked.

"I mean, you were just a girl."

"He didn't do anything wrong."

"Think about all you'd been through."

That stung. I blinked. It was strange; I felt this pressure in my chest. To me, the one thing Axel did wrong was be a coward, not face up to everyone else and himself, and in that way he failed himself, and he failed me too. That was what I couldn't forgive. But hearing those words from his mother, I started to understand the burden he was under. Not that I was justifying his actions, but I realized he might have been scared, and that none of this was easy...

I wanted to free him from that, at least with his family. I put my silverware aside and took a breath.

"I know we've never talked about this before, I guess because it was easier to ignore it and just keep going like it was nothing..." Georgia was watching me, expectant, attentive, a little abashed. "But in all honesty, I didn't fall in love with Axel those months we were living together. I fell in love with him long before. I always loved him. And I wanted to be with him. What happened between us wasn't bad. It was anything but."

"Leah, you don't have to go on." Daniel reached across the table and squeezed my hand.

But I wanted to go on, because I needed things to be clear, and because Georgia's silence was killing me. I blinked to hold back my tears.

"If I'm here today, it's thanks to him. Because I didn't want to paint. I didn't want to talk. I didn't want to live. And Axel... awakened me. And in a way, despite everything, he's the one who gave me the future I have now."

Georgia got up, eyes glazed, and left the room. For a long minute, all was silence, it seemed it would never end, and then Daniel surrounded me with a warm paternal embrace.

"Don't worry about her; she thought she needed to protect

you. You probably just seemed to her like a fragile little girl then, whereas he…"

"Sometimes strong people hide behind a shield to keep from showing their fears and weaknesses."

He nodded, understanding what I meant to say. Because Axel wasn't as strong as everyone thought, and I wasn't as delicate. But appearances are deceiving.

"I'll go talk to her."

"No, I will." I suggested.

"Are you sure?"

I nodded, smiled, and went to the kitchen.

Georgia was cutting the cheesecake she had just taken out of the fridge into small triangular portions. I remembered how whenever she got nervous, she had to keep her hands busy. The thought tugged at my heart. I walked up behind her silently and embraced her. She stood still, but I could feel the sobs escaping her as she moved. When she turned around and looked at me with damp eyes, I forgot why I'd gotten angry with her, because that's how it is with family; you try and remember why you were mad, and it just doesn't matter anymore.

"I'm sorry," she whispered. "I felt like I had to protect you, that it was what your mother would have wanted, and when all that happened…it was like I had failed you. It hurt not being able to take care of you when Oliver had to go away to work; there was no room here, and everything got so complicated…"

I smiled and shook my head. "You worry too much."

"I don't worry enough," she joked.

"I'm not a little girl anymore, Georgia."

"I guess not... So you always liked Axel. How is it possible that I didn't realize that?"

I blushed and shrugged. "Mom certainly knew."

"Rose? And she never warned you away from him?"

"I don't think she worried about it." I stared at the tiles while Georgia rubbed my shoulders softly. "Anyway, it's done. It doesn't matter anymore."

42

Leah

WE WORKED SHOULDER TO SHOULDER the next two days until we had the layout of the rooms ready and all the pictures framed. It was easy. The way it used to be.

We took a break to get lunch with Sam at the café and then went back to the gallery one day; on the other, we went to Axel's office to go over last-minute details. That afternoon, it grew hot.

"Looks like everything's ready," I said.

"Yeah, and tomorrow we'll finally be able to try the menu Justin's put together. There aren't many dishes, but he seems to have taken it super seriously."

Hearing that made me feel elated.

"Great. Anything else?"

"There's a newspaper that's interested. It's not a big deal, but they want to do a short interview for their culture section." He leafed through some pages on his desk. "When the pictures are up, we'll work on lighting. Then there's the most important part of the exhibition: you, the artist."

"Are you talking about socializing and all that?"

"Yeah. This is an event, after all. When people come to see the works, they also want to talk to the artist, ask questions, have a conversation..."

"I'll be awful at that."

"I'd say the opposite."

"You've got a lot of faith in me."

"We'll practice; don't worry."

"Okay." I looked at him indecisively, not knowing if it was time to say goodbye and go, or if we still had details to go over.

"Do you have something you need to do right now?"

"Nothing concrete. Why?"

"I was wondering... The waves are good today, so I was thinking you might want to take the board out for a while, you know."

"I'm not sure that's a good idea..."

"Why not?"

"To start, because I haven't done it in three years."

Axel looked confused. Then he rested his hands on his desk and leaned in toward me.

"Did I hear that right? You haven't surfed in three years?"

"That's right." I giggled.

"Give me a fucking break."

"It's just how things are." I stood up.

"Wait. Come do it. This afternoon."

"Axel..."

"Just for a bit."

"I'll think about it," I said before leaving.

43

Axel

HONESTLY, I DIDN'T EXPECT HER to show up on my doorstep, but still, her absence hurt. The sun was already setting on the horizon when I decided to grab a board and take the path down to the shore. The sea was choppy that day, the waves good. I got in and stopped thinking of anything as I slipped, fell, and got back on.

I don't know how long I was there when I saw her.

She was close to the shore, with a longboard she'd grabbed off my porch under her arm and a tiny red bikini that immediately captured my attention. I wanted to take it off and lick the skin beneath it and have everything go back to the way it was before. Every time I remembered how distant that possibility was, it felt like a blow to the stomach.

I swam over to her.

"Didn't think you were coming."

"Me neither," she admitted.

"What made you change your mind?"

"Like you said, it's *just for a bit*, and yesterday I spent all afternoon shut up in a hostel. But listen up: absolutely no laughing at me! It's been a long time, okay…"

"I won't laugh," I promised.

She turned away and headed into the water. I followed her, with a warm feeling in my heart, knowing she was back here, in my stretch of sea, under an orange evening sky, even if just for a fleeting moment, because that was better than nothing. Anything was.

I was so scared I'd screw it up, say something that would push her away, that I kept my mouth shut the whole time she tried to cleave the waves, even if she kept falling off too early. When she was too tired, she lay on her board, resting her cheek on its surface. She was stunning.

"I don't think I can move."

I laughed and sat next to her on my board. "Tomorrow we've got a lot to do."

"I hope I'm not causing Justin any headaches. Because of the unanticipated catering gig."

"He couldn't be happier. First to be doing it, and second because I'll owe him a huge favor."

"So things haven't changed with you guys."

"Nah, I was kidding." I narrowed my eyes. The last rays of sunlight were blinding me. "Everything's different now, honestly. We're friends."

"Are you serious?"

"Yeah. I took him out the other day for a walk, and he wound up scarfing a marijuana brownie and dancing with a group of girls. Can you believe it?" I laughed.

Leah sat up, curious.

"What changed in your relationship?"

"Nothing. Everything. I guess sometimes the person you least expect to understand you surprises you, and they're there for you when you need them. That's what happened."

She looked at the horizon, and we stayed there in silence, contemplating the rise and fall of the waves and the sea reflecting the dying light. That evening was different, the way it always was when Leah was there. Unique. Intense.

44

Leah

IT'S FUNNY HOW HUMAN BEINGS can get used to new situations. I'd only been in Byron Bay a few days, and it was as if I'd been there those lost three years, as if I'd never left. Maybe because I knew every street all too well. Maybe because, despite everything, it was my home. And there's no place as comfortable as home.

I didn't go to the gallery that morning because I had to meet with the guy who was interviewing me for the local paper. I was so nervous at first that he offered to get me a glass of water before the next question, but then, I just tried to focus on responding to what he asked, without thinking, and everything flowed. It was much easier than I expected.

I ate lunch with Blair and walked to the Nguyens' café that afternoon. That place had always been in my life. I'd spent so many long afternoons there with my parents, or with Georgia when they'd drop me off because they had something to do. Justin had renovated it when he took over the business, but I still recognized everything, right down to the last cup.

Everyone was there when I arrived: Emily, the twins, Georgia, and Daniel.

But there wasn't a trace of Axel. It was weird to me all of a sudden that I'd gone the whole day without seeing him. And I thought about how we get used to everything. It used to be so hard for me not to miss him, and there I was again, feeling strange because I hadn't heard from him in twenty-four hours.

"Come here." Justin smiled and grabbed my hand to take me over to the table he'd set up. It was covered in tiny pastries. "Sit down. Today, you're the boss."

"Me?" I laughed. "You say this like I've got some refined palate!"

Little Max sat down next to me, and everyone else took their places at the table. I loved being there with them, surrounded by what was also my family, the people I'd missed so much. I'd seen them these past three years, but only once in a while, and nothing had been the same, not the way it was in Byron Bay.

"Try the orange and chocolate puff pastry."

"You're stressing her out, Justin!" Emily smiled.

"Son, this is...*bodacious*." Daniel licked his lips.

Georgia rolled her eyes, chuckled, and shook her head before giving me a tender look. I felt a tickle in my nose, I was so happy, and I blinked through the beginnings of tears as I grabbed one of the pastries.

"You like?" Justin seemed nervous.

"Honestly, it's incredible. Everything's perfect." I took another look at the plates covering the tables. "This is going to be the coolest exhibition in the world."

My smile faltered when I looked at the café door and saw that it was still closed. I shook my head. Maybe Axel had things to do. Maybe it hadn't even occurred to him to attend a reunion more family than professional, even if we were looking over the menu that would be served at the gallery.

"You know I've got my own board now?" Connor said proudly.

"Really? Since when?" I asked.

"Since a month ago. Me too!" his brother, Max, added.

I mussed his hair, and he grunted before taking a sip of his chocolate shake. I did the same. It was delicious.

"Justin, thanks for everything. Really."

"I should be thanking you. I get to make Axel my slave for the foreseeable future after this. I love my brother, don't get me wrong, but nothing makes me happier than driving him nuts."

"Some things never change," Emily said to me, grinning.

"Speaking of Axel, where is he?"

Everyone suddenly stared at me. I felt strange, exposed.

"He didn't call you?" Justin asked. "His head hurt. One of those migraines he gets sometimes. It's just as well he stayed home to rest, because when he feels bad, he's absolutely unbearable."

"Don't say that about your brother!" Georgia complained.

"It's true!" He shrugged. "Mom, admit it: putting up with him when he's sick is torture. We all know it."

"He just can't stand feeling bad," she said, trying to justify him.

Daniel smiled and ran the back of his hand along his wife's cheek. It was a small gesture, very pretty... It must have been amazing to know that you had done all this: a family, children, grandchildren, a business.

We talked all the way through the meal. They brought me up to date on their lives, and I told them things they already knew about Brisbane. Georgia and Daniel were the first ones to get up and go, followed by Emily and the kids. I stayed a while because, to start with, I didn't have anything better to do, and then, I wanted to help clean up. Justin and I cleaned the table and arranged the plates in the dishwasher.

It was a comfortable silence. I hung my rag up to dry.

"So you're going to do it. Everything you ever wanted."

"I'm not really sure what it is I want," I conceded.

"Isn't this it? Making a living off your painting?"

"I guess. But I never really had a concrete dream; I just wanted to paint, that's all. It sounds conformist, right? Or naive, or something."

"Not at all. The only thing I wanted was to have a café. There are no big or small dreams, Leah."

"You're right." I took off my apron on the way out of the kitchen. "I guess I can always figure out what I'm looking for along the way."

We said our goodbyes just before nightfall, and I took off walking for the hostel. Maybe I should have been more surprised when my steps changed direction two streets later, but I wasn't. A part of me wanted to do it, even if another shouted at me to turn around.

And so, fifteen minutes later, I reached that place I knew so well. I didn't ring the doorbell, because I thought he might be sleeping, and I walked around the house until I reached the back porch where we had spent so many hours. The surfboards were piled up against one wall, the wind was making the hammock sway, and wild ivy was creeping up the handrail of the steps. Everything was the same, as if time had stopped there.

I climbed the steps and stopped. I still had time to turn back. But I didn't. I hesitated a few seconds, nervous, before deciding to open the door and sneak into that house I knew so well.

I walked inside slowly. The living room was empty. As my eyes settled on the familiar furniture, objects, details, I felt a sharp pain in my chest, as if I'd traveled back in time, but as a different person, one who was seeing everything through a much broader prism.

As I stepped forward, I left my fears behind, and when I entered the bedroom, I held my breath.

Axel was asleep. He was wearing swim trunks and had one arm draped over his face, as though trying to protect himself from the afternoon sun that had come through the windows hours before. His chest rose and fell with each breath. And above him, the picture we painted together while we made love was still hanging over the bed. I grabbed the doorframe when I felt my legs trembling.

Why had he kept it?

I wanted to wake him up and shout all the things I'd never said. How he'd hurt me. How he'd broken my heart. How I couldn't understand that all we'd lived through had meant so little to him. How I had slept all those nights with tears in my eyes. How I was still that same silly little girl who thought and didn't act and did the things she promised she would never do again.

Because there I was.

Looking at him...

Shaking...

I turned around and went back to the living room.

I stood there a while until I calmed down and remembered why I'd come to see him. I went to the kitchen and opened the cabinets to see what was inside them. Too much alcohol, to start with. Not much food. I smiled when I saw the envelopes of powdered soup Georgia must still buy him regularly. I grabbed one and turned on the light to read the instructions, because I couldn't remember how much water they needed. As the light bled into the living room, I could make out above his desk the painting I'd given him weeks back in the studio, the one that showed our stretch of sea.

I took out a pot and boiled water in it. I'd make him dinner, wake him up, and make sure he was okay before I left.

Nothing else.

45

Axel

I DIDN'T KNOW WHAT TIME it was when I woke up.

The pain had died down, but my head was still throbbing. I got up slowly, trying not to make any sudden movements, and walked barefoot to the living room. I stopped when I noticed the scent pervading the house and I saw her there, sitting on a stool in the kitchen looking at me.

"Am I still dreaming? Because if so, I don't know what you're doing still dressed."

Leah rolled her eyes and smiled.

"I wanted to see how you were," she said.

I sat on the free stool next to the wooden counter across from her and tried to figure out what she was doing there. Happy as I was to see her, I was also surprised.

She got up and poured the soup into a bowl and set it down in front of me before handing me a spoon. I struggled to grasp what exactly was going on.

"I feel better now. You don't need to do this."

"It's just dinner," she replied.

I'd been sick to my stomach all afternoon. I was no longer nauseated, but when my migraines struck, I preferred to pick up a bottle or stay confined to the bed. Hot soup was a no-go.

"Your family's right, Axel. You're unbearable. When someone comes to your house to take care of you, the best thing is to just say *thanks* and put whatever they've made you in your mouth. It's called manners."

"You know I don't have those."

"True. I've got to go, so…"

"No, wait. Have dinner with me. Take half."

I pointed at the bowl with my spoon and gave her a pleading look. If my idiot face didn't melt her resistance, nothing would. I was starting to feel ashamed of myself.

After a moment's hesitation, Leah sat down.

We divided the soup into two bowls and sank into a silence that said all too much. Or maybe that's just what I thought. Maybe it was easier for me to believe that something was left of *us* than to accept the reality, the pain.

I got up to gather the dishes.

"I should go," Leah said.

"You can't walk back alone at night."

"Don't be stupid," she said.

"I'll take you. Just wait a while so I can smoke." I grabbed my pack of cigarettes. Her look was doubting, but she followed me onto the porch. "If they didn't know you, a person would say I had just kidnapped you or something. You don't need to glare at me."

She grunted while I lit up, and stood there beside me with her hands on the railing. The dark night sky was dappled with stars.

"So…" I asked, "What's this all about?"

"About? I don't know what you mean."

"You being here…"

"I just wanted to know how you were," she repeated.

I tried to be strong and ask her the question I feared most, because maybe deep down I already knew her well enough to feel what she was feeling, and so I knew it would make me suffer. And it was still hard for me to face things. To accept them.

"Does this mean you've forgiven me?"

She waited a moment before responding.

"I've forgiven the Axel who was my friend, my family."

"What about the one who used to fuck you?"

"No. Not that one." I felt her staring through me. It stung.

And yet, in the midst of that pain, I understood her need to separate things, and that perhaps that was the only way she could get close to me again without reproaching me. We hadn't talked about *it*. She hadn't asked me to explain myself. And her reactions hadn't been what I expected. It was as if nothing had happened, and we could go back to before, back to what we once had before the two of us decided to cross that line and everything changed.

I took a long drag and blew out the smoke.

"I get it," I whispered.

Leah suddenly looked away, discomfited.

I leaned against the post as she stepped back, seemingly needing to leave, then started pacing nervously from one end of the porch to the other. I don't know how many minutes passed that way. All I could think of was cutting through the distance between us and kissing her until we both forgot who we were and the history we were dragging behind us.

I clutched the railing.

"It's fine, Leah, everything's fine. Stop doing that." She stood still then and ran a hand over the back of her neck. "I was serious when I said that. I understand how you feel."

"Bullshit."

"Babe..."

"You'll never understand, Axel."

I knew then I was never going to win that war. She had locked the door and thrown away the key, and I wasn't sure knocking it down or waiting until she figured out how to let me back in were the right options.

"What about him? Does *he* understand?" I asked.

Her eyes opened like saucers, and she shook her head.

"I'm not talking about him with you."

"Why not?" I decided to bet everything on that card. "You've forgiven me, as a friend anyway, right? Then show it. I'm here. All I want is to talk. According to your reasoning, that should be easy."

"He's a good person," she said.

"What's his name?"

I don't know if I needed to torture myself, but the one thing I wanted to do then was keep pulling harder and harder on that frayed fragile cord that united us until we were close enough that there was barely any room left to breathe. I didn't care if it hurt. I didn't care about anything anymore.

"Landon."

"Do you go to school with him?"

"No."

"He doesn't paint?"

"No. Do you?"

"Me?" I asked, confused.

"You're still not painting?"

"Correct. Did you expect otherwise?"

"I don't know. I never know what to expect with you."

"Is that good or bad?"

She shook her head, as if she weren't sure what she was doing there on my porch, and she brought her fingers to the bridge of her nose.

"Could you take me to the hostel, Axel?"

"I can. Now ask me if I want to."

"Do you want to take me…?"

I was going to respond. I was going to say no, goddammit, she should stay, forever, but when I saw how her eyes were pleading with me, I had a change of heart. I could almost hear her in my mind saying, "Please don't do this. Please, please, please." And however shitty it was, I thought: better to have a bit of her friendship than lose all of her again forever.

"Wait here, I'll go get the keys."

Five minutes later, we were in the car.

We barely talked as we passed through the streets on the way to the hostel. When we got there, I didn't cut the motor; I just pulled over to one side of the road.

"Thanks for coming. And thanks for dinner."

"It was nothing," she said.

We looked at each other in the darkness. The light of a far-off streetlamp glanced off the windshield. The street was deserted, and it had started to drizzle.

"So...friends?" I asked.

"Friends," she answered calmly.

I stopped her as she opened the door.

"Are you really going to leave without giving me a kiss?"

"Axel..." Her eyes drilled into me.

"Sorry. I'm a bad little boy."

I pointed to one of my cheeks, and I could see she was trying not to grin as she bent over and gave me a kiss so soft I could barely feel it. She got out before I could complain, and I stayed there smiling like an idiot while she crossed the street and went upstairs.

46

—

Leah

I WAS READING A MAGAZINE on my parents' porch when Axel appeared. I remember it was summer, I was on break from school, and I couldn't stop thinking about what Jane Cabot, a classmate, had told Blair and me a few days before: she had kissed a boy. She was the first girl in our class to do it.

"What are you doing out here, babe?" Axel asked. He looked so much older...

The week before, he had turned twenty, and we had gathered in the yard to celebrate, even though he complained he was too old for that kind of party. I didn't understand how you could be *too old* for your birthday, and I wanted all of us to keep getting together for that kind of meal forever, even if he was ninety or more and we all had wrinkly skin.

"You here to see Dad?" I asked.

"Yeah, is he inside?" He pointed to the door.

"He's arguing about something dumb with Oliver." I rolled my eyes, and he laughed and rubbed my head. "Wait, stay here a bit. I need to know something."

Axel sat down beside me on the wood floor. The wind was warm, and he was wearing a shirt with rolled-up sleeves and a palm tree print. I liked it.

"What do you want to know?"

I'd almost forgotten. I tucked away the magazine I was reading because it had something on the cover like "Three Foolproof Tricks to Kiss Him until He Has a Heart Attack." I blushed while I looked for the right words, but then I just came out with it:

"Axel, what's it feel like to kiss?"

"Kiss?" He looked shocked.

"Yeah. When a boy kisses a girl."

He hesitated a moment before replying, "At your age, you shouldn't be interested in that."

"The other day, a friend of mine kissed a boy."

"Well, then...your friend made a mistake. And the thing about making a mistake when you kiss is, you can't take it back. You should only kiss a person you really love, Leah, understand?"

"Yeah. Like how I love you," I said.

Axel grinned and looked away.

"Not like that, babe. What I mean is one day you'll meet a person you like so much that you won't know how to tell them what you feel without using your mouth."

"Ugh! Gross, Axel!" I laughed.

I thought about what he said awhile as I toyed with the end of one of the braids my mother had put in that morning.

"What about you? Have you kissed lots of people?"

"Me?" Again, Axel looked surprised.

"Yeah, dummy, who else?"

His expression turned serious. I loved that about Axel, the way he seemed to believe I would understand everything he said to me. That made him different from my brother and everyone else. With him, I felt stronger. Older. When I needed an honest response to a question, I always turned to him.

"Can I tell you a secret?" I nodded right away. "I was a little like that friend of yours, and I made a lot of mistakes. That's why I can tell you what you shouldn't do. And you know what? I never have given a real kiss."

I didn't know exactly what a *real kiss* or what a *fake kiss* might mean. Maybe it had to do with how long they lasted, I thought, and I was about to ask him when my father came outside.

"Axel! I didn't know you were already here. Be a good boy and come up to the studio for a moment before you take off with Oliver."

I stretched out on the ground as they went inside and their voices trailed off. And I thought of kisses on that summer night, about how hard it was to make the right choice and about how I needed to talk to Blair about all this as soon as possible.

47

Axel

I SAT DOWN IN FRONT of the desk and looked at the painting Leah had done of our sea beneath a stormy sky. I ran my fingers over it, as I'd done before, feeling the irregular edges, the layers of paint, the mistakes she'd tried to cover up. Then I did it: I grabbed a kitchen knife and very slowly scraped the paint off one of the corners with the tip. I bent over and gasped as I saw among the dark flakes a few lighter ones, cobalt blue in color.

At one point, that somber sky had been clear.

48

Axel

WITH SAM AND LEAH'S COLLABORATION, getting the exhibition ready was easy. We worked tirelessly over the following days. My head stopped aching, maybe because I started wearing the glasses Leah thought were so funny more often, and I made sure every detail was perfect.

By Friday morning, we were ready.

With Leah on my heels, I walked through the three rooms, admiring the final result as though I hadn't seen it a dozen times already.

"Satisfied?" I smiled.

"Yeah. And nervous."

"In less than twenty-four hours, this room will be full of people." Word had gotten round that the Joneses' daughter was an artist, and that got people interested. If that wasn't enough, I'd also convinced my nephews the afternoon before to stick up posters on the nearby streets in exchange for the use of my surfboard. "I'd say the time's come for a dry run, what do you think?"

"I think I'll die of a heart attack."

"Always exaggerating." I laughed.

She followed me back to the door of the gallery.

"What are you doing?" she asked.

"A simulation. Imagine people are around you munching on something, chatting, looking at the pictures, and I'm a very demanding visitor who's just come in." I walked down the hall to the first room, and when I got there, I looked at the pictures for a few seconds. Then I turned to Leah and asked, "Are you the artist?"

She laughed a second, then turned serious. "Yes." I looked at her as if to say that wasn't enough, and then she spoke again: "Sorry. It's my first exhibition, I'm a little nervous."

"Well, you've got a lot of talent for a beginner."

"Thanks. Actually I've been painting my whole life."

"Interesting. So this was your dream then?" I asked, walking on to see the remaining pieces in that room.

"Painting, yes. Exhibiting... I don't know."

For a moment, I dropped my role, because the response threw me off. I looked at her intensely, as if doing so might help me see beneath her skin.

"Why else would you paint?"

"Just because. For the pleasure of doing it. Of feeling."

"You've never wondered what another person might think of the art you're creating?"

"You're a very curious visitor, aren't you?"

I laughed and shook my head, because she was right, I had gone off script a little.

"Okay, fine, let's start over." I walked to the next room.

"Imagine you're here and all of a sudden someone comes over to ask you a question."

"Shoot," she said.

I pointed to the picture of the girl with the heart.

"What does this picture mean exactly?"

I could tell that made her nervous. Because it was something personal, something deeply hers, and then all at once it was going to be on display before the eyes of anyone who felt like looking at it.

"It's lovelessness."

"I don't understand."

Maybe I was playing dirty, but I needed to know. And anyway, it wasn't something Sam or another person couldn't have asked. Collectors and art lovers came to openings for this reason: to meet the artist, learn the secrets behind the work, and decide whether it was worth buying, because they wanted that little extra that made it different, special, unique.

"It's the exact moment when a person decides to give you back your heart even though you gave it to them. That's why she's holding it in her hands. Because she had given it up, handed it over to him, and she doesn't know what to do with this thing that doesn't really belong to her."

Lord. That girl could kill me with words alone. With her eyes. With anything. She could make me turn to stone even when I thought I had the advantage. I understood then that she would always win. Always.

I was one step behind, trying to understand myself when she already understood both of us. I cleared my throat.

"How can I purchase it?"

"You'll have to talk to my agent." She smiled. "He must be around here. He's tall, he usually has a furrowed forehead, and he's wearing funny-looking glasses."

I grunted in response, but I was happy to see the tension had been relieved. We went on playacting for a while more, considering the different questions a person might ask and the best way to answer them. When it was time to close the gallery, we said goodbye to Sam, and I walked Leah back to the hostel.

"The big day's just around the corner," she sighed.

"You still nervous?" I asked.

"I doubt I'll be able to sleep."

"I'll bet."

"My brother will be here tomorrow."

"I know. Your boyfriend too, right?"

Her back stiffened, and she licked her lips, unaware of that gesture's effect on my self-control. She grabbed a flower from the creepers growing on the roadside behind a fence and plucked off the petals slowly.

"He's not really my boyfriend, you know, not exactly. I wanted to tell you before, but honestly, it wasn't something I felt like talking to you about. Landon is... I'm in a relationship with him. Without labels. It's different."

"Different..." I savored the word.

"We're together," she added.

"I hear that. I guess you'll introduce us."

With a thankful expression, still nervous, Leah kissed me on the cheek and disappeared through the door of the hostel. And a part of me thought if she didn't have a boyfriend, I wouldn't have stood there like an idiot; I'd have eaten her alive with kisses, even running the risk that she might reject me. But then, I was also starting to grasp that things aren't always as simple as what one person can or can't do. Sometimes, there's a lot more to it.

49

Leah

ASSOCIATIVE MEMORY IS DANGEROUS, I'VE always thought. The memory we don't control ourselves, that awakens forgotten sensations just because someone brushes past us. I had lots of things tucked away in boxes piling up inside me.

My mother was the scent of lavender, hands untangling my hair before braiding it, calm. Dad was a vibrant laugh, the scent of paint, color. The flavor of a strawberry lollipop and the sea breeze, that was my school days and afternoons walking through Byron Bay. The Nguyens were Sundays, cheesecake, family. And Axel...

Axel was many things. That was the problem.

Associating him with all those details had dangerous consequences, because the memory of him trapped me. Axel was dawn and dusk, tenuous light. He was printed shirts half-unbuttoned, tea after dinner, nights on the porch. He was the sea, the sand, and the foam on the crests of waves. He was the tattoo I had on my ribs, that "Let it be" drawn by his hands. He was the first time I'd been with someone between the sheets. He was that gesture of raising his chin to look at the stars, and the soft music that enveloped me...

The only person who, if "Yellow Submarine" started playing somewhere, would also hear an "I love you" behind the words *we all live in a yellow submarine*.

And it didn't matter how much I ran, I could never escape what I'd been unless I was ready to erase those parts of myself.

50

Leah

NO SURPRISE, I COULDN'T SLEEP, so I tried to calm myself down after turning over in bed and staring up at the ceiling. I thought of all that would happen in just a few hours and felt my stomach turn. My paintings would be hanging on the walls of a gallery in front of a bunch of people who would see different things in them, translating the brushstrokes in their way, taking what they wanted from here and from there, and that frightened me. Not being able to communicate what I wanted. When I left them there, I would renounce them in the sense that they wouldn't just be mine and couldn't have just a single meaning, they would mean many things and would belong to whoever wanted to see them.

I breathed deep and closed my eyes. And then I heard it.

A soft *tick* followed by many others. *Tick, tick.* I threw aside the sheets and got up. *Tick, tick, tick.* I walked to the window and jerked up to open it. I had to rub my eyes to be sure what I was seeing was real. Axel dropped the pebbles he still had in his hand and shrugged when he saw my disconcerted expression. I grinned.

"You're thirty-three years old. That's too old to be doing this kind of thing."

"I guess I feel young when I'm around you."

"I can't believe it."

"I knew you'd be awake."

"It's midnight, Axel."

"Come down. It's Friday; there are places open."

I thought about it for a moment, but who am I trying to fool? I'd been tossing and turning in bed for hours and wasn't going to say no. I sighed and told him I'd be ready in five minutes. I put on a pale blue summer dress with white spots and a pair of flats and walked outside.

Axel was leaning on the fence.

"Couldn't you have just called me?"

"I thought that was too conventional," he joked.

"And the pebbles striking the window wasn't?"

"Seemed more fun."

He smiled in that way that seemed to stop time. I hated it! His magnetism. How easy everything was for him. I shook my head and walked up beside him, and the two of us went downhill.

"Where are we headed?" I asked.

"To grab a drink. Perhaps."

"I'm so nervous! I've got this feeling like everything's going to fall apart, or I'll draw a blank when someone talks to me, or I'll open my eyes and find myself standing there naked in the middle of the gallery."

"I wish that would happen! I'd be in the front row."

"Idiot!" I pushed him and he laughed.

"It's going to go great. But that's why I came to find you, because I know you and I knew you'd be getting all dramatic. Anyway, I've got a surprise for you. I think you'll like it." He looked a little uncertain, and I couldn't read his expression.

I felt that tingle all over that I used to feel whenever I was going to get a present or someone was trying to surprise me. I remember how I used to rip off the wrapping paper, anxious and elated, unable to think of anything else. Those evocative streets dusted off parts of the girl I had left behind years ago.

But I kept myself in check and asked no questions.

We reached the boardwalk and continued along to a place where there were bars and gatherings of people. We decided to stop at one next to the shore that was little more than a shack. When we got inside, I kicked off my sandals and felt the wood floor and the sand on my toes.

"You still like mojitos?"

"Yeah," I replied, and he ordered two.

"I trained you well..."

I felt breathless as I remembered the night when I told Axel I wanted to get drunk, and he gave in and we danced together to "Let It Be" with our eyes closed. He had made a pitcher of mojitos, and later he'd kissed me for the first time under the stars.

How far away it seemed, and how close at the same time.

I took a long drink. In the background, "Too Young to Burn" by Sonny & the Sunsets was playing, and the night owls were laughing and trying to dance in the middle of the bar while farther off, some people were taking a late-night dip.

"If you tell me what you're thinking, I'll buy the next round," Axel said.

"Trying to make me an offer I can't refuse? Nah, I'm not having another."

I stirred my ice and sucked up the dregs of my mojito through a straw. Axel leaned on the bar and gave me one of those twisted smiles I remembered so well, the ones that turned my world upside down.

"Remind me which of us has ten years on the other?" he joked.

"How about you remind me which of us is still just a big baby?"

He laughed. He was wearing a loose blue shirt with the first few buttons undone. The warm wind disheveled his hair. He still had that same captivating look that attracted me and frightened me in equal measure.

I ordered another. I don't know why I changed my mind. He did the same, and we clinked glasses.

"For successes to come," he said, and I smiled and drank, keeping my eyes on him the whole time.

"So it's one of two things," he said. "Either I'm incredibly attractive or you're studying the best way to finish me off and hide my body."

"It's obviously the second."

"I should have guessed." He set his glass on the bar.

"Really, though," I said, turning serious and a little timid, "there's something I've been thinking about for days... I don't think I thanked you yet for everything you've done for me."

"You have, Leah, and anyway, there's no need."

"Let me finish. You did it unselfishly. You let me into your home. You took care of me. You got me to feel again, to paint, to live. Only you and I know what happened during those months, and I don't care what anyone else thinks, because they'll never understand it. So thank you. Because you were generous. A friend. Family."

His eyes were a stormy sea full of feelings I couldn't really read. He looked moved, anxious, agitated. He licked his lips and froze for a moment before saying:

"But you still haven't forgiven me..."

"Don't confuse one thing with another."

It was almost a plea. Because I wanted to keep the good. His generosity. His loyalty. His sensibility. But if I thought of the Axel who used to make love to me, I saw other things. His cowardice. His selfishness. His weakness. His fears. His harsh words.

He knew neither of us wanted to go down that road, because he changed the subject right away, ordered two more drinks despite my protests, and hid himself again behind that crooked smile.

51

Axel

LEAH TALKED TO ME ABOUT her classes—just one more, plus a final project she'd work on next semester—about her uncertainty as to what to do afterward, the vacations she'd spent with Oliver and Bega the past few summers, the new drawing techniques she'd tried...

I listened rapt, following the movement of her lips as we drank our way deeper into the morning. At my insistence, we had one last drink, a red strawberry something, because that flavor always reminded me of her. She smiled when I whispered this into her ear.

"Payphone" by Maroon 5 started playing, and I got up.

"Dance with me." I stretched out my hand.

"No," she said and chuckled. "I've had too much to drink."

"Come on, I won't drop you. I'll hold on tight."

She laughed again and pushed me away when I tried to show her how tight I could hold her. She knew it was just an excuse to have her close. She grabbed my hand and jerked me out to the middle of the dance floor. She'd kept her shoes off. I was barefoot too. Her feet were close to mine, and I gawked at her like an imbecile thinking of everything she'd told me about her life in Brisbane.

"You've met a bunch of guys, then…"

"Quite a few. Isn't that what you wanted, Axel?" She twisted around without letting go of my hand.

I pulled her in, and my hands slid from her waist to her hips, which were swaying with the music. Her eyes stared into me beneath their thick lashes, and I wanted to hold on to that look forever.

"What was it you said, exactly? I'm trying to remember…" She brought a finger to her lips.

"Don't bother, I remember perfectly."

"What else do you want to know, then?"

"Whatever."

We went on dancing as though there was no one else around. Maybe the alcohol was speaking for her, but despite the words of thanks from an hour before, at that moment, I sensed she was enraged. And resentful. And disappointed.

"You don't remember anything interesting about them?"

"About the guys I was with?"

"Yeah."

"There's not much to tell."

"Did you enjoy them?" I held her tighter. I was horny and angry and jealous at the same time.

"Sometimes. With some more than with others."

I struggled to keep up with the song while I imagined those other hands caressing her and my own voice encouraging her to live, go out, fuck, when deep down what I wanted was to be the only person who ever touched her.

"Did you always come?"

She squeezed me around the neck.

"Axel, you're going too far."

"I thought friends talked about stuff like that."

"Don't ruin the night," she begged.

I didn't want to, so I closed my mouth and danced and watched her and felt my hair stand on end every time our bodies touched. Leah let herself go, closed her eyes, uninhibited, tranquil. I smiled, knowing that I'd at least managed to keep her from spending a sleepless night in bed. When I realized dawn was just a few hours away, I convinced her it was time to go home.

We returned to the bar to get her sandals.

"They're gone!" she shouted indignantly.

"Wait, I'll help you look for them."

I put mine on and tried to find hers among the barstools we'd been sitting on. But she was right. There wasn't a trace of them.

"Now what?" she slurred.

"You can walk barefoot. Who cares, babe?"

"Don't call me that! We've got to walk on a dirt road. I'm gonna step on a rock!" She was hilarious, yelling and screaming like that.

"I'll carry you, come on."

She followed me toward the boardwalk. When we reached the dirt path, I crouched down and told her to hop on my back.

"Are you kidding? I can't even add two and two right now."

"I think it's five. Jump on!"

"This is ridiculous! What if someone sees us?"

"Since when do you care what other people think?"

That was enough to get Leah moving. I loved daring her. She wrapped her hands around my shoulders, her legs around my waist, and sat on my back like a monkey. I stood up and started walking. She couldn't sit still.

"Stop doing that with your damn leg."

"Why?" she asked.

"You're tickling me!"

Leah cracked up and tickled my ribs, and my legs started to give out. Our laughter tore through the silence of the night. It was the best sound in the world.

"Axel! We're going to fall!"

I tried to keep my balance, but I wound up falling to the ground. My stomach was hurting from the laughter, and I tried to take a deep breath to stop acting like a little girl. I turned my head to look at her.

"I missed this..." Leah whispered.

"My amazing company?"

She sighed with satisfaction.

"This. Byron Bay. The stars. You."

"Good to know," I responded, contented.

"And your family, and the scent of the sea."

"Come back then. Stay here," I said.

"My life is in Brisbane now..."

I stood up slowly and grabbed her hands to help her up. Without much effort, I got her on my back again and walked until we hit the paved road. I set her down softly, and we continued on to the hostel. At the bottom of the steps, I grabbed her wrist.

"You're forgetting my good night kiss."

Leah's face was mocking, but she bent over anyway, and the kiss wasn't fleeting; it was real, sincere, and lit up my cheek.

"Good night, Axel."

52

———

Leah

MY HEAD WAS POUNDING.

I don't know how, but I managed to get out of bed and drag myself to a shower. The water woke me up a bit, but my stomach was still aching. Fucking Axel, the way he could just blink and convince me to do whatever without thinking of the consequences, like how I was about to have a terrible day, or how at midday I was supposed to see my brother and Bega at the Nguyens' for lunch.

I didn't even have time to get nervous, because I'd slept so late I had to do my hair, throw on some clothes, and go, walking five minutes to downtown Byron Bay. I was the last one to arrive.

It felt strange, entering the Nguyens' home. I don't know if it was the hangover or the sight after three years of them all gathered there, but when Oliver got up to hug me, I hid my head in his chest so no one could see the single tear that had escaped me. I hated being emotional, but I couldn't act like it was nothing, and still... we were family; the bonds that brought us together lay beyond words, and the feeling of seeing them all around the table was so poignant, so warm.

"Pixie, you're such a sleepyhead," my brother joked.

"It's not true!" I shouted. "I went to bed late."

Everyone got up to say hi, starting with Bega and ending with Axel, who was the last one to come over and give me a kiss on the cheek.

Then I took my usual seat. Next to him. In front of my brother. While Georgia set out the plates and pushed everyone to eat more, I thought about the discomfort that might await us, because it was the first time Axel and I had been together in my brother's presence since he found out about us. But Oliver didn't look tense, he wasn't tapping his fingers on the tablecloth; instead he was calm, with one arm around the back of Bega's chair.

"Couldn't sleep?" he asked.

"You must have been nervous," Bega said.

I nodded and grabbed a roll. I couldn't help but feel strange sitting next to Axel in front of his family, my family, ours. If I didn't know him so well, I'd think he was invulnerable, as usual, but it wasn't true; I could see how stiffly he was moving.

"Oliver, what we're all asking ourselves is"—Axel looked at my brother with a mischievous smile on his lips—"how the hell did you manage to trick this woman into agreeing to marry you?"

Daniel laughed despite Georgia's sour expression, and Justin did the same as he picked at his salad. Oliver smiled back at Axel. There was something in that silence full of words only the two of them could perceive that moved me.

"If I'm honest with you…no fucking idea."

Bega nudged him sweetly.

"He's gentler than he looks," she said.

"I know. A true gentleman, this one." Axel swallowed the bite of food in his mouth. "You want to hear some stories from when he was a kid? I could go on for days."

"Axel, drop it." Oliver tried to kick him under the table, but he missed. And in a way, it was like they were boys again, the same two who'd promised they'd never separate before they even knew what that meant. "I know some shit about you too," he warned.

Georgia exclaimed, "Young man, watch your mouth!"

It was funny to watch my brother look straight down into his plate, even if he was now far from a young man.

"Don't leave me hanging," Bega said.

"A woman who knows what she wants. I like that," Axel said.

"I've got the dirt on both of them," Justin said malevolently. "Those two little angels there, Bega, have been arrested no fewer than three times. Twice for being plain idiots."

"Cool!" Max and Connor said in unison.

"What?" Georgia brought her hand to her chest.

Justin looked at Axel and raised his eyebrows.

"Mom didn't know?"

"We didn't want to upset her," Daniel added, but then turned meek when his wife glared at him as if ready to tear off his head. "Honey, it was for your own good. Douglas and I thought it was best. And we did chew them out for it, didn't we, son?"

"You bet you did. I still remember it today."

Axel frowned when his mother got up to take some plates to the kitchen and Daniel scurried after her. Then he bent over and whispered to Bega:

"Actually we got arrested for fighting, they bailed us out, and we were out with them all night until dawn."

Bega and I laughed to ourselves while Oliver smiled, apparently remembering that day as he stared at Axel. When the elder Nguyens were back at the table, we returned to less controversial topics like the exhibition, Oliver and Bega's life in Sydney, and their plans for the near future.

"You haven't considered moving here?"

My brother seemed uncomfortable with Georgia's question.

"It's complicated. Work, you know. Bega is director of the company, her role's important, and she has a ton of responsibilities."

"This place is precious, though," Bega said.

"It is," Axel agreed.

"You never know," Bega mused, and I couldn't help but notice my brother's surprised, even hopeful expression.

For the rest of the meal, I didn't talk much, preferring to watch and listen and retain that moment in my memory. After dessert, Daniel uncorked a bottle of champagne, and once he'd assured us the exhibition would be a success, he raised his glass to toast.

"To family," he said proudly.

53

Leah

I HUGGED LANDON BEFORE HE could shut the car door. He smelled of the same cologne as always. His body and mine merged just as they had eight days before, even if it felt like it had been far longer since I'd seen him, a month at the very least.

"You'd think I'd been off fighting a war," he joked.

I laughed and separated from him. Landon bent over and gave me a soft kiss. I wished I had taken the initiative, that should have been my first impulse. I stood on tiptoe to reach his lips.

"Am I on time?" he asked.

"Yeah, there's still a couple of hours to go." I'd left lunch early to meet him before the exhibition. "You feel like taking a walk? I'd love to show you everything. You know what? I don't know why I never came back before. We should have done it together. Come here, spend a day on the beach, eat the best ice cream in the world..."

"Breathe, Leah," he remarked sarcastically.

"Sorry, I'm excited. And nervous."

"Everything will be fine. I promise."

Even though Landon didn't know a thing about art, exhibitions, or anything else related to them, I believed him. Because unlike Axel's promises, Landon's had always been real; he'd always made them with a serenity that left no room for questions.

"Thanks for being here."

"I wouldn't miss it for the world."

I smiled and tugged him after me.

"Come on," I said.

Night had started to fall when we reached the gallery. I wanted to show up late, when the public was already there, so I wouldn't have a heart attack every time I saw someone come in, or, just as bad, see the rooms sitting empty. So we spent the afternoon walking around, and I told him stories about my childhood that he listened to with interest, and we shared an ice cream cone. Then we went to the hostel so I could change clothes.

"Ready?" He squeezed my hand.

"Not even close." But still, I put one foot in front of the other till we were on the stairs outside. "If I ever look like I'm about to puke, try and help me make it to the bathroom."

His giggling calmed me down.

"Consider it done."

I didn't tell him that, apart from my nerves, I was anxious about him meeting Axel. I don't know why it was so hard for me to imagine them together, but still, it irked me. Something about it just didn't work. And that made me feel guilty, because Axel wasn't mine anymore and I'd need to learn to live with that without every situation awakening slumbering memories.

There were people inside. Lots of them.

I was terrified as I walked through the rooms. And then, I recognized the surprise Axel had mentioned to me the night before. Or better said, I heard it. The surprise I'd forgotten because of everything I'd been feeling.

A Beatles song was playing softly through the speakers scattered throughout the gallery. And when it finished, the notes of the next one rose up amid the voices of the visitors chatting loudly, unaware that I was about to break down. In some way, thanks to the paintings and the music that had been my life's soundtrack, I felt my parents were there with me, accompanying me in memory.

"Leah, are you all right?" Landon asked. He seemed worried.

"Yeah, sorry." I managed a smile.

I forced myself to breathe before I plunged into the multitude. To be sincere, I barely understood what was happening for the next thirty minutes. I was overwhelmed and a little dizzy. My brother hugged me proudly, and everyone else did too: the Nguyens, Blair, Kevin, some friends, some old classmates who'd decided to show up. The rooms were full, Justin was in charge of the catering in the reception area, the music was sounding like an unexpected gift. I let myself go. Everything was perfect. Almost everything.

I saw Sam and stopped her.

"Have you seen Axel?" I asked.

"I think he went to his office earlier. I'll go find him."

"No, I'll go."

"Okay. Wait, Leah." She placed a hand on my shoulder and smiled. "I wanted to tell you we've sold a painting, and there's interest in the other three. The opening's a success. And this is only the beginning."

I was about to ask which one they'd bought, because losing something that had been so mine was strange, but I forgot about it when I remembered Axel while the notes of "Let It Be" floated around me. I advanced down the hall, leaving behind the crowds, and opened the door to his office without knocking.

"Axel?"

My voice faded into the shadows, and a pair of solid arms surrounded me and pulled me into a chest I knew all too well. I felt the warm air of his breath on the nape of my neck, and I felt him shaking against me. And something damp on my skin. Fingers around my waist. Relief. Pain.

I shuddered when I realized he was crying, and I tried to hold in my own tears, but in vain.

I hugged him tighter and wished I could melt into him, see all he was feeling, dig around in his heart. I didn't know what that meant. I didn't want to think about it either. For a few minutes of silence and darkness, we were just two people who, despite everything, still loved each other, and shared too much.

"I promised him…" His voice cracked as it overtook the room.

I closed my eyes when I realized what he meant.

The promise he'd made my father when he realized that he'd never exhibit anything himself, and he assured him he'd get me to do it instead.

I held him tight, pressed my head into him.

"Thanks for everything, Axel. For the music."

"Thanks for letting me back into your life."

54

Axel

A PART OF ME WAS still afraid, and just wanted to stay there in that office forever with Leah in my arms. But the other part was trying to find its way forward slowly and knew that I needed to learn to face reality. Like the reality that our hug was ephemeral. Or that just a few feet away were tons of people who wanted to share that night with her.

So I relaxed and pulled away from Leah.

"We need to go back out."

"I know," she said.

"You go ahead. I'll follow."

She realized I needed a minute to myself and left noiselessly, almost on tiptoe. I took a deep breath when the door closed. It was done. I had kept my promise to Douglas. And being true to my word was heartening in a way I'd never known before.

Satisfied, I walked down the hall to the biggest exhibition room and greeted some acquaintances before a woman interested in one of the pieces rushed me. From that moment on, help out as Sam might, I didn't have a minute free all night. Now and again, I caught a glimpse of my family enjoying themselves. And of course, Leah lit up every room she walked through.

When the evening reached an end and the gallery was emptying out, Leah came over. She was holding hands with him. I forced myself to breathe, but my lungs were on fire, I felt... Really, I couldn't put a name to it, because I'd never felt that way. And if I thought I was ready for that moment, I was wrong.

She spoke faintly.

"Landon, this is Axel," she managed to say.

The kid looked friendly, and his handshake was too. Still, it was hard to ignore the tension. Anyone who knew me would know I wanted to get out of there, the same way I always wanted to escape when things got to be too much, and I felt everything drowning me and just wanted to make it all go away... But I dealt with it...

"Pleasure," I said.

"The same." Landon looked around before pinning me with his chestnut eyes. "This is amazing. You all have done a tremendous job."

"Thanks."

I wished he was a dickhead. But he wasn't. He was the picture of cordiality. Probably a thousand times better person than me. More attentive. Braver. A fighter.

Like a miracle, Oliver appeared.

"How's it going? This is fucking amazing, right?"

I nodded, unable to take it all in. "Yeah... Actually, I should go see how Sam is doing."

Not until I was all the way in the other room did I realize

I hadn't looked at Leah once. And in that situation, it was so hard to do so. Pain. Jealousy. Goddammit. I'd never even known jealousy before. There was a time when I didn't know what the fuck anxiety and insecurity were. But then I fell in love with her.

A little later, we closed the gallery.

Outside, I found my family and everyone else gathered by the door. They asked me if I wanted to go out with them to celebrate with drinks, but I shook my head.

"I barely slept. I'm gonna head home."

"Come on," Oliver said. "You never say no!"

I saw Leah looking at the ground.

"I think we're going to go too," my brother said. He supported me, read my thoughts even when I couldn't, and I was grateful for that.

"See you tomorrow." I clapped Oliver on the shoulder. "Have fun."

I took off walking before they could try to change my mind. I was happy my house was a couple of miles away. I needed to walk, clear my head, stop thinking about their hands touching.

I tried to sleep. It was impossible. So I ended up on the porch smoking another cigarette. God knows how many I'd had since the exhibition ended. I was looking at the waning moon and thinking of all the dumb things I'd done in the course of my life when I heard a noise in the bushes growing beside the cabin.

Before I could react, Oliver appeared.

"Jesus! You scared me! What are you doing here?"

He laughed and climbed the porch.

"Thought I'd come see you a while."

"It's four in the morning."

"I knew you'd be awake."

He grabbed my pack and took out a smoke. I passed him a lighter, still confused, and waited a while in silence until the words came to me.

"I promised your father, you know? That I'd do this."

Oliver blew his smoke out slowly. "I know, Axel."

"How? Did he tell you?"

He nodded, ill at ease, maybe. "He talked to me about that night."

"Did he tell you he encouraged me to stop painting?"

He snuffed out his cigarette and breathed a sigh. "You don't get it, Axel."

"Then explain it to me."

"My father told you what you wanted to hear."

"You don't know what you're saying…"

I walked back and forth on the porch feeling a strange tension, because of everything, that night, the past three stagnant years. I didn't get it. I'd never talked to Oliver about what Douglas and I had shared that night, and for me, it had been significant, a before and after, but for Oliver…nothing. He'd never said anything. I tried to calm myself down as I stopped in front of him.

"I want to understand," I said, almost begging.

"You didn't want to paint, Axel. It was an effort you weren't willing to make, because you'd have had to open up and you weren't willing to. And I get that, okay? I didn't know what it meant to make a real sacrifice either until my parents died."

"That isn't true."

"It is. And you were suffering because you wanted something at the same time you yourself refused it. Like trying to run a marathon and putting obstacles in your own way. It's ironic, right?"

"I don't know what you're talking about…"

"Axel, look at me. You told my father the only thing coming between you and the canvas was you. I know that because I tried for months to get him to tell me; you want to know why? Because it fucked me up that you never talked to me about it, but you talked to him, even though it meant so much to you, and I was supposed to be like a brother to you, and I couldn't hide a damn thing from you, not even what I'd had for lunch the day before."

"Oliver…"

"Let me finish. You told him, and he answered that you didn't have to do it, that no one was forcing you, that you were in a war against yourself, and you'd never win."

I didn't want to cry again. And I wanted to punch him in the face for reminding me of my own words. That's how much sense my behavior made. Cry or hit someone. I needed to calm down.

"Your problem's here." He touched my head.

"I ought to kill you," I answered quietly.

"Half the time, when I see you, I want to hit you. And the other half, I feel guilty. And with all that shit, you're still one of the people I love the most in the world, and I hate loving you because the opposite would be easier. Much, much easier."

Oliver took out another cigarette, lit it, and took a drag. His hand was shaking a bit as it rested on the railing.

"I want to strangle you every time I see you, and then I ask myself, 'Why the hell do I want to see you then?' Like tonight. I saw you there looking at her, and then I knew I was wrong."

What the hell? I hadn't expected that. "You were wrong?"

"You really were in love with her," he said.

"You're three years late on that."

My heart was thudding, and he laughed mirthlessly. I didn't understand why he'd shown up at my house at four in the morning, or how it was possible for us to be having this conversation after so long in silence.

"I'm not late, Axel. I did what I had to do. She's my sister. My obligation is to protect her. I sacrificed everything so she could go to college, and I trusted you, and you failed me. You lied to me."

"What the fuck do you want then? It's over! It all went to shit. Are you happy now? What else is there for us to talk about? I thought everything was clear."

"Listen up: I wasn't late, but you were, or worse, you never really even showed up." That truth was like a knife boring right into my chest.

"You asked me to let her go," I said.

"And you did. Without fighting. Without even trying."

"You asked me to," I repeated, just barely.

"Goddammit, Axel, don't you get it? If I didn't know you as well as I do, I'd think you didn't even give a shit about my sister. Same as painting. Same as everything."

"I'll kill you…"

I could feel lava flowing through my veins.

I could hardly breathe. And despite the rage, the blind fury, I could hardly figure out if I was angrier with Oliver or myself. At the same time, I felt that wall between us crumble at our feet as we finally screamed out all the shit we had inside us.

"Remember what you told me the other day?" Oliver asked.

"No. No, goddammit. I can't even think right now."

"Axel, get ahold of yourself. Look at me." I did, but I was lost; everything seemed to be slipping from my grasp. "I remember when you went to the exhibition. You told me that day I was important to you, but I always knew she would be more. You faced up to me; you told me to go to hell."

The hole in my chest kept getting bigger and bigger.

I needed a goddamn time machine. "I can't change what I did."

"I know."

"I failed you."

"It's forgotten."

"I'm a moron."

"You always have been."

I snickered and rubbed my face. "I don't even know what you're doing here."

"I'm here because you're my friend. And after seeing how you looked at her, I knew you had it bad. And we all fuck up sometimes, Axel. Me most of all."

I should have answered him with words, with some kind of deep bullshit, but I just couldn't speak. So I went over to him, hugged him, and breathed a sigh of relief. I'd been doing that more lately, and it had to mean that a fucked-up period of my life was finally over.

Oliver squeezed my arm and pulled away. "When you fall, I'll pick you up, bro."

I nodded, grimaced, and took out a smoke. He did the same. For a while, we said nothing. I couldn't stop thinking that it was true; it took everything I had to face up to things, to change, to go for it. And I was ashamed, in a way, that Oliver had to be the one to come find me two and a half years after the fact, that he was the one who missed me, the one who tried to fix things...

Like that night. Like always.

"Listen, Oliver. I love you."

"Okay, now you're going off the deep end."

"You know words aren't my thing."

"Don't start making declarations..."

"You know my speech will be absolute garbage."

"Axel..." He grinned.

"Still, if you want me to be your best man..."

"Who else?"

I wound up smiling too.

55

Axel

"WE SOLD SIX PAINTINGS. SIX," Sam said. "It's incredible. Can I ask why you're not more surprised?"

"I figured she would. The girl's good, but... You don't understand." I looked up from the papers I was rifling through on my desk. "Leah isn't the best, and she's got a lot left to learn. There's thousands of artists out there who are technically better than her, who know more, and who can find a million errors in each of her pieces. You know that. But she's got soul. When someone looks at one of her paintings, they can see and feel the emotions she's put into it. She can transmit things. And isn't that what it's all about in the end?"

56

Leah

MY LAST DAYS IN BYRON Bay, I hardly saw Axel. He claimed he was busy with the sale of the paintings and other issues. I almost felt like he was avoiding me, and even though I needed the breathing room, I was also addicted to being by his side. He was like the chocolate cake they put in front of you when you're on a diet, the gossip you don't want to hear but can't help listening to.

I didn't have much time to think about him, because the day after the exhibition, when Landon left, I could hardly get away from the Nguyens and my brother and his fiancée. On Monday, when we all had our last meal together, Axel seemed more pensive than usual, off in his own little world. He hardly even spoke.

"Honey, are you okay?" Georgia asked.

"Yeah, brilliant." But his eyes were distracted, and he looked back into the center of his plate and remained that way until it was time to say goodbye.

He gave me a kiss on the cheek and told me he'd call me that week to talk business. Then he left, and we walked to the hotel where Oliver and Bega were staying. When she said she had to pack her bags and take a shower, my brother asked me if I felt like going for a walk. I said yes, because we still hadn't spent much time alone, and I was used to having him all to myself every time he came to see me in Brisbane.

I hung off his arm as we strolled.

"It was nice coming back here," I said.

"It has been." He smiled. "I missed it."

And then something occurred to me. Actually, I'd thought of it more than once those past few years, but I'd never had the courage to seriously propose it.

"Would you like...to go to our old house?"

"Leah, I'm not sure that's a good idea for you."

"I want to," I assured him.

"Okay, let's go." He grabbed my hand.

We took that route we knew so well, and I could almost see Oliver's excitement mingling with mine, like colors: the blue of trust, the intense yellow of uncertainty, the violet of longing...

We had grown up on the outside of town, next to the Joneses' old place. Both houses had two stories with a small backyard surrounded by trees that had grown tall.

Everything was the same, but at the same time, so different...

"It's abandoned," I cried, seeing the house.

"Not exactly." Oliver squeezed my hand. "Some English people bought it a few years ago. You know how it goes. They got this idea of coming here when they retire; eventually they'll tear it down and build something new. Or so I heard."

Despite the pain of imagining those walls turned into a pile of rubble, I told myself it was better that way. Because that place held too many memories for new ones to be created there. If it was never going to be the same—and it wasn't—maybe it was better to just start from zero.

"I remember when you used to climb that tree over there," Oliver said. "You'd shoot up like a monkey and stay there for hours hanging from one of the branches. Only Axel could ever get you to come down."

"Mom threatened to cut it down."

"It's true." He laughed. "She was amazing."

"She had character."

"Like you. She was emotional..."

"You're more like Dad."

"You really think?"

"Yeah. You're honest. Transparent."

He smiled and squeezed my hand tighter.

"I love you a lot. You know that, right?"

"I love you too. Always."

The wind shook the treetops and swept away a couple of leaves that had fallen to the ground.

"Oliver?"

"What?"

"What did you do with all our things?"

"I grabbed what I could." He looked away. "The Nguyens helped me. I have a few boxes; they kept the others. I donated a couple of Dad's paintings to a gallery that wanted them, and the rest..."

"What about the rest?"

"I left them there."

"In the house? Do you think they threw them all out?"

"I don't know, and I'd rather not think about it. We should go back, Leah. It's getting late; we need to drop you in Brisbane. It won't be long before our flight leaves."

As we returned to the hotel, I tried to clear my mind of all I was thinking. I wish I could say I succeeded. But I didn't.

February

—

(SUMMER, AUSTRALIA)

57

Leah

I WENT BACK TO BRISBANE. To my routine. To painting.

Since I didn't have to go to class, the days just slipped past. I spent hours in the attic, went out now and then for a drink with friends in the evening, had dinner at Landon's some nights, and slept curled up by his side.

But there was a crack in that monotony.

And that crack was named Axel.

58

Leah

"AN ART FAIR, HUH," LANDON said while he helped me take a shell out of a cabinet over my head. I'd just told him I'd be going away that weekend with Axel and exhibiting five pieces. "Will you sleep here?"

"Yeah, it's just an hour away by car. You want to come?" I looked at him doubtfully, knowing that if he said yes, the situation would be weird, but at the same time, I desperately needed everything to be normal. For now, I was far from achieving that.

Landon shook his head.

"I can't, I've got things to do."

I admired Landon's serenity. Maybe because that was the opposite of me; I was pure nerve and impulsivity. I let my emotions carry me away. I could cry over something silly; I could laugh until my stomach hurt, go from black to white in the blink of an eye, and turn things over and over in my mind till it felt like a centrifuge.

"Tell me what you're thinking."

He came close and kissed me softly. "I'm thinking about how incredible you are."

"I'm serious," I laughed.

"So am I. What are you worried about?"

"You know. The situation." I sat on the kitchen counter, while he put water on to boil and took a packet of pasta from the pantry. "I want you to tell me what you're feeling, especially if something ever makes you uncomfortable. Please, don't keep it inside."

With a slightly preoccupied air, he said, "That would only make things more complicated."

"Fine," I said. "Make them complicated."

I always preferred that to silence.

"I don't like the way he looks at you," he said.

"He doesn't look at me any way."

Landon tossed the pasta in the boiling water.

"I also don't like that you refuse to admit it."

"If you knew Axel, you'd understand."

I bit my lip. I didn't want to go further and tell him not to trust his first impressions of Axel, who was less intense than his appearance promised, and who didn't *love things enough*, as he had told me.

"Have you all talked?" he asked.

"What do you mean, exactly?"

"Dammit, Leah. About your relationship. About what happened."

"There's nothing to talk about."

"How can you say that...?"

"We're friends," I cut him off. I was getting angry now. "And I'd prefer to forget we ever shared anything else, because when I remember all that, I can't forgive him. We haven't talked, and I doubt we ever will; that's something that happened, and sometimes it's better to leave things behind so you don't have to drag a burden around with you forever, understand? That's how it has to be."

Landon nodded, but his look was serious.

"Do you still hold it against him?"

"Yes," I lied. I lied because I couldn't face the truth and wasn't ready to answer the question honestly. If I said no, I'd be destroying the fragile edifice of my new relationship with Axel.

59

Axel

THE FIRST TIME I FELT the need to paint, I was thirteen years old. Oliver hadn't gone to school because he had a fever, so I went to his house on my way back from class. Rose opened the door and smiled before letting me in.

"Come on in, honey. Oliver's asleep."

"Still? What a wimp."

Rose laughed, and I followed her to the kitchen.

"You want an orange juice?"

"Okay." I shrugged. It's not like I had anything else to do that afternoon, and I didn't want to be by myself. "Douglas isn't here either?"

"Yeah, he's in the studio. Go up and see him. I'll bring you your juice."

I climbed the stairs two by two to the second floor. The notes of "I Will" guided me to his studio, and when I got there, I looked around with fascination. Douglas was humming the song with a brush in his hand while Leah danced around him. I gawked until he realized I was there.

"Hey, son! Come here."

He stopped the music and smiled at me.

I walked in. I'd been there before, but usually with Oliver, and I hadn't paid much attention to the colorful paintings placed all around the room. Only once, years ago, had I really noticed one, that picture of Douglas's with the beetles sliced open and filled with daisies.

"What are you doing?" I asked.

"What's it look like?"

"I mean, because the music is so loud."

"Music is inspiration, Axel." He put the same song on again and pinned me with his eyes while he took from Leah's hands a brush that had fallen to the ground. "Didn't I ever tell you how I realized I was in love with Rose?"

I shook my head, a little embarrassed that Douglas was talking to me so openly about that subject. At that age, a stolen kiss from a classmate on the walk home from school was enough, and the word *love* struck me as silly.

"It was simple. I was on the boardwalk with some friends, and I saw her in the distance. She was skating, her hair was disheveled, she looked wild. As she came closer, I heard the notes of this song in my head, and then I heard the words. All of it. I was hearing myself fall in love with her."

"No way."

"I'm serious," he said. "I swear."

"Then what?"

"Then I spent weeks looking around for her."

"She must have thought you were nuts."

He smiled and put the song on again. I watched him mix two swatches of paint on a palette full of color, and as the minutes passed and neither of us said a word, I sat on the ground, my back leaning against the wall to observe him painting. Leah started dancing around again to that song. Then she got tired and came over to me.

She was three, but she was still using a pacifier sometimes, and that day she had it with her. Her wavy blond hair brushed her shoulders; her cheeks were rosy. I let her sit in my lap. I usually never paid much attention to her; at that age all I cared about was hanging out with Oliver and getting into trouble, or watching the surfers all afternoon and trying to do like them, or looking at the girls' butts in their tiny bikinis.

But that afternoon, I had everything I needed.

It was relaxing to watch Douglas move his hand and drag the brush across the white canvas, filling it with color. I looked away from him when Leah gurgled and I saw she'd fallen asleep in my arms with her ladybug pacifier still in her mouth.

"Here, let me take her off your hands."

Douglas picked her up to go lay her down. When he came back, I was standing up, ready to go, but I lingered a moment to look at the painting.

"Like what you see?"

"Yeah," I responded.

"You want to try?" Douglas passed me a brush.

"I don't think I can," I said, anxious. "I'm afraid I'll screw it up."

"I doubt that," he insisted, and I gave up as he stood beside me with his usual sincere, immense smile. "I'll tell you what to do, okay?"

"Okay." I agreed.

"Close your eyes, stop thinking, then open them and paint."

"That's it?" I replied, incredulous.

"This is just the first contact."

"Right. Sure."

"Ready?"

I nodded. Then I closed my eyes and tried to force every idea out of my head until all I saw in front of me was a clear sky. I opened them back up. I stretched my hand out toward the palette, got a little blue, and left a small blotch on the sky over that open field Douglas was painting. The uncertainty of that first trace dissipated as the white ceded to more and more blue, and that became the strange satisfaction of inventing something, representing, leaving behind, depositing, spilling out, vomiting up, scattering, expressing, shouting...

"I can see you want that sky to be clear."

"I like that. I like a clear sky."

"Me too," he said. "And do you like this?"

"What? Painting?" I wrinkled my nose. "Yeah."

"Well, you can do it as often as you like."

That was silly, I thought. Oliver would probably laugh if he saw me painting like his father. I shrugged with feigned indifference.

"Maybe. Maybe one day," I said.

"I'll be waiting for you."

Years later, I realized that there are smiles that conceal truths. Lazy afternoons that turn into important memories. Decisive memories etched out when you least expect them. That life's charm lies in that unpredictable something.

60

Leah

IN THE CAR, I LOOKED at Axel as he clutched the wheel. Two days earlier, we had selected the pieces to send, and someone had come to box them up and ship them. Only artists with representation could participate in the fair, and Axel had decided to take me.

"Wasn't there someone better?" I asked him.

"Don't you want to go?"

"Yeah, but...I don't know."

"You think there's an ulterior motive behind me choosing you, Leah? Well, you're wrong. First of all, this was Sam's decision. She's the one in charge. Second, it's time for you to admit it: you're good. Of all the artists we represent, you're the one who's sold the most in her first exhibition. Does that convince you?"

"It does," she agreed.

"Better."

Axel turned up the music and said nothing else the rest of the trip. I didn't feel like thinking too much, so I just looked out the window. In the weeks since the exhibition, I'd been thinking about my future, my expectations, trying to decide what I wanted to do with my life. And I didn't know. I wanted to paint, but beyond that, everything was blurry. It was as if I'd put myself in Axel's hands, but without knowing for sure whether the road he was taking me down was the right one, or whether it was okay just to close my eyes and follow him without worrying.

The art fair took place in a giant building with many rooms. When we went inside, they gave us ID badges and told us our space was on the second floor to the right. My pieces were already hanging up when I got there. Even if there was only space for five, Axel had said, it was worth it, that this was a way I could get my name out there. The place smelled of disinfectant, and the smooth walls were a little impersonal, but at least it was open and airy.

Axel adjusted his collar. He had gotten dressed up. I wasn't used to seeing him like that, freshly shaved, in long pants and a tailored shirt. He was so sexy that in a moment of weakness, I could think of nothing but him. As if he permeated everything, even me.

I tried to shrug that feeling off and asked him why he was being so quiet. I preferred the funny Axel to this hushed and pensive one. Something about him seemed to have changed since the exhibition.

"I didn't get much sleep."

I couldn't think of anything else to say, and the day crept by slowly.

If Axel had been the same unworried guy as always, the calm one, the unfiltered one, the one who made me laugh even when I was angry with him, the minutes might not have stretched on like hours. But he lingered to one side every time someone came over to ask about the pieces, almost as if he didn't want to get involved. At least until we sold one of the pictures to a couple, and he had to take care of the details.

Around 6 p.m., we left.

"What about the other pictures?"

"Don't worry, they'll take them to the gallery."

"Okay." I bit my lip. "Are you sure everything's all right?"

Axel was toying with his keys. Instead of putting them in the ignition, he leaned back in his chair and exhaled wearily. Then he rubbed the bridge of his nose and clicked his tongue.

"I talked to Oliver last month…" Just hearing that made me nervous. "We talked about you. About everything that happened three years ago. About me. About what I did wrong, what I screwed up back then, and…"

"Please, no," I begged him.

"Leah…"

"No."

"Why?"

I realized this was an important moment, one of those that shifts the scale. I thought while my heart began to pound. I had the answer, but it hurt me to have to say it.

"Because then I'll hate you, Axel. And right now, I can't do that. You just appeared in my life again, and…I need you. I don't want to think about everything that happened or why you did it. Still worse, how you *could* do it. I don't want to think about what might have happened if the university hadn't offered me that exhibition, if you'd never had the balls to come back into my life. I don't want anything to break now, when we're finally rebuilding our friendship."

"I'd have found you sooner or later," he said.

"Maybe. We'll never know though."

"I know, babe. I swear to you, I know."

I swallowed, on the verge of tears, and noticed a bitter aftertaste, as if the words didn't want to go down, and my thoughts were so wrapped up in all he was saying that I struggled to find the thread.

"Axel, I don't want to lose you again."

"I'd never let that happen."

I'd never seen him like this. Weak. Insecure.

"I need more time," I managed to say. "Then maybe one day…"

Maybe one day I'll be able to look you in the eye while you tell me how the hell you were capable of giving up all we had, a story I was ready to sacrifice everything for. How you managed to sleep every night without crying. How things could be so volatile for you. And then, maybe I could start to believe you when you say you would have come back for me sooner or later, because three years is too long. Three years is enough to build something new. In three years I almost forgot the shape of the scar on your forehead and the exact tone of your dark blue eyes.

I thought all that with a weary heart.

"What do you want now?" There was fear in his voice, but also impatience, as if he needed to finally know.

"I want you to be my friend. I want you back in my life. Don't you want that, too, Axel? To be able to spend time together, like the other night?" As I reminded him of this, I grinned slightly, recalling how we'd both ended up lying in the middle of the road when he'd carried me piggyback and I'd tickled him. "I want the old Axel," I concluded.

61

Axel

MAYBE LIFE IS MOMENTS. JUST that. Moments. And sometimes you show up at the right time, and sometimes you don't. Sometimes a second changes everything. Sometimes time draws a line. Sometimes, when you want to talk, the other person isn't in the mood to listen. These things happen, I guess. You want something, and weeks later you can barely remember what it is, or else it's lost all its value.

And the worst of all that is that I understood Leah.

I'd needed three years to be ready. Three years of silence after telling her maybe I didn't love her that much, and seeing how her face crumpled, and she was hurt and cried, and she ran off in the middle of the night. Three years being an idiot. She deserved an explanation. She did. I wasn't even sure what to tell her or how, but I needed to try; but then I stopped to think about what Leah needed, and for the first time, I realized I should stop looking at my own belly button and put her feelings before mine, because that's what you do when you love someone.

And so I swallowed my words.

62

Leah

AXEL SAID NOTHING MORE, JUST nodded slowly and pensively before putting the truck in drive.

We left the city behind and pulled onto a highway flanked by a tropical forest. I smiled to see him looking over at me when the road straightened. That calmed me.

I was exhausted after a day of frayed nerves and that unresolved conversation that seemed to be floating between us in the air. I thought I might sleep a while, but that possibility vanished when we turned right onto a narrow unpaved road.

"Where are we going?" I asked.

"Thought you were in the mood for an adventure."

His sly expression reminded me of the old Axel, the one I wanted him to be, and a familiar sensation warmed me up inside.

He parked in front of a deserted beach.

"What are we doing here?"

He didn't answer. He hopped out of his pickup, unzipped the plastic bed cover, and started pulling out the surfboards.

"I hope you're kidding," I said between clenched teeth.

"Aren't you in the mood? Come on, get out."

"That's not what I mean. I don't even have a bikini with me."

"Don't you have underwear on?" The idiot grinned when he saw me blush. I pursed my lips. "It's not like I'm going to see anything I haven't seen before, babe," he said.

I rolled my eyes, and he walked off toward the beach. I stayed there a minute watching him under the afternoon sun and asking myself if I wouldn't rather be with the new, unknown Axel instead of the one who always threw me against the ropes, as if he wanted to coax out my most impulsive side, the side I tried to control.

I insulted him a few times in my mind before letting desire and the envy I felt seeing him in the water push me forward. I pulled my dress over my head and gave thanks that I had on dark underwear. I grabbed one of the two remaining surfboards and walked down to the beach, observing the orange sun.

"Took you a while," he reproached me when I reached him.

"Sorry, I was just counting up all the dumb reasons I play along with you."

"I love it when you get mad."

He took off into the water, and I followed him.

I couldn't catch the first three decent waves, but on the fourth, I managed to stay standing on the board, body bent forward and flexing, gliding softly while the sea and its aroma enveloped me, and everything was perfect. Perfect. Those moments of plenitude that occur when you least expect and that shake you, reminding you that they do exist, they're possible, and they fill you with energy.

When all my slips and falls started to make me achy, we got

out and sat on the damp shore to dry off. The sun was almost gone. Red and orange rays were splayed across the sky, which was darkening, and the birds that crisscrossed it were like little shadows over the murmur of the waves.

"How would you paint this?" I asked without thinking.

"The sky?" he said. "I don't know."

"Something must come into your head."

He exhaled and relaxed his shoulders.

"With my hands..."

"What?" I laughed.

"Exactly. With my hands. I'd daub my fingers with paint, and I'd move them upward," he said, squeezing his hands into claws.

I imagined the rays like that, drawn in a single trace by his soft fingertips, and I shook.

"We ought to go," I said.

"Yeah. Come on," he replied, standing.

We didn't talk the rest of the way, but it wasn't uncomfortable. I had the feeling we'd put back in place some loose pieces that had long been scattered around. Maybe the puzzle wasn't perfect, but for the moment, it looked okay. When I watched him driving and singing along with the radio in that deep voice of his, I realized I needed him again in my life. Running away from him wasn't an option. It never was until I forced myself to do it. Axel was like that strawberry lollipop I didn't taste for years and years, and then I did, and it became a flavor I couldn't do without. Addictive.

He drove me to the dorm when we got to Brisbane.

I could see Landon sitting on the steps. I opened the door of the truck before Axel had even parked and got out.

"What are you doing here?" I asked.

"I thought we might see each other tonight."

"Of course. I didn't know what time we'd be done, though."

I could see Landon staring at my tangled wet hair, still flecked with grains of sand. I wanted to rid myself of the feeling of guilt tightening around my throat. I didn't like feeling that way, so tense, so uncomfortable. "We stopped once the fair was over, and time got away from me."

"Did everything go well?" He kissed me on the cheek.

I nodded, but I stopped talking when I saw Axel get out of the truck and come over to say hi. He was imperturbable as he shook Landon's hand, wearing that mask that I hated but that intrigued me in equal parts. Landon asked him if he wanted to go for a drink, and Axel declined, saying he had a long drive ahead of him. He told me goodbye with a kiss on the cheek.

"Why'd you do that?" I asked.

"What?" Landon followed through the open door behind me.

"You know what. Invite him out with us."

"Is there something wrong with that?"

"No, but..."

"You said you didn't hold anything against him."

Frustrated, I sat on the bed when I reached my room and toyed distractedly with a thread hanging from the edge of my dress while Landon observed me as if thinking something. I looked back up.

"This is uncomfortable," I whispered.

Landon, clearly stressed, replied: "It shouldn't be, Leah."

"I know, but it is."

"What does that mean?"

"Nothing. It doesn't mean a thing."

Landon walked over to the window and opened it. The warm evening air flooded the room. I don't know how long we remained there in silence, each thinking our own thoughts, before I got up, unable to bear the awkwardness any longer and the way it took over everything beautiful we had built up over the years: friendship, trust, safety.

I embraced him from behind and rested my cheek on his back.

He didn't move, but he also didn't push me away.

And for the moment, that was enough.

63

Axel

JUSTIN LOOKED AT ME. WE were on my porch. I had hardly talked to Leah that week. I lit a cigarette and blew out.

"What's up with you?" my brother asked.

"Nothing. Thinking about all this drives me to distraction."

"If you're not going to talk, I'm leaving."

"Wait, I'm trying to find the words... I've been thinking about myself lately. About people in general. You think the reality of ourselves is anything like who we think we are? I mean...I'm not sure I've always been honest. Deep down, I think we have a concrete ideal of ourselves, and we're always trying to reach it."

"Is that bad? It seems like a good plan to me."

"But who are we really, in the end?"

"I guess there's no answer."

"Well, there should be one." I snuffed out my cigarette. "Sometimes I feel like a stranger in my own skin. I have this feeling I'm showing up late to my own life, that I'm at the wrong place at the wrong time. That I'm missing something, but I don't know what. And I'm scared, because every time I try to change that, I end up taking a step back."

64

Axel

SAM KNOCKED ON MY OFFICE door before coming in.

"Hans is on line two; he's been trying to get ahold of you since yesterday afternoon."

"Shit." I'd left my cell phone God knows where. I picked up my office line to speak to the gallery's owner. "Hans, sorry, what's going on?"

"Listen, that new girl...Douglas's daughter..."

"Leah Jones, I think you mean."

"Yes. Sam told me she sold nearly half the pictures from the exhibition, and she sent me the photos of the pieces you'd cataloged last week. I think she's perfect for a project we're involved in. But I need you to be the point man on this. And of course, I need her to agree."

"What's the project?" I asked.

"Are you sitting down? Good. Listen close."

65

Leah

"ARE YOU HAPPY? WAS IT what you expected?"

I nodded as I accompanied Linda Martin out of the classroom. The hallways were full of students. It was the end of a Friday, and I'd gone there to talk to my professor about internships for the upcoming semester.

"Honestly, I didn't have any concrete expectations. I guess anything works for me. I'm...waiting. I guess that's it. I'm in a wait-and-see phase."

"It's good to try things out and learn what we do and don't want." It started to rain outside. "The art world is tough. The secret, I think, is to find your niche, a place where you feel comfortable. As far as internships, just think it over. Both options are good, but it's your decision, Leah."

"I know, but I need to choose something soon."

We said our goodbyes, and I walked out the door and into the rain, which was falling harder and harder. I hugged my portfolio to my chest to protect it from the rain, remembering I had a few prints inside I didn't want to get smudged, and I cursed under my breath because I'd forgotten my umbrella despite knowing storms were frequent here in summer. I groaned when I stepped in a puddle, and just afterward, I heard a familiar hoarse laugh right beside me.

"Axel?" I squinted.

"Come on, my wheels are nearby."

"What are you doing here?" I followed him.

"You told me you had a meeting with Professor Martin today." We'd texted two days before, and, I don't know why, I'd had the urge to talk to him about internships and my insecurities, because neither of my options satisfied me fully, and I knew he'd have something to say. "I had some errands to run," he said. "Plus I wanted to talk to you."

His nervous expression wasn't lost on me.

We got in his car, and as he turned onto the road, I watched the movement of the windshield wipers.

"What did you want to talk about?" I asked.

"It's something touchy. Can we wait?"

"Landon's coming to get me from the dorm in a half hour. Plus you're scaring me. Is this anything I should be worried about?"

"No, it's nothing bad. The opposite, actually."

He didn't say anything else until he parked in front of my building. He took the keys from the ignition. The rain was plunking against the windshield and soaking everything. It would be nice to paint something like that, I thought: blurry, diffuse, chaotic.

Axel took a deep breath, then began: "A few days ago, Hans called me to discuss a project he wants you to take part in. He needs someone young, no more than twenty-five. There's a grant to participate in a series of exhibitions with artists from a number of countries. It's a big opportunity. The grant will cover all your expenses, including room and board and a studio..."

"I've got a studio, though," I said.

"It's in Paris."

"Are you kidding?" I replied.

"No, Leah. Listen..."

"There's no way! I can't go!"

"Why?" he asked.

"There's a million reasons. I have to do my internship. And my life is here, Axel. I can't just up and move thousands of miles away. You know how hard it is for me to be alone, how hard it was for me to come to Brisbane. I was so scared..."

He held my chin between his fingers.

Our eyes locked.

"I'll go to Paris with you, babe."

And those eyes...that way of touching me...

I looked away and opened the door. I got out, despite the rain, and I ran to the dorm. I'd just stuck the keys in the lock when I felt his presence behind me. I didn't turn around. I headed straight for the stairs. As I climbed them, he was hot on my heels, leaving a trail of water behind us.

"Axel, you need to go," I said when I reached my room.

He ignored me, standing instead in the middle of the room with his back stiff and his jaw clenched while I opened my closet to take out dry clothes.

I was so nervous I wanted to giggle. How could something like this occur to him? Going with him to the other end of the planet was riskier than Russian roulette. It had only been a month that I'd even been able to tolerate his presence, forcing myself to remember he was a friend, that what happened in his house was just a ripple in our story compared with his being family my whole life.

I tried to go into the bathroom, but Axel blocked my path. His overwrought eyes roved my face and settled on my own eyes.

"What are you so scared of?"

"You know. I told you already."

"And I promised you that you wouldn't be alone."

"I don't care. Let me through; I need to change."

He didn't move. My legs trembled, knowing he was so close.

"Are you scared of what might happen? Tell me."

"I don't know what you're talking about."

"Yeah, you do. I'm talking about us."

"That's not even a possibility," I said.

He stepped aside, and I entered the bathroom, taking a deep breath after locking it, as if I'd just gotten out from under a weight and finally felt safe from him, far away from him. I couldn't grasp what had happened, and it scared me so much I didn't even want to think about it. I didn't realize my arms were shivering until I lifted them to take off my soaked T-shirt.

"Fine, I'll talk through the door," he said.

I clenched my teeth when I heard his muffled voice. How could he be so stubborn and impossible when he really wanted something, and then leave it behind so easily?

"The grant is just for two months. I'm not asking you to leave your life behind here, Leah. As for internships, look, I could talk to your professor and probably get you credit for this. You'd be killing two birds with one stone."

"I see you've got it all planned out," I grunted.

"Yeah. 'Cause I'm the world's best agent."

As I buttoned my pants, I told him there must be other people interested.

"You're the youngest artist we have."

"You should find another one," I responded.

"Could we have this conversation face-to-face and not through a door?"

I opened it slightly. I was more relaxed now. I didn't want to be vulnerable in front of him again.

"Axel, I realize this is a big opportunity, and it sounds amazing."

"It's a huge opportunity. Hans has a lot of contacts."

"Still, it isn't for me. I'm sorry."

I looked around for a hairband on my counter.

"What do you want, then?"

By his voice, I could tell he was frustrated.

"In what sense, exactly?" I asked.

"Your career. Painting. Tell me what your goals are, and I'll try to help you reach them, but to do it, we need to have this conversation before we take another step. What are you thinking of doing when you finish school? Do you want to get a job in some other field and paint in your free time, or is the idea to live off your work? I think I deserve an answer."

I shut my eyes.

I knew he was right. I needed to choose. I didn't want to make him waste his time, and this wasn't a game. But I hadn't thought about concrete objectives, not seriously. All I knew was that painting was my life, but I didn't know where that should lead me. All I was certain of was that I wanted to go on painting, however simple that might seem. It's not like I dreamed of exhibiting in a gallery in New York and getting famous, or selling my pictures for a fortune and getting rich. None of that had occurred to me. I'd never worried about it; you just don't, I guess, until you realize you're on the verge of having bills to pay and you'll need a job to pay them. I tried to imagine that other life, but I just couldn't.

"Yeah, that's the idea, I guess, making a living from art," I said quietly.

Axel's hair was still wet, and I remembered seeing him come home after whiling away his time among the waves.

"Then I don't understand..."

"It's all just so complicated."

"Are we the problem, Leah?"

I didn't want to answer, because if I said yes, I'd be admitting things weren't right. Which was true. Our relationship was so complex, so knotty, that we had no idea how to start untangling it...

I opened the window for some fresh air.

"That's not it. I'm just stressed out, Axel. I need time, okay? It's not a good idea to keep talking about this now."

"Does that mean you'll consider it?"

I wavered. But before I could answer, there was a knock at the door, and I remembered I was supposed to see Landon. The last thing I needed was things to get uncomfortable. I opened the door and tried to shrug off the tension when he kissed me briefly on the lips. I was on edge. He and Axel greeted each other, shaking hands.

"I've got to go," Axel said.

"All right." I wanted to cry. I don't know why, but that room felt like a vacuum, and with the two of them there, all I wanted was to break down in tears.

"Think it over, okay? I need an answer."

I trembled when his lips touched my cheek. He shut the door, and Landon and I stared at each other for a dense, unpleasant minute. I didn't want to associate all this with him.

"What do you need to think over?"

"I think it's best if you sit down."

66

Axel

"I SWEAR I HAVE NEVER shown that much self-control in my fucking life. When I saw him kiss her, I wanted to kill him. And he's just a kid. Not only that, but he seems like a good guy…"

My brother poured me a coffee.

"Would you rather he be an idiot?"

"No, dammit."

Because if he was, he'd be dead, I thought. Justin stepped away to attend to some customers who'd just entered the café. I'd never been jealous, but in recent months I'd felt a pain in my chest that wouldn't stop growing. Insecurity was eating me alive. And fear. I was terrified of spending the rest of my life like that, confused, self-involved, never able to touch her again.

I saw my father though the glass and forced myself to put on a good face when he came in, clapped me on the back, and sat down on a stool next to me.

"How's it going, dude?" he asked cheerfully.

"I've had better days," I admitted.

"Tell me what's the deal then."

Justin pretended to be looking for a rag under the counter to keep from laughing in front of him, and wound up with a twisted grimace, while I thought how lucky I was to have a family like that. Despite their defects, I wouldn't change anything about them.

"The deal is Leah. I think you've heard of her."

My father eyed me warily, because we hadn't talked about her again since she reappeared in my life. Not like that day, when I wasn't sure I could keep up my filter. Justin closed out someone's check and came over to us.

"I can listen; I'm good at it," Dad said, by way of encouragement.

"Okay. So there's several problems. The first is I need to convince her to take this grant she's up for and go to Paris."

"She should. It's a big opportunity. Maybe your mother can talk to her..." Dad said.

Justin looked anxious on the other side of the bar, almost enchanted by the spectacle. Sometimes it surprised me how well my brother knew me, but that was to be expected, after all the trouble I'd given him over the years.

"Second: I want to kill this guy she's going out with."

"Son, that's, uh...whew...that's not good."

"Third problem is, I want her in the sack."

"Axel!" my father said.

"Honestly, it's all I ever think about. So you got any advice, Dad?"

"This is better than I thought," Justin laughed, cracking up, and soon my father and I had joined him, even if Dad, a bit startled, was red-cheeked and coughing too.

"You've got a lot on your plate," he said.

"Yeah. Not too bodacious," I joked.

"Not at all." He smiled.

"Let's go take a walk."

We said goodbye to Justin and left the café, heading toward the boardwalk, which we walked along in silence, enjoying the time together. When we sat on the wall, I looked at him, in his plastic glasses, with his eternal smile and the wind whipping through his hair, which was longer than my mother liked. I wanted a cigarette, but I abstained, knowing he wished I'd quit.

"Dad..."

"Spit it out, dude."

"If I ever have kids, I hope I'm half as good with them as you were with us."

"You both made it easy on me."

He blinked, trying to hold his feelings in, and I put an arm over his shoulders while we looked out at the blue sea with the surfers looking for waves under a calm morning sun.

67

Leah

FOR SOME REASON, WHEN I thought of Paris, Claude Monet always came into my mind. My second year in college, I did my final project on him. His determination fascinated me, even if the upper classes rejected him at first because he broke with the artistic values of the time. I loved his obsession with color and the ethereal qualities of light. His free brushwork, with short, heavy strokes, his bright, vibrant tones. That interest in capturing the instant, the impalpable, the fleeting. It was comforting to me, like those moments you store in memory and that you know you'll never experience again. He was magic. Representing the volatile in pure, juxtaposed colors.

His most important work, the one that gave impressionism its name, was called *Impression, Sunrise*. I tried to pretend that wasn't a sign. The sunrise. Him.

All I thought of in those days was Monet.

All I thought of was Paris...

68

Leah

WE WENT OUT TO EAT and spent the night trying to act like nothing was going on, but we both knew we weren't doing well. I wasn't even sure what the problem was, but I could sense the uncomfortable silences, the topics we were avoiding, the looks that concealed doubts and fears.

I took off my shoes when we reached his apartment and walked barefoot to the kitchen for a glass of water. When I drank it and came back, Landon was leaning on the counter and watching me gravely.

"What?" I walked toward him.

"We need to talk about Paris."

"You think I shouldn't go?"

"That's not it. Actually I think you should. It's a once-in-a-lifetime opportunity. But it makes things harder..." He ran his hand through his hair, stressed. "I love you, Leah, but you're going there, with him, thousands of miles away, and I'm not sure I can go on pretending nothing's up."

"What are you trying to say?"

"We can talk about it when you get back…"

"Are you breaking up with me?"

"No, because there's nothing to break. You're the one who never wanted to label what we had, so now we don't know what we have. Go to Paris. Take the opportunity, and…figure things out. Figure out what you really want. I don't want to know what happens between you and him for those two months, though."

"Nothing's going to happen."

"Leah, I'm not fucking blind."

"What do you mean?" I was about to cry.

"I see how he looks at you. And I know you too well to believe you don't feel anything for him." He closed his eyes, bit his lip, and rested his hands on his hips. "You go do what you need to do, but when you come back, give me an answer. If you want to keep going with me, then we'll have something real, boyfriend-girlfriend real. That's the deal. Because I can't keep going like this, understand?"

I nodded slowly, with a knot in my throat.

"So what are we right now, Landon?"

He wiped away my tears.

"We're two friends who will love each other forever, no matter what happens."

69

Leah

IT WAS ALMOST NIGHT WHEN I got off of the bus. My heart was pounding in my chest as I walked down the path to his house, but I needed it. I needed...I'm not really sure what, but the idea had gotten stuck in my head and made me hop on that bus. My brother or Landon would have thought I was being whimsical, but Axel would have been as tempted by it as I was. Deep down, I had the feeling that there were things I could share with him and him alone, as if I were afraid the rest of the world wouldn't understand them the same way.

I decided to knock on the front door instead of walking around to the porch and finding out Axel wasn't alone. I was apprehensive as I did so. Axel looked surprised when he opened it.

"Can I come in?"

He stood aside, and I went in and left my bag on the sofa. I tried to remember the words I'd wanted to say to him, but I got distracted watching him grab a T-shirt from the back of the chair and put it on. His shoulders and the muscles in his back, the straight lines suddenly curving, his golden skin...it looked so entrancing...

"What are you doing here?"

"I wanted to see you. And ask you for something."

"Is it about Paris?" I shook my head. It was true that I still hadn't given him an answer. "Is everything okay, Leah?"

His dark blue eyes shone unsteadily in his tense face, and I wanted to reach up and smooth out the wrinkles between his eyebrows.

"No. I just need to do something."

"If by something, you mean something in bed, babe, all you've got to do is ask."

I stared daggers into him and he laughed, turning toward the porch. I followed him out.

"Spit it out, Leah; you're worrying me. You know you can ask me for anything, right?"

"Anything?" I asked quietly, standing next to him.

"Absolutely, Leah. Any and everything."

"Even breaking into a house?"

"What?" He blinked.

"Breaking into an abandoned house."

"Now why the hell...?" He closed his lips when he understood what I meant, and a thin grin spread across his lips. "Just say when."

"Tonight?"

"Sure. You had dinner?"

"No. Anything you've got will be fine, though."

He went into the kitchen. "I've got a little leftover lasagna from yesterday and..."

"That'll do," I said, interrupting him, then sitting on one of the stools.

He heated up two plates, and we ate in silence, looking up at each other now and then, otherwise lost in our thoughts. For a moment, I felt I'd traveled into the past. I finished my glass of water in one sip.

"How will we do it?"

"There's not too many neighbors. We can go around the back and climb the wall. I'll take something to jimmy the door. You're sure about this, right?"

"Couldn't be surer," I responded.

70

Axel

I WANTED TO ASK WHY she hadn't gotten Oliver to help her instead. Or Landon. Or anyone. She could have saved herself three hours on a bus, and the bother of having to see me, or so I thought, because despite our so-called *friendship*, I wasn't always sure she could even stand to be around me. At least, that was the conclusion I'd come to after realizing one of the problems with Paris was that I would be there.

But I was so happy to see her that a part of me knew I'd do anything she asked. Because my heart raced every time she was near. Because I got hard when I saw her. Because she had the prettiest face in the world and I wanted to kiss her all over.

"You ready, Leah? Come on."

We'd walked around the property and had our flashlights off, so we could only see by the light of the moon. She stepped into some bushes, I grabbed her by the waist, lifted her up, and got her close to the edge of the wall. She climbed up and jumped off, and I did the same. I stretched my arm out to her.

"Give me your hand," I said.

Her fingers met mine in the darkness, and I ignored the shiver that ran up my spine as I pulled her toward the house through the overgrown grass and weeds. We walked up the back porch, and I let her go when we were at the door. I crossed my fingers, hoping it would open easily.

"Let me light it up for you," she said and turned on her flashlight.

I bumped the door with my shoulder, and the wood cracked loudly. I closed my eyes and did it again, I heard a snap, and it tore open.

"Ready?" I asked.

She nodded.

This time her hand sought mine on its own, and when we set foot inside what had been her home for so many years, she squeezed mine, and in that gesture I felt trust. There were memories in each corner and on each of the furnishings now covered with sheets.

"Babe, if you want to go, just tell me."

"I'm fine." She sniffled. "I swear, I'm fine." She seemed to want to convince herself that it was true. "There's so much stuff here, so many..."

Her flashlight moved through the living room and across the stairs, which creaked beneath the weight of our steps as we mounted them. I waited patiently on the threshold as Leah peeked into her bedroom.

Then we went to Douglas's studio.

I wasn't ready for everything I felt when I walked in. Seeing his pictures leaning on the wall, his paints, his easels. I tried to keep my cool as I heard Leah sobbing.

"Everything's okay," she whispered. "I'm just...feeling a little weak. I can do it, though, Axel. I want to."

She looked through the paintings. I helped her set a few of them aside. Then I saw one that made me freeze.

"Wait." I grabbed it.

"What is it?" she asked.

Leah leaned in as I tried to wipe the dust from the canvas and placed it on one of the easels still standing. I took a deep breath.

"I need to take this one with me."

"What's so special about it?"

"It's the first time I ever painted. I don't know why your dad kept it. It never would have even passed through my mind." I brought my hand to my mouth while Leah shined her flashlight on it. "You were three years old, and you were dancing around here while he painted. He gave me a brush, and I did this. A clear sky..." I ran my fingers over it.

"You and your clear skies..." she said.

I looked at her and saw her smile in the shadows. We gazed at each other in silence, connected in a way I couldn't even understand.

"Thanks for coming with me..."

I nodded, and we went on looking through the studio. Maybe it was stealing, but whatever, I was planning on taking several of those pictures. They didn't have any value. Not for the current owners of the house. They did for us, though. For us, they were priceless.

For some things, it's worth it to close your eyes and take a risk.

As we walked out, I promised her we'd return another day

with a car to bring back some memories with us. I lifted her again so she could get over the wall. How I wanted to pull her into my body. We kept glancing back and forth, tickled, as we walked down the street. If I'd thought Leah had changed, that she was calmer, more like a grown-up, I was wrong. She was still the same girl, adventurous, up for a dare, and here she was walking with me amid the soft breeze on a random Thursday night.

"What are we doing?" I asked.

"I don't know." She laughed, but under the streetlamps, I could see her eyes were still a little red. "I don't know where I'm going to sleep."

"You just caught a bus and didn't think about it?"

"I was making it up as I went along!"

"Let's go to my place." I reached out, but she looked at my hand, shook her head, and kept walking. "What are you thinking?"

"Let's just stay up all night," she said. "We'll walk, talk, or just sit there." She didn't say she wasn't ready to sleep at my house yet, but I could see these things sometimes just looking at her.

"Sounds fantastic."

And that's what we did.

We let the hours slip past strolling over empty streets, seeing them from a different perspective, not at all like the daytime, when they were full of people. We walked down to the boardwalk, and I tried not to do anything stupid while we were lying on the beach and she told me her relationship with Landon was passing through a rocky phase. I tried to listen. I tried to be her friend. I tried not to want to fuck her then and there. But it was in vain. And when we retraced our steps and stopped in a lonely park, we sat on the swings. I laughed, and she swung back and forth, and her hair went to and fro. I sat there holding the ropes and I felt alive again. When we were together, the world felt more colorful, more vibrant, more intense. That's what she was for me.

"Be careful," I said as I saw her start to twist in the air.

"If I fall, will you catch me?"

"What's that question mean?"

She stopped.

"In Paris. If I fall, will you pick me up, Axel?"

Now I understood.

"Always, babe. I promise."

"I'm scared to walk on my own."

"I know. But I'll be there."

She seemed doubtful. But she went on:

"When will I see you then?"

It had been years since I'd seen her smiling like that.

71

—

Leah

THERE ARE WOUNDS THAT CUT straight into the flesh, and those are bad, but still worse are the ones that don't bleed, that seem scarred over, but when you touch them, they hurt just like the first day.

Axel was my wound.

March

—

(SPRING, PARIS)

72

Axel

I LOOKED AT THE IMMENSE blue sea through the oval window, heart still uneasy, because flying wasn't my thing.

"What are you thinking about?" Leah asked.

I turned to look at her. She was gorgeous.

"Trust me, you don't want to know."

"Just say it."

"Fine." I leaned my head into hers to be able to talk without others hearing. "I'm thinking about how we're more than twenty thousand feet in the air in a tin can, and I don't trust it, and neither of us can get out..." I looked down at her lips, which were moist. "And I guess if I was looking for the perfect moment to tell you that I'm still wild about you, this would be it. Or to tell you I don't know how, but I'll keep trying every day to get you to forgive me. Or that I've been about to kiss you so many times..."

"Axel..." She was tense, her breathing accelerated.

"But those are just suppositions."

I smiled innocently, and she released the breath she'd been holding in.

73

Leah

WE'VE ALL GOT OUR DEFENSE mechanisms. Against pain, betrayal, danger. Channeling emotions, knowing how to digest them and internalize them, isn't always easy. In my case, the hardest thing was the end point. I'd think and think and think about the same thing over and over, turning it over, looking at it from different angles and perspectives until I'd found what for me was a valid conclusion. And then…I wouldn't know what to do with that conclusion. What do you do with feelings once you've labeled them in your mind? Order them by color? Put them in a box? Let them accompany you throughout your day, learning to wear them like a scarf that squeezes your neck tighter and tighter?

I didn't know how to let go. How to let my thoughts be.

Maybe that was why I still hadn't talked with Axel, because a part of me resisted it. I had infinite reproaches, but I couldn't let them out, even though carrying them around was eating me up inside and they seemed to weigh on me more every day. I was scared. I didn't want to open the box where I kept all that ugliness, all that happened between us.

It scared me that the line between hate and love was so fine, so slender that you could jump straight from one extreme to the other. And I loved him... I loved him in my entire being, with my eyes, my heart. My entire body reacted when he was near. But another part of me hated him. I hated him with my memories, with words never uttered, with scorn, and was incapable of opening my arms and offering him forgiveness, however much I wanted to do so. When I looked at him, I saw black, red, throbbing purple: emotions welling over. And feeling something so chaotic for him hurt me, because Axel was a part of me. He always would be. Despite everything.

74

Leah

A TAXI DRIVER WAS WAITING for us at the airport.

He took us to the apartment where we would stay in the upcoming months, and after helping us with our bags, he gave us the key Hans had left with him. When he left, the two of us were standing in the middle of the street looking up at the leaden sky and contemplating the old building done in the style of Haussmann.

Axel opened the door, and I followed him inside. The prehistoric elevator had a sign on it that read *hors service*, which, to judge from the chain and lock running through the grate, meant that it didn't work. The stairs were narrow, but I still felt a tingle as we dragged our luggage up them.

"Just leave them if they weigh too much," Axel said.

"I'm fine," I replied.

We reached the third floor, the top one. After walking in, Axel cut on the lights and stepped to one side. I turned around, looking up at the high ceilings, the molding, the rosettes, the huge windows. The light glowed off the bright wooden floor, and I asked myself how it was possible that a building so old could harbor an apartment so beautiful.

A metal staircase spiraled up toward what looked like the attic, and I assumed that would be my studio. I took off my thin jacket and left it on an arm of one of the sofas, then opened the three doors that led to the bathroom and the two bedrooms.

"You can take the one with the big bed," I said, and I felt briefly paralyzed, because I hadn't realized before then how hard it was going to be to see Axel every morning, every night, every day. "That'll give you room to spread out, you know. Anyway, I like the view from the other room."

"Fine," he responded, not really paying attention.

As he took the suitcases to the bedrooms, I climbed up to the small attic. I smiled when I saw how clean and comfortable it was, with its easels already set up, white canvases spread around, and a few tubes of paint and brushes. I knew I'd need to buy much more material.

I heard Axel coming up behind me.

"Man, the light's great in here."

"It's perfect," I agreed.

He opened a window to let the cool air ventilate my studio. I was content as I looked in every corner and felt impatience overtake me. I was ready to break it in, start painting, look down at the street for hours on end, let myself go, thinking of nothing else, with those walls protecting me.

"You happy with it?"

"Absolutely. But I'm nervous too."

"We'll look it over more closely later. We need to meet with

Hans in half an hour, and I hope the place is close, because I have no idea where we are."

We went back outside. The wind was cold, especially compared with the mild temperatures we were used to. We were wearing thin, comfy clothes. As we walked along, following the directions on Axel's cell phone, I realized we'd need to buy something heavier to wear unless better weather was right around the corner.

The restaurant where we were meeting Hans was nearby, just a few steps from the famous Moulin Rouge, below the famous bohemian neighborhood of Montmartre. Le Jardin d'en Face had a facade of Veronese granite, and inside was cozy, almost rustic.

A gray-haired man with a pronounced smile stood when we walked in, and he and Axel hugged each other briefly. Then he looked over at me and surprised me with a kiss on each cheek. "A real pleasure, Leah."

"The pleasure's mine, sir."

"You can skip the *sir*. I'm still a young man at heart. Come on, I've got a table reserved. What are you in the mood to drink? Should I order a bottle of wine?"

We said yes as we were sitting down.

"How was your trip?"

"Good, but I'm still not sure what time it is," Axel said, making him laugh. "The apartment's incredible. Same goes for the studio, right, Leah?"

"It's beautiful. The light is amazing."

"Great. That *was* the idea."

We ordered a few dishes, and I focused on my salad while they talked about the gallery in Byron Bay and our plans for Paris. We had to attend an art fair that same week. With all the proposals Hans was making, it looked like we were going to be pretty busy.

Axel got up to go to the bathroom. Hans was looking at me. I felt nervous.

"So you've got art in your genes…"

I cocked my head to the side and looked at him with surprise.

"Did you know my father?" I asked.

"I did. I bought some of his work years ago. He was talented. Your mother, too, but she wasn't as taken with art as he was. When she put her mind to it, though…" He toyed with his napkin. "Don't be nervous, Leah. I trust you even more than you trust yourself. This will be good for you."

"I wish I could believe that."

"Are you worried about it?"

"I'm worried about everything. The newness of it all. The people. The language."

Hans seemed to understand. "My mother was Australian and my father French," he said, "so I spent a lot of my life traveling back and forth. Believe me when I tell you the only thing you'll need to know your first days here is a bit of small talk."

Axel sat back down and smiled. "Why, do Parisians like to chitchat?"

"They do. And they have very specific ways of doing it. On Mondays and Tuesdays, *bonne semaine* is best; on Wednesdays and Thursdays, they use *bonne fin de semaine*; and on Fridays they say *bon weekend*."

I laughed. I don't know why, but it all seemed so funny to me. And the tension that had taken hold of me since we'd landed in

Paris disappeared all at once. I wrote those expressions down on a napkin. Axel made fun of me for it. I enjoyed the meal without thinking any more about my fears, enjoying the desserts and listening to Hans's entertaining stories.

75

Axel

MY HEAD WAS ABOUT TO explode. I tried to hold out till lunch was over, and when we got to the apartment, I took a pill.

"Are you feeling bad?" Leah asked.

"It'll pass. We can go for a walk later, get to know the area, maybe grab some dinner. What do you say?"

"Sure. You need anything?"

I smiled mischievously and pointed at my cheek.

"I'd never say no to a kiss."

"You are truly an idiot, Axel." She walked upstairs, but I could see her lips tugging upward before she disappeared into the studio, and that warmed me up inside.

I swallowed the pill and fell back on my bed with my hands behind my head, looking at the ceiling and thinking...thinking how a part of me felt that being here in Paris was like starting over from zero. There was no logic to it, but it seemed as if, exiting the airplane, I'd become a different person from the one who'd climbed into it, and I asked myself if we would be the same people when we went back home or no. Because in some weird way, Leah and I were stripping ourselves bare layer by layer every time our lives hit one of these crossroads and we had to decide what direction to take.

76

Leah

THE FIRST WEEK WAS RELAXED. We barely had any free time. When we weren't buying art supplies, clothing, or food, we had to go to Hans's gallery and meet people. I was incapable of remembering all their names.

"What was that guy's name, supposedly?"

Axel suppressed a smile and bent over to whisper in my ear. His breath was hot, close, almost tingly on my neck. He was wearing dark pants and a white button-down shirt. I'd never seen him in anything so formal. I was painfully conscious of how attractive he was: his freshly shaved chin, the cologne he'd put on before leaving, his penetrating stare.

"Armand Fave," Axel reminded me.

I finished the drink I'd been served in one swallow and stared at Axel's neck in his shirt and his badly tied tie. We didn't fit in there at all. What were we doing here, I wondered and grinned.

"What's so funny?" he asked.

"Nothing. Come here and let me fix that..."

We were in a sterile space full of chatty people drinking and remarking on the works of artists who'd made it after an opening in that gallery. I didn't know any of them, and I felt a little bit lost. As I cinched Axel's tie, he said, "You shouldn't get so close."

"Why? Am I in danger?"

"I'll bet Little Red Riding Hood asked the Big Bad Wolf that same question," he replied, so I tightened the knot more, until he said, "Jesus, babe," and stuck a finger in his collar to loosen it.

I was aroused, but I was still struggling to get over what he'd said to me on the plane, still dealing with how hard it was seeing him at all hours of the day, and still trying to remember all the reasons why I couldn't let my guard down.

"Here you are," Hans said. "I wanted to introduce you to one of our partners at the gallery, William Parks. This dazzling lady is his wife, Scarlett."

I greeted them both. They had noticeable English accents and a distinguished air it was hard not to be impressed by. They were enchanting, the kind of people who command attention in any room they enter. Everything about them spoke of elegance, luxury, and sophistication.

Axel took the wheel in the conversation, and Scarlett grabbed me by the arm, saying we were going to step away for a drink. I couldn't say no. I crossed the room with her and felt uncomfortable as she stopped me in front of a huge picture of geometric shapes, broken lines, and cool colors.

"What do you think of this?" she asked.

"It's interesting." I didn't add that, to my mind, there was something missing from it. It was hard to explain. It needed soul, feeling, purpose.

"The artist's name is Didier Baudin, and a little less than a year ago, he was only showing his work at fairs and a few restaurants that agreed to lend him a hand. My husband and I saw he had talent, a future. Believe me, we've been doing this for years, we know how to pick out a diamond from the dull stones around it, and the catalog Hans showed us with your work in it was... refreshing. I think that's the word. Something unexpected in the midst of monotony. Trust me when I tell you that, if we work together, we can achieve great things."

She winked and I thanked her quietly, unsure how to respond, unsure even if her interest was flattering or discomfiting.

When the opening was over and we were leaving, it was eleven at night, and the streets of Paris were almost empty. It was cold, but over my dress, I had on the coat I'd bought the week before. And, unfortunately, my only pair of heels, which I'd worn out of the store.

"They're killing me," I said.

"Take them off, then."

"We're not in Byron Bay," I reminded him.

"Who cares? Come on, I'll help you."

I laughed and shook my head, amused at how little Axel let the environment influence him. I grabbed the hand he held out and let him support part of my weight until we made it to the apartment. As soon as we opened the front door, I took off my shoes.

"Do we have to go to more parties like that?"

"I'm afraid so. You feel like a nightcap?"

I shook my head while he served himself two fingers' worth of amber liquor. He took a long sip as he sat beside me on the sofa.

I was anxious as I watched his eyes descend my neck and come to rest in my cleavage where my black dress ended.

I trembled, and I hated the desire I felt.

The longing. The memories.

I got up and told him good night, barely even looking at him. Closing the door to my room, I took off my dress, put on pajamas, and walked to the window to look out at the lights of the city and the sky, almost bare of stars, so different from the sky at home... and at the chimneys and rooftops of Paris...

77

Axel

I TRIED TO GIVE HER space for the following days. She wasn't too happy with her work, no matter how many hours she spent shut up in her studio, a prisoner to her own chaos. When she ate one of her lollipops, it wasn't slowly, distractedly, as usual. Instead, she'd immediately bite it into little pieces. She'd thrown out three half-finished canvases, and I agreed, in a sense, because I knew she could do much better, and plus, I wanted her to be satisfied with her results. She obviously felt pressure to show Hans something next week, but I didn't think too much of it. We were there for a grant; I wanted her to take it easy and enjoy the city and the experience. I told myself that every time I saw the closed door to the studio and felt the hours that stretched out silently.

I developed my own routine pretty quickly: climbing Montmartre at dawn.

Since I couldn't wear myself out among the waves, I followed the steep stairways and hills leading to that artsy neighborhood. Every morning, while Leah was still asleep, I'd cross the square with the painters in it and head right toward Sacré-Coeur. Then I'd retrace my steps, and before returning to the apartment, I'd have a leisurely breakfast on our corner, thinking about her, about how to knock down the locked doors that separated us, the ones built of all the things we still hadn't said.

78

Leah

IT TOOK DAYS FOR ME to create something I was satisfied with, even if it wasn't close to the best thing I'd done. *But it'll do*, I thought as I took one last look at the canvas on the easel before cleaning my brushes and putting in order the disaster area around me. I went downstairs and took a shower. Only then, while I dried my hair with a towel after putting on comfy clothes, did I realize I hadn't seen or heard from Axel in hours. Normally he was always nearby, looking at my work or proposing a million plans that I rejected out of fear of getting too close and burning myself.

When I passed by his room, I saw the door was cracked and the lights were off. I wasn't sure, but I opened it anyway, trying not to make noise. He was lying in bed with the curtains drawn to keep out the afternoon sun. He sat up when he realized I was there.

"You okay?" I asked.

"My head, these goddamn migraines."

"You should really wear your glasses."

"Sure," he hissed.

"Wait here; I'll bring you something."

I went to the kitchen, got a glass of water and a pill, and wet a washcloth for his forehead. I turned the light on in his room and saw him squint.

"The light bothers me," he grunted.

"Stop being whiny. Here, take this."

He leaned back against the headboard, and the sheet slipped off his torso. I looked away from him as he handed me the glass and I set it on the table. I turned the light off again, told him to lie down, and applied the damp cloth.

"Does it help any?"

"It helps that you're here."

I rolled my eyes.

"If you need anything, call me…"

"Wait. Stay a while. Please."

He made room for me on the bed. There were extreme sports less terrifying than sitting down on that stretch of mattress. I don't know how long I hesitated there with Axel daring me, as always.

"What are you afraid of?"

It was as if he could hear the words in my head, and as I sat down and he pulled on me, trying to get me to lie down, I wished he couldn't see right through me. I remained stiff, looking up at the ceiling as our arms touched in the bed. I could hear his relaxed breathing. It was all so intimate, so dangerous…

"What is it you want, Axel?"

"I don't know. Talk to me. Tell me something. Anything."

So I did. I confessed to him that I wasn't entirely pleased with the work I'd done in recent days, even though he already knew it.

I told him about my brief encounter with Scarlett at the opening and how everything was overwhelming me.

"Just remember, Leah, it's temporary."

"Yeah, but even so…"

I didn't finish the phrase. My skin was prickly, my stomach turned. At some point, I stopped counting the seconds I was there, stopped cursing the jolt I felt every time he moved and his arm touched mine. I closed my eyes and saw colors: bright, soft pastels…

I blinked, confused.

And then I felt it: his body against mine, his hand on my waist, his lips by my cheek, his presence enveloping me in a warm embrace. I tried to tell myself to breathe when I felt myself getting light-headed. I remained still, very still, asking myself why I didn't just get up and go.

Maybe because, for a moment, I wanted to live again in that possibility we'd lost. But no. He'd thrown that in the trash. And I couldn't stop remembering how very happy I'd been in his arms before he did that.

As Axel moved, I felt his fingers slowly climbing my ribs. Then I understood. Over my T-shirt, they were once again tracing the outlines of the letters I'd had tattooed there, wanting to hold on to them forever: *Let it be*.

"Axel…" I said almost silently.

"Let it be, babe."

And a second later, his lips met mine, and all I could do was feel. Just as he once taught me, mind blank, heart open, I felt his perfect mouth, his tongue caressing me, his abdomen twitching as he let loose a moan, his hands under my shirt and his fingertips burning my skin, leaving an invisible but permanent mark.

I felt everything. Lust, hate, love, friendship, the sea, disappointment. I felt all the things Axel had been for me, and I saw the emotions spilling out onto a paper painted in watercolors so wet they dripped past the edges.

79

Axel

I COULDN'T THINK. I COULDN'T. I couldn't.

Because her mouth was an addiction.

Because I was out of control.

Because I loved her so much… I moaned when Leah bit my lip, but the pain only turned me on more. I pulled up her T-shirt and inhaled a deep breath of air. She whimpered when I pressed my hips into her thighs and she felt how hard I was. I needed to breathe. I needed to be inside her. I needed to fuck her until she understood that she had to forgive me, and no one could feel for her all that I felt, all those things filling my chest and suffocating me.

But it wasn't going to happen. Because before I could tear off her clothes, I fell still, tasting the salt of her tears on her lips along with the saliva from her kisses.

"Don't do this. Don't fucking cry."

"Stop. Please, Axel. Please."

I had never heard words that hurt so bad, but I freed her from my arms. I let her go. Leah got up sobbing and left, and

I heard her slam the door to her room; it echoed through the whole apartment. My heart was pounding, and I asked myself if I would keep doing the same thing forever, not fighting, not reacting, letting the days pass between us as if this was it.

I had to go after her. No, I needed to.

80

Leah

I BROUGHT A TREMBLING HAND to my lips and touched them as if they were a stranger's, unsure who that girl was who had been moaning beneath Axel's body moments before, while the world drained away in the kisses and darkness.

I wanted to erase the memory. I wanted to hold on to it forever.

I wanted...to be someone else. Stronger. Firmer.

Axel was savagery, necessity, impulse. But I couldn't stop thinking about Landon, who was tenderness, security. I couldn't stop comparing him when I understood I would lose him. Maybe I had lost him already. And even though we'd talked before I went to Paris, I still wasn't ready to face it. I needed a pillar. And Axel would never have his feet on the ground. He'd always be airborne: vertigo, risk.

Axel opened the door without knocking and came in.

His eyes were inflamed, his lip bleeding. I tried to tell him to leave, but my voice failed me. He huffed as he walked back and forth, one hand resting on the back of his neck. Then he stopped and stared at me a long time.

"I need us to talk, Leah."

"Nothing's changed."

He crouched in front of the bed where I was sitting and closed his eyes, almost as if he were doing some kind of self-control routine, resting his head on the wooden edge of the frame. When he looked up, the grief made me want to die.

"I tried... I promise I tried. But I can't go on like this, pretending I'm not in love with you. I am. And every morning when I pass by your room, I have to stop myself from kissing you awake, holding you all day long, and at night... You don't want to know what I think about doing at night. I need to know what I have to do so you'll forgive me. Just...just tell me. And I'll do it. No matter what it is."

I wiped away my tears.

"You say it like it was that simple. But it's more than that, Axel. Much more. I'm talking about years of not understanding. I'm talking about everything that's broken. Everything that could still be broken. Plus there's another person involved."

His jaw twitched.

"Are you in love with him?"

Yes, I wanted to shout, but I couldn't. There had already been too many lies and empty words between us to add more. I heard that song in my head that we danced to the day I thought Axel was finally mine, when I was so naive I thought things really could be that simple. The sad notes of "The Night We Met" swirled around me while I realized that question wasn't the right one. It didn't matter whether or not I was in love with Landon, what mattered was why I didn't want to be in love anymore.

"Everything with him is different."

"How? Tell me."

"We don't argue…"

"Couples argue, Leah…"

He paused a second, then went on: "Dammit, I never wanted…"

"I know," I interrupted him.

"What does he have that I don't?"

It was hard for me to let the words out, to be sincere.

"Security. Trust."

"You don't trust me, babe?"

"Trust is something you earn, Axel."

I ignored the pleas in his eyes and looked away when the pain got to be too much. I didn't want to hurt him, but I didn't want to lie to him either; the truth was all I had now. With Landon, I felt protected. With Axel, I felt like I was skydiving. Maybe that was why I didn't say as much as I might have said just then: that trust had to be earned, and that a person could do it with effort, good intentions, honesty… but love? No, real, passionate love, the kind that makes you shake from head to toe, that gives you butterflies in your stomach, wasn't something someone could earn; it just came, whether or not you wanted it. Because the heart is more powerful than reason. Because there is no secret formula to keep you from falling in love with the wrong person, a person full of defects, someone who's taken, someone who might never even notice you exist…

And that scared me. Bad.

But even as scared as I was, when he got up, I told him, "You shouldn't have asked."

With one hand on the doorknob, he said, "What was I supposed to say, then, Leah?"

"You should have asked what I was looking for. Because you know what?" I sniffled, feeling empty, broken, and lost inside. "You were right. I needed to go to college. I needed to get out of Byron Bay and face things on my own. But when I did it, I realized I didn't need you. Life went on."

In his face was an infinity of emotions...

"I'm proud of you for it."

"You shouldn't be. Because when that happened, I understood you weren't irreplaceable. I understood that nothing is, that romance like that doesn't exist. And a part of me was lost the day I pushed that idea out of my mind. The part that believed in idyllic loves that were worth fighting the whole world for. It sounds silly when I say it out loud, right? I guess it is. So, as always, you win."

His entire body was frozen, apart from his heaving chest.

"Goddammit, Leah. I'm sorry to tell you, but I was wrong. So I guess that means we both lose. You for listening to me and not trusting yourself. And me for being a fucking idiot."

He walked out.

And all I could do was try to breathe...

81

Leah

WE BARELY TALKED THE NEXT three days. If Axel cooked, he'd tell me he'd left me something in the fridge. If I went out for groceries, I'd ask him if he needed anything. The tension gathered in the corners like dust. And the silence. The fleeting glances. Weirdly, the situation felt familiar to me, because it wasn't the first time we'd lived like that under the same roof, avoiding and seeking each other out at the same time, walking around each other in circles as if we were expecting something.

A part of me that I wished I could silence kept remembering the electrifying feeling when I felt his lips on mine. So warm. So hungry. So wild. And I felt guilty for it, and angry with myself for remembering.

Another part of me was still mad at him.

I'd tried for years to digest what had happened. Constantly chewing it over, never managing to fully process it. Maybe that's why I couldn't forgive him. It wasn't what he did, but how he did it and why. I was frustrated that he'd been so weak, and worse, that he'd made a decision for me, but at the same time in spite of me. Treating me like a girl after all we'd lived through together. He wasn't the sincere boy I'd fallen in love with. He'd let me down...

Disappointment. That was the word. The fault must have been partly mine, because believing he was perfect, idolizing him in that way, melting every time I saw his crooked smile for as long as I could recall, gushing over his intense eyes, his casual stroll... Saddest of all was the way Axel used that image of himself as free and sincere to hide how, in reality, he'd always had his hands tied. Or had tied his own hands, actually, limiting himself, deciding it was easier to stay on the cliff than to dare to jump. And even worse, had I known it all since the beginning, I wasn't sure it would have changed our story that much. Because it was Axel's lights and his shadows that had always drawn me to him, his complexity and his contradictions.

All the things he was in Paris, but with more intensity.

I was so scared of falling into temptation. Of curiosity getting the best of me.

82

Axel

IT WAS LIKE A SLOW, painful torture, having to see her all the time. I wanted to reach her, but I didn't know how. I wanted to be able to say or do something that wouldn't fuck the whole thing up even worse. I wanted her to trust me. And all I did was make mistakes, over and over again.

That night, when I saw her coming down from the studio, I couldn't help but notice the bags under her eyes.

"Bad day?"

"Not really, to tell the truth."

"You want me to go to the place downstairs and grab some Chinese for dinner?"

"Fine."

I didn't hide how much her response surprised me. I should have gotten used to how odd Leah was by then, but I couldn't. Sometimes she looked at me as if I were the center of the world. Other times, hatred and disappointment filled her stare. I asked myself how she could stand living with me around when her feelings were so contrary and extreme, when she barely knew how to manage the simplest situations.

I went outside and returned a bit later with a bag of food, which I left on the table in front of the sofa while she grabbed glasses and napkins. I passed her some chopsticks before opening the boxes. Leah tried her noodles absentmindedly, sitting on the rug with her knees pulled up to her chest, and I did the same, settling in beside her. We both were staring at each other out of the corner of our eyes. And her stare said so much to me...

"Don't cry, please," I begged.

"I hate this. I hate being like this. I hate hating you."

"Then don't do it," I replied, almost implored.

"I've tried, I swear..."

I leaned my head back into the sofa. "One of these days, we're going to have to talk for real."

"You think that's going to fix everything?"

"No, but I need it. And the only reason I still haven't done it is I'm trying to think about what you need." When she pursed her lips, I guessed at what she was thinking. "You're going to tell me it's a little late for that?"

"Why do you have to know me so well?"

"Because I was there when you were born, jeez. Not literally, thank God. But I've got a few years on you."

She smiled weakly as she twisted noodles around her chopsticks, dropped them, and started over. We were so close that we were breathing the same air, and I had to remind myself that kissing her wasn't the best idea.

"Axel, it scares me... Everything I feel scares me, everything I've kept inside all these years, the ugliness... You know I'm not good at channeling my emotions; that's a problem I have, and I feel like if I open the door, I'll hurt you."

"I can take it," I whispered.

"But I love you."

I trembled, and I wished she had said, "We all live in a yellow submarine," because that phrase was ours alone and was the special way we loved each other.

She continued. "I thought with time those feelings would abate, and you and I could be friends, but I'm not even sure of that. Because it still hurts. And it's still complicated. And I still don't understand what I'm thinking half the time..."

"Breathe, babe." I ran my knuckles across her cheeks, and she closed her eyes in response and inhaled deeply. It was enough for me to feel I had her there beside me and that a part of her wanted to stay there with me, because that meant, or I hoped it meant, that there was at least still something left. I asked myself if that might be enough, if I could be happy with her just being a part of my life, but the hole in my chest grew, and I cast that idea aside.

I got up when I was done to take the empty boxes to the trash. I made some tea, opened the living room window, and leaned on the sill before lighting a cigarette.

"What's going on up there?" I nodded toward her studio.

"What's not going on up there, you mean," she corrected me. "Nothing at all."

"Is it because of me?" I took a curt drag.

"No."

I knew she was lying. And I guess she knew I knew that, because she stopped looking at me and started rubbing her fingers across the shag carpet.

"I guess it's all the changes, you know? I'm used to working in my own space."

I rubbed out my cigarette and stretched.

"You want to come with me tomorrow morning at dawn?"

"Okay." She looked at me a long time, then smiled.

83

Leah

CLIMBING MONTMARTRE EVERY MORNING HAD a magical effect on me. Not so much for the walk in itself as for the way it made me face the rest of the day differently. Channel my frustration. Try to keep calm. Sitting there in the heights of the city after the laborious ascent, Axel and I would let the minutes pass while the sun rose in the sky and the day began.

The third time we did it, Axel looked at me, intrigued.

"What are you thinking about?"

"Butterflies." He raised an eyebrow, and I laughed as the morning glow bathed the roofs of Paris. "I was remembering how, when I was little, I loved to lie in the grass in my yard and watch the butterflies for hours, the way they'd flap around the trunk of a tree. I was thinking about that feeling you get when you're little, when you don't have any obligations or goals, and you're not living by the clock. That was so nice. Being able to just watch without a care. I wish it was like that now. But all I can think is how next week Hans wants to see something, and I don't have anything halfway decent. And all I want to do is spend the rest of the day watching a million butterflies whirl among the flowers."

Axel smiled. With tenderness. With love.

84

Leah

I SPENT HOURS LOOKING AT the blank canvas. Blocked, but at the same time with emotions bubbling up inside me. The problem was, if I let them out, I knew Axel would understand each and every one of them when he saw my work. He'd know if it was about Landon, about me, or worse, about him.

I was startled when he knocked at the door and came in with a bag and a package in wrapping paper that he set down in the middle of the studio to my evident disconcertment.

"What is that?"

"Isn't it obvious? It's a gift."

"But…"

"Come on, open it!"

I knelt in front of the rectangular box and tore into the paper with the bright red bow. I smiled until my cheeks twitched with happiness and got up to hug him, even though my body screamed at me not to, because having him so close was complicated: hearing his heart beat against my chest, feeling his hands on my back, his hot breath on my neck…

"It's precious! Thank you!"

"Wait, I'm going to turn it on."

Axel grabbed the record player and put it on top of a wooden shelf full of art materials. It was a classic model, similar to the one he had at home.

"Where'd you get it?"

"In a secondhand shop."

"We don't have any records here though…"

He passed me the bag, which was still in his hands, then busied himself with the record player. I pushed some junk off the table and took the records out. I blinked to keep from crying, but at the same time, I was grinning. Frank Sinatra, Nirvana, Elvis Presley, Supertramp, Bruce Springsteen, Queen…and the Beatles. Always the Beatles. I slid my fingers slowly over the cover with the drawing of the yellow submarine on it and shivered when I realized he was looking at me.

"Why'd you do all this?"

"I already told you. It's a gift. I thought you'd like it; I thought it would help you get your work done. Listen, Leah…" He looked away, picked up a record, and placed it carefully on the turntable. "If you have to paint something you don't think I'll like, just do it. There are artists who paint external things, landscapes, or faces, but you're not like that. That doesn't work for you. Just pay attention to that tattoo of yours and let be whatever has to be. Understand? Because it's a problem if you repress what you feel when your feelings are the basis of your art. And they always have been." He set the needle down as he finished talking.

"My Way" by Frank Sinatra started playing.

"I think I can find a solution."

"I'm glad," he said, apparently relieved.

"What about you?" I asked. "Are you ever going to be able to do it?"

"What?"

"You know. It. Paint."

He laughed humorlessly and shook his head.

"I gave up a long time ago."

I saw then a change in his expression as he realized what he'd just said, how he recognized all at once that those were the same words he'd once used with reference to us.

"I didn't mean... This is different, Leah. I wish I could, but..."

"How about you let me try something?" I said, tense as a bowstring.

His eyes were suspicious, but he didn't put up much resistance when I asked him to sit on the wooden stool in front of a canvas. I stood behind him.

"Relax."

"I know more effective techniques than this..."

"Shhhh. Wait a moment."

"What are you trying to do, exactly?"

"Paint through you. Or with you. I don't know."

"This is a bad idea."

I held his shoulders down when he tried to get up, and he yielded again with a sigh. I grabbed my palette and looked down at the still-damp colors. What tone was Axel? Red, certainly. Intense red. Like a cherry. Or a red sundown, more enigmatic. I dipped the tip of the brush into the paint.

He was so close that my body could feel his back, and the scent of his hair distracted me. I grabbed his hand when he closed it around the brush. Frank Sinatra's voice boomed in the walls of that attic somewhere in the middle of Paris, and for a perfect second, I felt we were alone in that phantom city. Axel, me, color, music, the rough skin of his fingertips...

"Close your eyes; you need to feel it."

It was stirring to see him so powerless, so defenseless.

"Why do you take so long?" he growled.

"Picasso said something one time, '*The paint is stronger than I am; it always gets me to do what it wants*, That's exactly how it is when I sit down in front of a canvas, and I'd like that to happen to you too. Don't tell me you don't want that, Axel." I closed my fingers tighter around his hand and guided him to the canvas. He obeyed, eyes closed, breathing slowly. "It would be so wonderful if you could wake up one day and get all the things you feel out there somehow, all those feelings you have trapped inside..." His hand glided beneath mine, and lines of color filled the canvas. They spoke of inhibition, survival, dread. "You know what? Sometimes I've been afraid of being close to you when that happens. The day you finally pick a brush back up of your own free will. You think that will ever happen?"

"Goddammit, Leah, don't do this."

"Open your eyes. Isn't it pretty?"

It was just splatters and red lines, some pressed down harder than others, thin ones, thick ones, some self-assured, some diffident, but all of them shaped by his hands. Our hands. For an eternal minute, Axel said nothing.

"Are you okay?" I asked him.

"Yeah, I'm fine."

But he wasn't. he got up and dropped the brush before turning around, kissing me on the head, and leaving me alone in the studio.

And my fingers burned with the longing to transform every heartbeat to a color, and every color to a heartbeat that would shake the canvas until it came alive.

85

Leah

THE DAYS WERE FULL OF music again, paintings and shared dawns. Every morning, coming down from Montmartre, we'd have coffee and toast together for breakfast, or a baguette with marmalade and butter, and then I'd go up to the studio and start working while Axel met with Hans or got lost in the city till lunchtime.

He gave me space. He didn't come back into the studio, and I focused on the canvas in front of me as if nothing else in the world existed. Before I knew it, I'd finished something I was satisfied with. That day, while I kept glancing over at the picture as I cleaned my brushes and tried to clean up a little, my phone rang.

I took the needle off the record and picked up.

"How's it going, pixie?" Oliver said.

"Good. Better."

A few days before, I'd called him up to vent and tell him how stressed I was at the idea of painting for someone else instead of myself. He had calmed me down, telling me the steps I needed to take.

"I managed to finish something decent for the exhibition."

"I knew you could."

I sat down on the stool, exhausted, thinking about how in just a few days I'd be back in a gallery full of people, and I hoped I didn't feel as out of place as last time. Twenty artists would be exhibiting this time, young promises, Hans had told me when we had lunch with him a few days before.

"How's everything with Bega?"

"Good, planning the wedding; she doesn't seem to understand that we've got almost half a year to do it. How's Axel? I haven't talked to him since a week ago."

"Same as always."

"Are you guys...having problems?"

"No. It's complicated," I confessed.

"He loves you. You know that."

"Why are you doing this now?"

"You're right, sorry. Forget about it. It's none of my business."

"That's not what I meant, but..."

"As long as I know you're okay, that's enough. Call me if you need anything, even just to talk, okay?" He hung up right afterward.

———

I tried to put on my best smile every time Hans came by to introduce someone to me, or whenever someone was interested in my work, but since they were talking in French, I barely understood anything, and I spent most of the evening watching Axel conversing with William and Scarlett. I think I was the only person in the entire room who could tell how fake his smile was, how rigid his shoulders under that tight button-down shirt that he must have been wanting to tear off. And I imagine he was the only one there who could read what was hidden in the lines of that painting hanging on the wall: the love, hate, doubt, guilt, the indecision in those strokes that changed direction just as they seemed to know where they were headed.

In some strange way, everything connected us.

As if he could hear my thoughts, he turned and looked at me, then walked over slowly, rolling his eyes.

"How's the night going?" I asked.

"Good. Interesting," he replied.

"You don't have to lie."

He tried not to smile and adjusted his cuffs before grabbing a drink off the tray of a passing waiter.

"I've never had a knack for putting up with swollen egos."

"Are there a lot of those here?" I took away his drink.

"Honestly, I don't know how these four walls can contain them."

I tried to suppress my giggling when Hans came over to congratulate us. The public and his friends had praised my work. I felt an unavoidable satisfaction. He looked at my painting again, nodding without realizing it.

"This is promising work indeed. Good girl."

I noticed a slight change in Axel's expression as Hans walked away to greet some acquaintances, but I wasn't sure what it meant.

86

Axel

IT WAS NIGHTTIME WHEN THE exhibition ended. Hans insisted we go to dinner with him and some of his guests, and I was relieved when Leah bowed out, telling him she was exhausted. We were taking a walk through the City of Light at nighttime, trying to find ourselves somehow in that maze of cobblestone streets, when I said:

"We should celebrate. Have dinner or grab a drink."

"Okay," she said, eyes focused on the rooftops.

"Okay? Just like that?" I joked.

She didn't respond, so we kept going in the direction of the apartment. Not long before arriving, we decided to stop in a bar with vintage wood décor. In the back, past the table where we were sitting, there was a dartboard and a pool table that brought back happy memories of the nights Oliver and I spent in Brisbane in our university era.

We ordered two beers, a plate of pasta, and another of vegetables.

She let her hair down, and it cascaded down her back, almost reaching her waist. I tried not to get lost in her cleavage, but with the dress she'd chosen, it was no easy task. We talked about work and the upcoming weeks while we ate. The last thing I wanted to do when we had finished was return to our shared apartment and watch her close herself up in her room. I couldn't stand more nights pretending I didn't want to open the door and show her we deserved a second chance. I wanted answers, words. Silence wasn't going to solve our problems.

Looking over at the pool table, I asked her how she felt about a game.

"Fine. I won't know what I'm doing, though."

We ordered two more beers and walked over to the pool tables. The lights were dim in that section of the bar. I slipped a coin inside after handing her a cue and picking my own.

"How about we do one question for each ball you sink?"

She nodded mistrustfully and rubbed a little chalk on her cue before asking permission to break. I let her have it. She bent over, squinted, and struck the cue ball hard. Nothing went in.

"Tough luck, babe. My turn." I hit the cue ball and knocked one in. I was hesitant at first, but then I said to hell with that voice whispering to me that it was a bad idea to proceed this way. "Is what you have with him anything like what you had with me?" I asked.

With eyes like saucers, she responded, "Honestly, Axel?"

"You gonna answer?"

"You honestly want to have this conversation standing over a pool table?" She clicked her tongue and shook her head. "You're out of your damned mind."

"You want an easier question? Like, uh, are you more of a beach person or a mountain person? Sweet food or savory? Cats or dogs?" I could see I was making her tense, but I didn't let up.

"Fine, if that's what you want... It's not the same. It's more real."

I ignored what felt like a blow to the chest.

"More real? So you think what we had was a joke?"

"That's another question."

"Goddammit," I said, bent over, and sank another shot.

"More real means more the way things are supposed to be. Living in a house all isolated so no one could see how you looked at me wasn't real. It was a fling. An adventure. Or at least that's how *you* treated it. Your turn."

It was hard for me to look away from those eyes that were piercing me. I don't know if it was because my hands were trembling, but I missed the red ball I was aiming for.

"You're up," I said, stepping back.

And then I saw her ass in that formfitting dress, and I couldn't think of anything else. When she turned back to me with a satisfied look on her face, I was still struggling not to let my horniness get in the way of the most important conversation I'd ever had.

"You ever think about coming to find me?"

"Every damn day."

Leah looked away and took another shot. I realized her "I won't know what I'm doing" had been a bluff. I smiled as she sank a second ball, in case there were any doubts.

"Why do you still have that painting over your bed?"

"Because I look at it sometimes, I remember that day, and I jerk off thinking about you."

With pursed lips, she responded, "I want the real answer."

"That one wasn't a lie."

"Axel…"

"Because I still love you."

She bent over and I could see her knees trembling over the high heels she hated wearing. I wanted to take them off, kiss her ankles, follow her calves up to her thighs, tear off her underwear…

"Your turn," she said.

Thankfully, I sank a yellow ball.

"If what you've got with Landon is so real, how come you're not with him?" Her eyes started to water. "Never mind, don't answer. Sometimes silence is a good enough answer."

"Fuck you."

"I wish, babe, I wish…" I had crept up behind her to whisper it in her ear, and I ran my hand over her waist.

She was clearly struggling to control her nerves, and I forced myself to stop being an animal and concentrate on the cue ball. I missed. I felt her take her position, but I kept my eyes on the table so that the tension closing in on us wouldn't asphyxiate me and I could keep my impulses in check. She knocked a green ball in, and I gripped my cue tight before looking up.

"No questions this time?"

"I'm good," she said.

"Well, that's no fun."

"Are you trying to tell me that what we're doing right now is?" There was pain in her voice. She turned around and walked off.

I cursed to myself, paid the bill, and took off down the street, managing to catch up with her thanks to her shoes, which slowed her down.

"Leah. Wait. Please."

She walked on to the door to our building, only stopping when she realized she didn't have the keys. She looked so defenseless in her white coat with her cheeks glowing from the cold. I felt the way I did years ago, when all I wanted was to hold her and take away her pain, but instead I pressured her and pushed her and tried to make her feel things she didn't want to. I did it because a part of me knew I had to. With Leah, it was always that way. I had to force her to open the doors to her heart and let her emotions come flooding out, even if there was a risk that I'd end up carried away by the uncontrollable current.

"Ask me something," I begged her.

"Open the door, Axel."

"Do it, Leah. Ask me."

A gust of wind blew through her hair.

"That night, when I went to look for you..." Her voice gave out as she tried to meet eyes with me. "I screamed at you that I didn't understand why you wouldn't fight for the things you loved. Like painting. Like me. And then you..."

"I said maybe I didn't love them that much."

"So was it true?"

I walked toward her, dying inside as I saw her so shrunken, so broken, waiting for an answer that for me had been so obvious, at least until I made the effort to step into her shoes and understand that she had been waiting three years to hear those words, three years doubting, three years asking herself.

"I lied to you, goddammit. I lied."

"How could you? How could you spoil everything that way? What is there even inside you?" She struck her fists against my chest. "Because I still don't know, Axel. After all this time, I don't know..."

I muffled the pain of those words with my lips. I kissed her with rage, with guilt, with a lust I could no longer suppress, with my teeth, with my body pressed against hers in the doorway of the building as her throbbing hands roved my chest. I wanted to sink into her, make her see that I loved her as I'd never loved anyone else, make her understand that what I said then was so far from reality that I didn't even know where I'd found the balls to utter those words.

I somehow managed to get the key into the lock and push the door open while still kissing her. My hands were shaking in her hair as we climbed up the first step. And the second. And the third. And a few more, until I finally realized we wouldn't make it upstairs.

I could hardly see her face in the darkness. I clutched the nape of her neck and pressed my lips into hers, biting her, licking her, abandoning all pretense to sanity.

"I'm going to tell you what I want, because it doesn't make sense anymore to go on pretending I can be your friend without hoping for anything else. I want to kiss you good morning at the beginning of every day. I want to fuck you every single night. I want to come on you and in you. I want to be the only one who ever touches you here." I slid my hand between her legs while she stifled a cry. "I want you to scream my name. I want you to die to have me again."

"Axel..." Her face was pressed against my cheek as she groaned.

I was going to ask her whether or not I'd been clear, whether she needed me to be even more specific, but I was no longer capable of using my mouth to speak. All I could do was kiss her and try to climb another step, and then I'd stop, and I'd kiss her again. I lifted her dress and ripped her tights as I tried to pull them down. She grabbed the banister as I slid my fingers inside her; she was wet; she was quaking with desire, just like me. Her hands found my belt buckle, and I had to hold my breath to keep from coming. I closed my eyes and lifted her up. She must have thought I was going to carry her to the apartment, but I couldn't... I couldn't think... I couldn't resist anymore... I couldn't do anything but push her against the wall in the stairwell with her legs wrapped around my back.

"Axel...someone will see us."

"I don't care."

Leah bit my neck as I plunged deep inside her. I groaned with pain, with pleasure, then rammed even deeper, even faster, wanting her to shout, wanting her to let everything out, for her to think of me alone, of us, us being together, to realize just how perfect that was. Panting, mad about her, I vanished between her legs. I could feel her nails biting into my shirt and her moaning in my ear, her teeth on my skin, her lips...those lips. I looked for them, and she hung from my shoulders while we fucked desperately, and I tried to tell her with kisses that this was more, so much more than just sex...

Her body suddenly tensed.

"Look at me, babe. Look at me."

I needed her to do it when she finished, and I could tell she was close, just waiting for the next thrust. She did. She pulled her lips away from mine and opened her eyes slowly, looking for me there in the shadows. I pressed my forehead into hers and breathed in her warm breath before sinking back into her quickly, ramming her against the wall, feeling her so vividly, losing myself so completely. I howled as I came inside her, breathless, heart pounding against her pounding heart.

The silence embraced us. I set her down when my arms began to give out, and I looked for her mouth again, but she turned away. Before I could even button my pants and try to grab her, she picked up the keys and ran upstairs.

"Shit. Leah, wait!" But it was too late.

87

Leah

I LOCKED MYSELF IN THE bathroom and ran water into the tub, ignoring the knocks on the door and his shrill voice, because I couldn't face him. I muffled a sob as I sat on the ground with my back leaning against the wall.

"Just talk to me. Let's make peace."

"I can't. I can't right now," I replied.

I could feel him there, just a few inches away, divided from me by a wall and a past that was a dusty road full of memories and problems.

"Leah, please…"

"I need time."

After a tense silence, he said, "I'll give you half an hour to calm down, and then we'll talk about this once and for all. But if you don't open the door when I'm back, I promise you I'll knock it down."

I remained curled up on the floor with the murmur of running water in the background. It was as if Axel had torn open the wounds I'd been sewing closed and trying to let heal for so long. But the wounds were infested. With him. With me. With us.

I slowly stripped off my clothes. One garment, one layer at a time. My phone had been in my coat; it fell to the floor. I stood there looking at it for a few moments, trying to decide what to do. When I crouched to pick it up, sucking in a breath, tears burning my cheeks, I looked for his name in my contacts. Three words—no more—but it took me an eternity to write them and even longer to send this message to Landon: **Don't wait for me.**

Just that. No *I love you*, no *I'm sorry*, I needed it to be blunt, I needed him to listen. I knew him well enough to realize he would be waiting on me regardless of the conversation we'd had before I left. And I didn't want him to. Maybe in a certain selfish way I did, but as I sank into the bathtub full of hot water, I realized I'd never be able to love him the way he deserved, crazily, full-heartedly, and I wanted another person to have the chance to do it. I didn't even have the feeling I'd lost him since Axel formed part of the equation. Somehow I realized that I'd lost him even before we'd started, because I never gave him the most visceral, impulsive aspects of myself; I never yielded to him or threw myself into his arms with my eyes closed.

I breathed in deep and dunked my head under the water. From below the surface, the world seemed to make more sense, even if it was muddled, agitated, opaque. I came back up and filled my lungs with air. Everything was silent, and I stared at my legs and thought how just a few minutes before, they were wrapped around Axel's body as he sank inside me over and over... All I felt in that instant was him, him everywhere; I couldn't think of anything else. I couldn't stop it; I still belonged to him deep down.

I didn't ask myself if I'd fallen in love with him again. I asked myself if I'd ever stopped loving him. And I was so afraid of the answer...

Of being so weak. Of giving up control again. Of falling.

I didn't like being fragile, unable to resist.

I got out of the tub when I couldn't cry anymore. I threw on a white robe and rubbed the steam off the mirror over the sink with the back of my hand. I saw my reflection. A reflection that frightened me, because it looked too much like the girl I'd been years before. I was the same. So much so that it was as if I'd been afraid to change and get lost in that unforeseen change. And I needed that now, to get lost and find myself again.

I grabbed the scissors out of the top drawer, smoothed out a lock between my index and middle fingers, and cut, dropping the hair in the sink and doing it all over again.

Axel knocked at the door.

"Open up, Leah." I didn't answer. I snipped again. "Open up or I'll knock it down."

Maybe because I knew he was capable of it, I dropped the scissors, opened the door, and let him in, even though I still wasn't ready for that conversation. Problem was, I probably never would be.

"What are you doing, Leah?" Axel asked, looking at my uneven hair. "I don't want you to run away from me; I can't deal with it..."

He came over and I didn't stop him. I closed my eyes when he cradled my cheek in his palm and his lips grazed my forehead. So familiar. So warm. His thumb traced out circles on my skin and his deep, hoarse voice shook me, awakened me:

"Let's try again."

"It's not that simple, Axel."

"Why not? Look at me, babe."

And one by one, every crack split open.

"Because you ruined everything! You ruined me!"

I stepped back, trembling, unable to look at him.

"Let me fix it, Leah."

"Do you even know how?"

"All I know is that we love each other."

I looked up at him, his face full of uncertainty, his lips still red from my kisses, his neck with my teeth marks on its surface, his eyes deep blue like the sea, his hair looking gilded by sunlight, and his gaze that made me feel so transparent, so vulnerable...

"Axel, you're...you're the past."

"Well, the past is right fucking here, babe, in front of you, trying to be your present. And that past knows he made the worst mistake of his goddamn life the day he let you go, and he's going to fight to make sure nothing like that ever happens again." He grabbed my chin and pulled it up to make me look at him. "Babe, I know I screwed up, bad, but give me another chance."

"Don't do this to me," I sobbed.

"Leah, please. When you left..."

"No! I didn't leave! You threw me out of your life!"

"I know, and I'm sorry, but I thought..."

"It was the easiest thing for you. The most comfortable thing."

"I thought it was the best thing for you." I saw his jaw clench as he corrected me. "I lied to you because I didn't know how to push you away from me, and if I'd told you the real problem, that I loved you too much, you would never have given in. And

I wanted you to live, Leah. I wanted you to go out and live, and then come back and choose me."

"But why did you have to tell me you didn't love me? Why couldn't you choose another way to do things? I don't know, talk to me, tell me we needed to take some time, and then later we'd figure out how to repair everything." I was shouting. "But no. You destroyed me instead. You made me believe I didn't matter enough to you, and I actually thought that for months and months, and then it turns out I was just too much for you. Ironic, don't you think? Because it just so happens that you pushed me away, the same way you do with everything when it gets to be too much. The same as you did with painting. The same as you do with everything, dammit!"

I tried to leave, but he stopped me.

"Let me go!" I screamed in a rage.

"This conversation isn't over."

"It was over as soon as I realized you weren't capable of being sincere. I should have understood a long time ago you never would be, that you'd always go looking for excuses…"

His face twitched, but instead of letting me go, he pulled me tightly into his chest, and his lips touched my ear as he whispered, voice cracking:

"I'm sorry I was weak, Leah. I'm sorry I was a coward. I swear, it's still hard for me to believe that was me, but it was; it's a fact and I can't change it. I want to be different, I'm trying as hard as I can, but you're right. I wasn't perfect then, and I'm not now. Maybe I was wrong for pretending to be, and the undeniable truth is I'm a walking mistake, and I spend every day trying to change that and regretting all that I've done wrong. I've been a terrible brother, a worse friend, and as for you, I..."

I covered his mouth with the palm of my hand.

"Don't say more. Please, stop talking."

I sniffled, hugged him, hid my face in his chest, grateful, relieved, because I'd needed him to admit that he was a coward, that he'd been wrong, I needed to know he was aware of it, but I didn't want him to go on torturing himself, because even if Axel was all those bad things, he was many more good ones too. And what I had said that first day I let him into my studio in Brisbane was true. I'd hated him; I'd hated him a lot, almost as much as I had missed him.

We remained holding each other for an eternity. A perfect eternity, and I didn't want to let him go.

"I want to show you something," he whispered.

"Now?" I pulled away to look at him.

"Yeah. Or when we get through this." He sank his fingers in my hair and smiled, and I tried to preserve that smile in my memory forever. "Come here, sit down."

He grabbed the stool and placed it in front of the sink, pushing me softly until I sat down. In the mirror, I watched him pick up the scissors.

"Are you kidding?" I laughed between tears.

"It's not like you did any better."

I tried to sit still as he grabbed a long tuft, and I heard the click of the scissors as blond hairs fell all over the floor around me.

"I'm just going to try to even it up for now. Tomorrow, you should go and see a hairdresser. And hope they understand your French when you try to explain what you've done." When he was done, our eyes met in the mirror. Axel ran his fingers over the nape of my neck and kissed me on the head. "You're perfect," he said.

"I know you think this is funny, but it isn't."

I got up. He was trying to bottle up his giggles.

"I was being dead serious," he assured me. He put his hand out, and after a moment's hesitation, I took it. "Now come on. I said I wanted to show you something. I want to be sure we don't miss the last train."

88

Leah

He was the piercing
Apex of the stars. He hurt.
But on other days...
He was the curve of the moon,
Its smile, its mouth.
And the heat of the sun. Its light.
I traced all those lines,
Got lost in the vertices,
Trembling as I found myself in him.

89

Leah

"WHERE ARE WE GOING, AXEL?" I asked as we crossed the Seine and our steps echoed over the sidewalk on the Pont d'Arcole.

He didn't reply; he just walked faster toward the square in front of the cathedral of Notre Dame, then put his arms on my shoulders to guide me. The cold night bit into my flesh, and I shivered under my coat.

"What are you doing?"

"Just stand still right here."

And he walked off in a straight line.

We looked at each other, and I could hear him panting despite the distance. Then he brought his fingers up to the tip of his nose. He looked up at the dark sky and then back at me. The light of the streetlamps revealed the unease in his face.

"We both know we've been through bad times, but I want you to think of all the good things we've experienced together. The things you can't stop thinking of despite how painful all the rest of it is. Do it now, and..." He bit his lower lip before proceeding. "And every time a good memory appears, take a step toward me."

"I don't get it."

"You don't have to. Just do it. Please."

"This is weird even for you, Axel."

"Babe…"

"Fine."

I yielded when I heard him, though I wasn't sure any of this made sense, because if he meant good memories I had about him, I could have just taken off running toward him instead of walking. But maybe Axel didn't know that. Maybe he had doubts and fears too. So I did what he asked. I closed my eyes, thought of us, about the time he used to spend with me when I was just a girl and he had better things to do, when he could have hung out with my brother, how he spent the afternoon in my room, observing my progress when he would come visit my father, how he took care of me and opened the doors of his home to me, how he insisted I had to open my eyes, all those conversations we had, and how he gave in when I asked him to give me a kiss while we were dancing to "Let It Be" and everything started to change, to fill with color and joy and his skin touching mine…

Just as it did then, when I realized I couldn't take another step because he was already an inch away from me, as though the entire world had shrunk down to the two of us.

"I could have covered a lot more distance," I whispered as all those memories he'd given me passed through my mind.

He grinned.

"I was hoping that if you reached me, it might be a sign that you'd say yes."

"Say yes?" I could feel my eyebrows rising up.

"Look at your feet."

There was a circular stone embedded in the ground, and inside it, a bronze compass rose.

"This is the zero point of the country, and I thought...I thought it might be the perfect place to find out if there was any possibility you and I could begin again too. From zero. Because I want...I want everything we didn't have. I want to go on a real date with you. I want us to get to know each other, the way we are now. What do you say, Leah?"

I said nothing, but just because I was busy trying to convince myself the Axel I had in front of me was the same Axel as always. The boy who'd never gotten serious with anyone, who'd spent half his life staring at his own belly button, who had certainly never imagined himself doing something so ridiculously romantic yet so perfect. I blinked to hold back the tears as I thought how complex we human beings are, me first of all, with our ironclad ideas that wind up crumbling on some random night, with all the ways we can shape ourselves and change and go backward or forward.

"You want to go on a date with me?" I ask.

Axel smiled and leaned down to see me closer.

"Yeah, I do. That's not so weird."

"It's a completely disastrous idea."

"I love disasters as long as they're with you."

Then, for the first time in all those years, I stood on tiptoe and pulled on his jacket so he'd come closer to me and I could kiss him. It was a pretty kiss, with no rage and no pain behind it. One of those kisses that reflect nothing but the present, without promises for the future or resentment from the past. A kiss that made me want to cry and laugh all at the same time.

April

—

(SPRING, PARIS)

90

Axel

A DATE. I WAS GOING to have a date. I didn't even remember what those were like. The only time I'd ever done anything similar was in high school, when I invited the girl I liked out to dinner, but all I wanted then was for us to get it on in the back seat of my car before I took her home. Or there was that time in my last year of college when I was fooling around with a professor, and my intuition told me rightly that all it would take was a little conversation to get her back to my apartment.

But I didn't want anything to go anywhere back then.

I mean, I'd wanted to have sex with Leah again, but in a way, that impulse covered up something else. How I wanted her to enjoy something she couldn't have three years ago: freedom, walks down the street holding hands, kissing in any doorway we wished. I wanted...I don't know, I wanted so many things, and it made me nervous and overwhelmed, and at the same time, I wanted to go for it, no holding back.

I leaned on the windowsill in the living room and turned on my phone while I was smoking a cigarette. I had messages from

Justin, a call from my parents, and some work stuff, but I ignored all of it, looking for Oliver's number in my contacts. I phoned him, and he picked up on the third ring.

We talked about life without going into much detail beyond the exhibition and the progress Leah was making.

"I still can't believe you're holding up so long out there. You, in a big city, with no sea. You live and you learn, I guess. So Leah's good? She's happy?"

"I think so. I sure hope so."

"Take care of her, all right? I mean it this time."

I tried not to smile as I took another drag of my cigarette.

"Actually, I was calling you to tell you I have a date with her tonight. You were right; I was a bad friend, I lied to you, I screwed you over, so I've been thinking about it, and I've realized I owe it to you to tell you everything. So I need to go a few days back, to when I kissed her and, even though the stairs weren't the best place for it, we wound up doing it…"

"Jesus, Axel, can it! For God's sake…"

"You want me to filter the story for you?"

"Yes, filter it. Knowing you're going out with her tonight and you're serious is fine; just don't hurt her and we're good. Okay?"

"Okay. Then that's everything."

"You're an idiot." He started laughing. "I've gotta go; Bega's waiting for me. We've got another twenty wedding catalogs to go through together. Imagine the fun."

"Be strong, brother," I said with a chuckle and hung up.

91

Leah

SCARLETT STIRRED HER COFFEE WITH calm and elegance while she looked at me. Her big expressive eyes were as magnetic as the rest of her. When I got a call from her, and she told me Hans had given her my number so she could meet me for a drink and we could talk one-on-one, it made me nervous, but really, it had been pleasant, even if all I did was listen to the remarkable stories, some beyond belief, that Scarlett was telling me in her marked English accent.

"And so that night we spent in Thailand was one of the wildest ones I can remember; I didn't think we'd live to tell the tale…" she said, laughing.

"You sure have traveled."

She'd been detailing her trips to New York, Dubai, Tokyo, and Barcelona. I asked myself if she ever just got up in the morning at home and did something normal and uninteresting, like linger in bed eating junk food or cooking while relaxing to music…

"So what's happening in your world?"

"Honestly, this is the first time I've ever been out of Australia."

"Don't let that worry you; I'm sure from now on you'll be visiting all sorts of places and meeting many fascinating people. It'll be like opening your eyes, Leah. You know what I like most about my job? That. It's not easy to find a diamond in the rough, I told you that much, but grabbing it and polishing it until it really shines is something unique."

I observed her with curiosity. I still didn't have a clear opinion about her. Sometimes she seemed frivolous and superficial, but I couldn't help feeling attracted by her genuine smile and her self-assured air.

"I'm not sure if I'll fit in..."

"The good life has space for everyone, believe me." She looked around at the meals those in the dining room were enjoying. "Shall we go elsewhere for dinner?"

"I'm sorry, I can't today; I..." "I have a date" would have sounded so ridiculous that it made me want to laugh, but I also felt an agreeable thrill when I thought of it. Anyone who knew Axel and me would be taken aback by the formality of the phrase. "I have a prior commitment. But we can try for next week."

"Perfect. I'll call you."

Scarlett got up, paid the check, and left before I could even button my coat and grab my bag. I went outside and strolled back to the apartment, taken in by the sights of the city. Axel did that every day: get lost in the labyrinth of buildings. Whereas I felt as if I'd barely gotten to know Paris, all shut up in my studio and anxious about what all this meant for me. And yet, remembering I was going on a date in the City of Love, all I could do was smile.

92

Axel

I UNBUTTONED THE LAST BUTTON on my shirt. Tucking it in made me feel like an idiot, so I pulled it out, even if it was wrinkled, and let it hang loose. I looked at myself in the living room mirror. I was shaved, dressed, ready for a night on the town when Leah came in, looked me up and down, and laughed.

"Sorry, I got delayed. Give me a minute to change."

"Let me know if you need help getting your clothes off."

While she ran off to her bedroom, I lit a cigarette. I loved the way she looked when she emerged, in tight jeans and comfy sneakers. I grabbed her hand and we walked out the door.

"What were you thinking?" she asked.

"Honestly. Nothing. Make it up as we go along."

So I took off for the part of the city I liked most, the one that had become *ours*, in a way, after spending so many sunrises there. We walked on the Boulevard de Clichy, between the lights of the famous Moulin Rouge and the nearby bars under the dark dome of the night. My stomach growled as I smelled the crepes the street vendors were preparing to tempt the nearby tourists. I stopped in front of one.

"Are you in the mood for dinner at a fancy restaurant or something like that?" I asked. "I'd happily take you to the costliest restaurant in the city if that's what you want. One of those where they give you so many forks you have to look on the internet to know which to use when. But if you're not in the mood for all that, I'd just as soon buy a couple of crepes and some beers, and go up to the top of Montmartre for dinner. Or we can stop in a regular old restaurant."

I was nervous as I proposed this, but she chuckled, as if it amused her to see me unsure what to do. She was gorgeous. Her hair cut just above her shoulders, her eyes shining with happiness the way they always had before, when her face was barely big enough to hold her smile.

She walked past me to the stall.

"I'd like a *crêpe avec fromage, thon, et oignon,*" she sputtered to the worker, then looked at me. "What should I order for you? One with mushrooms and cheese?"

"Yeah, and another one with Nutella to share."

We climbed the 222 steps and took the Rue du Mont-Cenis, and when we arrived at Sacré Coeur, the imposing church on top of the hill, we sat on the stairs leading to it, smelling the flowers in the neighboring garden and looking at the tourists lingering around the parapets and the busker with his guitar.

The city was at our feet. During the day, the place is packed, but at twilight or nightfall, it empties out, turns magical, and you can relax and enjoy the view. Time seemed to stop, and the silence was not just tolerable, but seemed somehow necessary.

"Here, this one's yours."

Leah passed me my crepe, and I absentmindedly tore off the tinfoil, absorbed in my surroundings and thinking to myself that this spring night couldn't be more perfect. She bit into hers with satisfaction. She'd always been like that, I realized. She'd never needed much to be happy, and I hated all those bumps in the road we'd needed to cross through to reach that simple joy.

"What are you thinking about?" she asked me.

"You. How I think you deserve better."

"You don't think I have enough? I'm doing what I love most in the world, and right now I'm having dinner in Paris, and you're here beside me. What else could I ask for?"

"Are you happy, Leah?"

"Yes. Why wouldn't I be?"

Her lips pursed slightly, and in her eyes I noted a certain reluctance. I tried not to see it, but it was frozen in my memory. I sighed and bit into my crepe, grabbed the beer bottle, and raised it in front of her.

"A toast?"

"To this evening."

I took the last sip in it and grabbed the dessert out of her lap. She laughed, still chewing her last bite, and tried to take it back.

"What are you doing, you savage?" I asked.

"Don't you dare stuff the whole thing in your mouth!"

"Who do you think I am? We're on a date. Let me remind you that my intention is to win you over so you'll let me get to third base. Or is it home plate? I don't remember. Sex, that's what I'm getting at."

Her cheeks flushed.

"That's not going to happen."

"Are you kidding?"

"Nope. It's a first date. That was your idea, not mine."

"I guess I didn't think through the consequences."

I tried to slide a hand between her legs, and she shoved me so hard, I couldn't react when she grabbed the dessert. I laughed as I watched her bite into it and cover her face in Nutella.

"Is kissing also prohibited?"

"Depends on the situation."

I couldn't help but grin. There we were sitting on the steps, her arm rubbing against mine, unable to take our eyes off each other. It had been an eternity since we'd just enjoyed each other like that, without remembering the mistakes we'd made or worrying about what would happen tomorrow. We were just there, together, in the moment.

"This honestly looks like the perfect opportunity. You're covered in chocolate. You could let me lick your face clean. Or better, you could do it yourself, and then I could kiss you and see what it tastes like."

"I'm guessing you haven't been on many dates, Axel. Am I right?"

"You know I haven't. Gimme that!" I took away the crepe.

We shared it in silence looking down over the shifting planes of the roofs beneath the moon. The city glowed with the lights in people's homes, in their lives, around the monuments. In the distance, Notre Dame was visible, and the Hôtel des Invalides. What I liked most about the city, what I'd discovered in all those walks over the past weeks, was the way every turn led you to something more, something new. And yet... It wasn't Byron Bay. It never would be.

I wondered if Leah missed it too.

93

Leah

HARDLY A STAR WAS VISIBLE in the sky. I was happy, but still, I thought back to our home, how different it was from all that. Here time had its own rhythm, as if there were just so much more to do. In some dark corner of myself, all that weighed on me: the expectations, the rush, the pressure. And I still hadn't worked through it all; I was scared to, because everything seemed to tell me that being there, painting, going to events, was the next logical step for me to take. And I didn't want to bring it up to Axel, not after all he was doing for me.

So far from his sea, his home, his entire life...

"It almost doesn't even look like our sky," I said softly.

"Because it's empty," he replied.

Axel got up, and I followed him over to the stone barrier around the lookout. He lit a cigarette, and the smoke snaked around him in the darkness.

"Do you miss Byron Bay? The sea?"

"You are my sea now."

"Axel!" I laughed and shook my head. "I'm serious!"

"Me too…" He clicked his tongue. "I guess yeah, I do miss it. But I'm not so sure that missing something is bad. Maybe it should be the other way around. Maybe that's how you learn what you really love."

"You adore your home," I remembered.

"Yeah, maybe. Probably. Not like before."

"Why not?"

"You know. I bought that house because I was in love with the idea of what I could do there, but I never did it. I imagined myself there in those four walls painting and being happy and just having it all. But I'm starting to think there's a big difference between what we want and what we finally get or what we're capable of achieving. It's like if you see yourself in a mirror, and in that light you look out of this world, and you just let yourself get carried away with that image even though it isn't real."

"You could change it. We can go back. Soon."

A month. A month, then the residency would be over, then we would go back to Australia. I hadn't wanted to think about it too much, because I wasn't sure what we'd do when it happened. In Paris, it was as if we were living inside a bubble, with me under a spell again, gawking constantly at the boy I swore I'd never fall in love with again, with him bending over backward to show me he'd changed, that he wouldn't turn into a coward again. And I was afraid that bubble could burst at any second.

Axel looked at me with half-closed eyes.

"Tell me something I don't know about you."

It took me a minute, and I giggled and said, "Good Lord."

"What?" he replied.

"I don't know if it's a good thing or a terrible one, but I can't come up with one thing you don't know about me. You were probably there the day my first tooth fell out."

"Of course I was; who do you take me for?" He dropped his cigarette butt and crushed it beneath his foot. "You cried for hours. And your little gap-toothed smile was so cute!"

Looking around, I realized we were now alone. The tourists were gone, the busker had disappeared some time before. Finally I remembered something. With butterflies in my stomach, I looked over at Axel.

"Okay, there is one thing. My first few months in Brisbane, I used to put on my headphones, listen to the Beatles, and walk aimlessly through the city. And on one of those days, I found this flea market with all these stalls with weird junk. And for some reason, I couldn't figure out what I wanted to buy, and I finally settled on this shell. And when I went to bed, I used to put it to my ear and listen to the sea, because it reminded me of you."

Axel reached up and stroked my cheek with his knuckles. I closed my eyes. I felt his fingers in my hair, his body coming closer, his hot breath on my lips.

"I must have been the biggest fool in the world for having a girl who smelled like strawberries, could paint her feelings, could hear the ocean in a shell, and for letting her go. I keep thinking over and over about all the kisses I didn't give you during those years."

His lips then touched mine, slow, soft. His kiss was intense and profound. I felt my knees start to give, and I grabbed on to his shoulders. Axel held me, as if he wished to protect me not just from the cold, but from everything all around us, isolating us from the rest of the world. I could tell he was holding back, restraining the savage impulse that kiss had awakened, and I liked that, us rediscovering each other through a kiss there above the city without looking for anything more. We took so long to finish that when we pulled apart, I felt like a little girl, lips tingling, cheeks warm.

"Let's go home," I said.

We held hands and retraced our route almost wordlessly. Axel would stop on random corners, and we would kiss again, as if we wanted to consume each other before we'd even gotten home, and then we'd carry on downhill. When we reached the apartment, I took off my jacket and threw it over the arm of the sofa.

"Did you like your date?"

"A lot," I said.

"Enough that you'd be up for seconds?" I nodded, and he walked over to me after hanging up the keys by the door. He cupped my cheeks, kissed my nose, then kissed me again on the lips. "Enough that you'd be up for sleeping with me tonight?"

I tried to ignore the feeling in my lower body. "Not quite."

"Come on, babe. I said *sleep together*. That's all I mean. Sleeping beside you. I swear."

"Maybe next time. Good night."

"It won't be any good without you," he grumbled.

I tried to play it cool and walked to my bedroom, putting on my cotton pajamas. As I lay there, I looked at the ceiling remembering the night we'd spent together. When we were good, it was just like that with him: simple, fun, comfortable, easy, exciting, and different from being with anyone else. I sighed and turned to one side. A little while later, I turned to the other. A half hour later, I realized I couldn't sleep, at least not until I stopped thinking about how close his room was to mine and stopped hearing his deep voice asking for us to sleep together...

I don't know what time it was when I finally got out of bed.

I tiptoed to his room and went inside without knocking. My legs were shaking as I walked slowly over to his bed and crawled in next to him. I held my breath as he wrapped his hands around my waist and pulled me into his chest. I closed my eyes. I could feel him exhaling softly against my neck, and I concentrated on that soothing sound until I fell asleep in the shelter of his arms.

94

Axel

LEAH WASN'T HOME WHEN I got back from grocery shopping. As I was putting things away in the fridge, I remembered she had to meet that day with Scarlett and a group of artists to talk about an exhibition that weekend at a small gallery. I don't know why, but I climbed the stairs to her studio to take a look at what she'd been working on. She'd seemed so stressed during the early weeks that I'd tried to give her space, let her be creative without any unnecessary interruptions.

Her latest piece was different, but I liked it. An empty street in Paris, with the roofs and cornices of the homes melting as if they were made of water, and snow all around, marking a contrast to that feeling of warmth and fluidity.

I was making dinner when she arrived home. She put down her notebooks and her portfolio before coming into the kitchen and sitting on a stool while I stood there chopping vegetables. I asked her how her day had been.

"Amazing," she responded. "The gallery's different, more authentic, you know? I'm really excited to be exhibiting there.

It's just one painting, but I think it will stick out because all the other artists are doing more modern stuff. Scarlett says important people are going to be passing through there checking out the latest work to see if anyone's got potential. Come here, I want you to see the one I'll be showing."

"I already went up there."

"So...what did you think?" She looked nervous.

"It's good. Chaotic. It speaks to me."

95

Leah

THAT MORNING, AXEL WOKE UP with a headache, and after much pleading, he listened to me, took a pill, and laid back down for a while. So I went to Montmartre by myself for the first time, feeling aware of every step I took, asking me if they went in any concrete direction, if they were like the strokes of my paintbrush that always led me to the finished work of art. But this time, I didn't know where I wanted to go. Part of me felt a tingle of pride every time Scarlett told me I could go far, if only I'd let her guide me. But another part of me wanted nothing more than to go home, put on a record at dusk, and paint barefoot on the porch while the sky turned that red color that always reminded me of Axel.

It was so contradictory...

I sat on the steps while the city awoke, and thought how, if I really knew where I wanted to go, I wouldn't always feel so uncomfortable in my own skin.

I toyed with my phone a while before finally deciding to call him. Landon responded on the fourth ring. After a cordial hello, there was a silence I hurried to fill up.

"I, uh, I just wanted to know how you were."

"Fine. Just finishing my senior project."

Landon hadn't responded to the text I'd sent him a few days before. Not that I'd expected him to. I'd been thinking a lot about him ever since, about us, about how things happened. Putting that tangle of feelings in order—even if it was my fault they were that way—hadn't been easy, but that didn't mean it wasn't worth trying. And I'd never do that if I didn't put things right with Landon.

"I'm really sorry." I could barely get the words out.

"Don't do this, Leah. We already talked about this before you left. We need to be clear with each other."

"I just keep thinking that none of this has been fair to you. It's not about Axel, I promise. It's about me. I shouldn't have tied you down for so long just because I needed you and I wasn't able to let you walk away."

"We both needed each other, Leah."

"That's not true." I closed my eyes.

"It is. You needed someone to lean on and I needed to hold you up. I knew from the beginning you'd never forget him, but even so, what we had was enough, feeling useful to you, and it was all so easy…"

"Too easy," I said.

"Yeah, probably."

We stayed quiet so long that I thought he'd hung up, but no, he was there, breathing on the other line.

"Even though you're so far away, it's like I'm seeing the dawn with you. I'm up on top of the hill; you can't imagine how beautiful it is when the whole city wakes up and fills with noise. There's always noise here, you know. It's weird. This constant, unceasing murmur."

"Will we see each other when you get back?"

"As often as you want, Landon."

"Okay, Leah. See you soon, then."

I didn't hang up for a while after that. I couldn't stop thinking about how lucky I'd been to run into Landon that night so long ago. Maybe not every story is destined to be forever, but that doesn't mean the road wasn't worth it. I liked thinking we could hold on to all the things we encountered on the way before reaching into the bottom of one last drawer and finding out it was empty.

96

Leah

MY CHEEKS HURT FROM SMILING so much every time someone went over to my painting. I was trying to be agreeable with all the visitors, but I could hardly understand anything anyone was saying to me except when Hans or Scarlett came over to give me a hand with the language.

I looked at the other artists. All of them seemed comfortable in their own skin, proud, calm. I forced myself to stop tapping my feet and stand up straight. When I looked up, I found a pair of dark blue eyes looking at me from one corner of the room. Axel looked so uncomfortable in that tight suit, so repressed, so unlike himself...

The part of me that wanted to walk barefoot and paint without thinking wanted to go over there and whisper some joke to him that only the two of us could understand. The other held back and feigned a bright smile when William, Scarlett's husband, came over to say hello and ask me how the afternoon was going.

97

Axel

I WAS RELIEVED WHEN AT last the exhibition was over and we could leave. It was getting harder and harder for me to pretend I didn't want to bolt whenever I was around those people. I was tired of boring conversations and trying to keep up appearances when everyone seemed to be acting in a low-budget movie with their constant insincere compliments.

"You all right?" Leah grabbed my hand as we walked down the street looking for somewhere to eat. "You didn't seem especially comfortable in there."

"I wasn't."

"Why not?"

"Are you comfortable around those people?"

"I don't know. Yeah. Sometimes."

I didn't say anything else. I didn't know what else to say. I went on walking until we saw a decent-looking place where we grabbed a table and a couple of drinks.

"Come on," she said, "tell me what's up."

"I'm really not sure. I've just got this weird feeling, this instinct, like when something creeps you out. I get it whenever I'm around most of those people. Don't worry about it. This is our second date, and we're going back home in less than three weeks. I want to enjoy the evening."

Leah smiled, but her lips were trembling. I knew there was something she wasn't saying, but I decided to let it go instead of pressing her. I knew all this was dazzling her and I wanted to let her enjoy that if it made her happy.

The tension dissipated when we ordered dinner.

"Where should we go tonight?"

"I've got a plan this time."

"You, making plans?" she asked.

"Yeah. Eat up, otherwise we're going to be late."

A half hour later, I was watching her smile as we reached the door of a little cinema housed under a neoclassical facade. I grabbed her hand, bought two tickets and popcorn, and led her into an almost empty theater that reminded me of the ones you see in European movies, with the burgundy seats and the dim lights.

Leah watched enthusiastically as the first scenes of a silent film, *The Kid*, came on. Content, I brought a handful of popcorn to my mouth and bent over to whisper to her:

"See, this is what normal couples do. They go out to the movies together. It's interesting. Not especially practical, but nothing's perfect."

"Practical?" Leah raised an eyebrow.

"I mean, if you had a skirt on, maybe it would be different."

She laughed and elbowed me in the ribs.

I kept my eyes on the screen, trying to concentrate on the

movie, until I felt Leah moving next to me. Then I felt her lips on my neck. I held my breath. I turned to trap her mouth, and she moaned when I licked her lower lip. We bit each other. We kissed. We looked for each other there in the cinema until I finally felt her hand rubbing me over my pants, and it took everything I had in me to keep calm and not tear off her clothes right then.

"Babe...this is going to have consequences."

"I'm well aware of that." She smiled.

"Then why the hell are we still here?"

I got up and pulled her up as well while she giggled. We stumbled back to the apartment, stopping at each corner to kiss, or else I'd whisper in her ear that she drove me wild when I saw the old her again, so wild, so impulsive, so vibrant.

In the doorway, I told her she had one minute to make it upstairs before I started putting on a show for the neighbors, because I couldn't hold back any longer. She laughed as she ran upstairs and I started counting. "One, two, three," I said just as the key slid into the lock.

The door slammed shut, and my hands got lost on her body one second later. Leah arched her back, and I looked for the buttons of her pants as I sucked her neck, marking it, leaving my trail on her skin...

I pulled her T-shirt over her head quickly and then jerked down her pants. My eyes closed against her body, naked except for her black bra and panties. I could feel her trembling, but she didn't move, she let me look at her, she let me... I wanted to paint her like that, to have her that way, a way no one else would ever see. I unbuttoned the top buttons of my shirt; I felt stifled, but I didn't get around to the rest of my clothes.

"Take off the rest," I nearly shouted.

"What about you?"

"Later." I gulped.

Her gaze had something vulnerable in it as she started to bring her arms up to unhook her bra. She let it fall to the floor, and I licked my lips as I contemplated that image of perfection. She slid off her panties. I took a step toward her, then another, then another. I covered her breast with a hand, bent over, tried to stop her lips from shuddering, planting a kiss on them as I felt her all over, so slowly my hands hurt, exploring every curve and fold of her naked body.

I moved down her neck, the arch of her shoulder, her breasts, sliding my tongue across them, pausing when I heard her pant, progressing on to her side, where I looked for those three words I had traced out there years before. I kissed that memory. Then I descended further, lips pressing into her stomach, nibbling and licking and savoring her in a way I'd longed to do for so long. Drawing her with my mouth.

I kneeled in front of her, my shirt wrinkled, so hard now that my pants were starting to hurt me. And as I was down there, all I could do was look up at her. Adore her, her impenetrable stare, watery, so full...full of all we once had, all those things that were still alive...

I stroked her legs.

"You like this? Seeing me kneeling in front of you? Knowing I'd spend my entire life down here if only you asked..."

Leah was nearly panting. I liked her feeling powerful, knowing that she was in control. I smiled slyly and moved my hand higher up her thigh and then between her legs. Then I kissed her there. She was wet, jittery, eager. Her fingers wove through my hair when she needed to change my rhythm and I let her do it. I liked that; I liked her being forward, even demanding. I pushed my tongue inside her, fucked her with my fingers. Then I started licking slower, putting off the moment when she'd moan my name and gripping her thighs when her legs began wriggling and I knew she was coming. I kept going until she couldn't moan anymore, until I'd memorized the taste of her and I could tell she needed me to get up and hold her together. I squeezed her tight against my chest.

"You taste better than I remembered."

"Fuck, Axel."

"I hope that's a command and not just a curse, because I swear to you I was so close to coming without even being touched, and I need you... I need you like you can't even believe."

98

Leah

MY HEART WAS POUNDING SO hard I couldn't hear a thing but my own palpitations as I pulled him toward the bedroom and unbuttoned his shirt. I pulled it off his shoulders, looked for his belt, slid my hands down his pants, feeling his erection just as we crossed the threshold.

I was breathless, and I had him there in front of me after so long...so perfect, his bronze skin seeming to scream at me to touch him. I pushed him back onto the bed and he fell, elbows propped up on the mattress, looking at me so lustfully that I trembled at his intensity as I climbed atop him and our lower bodies touched.

I closed my eyes. Pain and love mingled together. I needed to have him inside me so bad that the wait was killing me, and at the same time, I wanted to put it off as long as possible to feel it more and more and more. Axel seemed to have different plans, though.

He sat up, moved back in bed until his back was leaning against the wooden bedstead, and hugged me, grabbing me around the waist to pick me up so he could slide in between my legs. I wrapped my hands arounds his neck while I felt him open me up inside. My eyes sank into his, his into mine, and our muscles tensed as his fingers gripped my thighs while mine caressed his hair. He grunted and rammed me and clenched his teeth.

"Jesus, babe, Jesus…"

"Let me," I begged him. "Please."

He heaved as I started moving on top of him, making love to him slowly, very slowly, because I didn't want it ever to end, that instant was perfect and I wanted to savor it: the feeling of having him there, of possessing him, of looking at him and seeing love in his eyes the way I had looked at him all my life, his eyes telling me so many things without any need for words and giving me control without hesitating or trying to hide. Brave in his feelings, brave in letting me see every trace of pleasure on his face, his mouth searching for mine every time I rose up over his body and came down and our bodies joined again.

He shivered, and I responded by moving faster, pressing down harder. I wanted…I wanted to give him everything. I whispered into his ear that I wanted to feel him come, and his hands clutched my thighs and he pushed inside me faster. I sought his mouth amid that whirlwind of feelings: pleasure, sweat, skin rubbing together, and then he roared and finished and gripped me tight and the silence of the room seemed to embrace us.

Axel had just soaped up my hair and turned on the faucet to wash off the foam. I felt his warm lips on my forehead while the hot water fell over us.

"I was serious about what I said, Leah. I want to kiss you good morning at the beginning of every day. I want to fuck you every single night. I want to come on you and in you. I want you to want me again. I want all that. For us to have it. To be a real couple."

I smiled and said to him, "We all live in a yellow submarine."

Axel cracked up laughing and whispered the same thing into my ear, sang it, sang me all the *I love you*s I needed to hear.

99

Axel

I WAS SURPRISED WHEN I reached over to the other side of the bed and found it empty. It wasn't like me to sleep so late, until the rays of the sun were pouring into the room, but the night before, we hadn't gone to bed until it was nearly dawn, we'd fucked and stared into each other's eyes until everything finally came together and it was all exactly as it needed to be.

I got out of bed, went to the bathroom, and stopped at the kitchen to make myself a bowl of oatmeal with milk. I put a spoon in my mouth and looked at the stairway leading to the studio. I put my breakfast aside and walked up, opening the door and readying myself to grab her and convince her to come downstairs and spend some time with me before she started work, but when I got there, I found her sitting on the floor, knees pulled to her chest, eyes full of tears.

"What's up?" I knelt down beside her.

"I wanted to look at the photos from the expo..." she responded, sobbing, before passing me her cell phone. "And I found this. I know my work isn't perfect, but the way they're saying this makes it seem even worse."

I read the article she showed me, which talked about the exhibition from the night before. It was in a little-known English digital magazine. It mentioned several of the pieces, and was especially nasty about Leah's: "Mediocre, lacking in creativity and coherence, almost boastful of its ignorance."

I grabbed her cheeks and forced her to look at me. I tried to smile, to let her know it didn't matter.

"Who cares, babe? It's just an opinion."

"But I think...I think they're right."

"I like your work. Doesn't my opinion count?"

"You're not objective," she sobbed.

"I damn well am. When I saw the early paintings you did when you got to Paris, I told you I thought you could do much better. And I didn't accept all your pieces for the exhibition in Brisbane, because some of them didn't speak to me enough. So trust me. Why do you care so much about what that guy who wrote the article thinks?"

"It just hurts so much."

"Don't let him do that to you," I said.

"You don't understand. You don't know what it's like to strip yourself naked in front of the whole world, create something, and watch them stomp all over it. It's personal. It's still mine."

"Exactly, it's yours," I reminded her.

I stood up, flipped through the Beatles records, and put on "Hey Jude" while I lay down beside her and pulled her into me. She hugged me there on the wood floor, calmer, and I kissed her on the head.

"This had to happen someday, okay? Better now than later.

You'll get past it, just like you've gotten past so many things. There are people who will pay money for your pictures and others who don't feel anything when they see them, but the important thing is how you feel, get it? You need to be happy with your work. Don't ever show a piece unless you're proud of it; otherwise if someone criticizes you, it really will hurt. And then we'll go back home and we'll do things our way. You can paint on the porch or in your attic, wherever you want. We'll go to little fairs, places where you really want to be."

"Do you regret this trip?"

"No. It's pushed you forward, plus you've got the credits you needed. So what? You got your first negative criticism today; that means you've gotten someone interested, plus you've got more experience, and that will help you understand what you want. Tell me you don't agree..."

She nodded, but she said nothing.

And I felt a strange pressure in my chest...

—

100

Leah

HANS'S HOUSE WAS LIKE SOMETHING from another era, with its classic wood furniture, its high ceilings, and the wallpaper on the walls. As I walked toward the dining room, I looked down at my own feet and at the carpet that covered the floors of all the rooms. The table was already set before our arrival. Hans had invited us to dinner with William, Scarlett, and three American friends who ran a gallery in New York and had just arrived in Paris.

"Have a seat," he said with a smile, pointing at the table.

We got comfortable, and Scarlett, who was in front of me, winked before turning to the server and asking her if she could have a glass of white wine instead of red. Afterward, Hans introduced us to Tom, Ryder, and Michael.

We started with duck confit, but Axel, who couldn't eat it, proceeded directly to the second course, a vichyssoise. I could see that, despite everything, he was trying to pretend that nothing pleased him more than a formal dinner on a Friday night. He could be charming when he tried, and he soon had everyone laughing at his jokes, and Hans was clearly pleased that he was livening up the evening. I tried not to think about how nervous I was sitting by him knowing that he must have hated every second of the situation. But I couldn't blame him.

"You're very quiet tonight, Leah. Is something wrong?" Scarlett pinned me in that direct gaze that always made me so uncomfortable. "Surely you didn't read the article in that magazine… What's it called, William?" she asked her husband.

"It's an English website. You approved their press credentials."

"Indeed. I'll be speaking with them." She drummed her fingers on the table. "Hans and I were talking about it the other day. It was unnecessarily cruel. But there's a positive side to it, we were thinking. Tell her, Hans."

I could feel Axel's hand touching mine under the table, and that little gesture calmed me down in that tense moment. I hated being the center of attention, I hated the food that was upsetting my stomach, and I hated that silence before Hans started speaking.

"We were thinking it could be beneficial for your career to focus on certain things."

"Like…?" Axel interrupted.

"Her work is so scattered," Scarlett explained. "She's good, and she could eventually be great, but right now, the market is looking for something very concrete. More modern, bolder. We'd like to make a deal for a series of pieces with a specific character. With a couple of large-format ones."

"A series of works? We're leaving in two weeks," Axel said.

"Not if you've thought about my offer."

When he realized what she meant, Axel let go of my hand. I

hadn't said a word; I felt like something was stuck in my throat, and I wasn't sure if I even could. I knew I should have told him, that he never should have found out...about something like that from another person. Doubt and guilt assailed me, but I managed to pull myself together.

"Could we talk about this another time?" I asked.

"Of course. Let's enjoy our dinner," Hans said, before looking over at Axel. "How did you find the vichyssoise?"

"Delicious," Axel replied bluntly, and I doubt I was the only one who could sense the hardness in his voice, even if everyone decided to ignore it.

The rest of the evening consisted of people telling entertaining stories while I sat there silently and nodded and tried to look enthusiastic. When it came time to leave and we stood up, I said I needed to powder my nose before going to get my coat. I wasted a little time washing my hands and looking at my reflection in that oval mirror that must have cost a fortune, while I asked myself who was that girl it reflected back at me and Scarlett's words echoed in my head: *She's good, and she could eventually be great.* It was a compliment and a snub all at once: bitter and sweet.

I was still saying bye to everyone as Axel stepped into the elevator. He held the door open for me and pushed the button without looking over. I wanted to say something, something that would make him understand, but I didn't know what, because I didn't even know what I was thinking.

It was cold as we took off walking.

When I felt brave enough, I said, "I'm sorry I didn't say

anything to you before. But I didn't know... I couldn't find the right moment."

"The right moment? We fucking live together, Leah."

Axel stopped in the middle of the street, looking anxious, hand on the back of his neck.

"Tell me now, then. Tell me what she said to you."

"She said I didn't have to leave when the grant was up. She said I could stick around a while longer working with them and they'd find an opening for me at the gallery."

"Is that what you want?"

That was the last question I wanted him to ask me, but it was also the most necessary one, the one that meant everything and that I still didn't know how to answer.

"I don't know," I whispered.

He rubbed his hands over his face.

"Well, tell me when you figure it out, because Jesus, I thought we were together in all this. I'm here, Leah; I've followed you to the other end of the earth. I deserve to know."

He walked off, but when I shouted, he stopped again.

"I didn't want to ask you to sacrifice yourself for me!"

"Are you kidding? I'm not leaving here without you."

My lower lip trembled, and I hugged him; I hugged those words and everything that they contained, praying that Axel wouldn't pull away. And he didn't. His arms surrounded me, protecting me from the cold, and then I calmed down as I felt his soft, familiar lips on my temple.

101

—

Axel

FOR DAYS I'D BEEN SMOKING and overthinking things. It didn't do much for my headaches. Or my nerves. No matter how much I tried to pretend otherwise, I knew things weren't right. It wasn't normal for Leah to shut herself up in her studio for so many hours painting things that didn't even look like her work. She didn't have long to make a decision. And I was frustrated that I didn't know what that would be.

I was incapable of telling her what I really thought, because I didn't want to fight and I was scared something would cause a breach between us. And in a strange way, I was being a coward again, but this time it was different: I wasn't trying to push her away, I was trying to avoid losing her.

I lit another smoke just as she emerged from the studio, watching her come down the stairs looking absent. I needed to do something to change that, I thought.

"Get dressed, we're going for a walk."

"Now? I'm beat," she said.

"You're missing out on the whole city."

Leah hesitated, but she knew I was right, and ten minutes later she was ready and we walked out of the apartment together. It was already nighttime. We took the Metro. As it chugged along, she seemed to forget the demons she'd left behind in the studio. She started smiling at all the silly stuff we said, listening to people speaking French and making up stories about what we thought they were saying.

"I hid the body in the freezer in the basement," I said, recreating the conversation of a man in front of us who was speaking to his wife seated at his side.

"Next to the turkey and the peas? Brilliant, you've just ruined Christmas dinner," Leah rejoindered, laughing when the woman she was imitating pinched her brows as if she really were angry at finding a corpse next to her food.

We walked out through the tunnel, relaxed. The Eiffel Tower was shining bright under the dark sky. We stopped close to the little carousel next to it, and I bent over to give her a slow kiss before rearranging the scarf she liked to wear on cool nights.

I felt frightened when I saw her eyes and asked her, "What's going on? What are you thinking?"

"How everything's good when I'm with you."

"What about when we're not together?" I asked.

"Then I'm not so sure."

I didn't know what to tell her, but I didn't like what she was saying; it meant something was wrong. I took her hand and pulled her up onto the carousel. It wasn't working. There weren't many people around. Leah climbed onto a wooden horse and smiled at me, and I felt shaken. She rested her cheek against the animal's head and stroked its mane.

"I need you to talk to me. To tell me what's going on so I can help you. That's what this is all about, Leah, getting through these things together..."

"That's one of the problems. I can't really tell you. I don't know what I'm feeling or why this is happening to me. I thought I didn't care what other people felt about my work, and now it turns out I do. I thought I was above all that; now it turns out I'm not. That's freaking me out, but at the same time I can't step back now. It's like I need to show that I can do it, that I'm good at what I do..."

I tried to ignore the pain. It hurt me no less than her to know that she was feeling these things and there was nothing I could do to help her, especially because I was such a poor example to follow.

"What's that got to do with us?"

"I don't want to need you the way I did years ago, Axel. I don't want to drag you into my chaos. I don't want to let that influence me. But you're here because of me, and that's not just some trifle I can overlook when I need to make a decision."

"Whatever you decide is fine with me."

"That's the problem," she replied, careworn.

I tried not to groan and kissed her to keep her from talking, because I had the feeling it didn't matter what I said. We were at a dead end and we weren't going to fix anything that night. All I'd even intended to do was take her for a walk so she could clear her head and stop thinking about work.

"Come on, let's play tourist."

I walked toward the tower and waited for her to catch up to me on the promenade. I took out my phone and tried to take a photo of us. We were laughing as I finally picked Leah up off her feet a bit so she'd fit in the shot with the tower in the background. Then we walked along the Seine's Left Bank. Leah climbed up on the stone wall next to the sidewalk, and I stood between her legs and kissed her until I got tired.

"Where should we go?" she asked.

"Anywhere. Or nowhere. You know what the word *flaneur* means? It's a person who just strolls aimlessly along the streets of Paris. That's an art. Tonight, we should be two flaneurs," I said in my horrible pronunciation.

"I love how that sounds."

And that's what we did until dawn overtook us. We walked across nameless streets and past corners we might never see again until we reached home and ended up in bed. I turned her on her stomach and pushed inside her, kissing the freckles on her back as I rammed into her. She clutched the sheets and moaned and pressed back into me. Then we embraced each other in silence in the shadows until we were too tired to look at each other any longer.

102

Leah

SCARLETT TOOK A DRESS FROM her closet and handed it to me.

"This'll do for you. It would have been easier to just go shopping, though. You're too headstrong, *têtue* as they say in French. Now you'll know what it means when people call you that. Do you have shoes?"

I nodded while Scarlett sighed impatiently. She'd invited us to a party the next week at the hotel where she was staying. I'd wanted to reject the offer at first, not just because I knew Axel would hate it but also because I didn't have anything to wear. But when she asked me why I didn't want to go, I omitted the first reason. She insisted we go shopping together, but I refused. Getting out of her lending me something was impossible, though. Scarlett was so persuasive when she put her mind to it that I couldn't imagine how her husband managed to carve out the least bit of independence.

I looked around at the huge suite we were standing in, with its own living room, two bathrooms, and a walk-in closet. More than a hotel room, it was like a snug apartment. Scarlett motioned for me to sit on the sofa.

"I'll order coffee," she said before dialing room service. She looked at me piercingly when she sat down. "Have you thought about my offer?"

"I'm still turning it over," I responded.

"If you're worried about that agent of yours, Axel, just remember that he's just a middleman. Actually, your contract is with Hans and not with him. Often people get their roles confused, but all that matters is the job you do for *your* gallery, and Hans has more than one."

"Axel isn't the problem."

I didn't like her bringing him into this. I didn't want anything pertaining to that decision to affect him.

Scarlett got up to open the door when room service brought up our cups of coffee. When the servers left, she returned to our conversation.

"Don't think I let every girl who's made a little splash come up to my room. If you're here, it's because I see something different in you, something big. But before you go down that road, there are some rules you need to follow."

"What am I supposed to do, exactly?"

"Wait here." She went to her desk and pulled out a dark, thick file folder she laid on the table. Calm and cool as ever, she took a sip of coffee before opening it. "This is what the market is asking for right now."

Inside were photos of paintings. Almost all of them were full of thick lines, without much contrast or detail. They reminded me of what Scarlett had shown me with such pride when I met her at the opening. I hadn't told her what I really thought that day: that the painting lacked soul and feeling. I tried to push that memory aside when I realized that I had done pieces like that before, when I was blowing off steam without really paying attention to the colors. It couldn't be too hard to repeat something I'd already done, I thought.

"I could...maybe I could do it."

"No *maybes*. I'm sure you can. If I thought otherwise, Leah... let's just say I have a lot of other artists waiting in the wings for an opportunity like this. But I want it to be you."

I liked how her words made me feel, but I hated it in equal part. I was content, unsettled, proud, and nervous, all mixed together.

"I don't know if there's time..."

"What if you stayed a few more weeks? Hans certainly won't have any problem letting you hold on to the apartment."

Undecided, I bit my lip.

When I got back, Axel was cooking, and the whole place smelled so good that my stomach started growling right away. I walked into the kitchen and stood on my tiptoes to reach his lips. Soft music was coming from upstairs, from the record player, I assumed.

"How'd it go? Good?"

"Yeah. Look." I grabbed my bag and pulled out the dress, which was of very thin champagne-colored fabric with an open back. "You like?"

"I'd rather see you naked."

"Axel..."

"Okay, it's nice, but I'd take a bikini now and again too." I laughed as he looked more closely at the dress. "You'll knock everyone off their feet."

"Did you take your suit to the cleaners?"

"No. Was I supposed to?"

"Yeah but it doesn't matter; you've still got a few days."

I took a quick shower, and when I came out, dinner was already served on the coffee table. Axel opened a bottle of wine and sat on the carpet. I settled down next to him. It was perfect. When I was with him, I felt the way I had years ago, when we dwelt in our own bubble in his home. Just us, as if that was enough. Everyone else was the problem.

We didn't talk much during dinner, but now and again, Axel forced me to try and guess the ingredients in each dish. I didn't have a refined palate, so I never got it right, but I liked listening to him describe the recipes afterward.

When we were done, I took the plates to the kitchen. Then I sat back down beside him and started drinking compulsively from my glass. Axel raised an eyebrow.

"You better go ahead and tell me what you've got to say before you wind up drunk."

"It's complicated... I told Scarlett that I'd think it over. I don't think it's such a terrible idea for us to stick around here a few more weeks."

"To do a job like she expects?"

I nodded, and Axel grunted and gulped down what was left of the wine in his glass. For a moment, I thought about how if he said he was leaving, I would leave too. The thought frightened me.

It was like an arrow that had pierced me and that I wanted to tear out. I realized that I was still scared to do things on my own, that I would always need someone by my side.

"Then that's that. We're staying."

He kissed me and I took a deep breath, relieved.

But I also felt something like bitterness. The way you feel when you realize you're weaker than you thought, that there's something inside you that keeps breaking down. I remembered the words Axel had uttered during our first date, weeks ago: "It's like if you see yourself in a mirror, and in that light you look out of this world, and you just let yourself get carried away with that image even though it isn't real."

103

Axel

OLIVER ANSWERED ON THE THIRD ring.

"We need to talk," I blurted out.

"Is Leah okay?" he replied, frantic.

"I don't know. I guess so. I want to think so. Have you talked to her lately? Did she tell you she wants us to stay here a few more weeks?"

"No. She didn't tell me anything."

I shared all the latest news. I told him about Scarlett, whom I didn't trust any farther than I could throw her. She was empty, a pretty envelope incapable of impressing anyone longer than five minutes. And yet Leah was captivated every time she opened her mouth. Plus there was this new side of Leah that had emerged in recent weeks: her ego, her vanity.

"I don't understand. That's not like her."

"What worries me is she doesn't know what she wants," I told him. "If this was what she'd been looking for all these years, I'd get it, if that was the future she wanted, but she doesn't even know what she's looking for, and that's dangerous."

I lit a cigarette. I couldn't stop ruminating. I wanted to understand, but I couldn't. And that was what it was all about, right, or...? I asked myself if this was what it meant to put yourself in the shoes of the person you wanted to share your life with.

"Let her fall," Oliver said.

"What the hell...?"

"Go back home. Believe me, it took me years to understand that she wasn't a little girl and that I couldn't just bend her to my will. When I left her in Brisbane after everything that had happened with you, I swear, I was freaking out for months. I thought she was my responsibility and I felt like shit for leaving her alone when I knew she was going through bad times and crying herself to sleep every night."

"Oliver, I don't need you to remind me of all that."

"That's not what I'm trying to do. I'm just saying, if she wants to stay in Paris, let her. But let her take responsibility for the decision."

"You don't understand," I said as I took a long drag.

"Then try to explain it to me."

"We're together now. And there's no way I'm letting her go again."

There was a long pause; then he started laughing.

"I never thought I'd be happy to hear something like that."

"What on earth are you smoking? Because you need to give me some."

"Maybe when you're back, we'll go out one night," he joked, but then turned serious. "It's weird, right? This is the dead opposite of what always worried my father. I remember hearing him say once that he was afraid she'd focus so much on her painting that she'd never set foot in an art fair or even share her work. The day of the accident, they were on their way to an art gallery in Brisbane... He'd spent days trying to convince her. And now look at her."

I stubbed out the cigarette, still on edge. "It's fine. Don't say anything to her. I'll do this myself; I don't want to cause you any headaches."

"Sure. You good otherwise?"

"Yeah, as long as we put aside the fact that what I'm most tempted to do is stuff your sister in a suitcase, hop the first plane, and go back home and back to our lives. After all these years, all these problems, I've got the feeling that we're farther than ever from where we should be right now."

104

Axel

"LEAH, DO YOU BELIEVE IN fate?"

"It depends."

"On what?"

"On the day. Sometimes I do; sometimes I don't."

"You think we were fated to be together?"

"Are you serious?" She laughed.

"Maybe there's some things we can't choose because they choose us."

"It sounds pretty when you say it like that." She was smiling. "I love this. Being in bed with you for hours and just talking. Or looking at you. Or touching you."

"I'm interested in this touching thing," I whispered. "Can you give me details?"

She giggled and hugged me.

105

Axel

SHE WAS BEAUTIFUL IN THAT dress that left her whole back exposed, even if all I wanted was to tear it off, and that was complicated, since we were surrounded by dozens of people who were talking and snickering. I ate and drank and tried to enjoy the festivities, but it wasn't easy. First of all, I couldn't stop thinking how wonderful it would be for Leah and me to be at home, our real home, lying on the porch and looking at the stars, maybe thinking about going to some simple art fair the weekend after or getting something ready for the gallery in town. Second, I was starting to realize that maybe I had been wrong the whole time. That this was what Leah really wanted. To spend her nights like this, among strangers with fake smiles pasted on their faces.

I looked at her. She seemed comfortable in her own skin. Or so I'd have thought if I didn't know her and couldn't see how rigid her back was, how tense her shoulders, how nervous she was when she greeted Scarlett, how she felt inferior or maybe dazzled around her.

I hung back while they talked. And eventually I turned around and looked at all the people there wrapped up like Christmas gifts in their finest outfits. It was smoke and mirrors. The entire party had this cardboard feeling about it; authenticity was notably absent. It didn't even seem real to me: each time I looked at the guests, they all seemed to me to be empty shells. And I didn't want Leah to be there with them. Were there exceptions? Sure, just as there are anywhere, but the air of refinement there, the appearances, the trifling conversations all bored me. I spent half an hour listening to a group talk about whether mauve was back in fashion, and I thought my head was going to explode.

I grabbed a drink and walked out, leaving the murmurs behind and climbing up to the top floor of the hotel. I emerged onto the rooftop.

The wind was cool, but pleasant. I took a deep breath, then lit a cigarette, looking down on the life that was throbbing below while I was stuck there at a party where I couldn't feel like myself. I was worried that she and I were looking for different things, and now, when it had taken us so long to learn to walk beside each other again...

I heard her behind me and turned my head.

"What are you doing up here?" I asked, then took a pull of my cigarette.

"I saw you leave."

"So you couldn't take your eyes off me," I joked. She leaned her elbows on the railing, and I continued, "Next time, tell me and I'll stay with you."

She smiled timidly, but not even my attempt to be jovial could cover up the mist that was settling over our night. Paris was at our feet, but I felt it was the other way around, that we were at the city's feet, scurrying from one dead end to the next.

"I hate seeing you like this. I just wish everything was easier," she said.

"It is easy. And I'm fine," I lied. "Come over here."

I hugged her from behind and rested my chin on her neck while she sighed.

"I feel more lost than ever, and this is the time when I'm supposed to be finding myself. Sometimes I wish I'd never even come to Paris."

"Don't say that. Think about all the good things!" My hand climbed her waist and stroked the bare skin revealed by her low-cut dress. "When we catch a plane and go back home, my number-one priority is shutting us up in the bedroom for days on end. We're allowed to leave only for good waves or if we run out of food, but that's it. The rest of the time, it's just going to be you, me, and my bed. Our bed." *Our bed.* I liked the sound of that.

She smiled and I nibbled at her cheek as I brought my hand down and slid it between her legs. I thought she would protest, but instead she arched her back against me, and I told her to relax and let me play a bit. I couldn't think of a better way to ignore the party taking place below us, the one I didn't want to be a part of. And all I wanted was for her to feel the same.

May

—

(SPRING, PARIS)

106

Leah

I STEPPED BACK A BIT to get a better perspective on the finished work. The afternoon light was coming into the studio and illuminating the canvas full of cold, distant strokes of the kind Scarlett had asked for. I was happy I'd done it. I had the proof that I could do something if I set my mind to it, and I felt a strange satisfaction as I started to clean my brushes.

Axel came into the studio and looked at the painting.

"What do you think?" I asked.

"I like it," he lied. I could tell from his eyes that he was lying.

That hurt, but I tried to ignore it. I'd wanted him to be more enthusiastic. It hadn't mattered to me before whether or not anyone liked what I did, but I'd also never felt so exposed, so weak and vulnerable; with that picture, I was opening up, it was as if anyone could look at it and see straight through my skin down to the bones.

I couldn't stop now, and I couldn't go backward. I was terrified to go running back into Axel's arms the way I had when I lost my parents and I needed to hold on to him so he would save me. I was thankful to him, I would be for the rest of my life, but I had to learn to hold on to myself, to save myself, before throwing myself into his arms and begging him to take me away from there on the very next plane. I felt Paris was giving me a kind of independence I'd never known, the possibility of a new beginning.

Axel put on "All You Need is Love" and walked over singing and acting silly. I snickered and took his hand when he put it out to dance with me, and as we kissed, laughed, and tickled each other, we fell down to the wooden floor, laughing and gazing into each other's eyes.

"You're a lunatic," I said.

"Takes one to know one."

He got on top of me and held my hands down over my head. I tried to push into him, but he pulled away, just barely letting his lips graze against mine. Then he sat up and licked his lips, and the gesture was so alluring that I could hardly keep from begging him to get to it and tear my clothes off.

"I want to know something," he said. "That first night we kissed and you said something about how you no longer thought of love as something idyllic...is that still true?"

"No, but I still think it's something different from that."

"Better or worse?" he asked.

"Better. More human."

"So with more mistakes, you mean."

"Sort of." I smiled. I liked us understanding each other. If only everything was like that. But that was impossible, because I couldn't even understand myself. "Now I feel like love is something more real, more intense, but it also has its bitter side. Nothing's perfect. Perfection could never be so addictive."

"So you're addicted to me..."

I started to pull off his shirt in reply, and remembered all those hours when I saw him barefoot, just wearing swim trunks, and I missed how unworried he'd looked back then. He hadn't looked that way for a long time now. If I had to draw him that way, I'd no longer remember exactly what he looked like. Instead of trying to rescue those details, I pushed the image aside, buried it the way I buried my fingers into his back and felt him slide inside me, bumping into my hips and then pulling away, getting harder, pushing in deeper until we peaked and I moaned and he covered my lips with his mouth.

We held each other. The moment invaded us fully. His hands touched my cheeks, framing my face, as if trying to make of it a living painting. My throat was dry as I asked him:

"What would you do if you had to paint me?"

He looked at me for an eternal second before getting up and putting on his underwear and jeans, which he didn't bother buttoning. I propped myself up on my elbows to watch him, confused to see him looking for some tubes of acrylics among my things.

He knelt down between my legs.

"Don't move," he asked, his voice hoarse.

"Are you serious? You're going to paint?"

"Yeah. Just something...small." He looked away.

I held my breath as Axel dipped a fine brush in blue paint and held my arm down on the floor next to my ribs, turning it around so that the palm of my hand was visible. He ran his fingertips up my wrist where he could feel my pulse. Then he touched me with the brush. It wasn't until he'd dragged it several inches across me that I understood he was tracing out my veins, looking for them under the pale skin and covering my forearm with intricate traces.

I stayed still, but I couldn't help shivering when he traced the same pattern in red. Just then, the first chords of "Yellow Submarine" played, the undersea sounds, those childish words about cities where we're born, about the ocean, about underwater voyages...

"Did you know your heart's actually in the middle of your chest? It's just that it tilts left and that's why you can hear it better there. Yours is right here." His paint-streaked fingers drew the conical shape of the heart so delicately that I wanted to cry, even if I couldn't really say why. "I love feeling it beat against your skin and thinking about how a little piece of it is mine."

That day, as we drew on each other, I realized there are words that are kisses and gazes that are words. With Axel, it was always like that. Sometimes he spoke, and I felt it on my skin, sometimes he looked at me and I could almost hear what he was thinking, and sometimes he kissed me without kissing me. Like that day when he painted one heart on top of another, sensing my racing pulse.

107

—

Axel

WE WERE ASLEEP ON THE sofa when her phone rang, and Leah got up to answer, suppressing a yawn. I sank my head in the pillows. When she came back, she was leaping and shouting, and she jumped on top of me.

Still groggy, I sat up.

"They sold the painting, Axel! They sold it! I just gave it to them the other day, and they already found a buyer; can you believe it? They aren't even going to hang it at the next exhibition. Scarlett says this is the best news possible, and…"

"The painting they told you to paint," I said.

"Of course. What else?"

"I don't know. I thought it might have been the one of Paris melting…"

Leah frowned. Maybe she didn't like my description of the painting, but she hadn't given it a title, as far as I knew.

"They'll probably have that one forever."

"Why do you say that?"

"It'll never sell."

I followed her to the kitchen and put on water to make tea, then cornered her against the counter. I couldn't help it; I needed to touch her constantly, and anyway, I wanted a clear and honest answer to the question I was about to ask her:

"That's it then. You got what you wanted. Does this mean we can go back to Byron Bay?" She gave me a look that made my soul wither. "Jesus, Leah!"

I let her go, closed my eyes, tried to calm down. But I couldn't. I turned off the gas.

"Scarlett says I'd be a fool to leave now after what's just happened. Not even she saw this coming. I'm not talking about a long time, just a few weeks, maybe, to see what all happens…"

"Why do we need to see what happens?"

"So we can make decisions. I don't know!" She brought her hands to her head. Her expression was frustrated.

"This is ridiculous. What is it you want?"

"I want to do things. I want to be better!"

"Better for who?"

"For all those idiots!"

"For God's sake, Leah, are you listening to yourself?"

"Why can't you just understand me?"

"Because you don't even understand yourself! If you could hear yourself, you'd realize what you're saying doesn't even make sense. If they're idiots, why do you care what they think? Are you trying to adapt to their expectations of you? Is that it? Look at me."

"I don't want to argue," she whimpered.

Shit. I didn't want to argue with her either, I didn't, but she was making it hard for me not to. She'd lost her perspective or was in one of those crises where you can't tell what really matters in life from what doesn't. Sometimes things are too blurry when you see them from the inside. But from my perspective, everything was clear as day, and it was torture to see her caught in that spiral of doubts and desires.

She hugged me. But that day, for the first time, I couldn't hug her back, because I didn't recognize her. Ironically, when I finally thought I had her, that she was mine, it was the very opposite: She wasn't even hers. She wasn't herself. She didn't know who she was.

108

Axel

"LET HER FALL," OLIVER HAD said to me.

The problem was, I couldn't forget that conversation we had the night we spent together in Byron Bay walking the streets till dawn, sitting on the swings, talking before she decided to take off on that journey. She asked me whether I'd pick her up in Paris if she fell. And I promised I'd always be there.

109

Leah

I COULD FEEL THAT I was doing something, but I didn't know whether that something was good or bad. Better than nothing, maybe, filling up that part of myself I hadn't even known was empty before then. There was an art website that had an article about still-unknown artists who were about to break out, and it opened with a photo of one of my paintings. At some point in all those weeks I spent shut up in my studio, I'd come to the realization that what mattered wasn't me being recognized, it was my work. People liking it. People seeing it and cocking their head to the side with interest, Scarlett smiling and nodding with satisfaction when she looked at it. I needed to feel people were understanding what I was trying to express. It was like putting a message in a bottle and crossing your fingers, hoping it would cross the sea and someone would still be able to make out the faded letters.

I worked from the time I got up to the time I crawled into bed. And when I curled up next to Axel's warm body, I tried to ignore the sour look on his face, the tension in his arms as they surrounded me, the increasingly dense silences.

I wanted to talk to him, but I didn't know how.

I wanted to tell him I wouldn't stay there in Paris forever, but that I felt I had to be there just then, and if I tried hard enough, I could find whatever I was looking for. I wanted to tell him that I hated holding him back, seeing him wither each day, smoking absently, leaning on the windowsill in the living room, and watching the city as it buzzed at all hours. I wanted…

I wanted things to be different.

But a part of me couldn't help thinking that if I gave in, if I left even though I was still unsure, it would mean putting Axel on a pedestal again, making him the center of my world. I liked the way things were now, that feeling that we were at the same level and could look each other eye to eye and not think about the difference in age or all we'd been through. Just being us. Starting over. Ready to paint the story we wanted to live with each other as if life were a blank canvas.

110

Axel

"ARE YOU SURE YOU WANT to come?" Leah seemed uncertain.

"Of course. It's not that big a deal. Or maybe it is. But I'll deal with it."

I kissed her on the forehead to try to ease the tension there, and we walked outside. The nights were getting warmer, and I left my suit jacket at home. It was a relief, a little victory that gave me back a bit of my former life. Leah nodded distractedly when I told her this, then took my hand as we walked to the restaurant where the gallery was hosting a dinner for a few artists and friends of the owners.

We got there early and sat at one end of the table across from Scarlett and William, who greeted us with their usual condescending attitude. Leah didn't seem to notice and smiled timidly. Not long afterward, Hans showed up, and the rest of the guests soon followed. Lucky for me, an artist named Gaspard sat to my left. He was one of the few interesting people I'd met in those months. At least I didn't wish I was deaf every time I talked to him. His English was rough, but we still chatted—I wanted to keep up appearances. Those past few days, the situation with Leah had been tense, and I wanted her to know that no matter what happened, we'd keep going. Together.

I don't know how, but I wound up talking about Byron Bay.

"That place sounds different," Gaspard said.

"It is," Hans butted in. "It's nothing like here; things there work in their own way. I'll bet you'd like it."

"Well, if I ever make it down there, I'll give you a call," Gaspard told me.

Unless I'm still here, I thought, but I kept those words to myself, digging around in my dish of ratatouille and trying to ignore Leah's stiffness and the roar of voices around me. Thinking about her barefoot, lying on the ground, smiling, her hair in disorder, I had to set aside my fork and take a long sip of wine. I could have used something a bit stronger. Something to give me a little strength.

"The market demands an immediate response," Scarlett said while the artists looked at her doe-eyed. "It's sad to say, but there needs to be productivity. We're not the ones asking for it, it's our customers, but they are the key to any business. Everything revolves around them."

"Things are moving fast," a young man said.

"We must adapt to the circumstances."

"Or change them," I said. I couldn't hold back anymore.

Next to me, Leah squeezed her fork.

"How do you suggest we do that?"

"I'm not suggesting anything," I replied. "And you're right, the customer is the boss, but a lot of times customers don't know what they want until they see it. It's not just about giving them what they're looking for. It's about surprising them."

"That's an interesting perspective," Hans said with a nod.

"That may work for the gallery in Byron Bay, but here, things are different. We don't have much margin for error," Scarlett noted before wiping her mouth with her napkin. "Surprising the customer is a risk."

"An appetite for risk is a requirement for this job. Or at least it should be."

The waiter interrupted us to place a tray of desserts on the table and took away the empty plates. I was thankful for the pause, because I didn't know if I could restrain myself much longer without telling her that her approach to the business was cowardly. Still pensive, I grabbed a *chouquette* dusted with powdered sugar and put it in my mouth.

I wasn't so stupid or so idealistic that I couldn't understand Scarlett's position. And in a way, she was right: there were times when the market demanded something, and to an extent, you had to give it. There were artists who were talented but lacked a personal style, and they needed guidance to find what they were best at. But then there were the ones like Leah, who poured their entire personality into the canvas and just had to do it that way, because anything else would be forced, dull, inauthentic. That type of artist you couldn't push, but only accompany. One thing was being by their side, helping them improve, polishing their strong points; another was standing behind them and telling them which way they had to go and how.

I didn't think there was a conflict between these two approaches.

You just had to take a personalized approach with everyone. That meant more work for the gallerist, because you couldn't sell everyone the same way, but the result was worth the effort. That was what I'd liked most about our work in Byron Bay: looking for talent, finding it, deciding how to place each artist, trying to fix weak points. It demanded time, study, interest. It would be easier to ask everyone to do the same kind of work and not bother with all the rest, but I couldn't imagine anything emptier compared with the pleasure of finding the perfect place for each artist and helping them get there. I thought of how revolted Sam would be if she had to listen to what Scarlett was saying—Sam, who treasured every detail of her work.

I held out for the rest of the night thanks to the two drinks I ordered after dessert. When Leah got up and started saying her goodbyes, I did the same with relief. An anguished silence enveloped us on our way home.

She went straight to the kitchen, took a bottle from the cabinet, and served herself a glass. Her hand shook as she took a long swig. Around us, the tension grew dense, stifling. I even had the feeling it was dangerous to breathe.

"You didn't drink at all during dinner," I said, taking the bottle and sipping straight from the neck. I licked my lips and met eyes with her. "Were you afraid of what they'd think of you? Does high society look down on it?"

"Fuck you." She blinked. "Sorry, I just..."

"Don't say sorry," I said and grabbed a glass for myself.

She followed me into the living room. When I told her not to excuse herself, I didn't say it out of angerI actually deserved her hostility. I had been looking for it, pushing her buttons; even when we were walking home, I'd wanted to grab her by the shoulders and shake her so she'd finally wake up from her trance.

"I told you not to come to the dinner."

"As if that would have fixed anything," I hissed.

I don't know if the alcohol had removed my filter or if I was just tired of being beside her and being unhappy, if I was angry about that pothole in the road we'd gotten stuck in. I sat down on the floor and drank and thought... I thought of all the things we were losing and all the time we had just let turn to dust. That stressed me out, and I drank even more. Leah left, and it was better that way, because even if it might have been the alcohol talking, it was the first time in my life I didn't want to see her. But it just lasted a few minutes, and then the bad things vanished and I remembered all the good things we had together.

Let her fall.

I savored those words of Oliver's for a moment, but then I shook my head and pushed them away. It didn't matter that I'd been repeating them to myself for weeks.

I downed the last sip of my last drink, and as I did so, I felt Leah's presence behind me. I got up and turned to face her, and I froze. She was there naked, looking at me glassy-eyed. Not a single thing stood between us. I remembered the first time I saw her like that, the night when it all started, when we came back from Bluesfest and I found her naked in the middle of my living room. Back then, she was more innocent, more vulnerable. More mine, even if I didn't know it then.

If I could go back to that moment, I thought, I'd do everything different. In my imagination, we'd never have reached this point; I would have taught Leah how close success and failure are, how those two streets often cross and often go in the same direction. I still saw her painting what she felt, and me there soaking it in and living through her brushstrokes. I imagined us, except together throughout those three years, her naked on the beach and not in an apartment in Paris with the murmur of cars and passersby in the background.

"Aren't you going to say something?" she whispered.

"This isn't the right moment..."

She blinked, wounded and surprised.

I forced myself not to look away. This hurt me as much as it did her. Maybe more.

"I'm not rejecting you. I'm rejecting the idea of just fucking you the way I would anyone else. And that's what I'd be doing right now."

Leah's eyes teared up with rage. I reacted quickly and grabbed her hand before she could slap my face. I gripped her wrists and clenched my teeth and forced myself to breathe deep and calm down. Then I let her go.

"If you can't control yourself, you shouldn't drink," I said.

"You're hurting me on purpose..."

"I don't want to hurt you. You're the one who's doing this to yourself, and I don't understand why. I'm trying to see things from your side, but it's hard, and it just keeps getting harder."

She grabbed a towel from the bathroom and wrapped it around herself as she bit her lower lip. There was something indecisive in her eyes, something new, something I didn't recognize. Rage, inner struggle, fear, ego.

"Maybe it's hard for you because you've never tried. You may not realize this, but sometimes dreams require sacrifices. Not everything's easy, Axel. Not everything's just given to you. But I guess there's no need to bring that up to you since you just turn your back on everything that requires the least bit of effort."

My pulse started racing.

"What about being true to yourself, Leah?"

"What does that even mean?"

"You know exactly what it means. None of this is you. None of it is what you really want."

"How should you know?" She frowned in disgust. "I'm tired of you telling me what I want! I'm tired of you making decisions for me! And this isn't the first time you've done it." I knew what she meant. She meant the night that I had decided what should happen with our future. But that was different. That was... There was no comparing then and now. "I feel like a puppet in your hands! And I knew you'd do this if you stuck around, manipulating me according to your will."

Without realizing it, I brought a hand to my chest. That hurt. I breathed deep, trying to find the words.

"Do you not understand it breaks my heart to see you becoming someone you're not?"

"Do you not understand that I don't know who I am anymore? I've gone through so many phases in the last few years that I don't even recognize myself when I look in the mirror! Is that enough for you, Axel?"

"Hell no, it's not enough for me!"

We kept going back over the same things, trapped in a vicious cycle, unable to break free. Frustrated, I went back to the kitchen and poured myself what was left in the bottle. When I came back, she was sitting on the ground with her back against the wall, still wrapped in the white towel. Tears streaked her cheeks, and she was staring down at her bare legs. I tried not to fall into the trap, not to hurry over and hug her, not to pretend that everything was okay. Instead, I sat down near her, in the corner, and we stared at each other in silence.

I don't know how long it lasted. That look. That attempt to understand what the hell was going on. That transformation of silence into pain, and pain into reproaches.

I was exhausted. It seemed no matter how hard I tried, I would never fix what I'd broken years before, and we would never be the people we were on those starry nights with music in the background that I missed so bad. I couldn't erase the three intervening years. I couldn't fill with memories of things that had never happened the void Leah was now trying to cover with things I knew would never be enough.

"We can't go on like this," she said.

"I know," I responded.

"I mean, I can't go on like this. Not with you here."

"What are you trying to tell me?"

She sniffled and looked at me.

"I'm telling you that if you love me, you'll leave."

I thought I'd misunderstood her at first; surely she wasn't actually saying this to me after all we'd been through together, the bumps in the road we'd gotten past, all the pain...

"You can't be serious, Leah. Don't play with me like this."

"I need you to go home, Axel." I could tell she was hurting, her cheeks were covered in tears, but me...I was dying inside, incapable of comprehending what was happening. "I need...to find myself. To know what I want. I can't be with you like this, dragging you to places you hate, hurting you. And I can't tell you to sit to the side and keep your mouth shut, it's not fair, and you know you could never do it."

I felt like I had a hole in my heart.

"You honestly want to tear everything up?"

"I'm just asking for a little time."

"Well, don't, dammit!" I stood up, angry, frantic, unable to see anything but the walls crumbling down for no reason. "Just think about things and make a decision. It's not that hard. It can't be."

"Axel..." She pleaded with her gaze.

"No. Fuck no. I'm not going to leave you here by yourself."

"I need you to. I'm not a little girl anymore. I want to make my own decisions without Oliver, you, or anyone else. I feel like I've spent my whole life hanging on other people's words. I can't get away from that feeling, and I have to show myself I can do more..."

"Show yourself or show them?" I replied.

She looked back at me as though broken, and I felt like a dog. I knelt down in front of her and hugged her even as she tried to get me to let her go. I hugged her tight until she replied in kind, crying against my chest for what seemed like an eternity.

"Don't you understand what you're asking me for, babe? You want me to run away like a coward and leave you here when I promised you I'd catch you if you fell. That's too much to ask, Leah."

"You told me you'd do anything for me."

"Leah, goddammit, anything that wasn't failing you again and feeling the way I did before. I know I fucked up and I know it was my fault everything went to shit. Probably that's why I never told you what it was like for me, because I felt like I didn't have a right to. But I regretted it every single day, I imagined a million times over what it would have been like if I'd made a different decision, I didn't want some damn guy to put his hands on you, and it killed me to have to remember I was the idiot who told you I wanted you to get to know other people. You don't understand how much it hurts to give up something you love so much because that's all you're capable of."

She pulled away from me and said in a broken voice:

"You're right, Axel, I don't understand. And neither do you. We don't understand each other."

"I guess for once we agree."

She looked away and stood up, holding the towel against her chest. Her eyes were red, and her unkempt hair flicked against her bare shoulders. She looked down and said she was going to get dressed. Then she left. I heard her shut the door to her bedroom. My God. I hated her doing that more than anything in the world. It brought back memories. I had hated it before and I hated it now. Maybe it was that, or the liquor still burning my throat, or the fact that I had opened up to her completely and no longer had anything to offer her and could feel her slipping out of my hands, but I walked down the hall and straight to her bedroom.

111

Leah

AXEL ENTERED WITHOUT KNOCKING. I was sitting in my pajama top and panties. It was weird to see him there. Since that first time I'd left in the middle of the night to crawl into bed with him, he hadn't set foot in my room.

"What do you want now?" I said.

"We're not finished, Leah."

"I already said everything I have to say..."

"Bullshit. You didn't. You know you didn't." He stepped toward me, grabbed my face, and kissed me.

I closed my eyes, enraptured by his scent and the addictive taste of his lips. He jerked down my panties and threw me on the bed.

"Why won't you?"

"Why won't I what?" I saw the tension in his face, felt it in his fingers when he touched me, everything about him screamed frustration. "Axel..."

"Say it. Tell me you'll never forgive me."

I felt him push inside me. My eyes were staring to water as he rammed into me.

"I understand, okay? I understand. You want your revenge. You want to do to me what I did to you, because I pushed you away when everything was fine, I wanted you to leave..."

There was no other pain like the pain I felt just then. None. Nothing hurt like Axel fucking me with rage, with disappointment, with the bitterness of kisses that taste like goodbyes and mistakes we can never undo.

I hugged him and he went on thrusting. I hugged him tight, as if with my arms around him I could make him understand how wrong he was.

"I would never want to avenge myself against you," I whispered. "Never, Axel."

He stopped, breathing hard, maybe on the verge of tears. I held him and kissed him softly and rested a hand on his pounding heart.

"Jesus, babe, Jesus..."

"This is about me, Axel. I forgave you a long time ago; no matter how much I told myself I wanted to take some parts of you and leave others, accept some and be angry with others, I was wrong..." Again, I felt he could see right through me. "I could tell you I fell in love with you again, but I think I'd be lying to myself, and that I just wish I could believe that, because if I stop to think about it...I'm not sure I ever stopped being in love with you, Axel. I feel like those three years were just a parenthesis. You were always there; in one way or another, you were always there... I don't know what it is to be alone, understand? I don't know what it is, I don't know if I'm capable of it, but I'm scared to never even try because that'll mean I'll have always had that doubt. I don't want vengeance. I don't want to hurt you. I don't want any of that."

I had never seen him looking so much like a defenseless little boy as when he realized that he couldn't give me what I wanted. We rolled over in bed, and now I was the one on top, seeking him, finding him. Axel looked at me so intensely as I shifted on top of him that I gasped. His hands felt nervous on my breasts. We never broke eye contact as we made love, and with every stroke we kissed each other and it was such sweet relief, knowing there was nothing left to add, feeling free.

I hugged him when we were finished and let his gravelly voice caress me.

"I love you more than anything,"

"I love you," I whispered.

"A thousand yellow submarines."

"Millions of submarines."

112

Leah

WHEN I WOKE THE NEXT morning, the bed still smelled like him, and it took a moment for me to notice the aroma of freshly brewed coffee. I walked over to the threshold of the living room and stood there, staring at Axel, who was sitting by the window and smoking, his neck covered in marks from my kisses the night before. I don't know why, but that image stuck with me: his fingers tense on the window frame, the sunlight breaking over the glass, his eyes focused on the new day sky.

I walked over on tiptoe and hugged him from behind. He barely moved, but he did squeeze my hand when it covered his stomach. I kissed his back, then let him go and poured myself a coffee. I dressed quickly afterward, because I had to be in the gallery in half an hour, and I was already running late. I said goodbye in a whisper: "We'll talk later." He gave me one last kiss.

That was our morning routine, sure. But sometimes a little detail is enough to break the routine and stick in your memory. Something silly. Like on the day of the accident, the day I lost my parents, how they looked so cheerful in the front seat and

"Here Comes the Sun" was playing, and then it was gone and the landscape looked blurry through the windows.

You don't think about those details until you realize you might be noticing them for the last time. Then you do, and they take on a different value. Like the kiss Axel gave me that morning, his fingers strong on my waist, his deep voice wishing me a good day, and the smile he gave me before I left, a smile that didn't reach his eyes.

Because when I returned that night, all I found was emptiness.

His things weren't there. Axel had gone.

113

Axel

PUSHING HER AWAY FROM ME years ago had been painful. Pushing myself away from her now was torture.

I couldn't stop thinking about the similarities between the two situations, about how maybe I wasn't fighting enough, wasn't pushing myself hard enough. Then I remembered the desperation in her voice, how she'd begged me just once to let her choose, to trust her, to give her space, to let her fall and learn to pick herself back up without anyone's help. Just the thought of it was killing me inside.

I looked out the round airplane window for hours, unable to sleep, unable to stop thinking about her. I hadn't called Oliver until I was already out of the apartment where we had experienced so much together because I needed to be sure he agreed with my decision and also know he'd take care of her from wherever he was and call her every day.

When we landed, I walked through the Brisbane airport toward the baggage carousel like a robot. I waited, absent, so focused on my own thoughts that I wouldn't have cared if it had taken hours for my suitcases to come through.

That was when I felt a familiar hand on my back.

I turned around. My father was standing there with his eternally cheerful smile. I heard the voice of Justin, who was beside him, but I was so surprised that I could barely tell what he was saying as my father hugged me and I closed my eyes...

I had a stupid thought, a memory of when I was little and a hug from my father could fix everything, in those days when I still hadn't grown up and saw him as a hero capable of resolving whatever problem arose without even blinking. How easy life had been back then. How simple...

I pulled away from him and looked at my older brother.

"What the hell are you doing here?"

"There's the old Axel. I thought you'd gone soft on me."

"Screw you, Justin," I said, but I pulled him close and mussed his hair. "Hold on, I think I see my suitcases." I walked over to the belt and grabbed them.

Once we were outside, they helped me put my bags in the car. I asked them to wait so I could smoke. The sky was clear. I hadn't seen a sky like that in a long time.

"So, Oliver told you..." I said.

"You're lucky. Seems like he's willing to forgive you and he still worries about you no matter what you do. If you ever wanted a friend for life, you've got one in him," my father said.

"Don't forget we're there for you too," Justin said, and I actually felt like smiling for the first time in weeks. It was a real smile. I threw my arm over his shoulders and pulled him in close as I took one last drag.

"Let's get out of here," I said, pulling the car door open.

Justin walked past me.

"Listen, Axel, if you need to cry…"

"One more word and you're dead."

I got into the back seat and watched my father try not to grin before pulling his glasses down over the bridge of his nose. They tried to chat with me, but they could soon tell how hard it was for me to come up with answers, and they left me in peace. Maybe they knew me well enough to realize I'd need time to digest all that had happened.

I looked at the landscape as we left the city behind. Soon vegetation covered everything. Finally I was home, I thought. But I wasn't sure I could really call it home if Leah wasn't there.

June

—

(SUMMER, PARIS)

(WINTER, AUSTRALIA)

114

Leah

THE FIRST NIGHT I SPENT alone in that empty apartment, I nearly opened my suitcase, stuffed my things inside, and caught the first flight out. To follow Axel. To tell him I was wrong, that I'd been wrong about everything. But I didn't do it. Instead, I stayed up all night and crawled into bed at the crack of dawn because the sheets still smelled like him. I always thought of the sea when I smelled him, the salt that used to cling to his skin, the sun, the beautiful light of summer.

I did that for a week. I tried to work during the day, shut up between the four walls of the studio, feeling how they seemed to close in on me, then I'd spend the nights thinking of him, of the last hours we'd been together, loving each other, struggling to understand each other amid all the doubts and silences.

After a few days in which I turned back into an emotional, vulnerable girl, something I didn't want to be, I made a decision, and one night I walked down from the studio and tore the sheets off the bed before I could give in to the desire to bury myself in them. I put them in the washer, sat down in front of it on the floor, with my legs crossed, and watched the last traces of him turn round and round and come to a stop. When I opened the door, the scent of fabric softener struck me, and it was a relief, but I also wanted to cry; it couldn't be healthy, missing him so bad...

Little by little, I started focusing more on my work. With Scarlett behind me, watching my every step, I forced myself to get going every morning. I did what she asked of me, producing two pictures similar to the previous ones. I also finished some other pieces, *my* pieces, but I didn't show them to her, because I had the sense she wouldn't like them.

Oliver called me every afternoon. We generally talked about his life, his job, the news, or silly stuff, but deep down, I was dying to ask him if Axel was okay.

"Tell me what you did today," he asked.

I took the wrapper off a lollipop and sighed.

"I ate with some friends from the gallery. We spent the morning there talking about the exhibition this weekend. Organizing things, you know, polishing the final details."

"Are you happy then?"

I hated when he asked me that kind of questions. It forced me to think, and I didn't want to turn those issues over and over, because when I did, I didn't find the answers I was looking for, and that frustrated me even more.

"I guess so," I answered.

"Is there something bothering you?"

I licked my lollipop.

"They told me I should sign up for a French class."

"Oooh. Sounds serious. What are you thinking?"

"I haven't decided yet."

"You don't sound like you're jumping for joy at the idea."

"Yeah." I bit into my lollipop and broke it.

"How's cooking for yourself?" he asked. When I lived in the dorm, I always ate at the cafeteria and I never had to worry about it.

"Terrible. One of these days I'll die of hunger."

"You're kidding, right?" He seemed genuinely worried.

"Of course I am! I'm fine, you idiot!"

"Okay. Well, talk to you tomorrow. Take care of yourself."

"You too, Oliver."

I hung up and stayed on the sofa until nightfall. I'd probably never been so aware of being alone. I looked at the phone and thought how ironic it was that I'd pushed out of my life the one person I trusted enough to share something that intimate. I dropped my phone on the side table, flopped down on the cushions, and stared at the ceiling, then closed my eyes and took a deep breath.

115

Axel

I WENT BACK TO MY routine. I got lost for hours in the waves, and when I came home, it was already midmorning, and I'd munch on whatever I had in the fridge. I only went to the gallery when I absolutely had to, but Sam did all she could to keep me busy, knowing that anything that filled a few hours was a relief. In the hours that remained, I tortured myself, thinking and drinking too much.

My mother showed up one Saturday morning without warning. That was the last thing I needed. I stepped aside to let her through and took off her hands the grocery bags she was carrying.

"What is all this, Mom?" I complained.

"Soup. And fruit. Vegetables. Actual food, Axel," she said, opening the refrigerator and looking at what little was on the shelves. "How long has it been since you've eaten right? You're so skinny. You look like a castaway. Go shave or I'll wind up shaving you myself, and I warn you, I don't have a steady hand. Or patience, while we're on the subject. What are you doing just standing there?"

"Mom, I'm not in a good mood."

"Do what I say," she responded.

I rolled my eyes, turned around, and went to the bathroom. After I finished with the razor, I looked at myself for a few seconds in the mirror, asking myself who I was, what was left of all I thought I was before Leah changed before my eyes. Not in a bad way. It's just that some people come into your life and stir up everything, open the drawers you stuff your fears inside, and force you to be better, more human, more real.

I heard a series of knocks on the door.

"How long are you planning on being?"

I opened the door and scowled at her.

"Dammit, Mom. Give me some room to breathe."

"You've had too much room to breathe these past few years. It's my fault for not realizing it, but you know, we all have our burdens to bear. Wrap it up and go sit down; lunch is ready."

I flopped down on the sofa and grabbed the bowl of instant soup she passed me. She settled down on the chair in front of me, picked up her spoon, and started eating. I grinned at her.

"What's so funny?"

"Nothing." I shook my head.

"Tell me or I'll come back tomorrow."

That was a threat, no two ways about it.

"It just makes me laugh when I think about how you're the only person in the city, probably, who buys this soup that tastes like... I mean, I don't know what it tastes like, that's the problem. What's your obsession with it? I remember..." I got a knot in my throat, but I forced myself to keep talking. "I remember Leah used to laugh every time you bought groceries."

"I should have realized how much you loved her back then, but it never passed through my mind. I couldn't even see what was right in front of me."

"Same here," I said and laughed.

I laughed because life was goddamn ironic, wasn't it? Someone you've barely even noticed has been after you for years, and then the tables turn and you're in love. Chasing after her. Wishing she'd remember you were here and would decide to come back one day.

"She'll come back, Axel," she said, seeming not quite sure of herself. This was the first time my mother had ever talked about anything serious on her own with me. "She'll definitely come back."

I followed her to the kitchen and rinsed the plates after she soaped them up and passed them to me. I was tense, waiting for her to tell me something I needed to know even though she really couldn't. No one could. No one but Leah.

"What makes you so sure?"

"Because she is who she is, son. This is her place. But sometimes you can't find yourself even inside yourself, and Leah has been through too much these past few years. She's a little lost. We don't always walk in a straight line, sometimes we go in circles, and it's hard to know it if you're looking straight ahead the whole time, you know? It's a matter of perspective. If she could see herself from above, she'd understand."

"I think I need a smoke."

I went out on the porch and stayed there thinking about what my mother had said. She was right. The problem was, I was frustrated I couldn't help Leah see things the right way, even if a part of me was starting to realize she had to do it on her own. That she had to get to know herself. Figure out what she really wanted. Learn to get up every time she fell. Experience solitude on her own, nostalgia, the burden of sometimes being wrong.

"Put on something decent," my mother said from behind me.

"Decent? What now?"

"This afternoon, there's a flea market, and we're meeting your brother, Emily, and your father there soon. So don't drag your feet either. The twins want to see you, and I told them you'll be there. Why don't you try out that shirt I gave you for Christmas?"

"Mom, I'm not wearing a button-down."

"If you keep grimacing like that, you're going to get wrinkles."

I clicked my tongue. She'd corralled me, but I agreed to shower and make myself presentable. A half hour later, I was walking with my family among stalls filled with handicrafts and artisanal goods, and the festive air grew as night started to fall, and everything seemed to be falling into place. For the first time, at least for a few hours, I didn't regret coming back, even if I'd left behind the person I loved most in the world.

116

——

Leah

I'D NEVER PAINTED SO MUCH. Not that way, at least. I didn't have the same feeling as I did back when I used to shut myself up in my attic in Brisbane and let myself go until night fell. This was different, stranger, heavier. At some hard-to-determine point, holding the brush stopped being liberating and turned into an obligation. I wanted to believe this was more real, more mature, because in the end, this was work, something serious, and yet, at the same time, I couldn't escape that feeling of discomfort that seeped further and further into every corner of my studio as the days passed.

I started going out for walks. Maybe I needed to clear my head when I noticed how empty the apartment was and felt the brushes in my hands sucking away my soul. I learned to appreciate what Axel discovered as soon as he'd set foot in Paris: how nice it was to walk aimlessly through the streets, just taking one step and then another. Sometimes I felt as if I'd discover the answer to my questions right around the next corner. At other times I didn't think of anything; I just let my mind go blank as I moved.

Painting was no longer a relief.

Compliments no longer mattered.

My smile lost its glow.

117

—

Leah

I ASKED MYSELF IF YOU could ever forget yourself. Not pay attention to yourself. Not look at yourself in the mirror. Not stop to think about what you really want and, more importantly, why you want it. I guess there are weeks when the days of the calendar pile up and you don't even have time to cross them off and life goes by so fast, and I got lost in that: everything I had to do, obligations, some real, others that I just imposed on myself at some moment I couldn't remember.

And all at once, you're not you anymore. You've turned into another person.

The same, but with different goals, expectations, dreams…

And I kept repeating to myself, *Who do I want to be?*

118

Leah

I WAS AT A PARTY at the same hotel where Axel had climbed up to the roof to run away from a world he didn't understand. I remember how I told him, not long before he left, that I was happy when I was with him, despite everything. Maybe that was the little push I needed to realize that this place wasn't for me, because with Axel gone, all that was left were the dresses, the parties, meeting people I'd never talk to again, trying to be pleasant with everyone. Not that there was anything wrong with that; it just wasn't for me. It didn't satisfy me. The void I was trying to fill was still there, deeper and deeper, harder and harder to ignore, as if it were growing.

I tried to enjoy the dinner, but not even a few drinks could calm the butterflies in my stomach. Everyone around me was speaking French. I'd thought about signing up for classes, but part of me knew I wouldn't stay long enough to make serious progress. After several weeks on my own, painting more than ever, getting better reviews and more congratulatory claps on the back, I didn't feel any more whole or more satisfied. I was unhappy, apathetic.

I talked to a few people I knew from the studio during dinner, and when it was over, I left the multitude behind and climbed the stairs to the roof. I swallowed nervously as I walked over to the exact spot where I'd been with him, where his hands had been under my dress while he nibbled at my cheeks and made me laugh whispering silly remarks into my ear.

I leaned on the railing and looked down at the city.

Down below, the lights formed constellations. I thought how nice it would be to capture that image on canvas: Paris, the night, the lives throbbing amid the streets and streetlights, the bridges, the cobblestone streets. I closed my eyes as the hot summer breeze blew over me. I imagined the soft brushstrokes, the dark tones, the dazzling lights, the shadows rendered in damp paint...

Then I took a step back.

I returned to the party even though I knew no one would notice if I didn't. That was a moment of clarity, a flash, right then, as I walked among unknown faces and tables laden with drinks.

"Where'd you get off to?" Scarlett grabbed my arm.

"I needed a breath of fresh air."

"Come here, I want to introduce you to a friend."

Claire Sullyvan was a charming Englishwoman who ran a small gallery in London. Her eyes were friendly, her smile timid, and she didn't seem cowed by Scarlett's presence. I said nothing while Scarlett spoke to her of the progress I was making and all I had accomplished since coming to Paris, but I did ask myself what it was about that woman that had fascinated me so much when I first met her. She had presence, sure, but somehow she made me feel...smaller. Pleasing her had for some reason become more important to me than pleasing

Axel or the anonymous people in Byron Bay who had chosen to spend their money on one of my paintings at an exhibition of works that were truly mine. I should have been astonished by those people and not by someone I'd never win over, because she didn't like my style or the way I expressed myself through painting. She didn't like the way I put my feelings out there. So why had I worried so much about getting her to accept me, to recognize me? Why do we often put more effort into people who don't deserve it than into people who do, even when they're right there in front of us?

The ground seemed to quake beneath my feet.

"Are you all right, honey?" Claire looked worried.

"Yeah, sorry, I just felt a little faint."

"Here, sit down." Claire walked me to a chair and Scarlett ran off for a glass of cold water. "You look pale. Are you sure you're fine?"

I nodded, but no, I wasn't fine.

Because life hits you hard sometimes and you don't see it coming, especially when you're the one responsible for it and you didn't see it coming.

"Here, take a sip."

I grabbed the glass. Scarlett sat down beside me. A moment later, Claire left to go find her husband, and I could see her tapping her high heels on the floor impatiently.

"I can't say you've made a stunning first impression, but I'll try to fix it. I'm hoping to convince her to put some of your work on display in her gallery. It's small but prestigious. It's good publicity for you. The day after tomorrow, she'll visit our warehouse, and if everything goes as we wish, we'll get a positive answer next week."

She seemed to be waiting for a reply. When none came, she asked: "Aren't you happy about it?"

"Of course I am," I lied.

"It's hard to tell."

I tried not to groan. I knew Scarlett well enough to see that she wasn't mad, she just regretted not having her moment of glory, with me gushing and smiling and thanking her for all she'd done for me. She was like a little girl performing her favorite trick for an audience.

I turned to her and asked, genuinely curious:

"Don't you ever get bored of all this?"

"Of what? The parties, living in a hotel...? Of course not."

I said goodbye to Scarlett at that party, even if she didn't find out until sometime later, when I sent Hans a message so we could meet up and I could tell him I was leaving. I owed it to him, and a part of me knew he'd understand.

That night, I painted something, something that once more was born inside me. I scattered around colors and let loose the emotions bubbling up inside me, anxious to get out: a dark canvas full of the lights of a city I was already beginning to say goodbye to. I enjoyed it. Every brushstroke, every second of it.

When the sun was close to rising, I sat down in the living room of that apartment that felt so big without him and picked up the bowl of strawberries I'd taken from the refrigerator just before. I held one up and smiled wistfully as I saw how much it resembled a deformed heart. If Axel had been there with me, I'd have said that and laughed and popped it into my mouth before giving him a kiss full of that flavor he loved so much.

———

119

Leah

I READ SOMEWHERE THAT THERE are times when you need to fall down because the world looks different from below. And once you're there, if you want to do something, you've got no option but to stand back up. You don't always need a concrete reason to react, but sometimes there is one, a blow that makes you open your eyes. And the veil that was in front of them disappears. You start to see. To see differently. The colors that used to be muted suddenly turn robust and vibrant. You relax. You gather your strength. And you get up.

And in some way, you start to feel like yourself again.

120

Axel

MY HANDS SHOOK AS I opened the stepladder. I climbed it, step by step, with a knot in my stomach and a feeling of urgency I never thought I'd feel again. The canvas bag where I'd put all my things was covered in dust. I brought it down and took it to the living room and dropped it in the middle of the floor. With Elvis Presley spinning on the record player, I sat down and opened the zipper, asking myself how I'd possibly taken so many years to do something so simple.

I made myself a tea, even though I wanted something stronger, and went back and took out my tubes of paint. Many of them were dry. I took one that was still unopened and squeezed it hard until the yellow paint dripped out onto the wood floor. I don't know why, but that color reminded me of her smile, her tangled hair, her eyelashes, the sun. I dipped my finger in it and spread it slowly over the floor, covering the wood, tracing out the grain that disappeared beneath the layer of color.

My heart was pounding out of my chest, and I could hear the blood rushing through my veins. I knew something had changed.

121

—

Leah

SOMETIMES, MOMENTS PASS SO QUICKLY you barely even notice. Other times, it's the exact opposite. My last week in Paris was calm, and throughout it, the minutes seemed transformed to hours.

When I wasn't painting the first thing that popped into my head, I made a habit of going out for walks. In the mornings, I'd head up to Montmartre, the way I had with Axel. I'd sit on the stairs and think about everything and nothing: our first date there, how pretty the city was under a silvery sky, how my father would have loved to walk those streets, and how sad it was that he never would. Strangely, in those days of solitude and silence, I thought of my parents more than ever, maybe because they'd always be like a nest I could curl up in when outside a storm was raging, or maybe because I couldn't stop asking myself whether they'd feel disappointed in me if they could see me from somewhere.

It might sound stupid, but even though they were gone, I wanted to make them proud of me; I wanted to show them I was doing the right thing, and that they'd been the best parents in the world.

I'd failed them. But above all, I'd failed myself.

I guess you have to fall completely apart to know what you have inside you. It turned out that I had my own demons too: my pride, my vanity. Things I'd never known were there because nothing had ever awakened them. Things I didn't want to fall victim to again. Remembering Axel and how he'd been brave and had fearlessly confronted his feelings even when I didn't believe in him gave me strength. All of us can learn to overcome our mistakes and leave them behind.

I forced myself to reflect no matter how much it hurt. It's never pleasant to look in the mirror and see not the thing that you wish you were, but the thing you are and that you're trying to run away from.

I accepted it: for years, I'd needed someone by my side. First it was Axel. When that was over, I held on to Landon to keep from falling. Then Axel came back into my life and reminded me of how magical it was to live surrounded by color.

I had never really been alone.

I envied Axel for that, because he seemed to enjoy his solitude; he didn't need anyone beside him. If he'd had someone there, it was because he wanted to, not because he felt suffocated by the idea of stretching his arms out and not finding some pillar to take hold of. But still, I wanted to be that for him. Free, not needing him, but choosing him. As I took my walks, as I worked in the studio, that idea started to come together in my head, and I remembered something Axel told me once: "I want you to live, Leah. And once you have, I want you to choose me." That didn't mean I agreed with the decisions he'd taken, but I was starting to understand them. I was starting to see things from his side when he was farther away than he'd ever been and when, despite everything, I felt him so close.

On one of the last days I spent in Paris, I stumbled—literally—upon a record store and secondhand shop. I had my headphones on and my head in the clouds and didn't see the chalkboard sign in the middle of the street advertising a special price for customers buying three records or more. I went in. I don't know why, but then, I didn't know why I'd spent the whole day walking from place to place. It was just what I was in the mood for.

I spent a long time looking at the covers, the titles, and names of bands that brought back memories. I grabbed a few Mom used to like that I hadn't listened to in years, and when I was about to go to the counter and pay, I saw another one I knew very well, *Yellow Submarine*, with its cover full of unmistakable colors.

I bought it on an impulse, then went straight to the nearest post office, hurrying, with an intense, even overwhelming need of a kind I hadn't felt in a long time. I liked that, feeling the way I used to years before, when I was a girl and I did things without stopping to think for even two seconds, even if it sometimes got me into trouble.

Then I went home and breathed easier. I was happy. I cooked for the first time in ages, played music, enjoyed being alone. Really enjoyed it, without feeling sad or unfortunate. I baked a lasagna and ate it still hot, with the cheese almost bubbling. And when I lay on the sofa and closed my eyes, the puzzle piece I'd been looking for so long appeared suddenly, as if by magic.

For months, I'd been asking myself who I was, opening doors and looking into them, hoping I'd find myself. The problem was I hadn't stopped to think that what really mattered wasn't that. What mattered was finding out who I wanted to be.

And just that—just asking the right question or the wrong one—changed everything.

122

Axel

"A PACKAGE CAME FOR YOU yesterday," Justin said.

Surprised, I looked at my brother, who shrugged and walked into the backroom of the café. He came out a minute later with a thin bubble-wrapped envelope with the name of a shipping company on it.

"Doesn't have a return address," I noticed.

"I'd suppose there must be lots of people who want to kill you. You just awaken that feeling in those around you. But I'm curious enough that I'm willing to accept the risk that I might be handling a mail bomb. Go ahead, open it!"

I grunted like an animal at my brother before opening it. Then I felt a nervous twitch in my stomach and smiled like an idiot. It had been weeks since I'd smiled that way.

"A Beatles record? *Yellow Submarine*. Who sent you that?"

"Leah," I whispered, running my hands over the cover.

"What's the story with that?" He looked confused.

Happy—elated—I told him, "The story is, she still loves me. I'm the luckiest bastard in the world."

July

—

(WINTER, AUSTRALIA)

123

Axel

I COULDN'T STOP. I COULDN'T. I kept getting up thinking of color and going to bed covered in paint. Paint on my clothes, on my skin, all over my hands...

When I grabbed a brush, I vanished, fully absorbed in the next line, concentrating on what I was doing, and thinking of nothing more, not even of her. It was liberating. Finding myself in those sensations I thought I would never relive again. Painting. Being in the present, feet on the ground, eyes focused on the tip of the brush as I filled edges with color, rounded off borders, splashed life into the monotony.

Time started to pass more and more quickly.

And as the days went by, I coated everything in color.

124

Leah

I WAS TEMPTED TO CHANGE my ticket and get one to Sydney. I imagined how nice it would be to find my brother waiting for me at the terminal in the airport. I could hug him as tight as possible and soak in his warmth and his familiar scent. Then we'd stop at some fast-food place and catch up over a meal. We could go to his apartment, and I could stay a few days full of smiles and good conversation with him and Bega.

It would have been nice. But I didn't do it. I didn't change my ticket.

I needed to learn not to throw myself in someone else's arms every time life put something in my way. For once, I wanted to hug myself.

So I reached Brisbane one afternoon at the beginning of July when it just wouldn't stop raining. I'd spent four months away from Australia, but it felt like half a lifetime. Soaked, dragging my suitcase, I climbed into the bus and looked out the window at the streets I'd walked for three years now. It wasn't until then that I realized that I'd been stagnant there, still hidden in my shell, carrying around a burden of reproaches, bitterness, and fear.

My dorm room was just as I had left it. I opened the windows to let in a little fresh air and took out my clothes to hang them in the closet. I felt strange because all of a sudden, I got the feeling Axel was right there with me, even though he was so far away...

I asked myself what he was doing just then and smiled as I imagined him barefoot in his stretch of sea, sand clinging to his skin, the soft winter sun glistening on the fringes of his hair. Himself again, just as I'd always liked him. Unique.

I called Oliver to let him know I'd made it in okay.

"I'm glad to have you back home," he said.

"We've got too many *homes*," I replied.

"And none of them where they need to be."

"Someday, maybe, someday..."

"What are you going to do now?"

"It's still early. I'll go to the studio; I need to get some things I left there. I need to take advantage of the time, because my grant is over in a month. Hold on just a second, Oliver, someone's knocking on my door."

I lowered the telephone after asking who was there and not getting an answer. What I saw then confused me so much I stood there blinking and trying to make sense of it. My brother smiled, walked in, and hugged me so tight I could barely breathe.

"I wanted to get you at the airport, but I didn't get here on time," he said, backing away and rubbing the top of my head. "I like the do, pixie. You look gorgeous." He hugged me again.

"What the...? How...? What are you doing here?"

"I was on my way to Byron Bay, so I waited for you to come back so I could work the dates out. I'm leaving early tomorrow, but we can spend all day together."

He helped me put away some things, and once my suitcases were empty, we took a walk through town and sat on a bench just as it started getting dark out. I tugged at the sleeves of my thin sweatshirt and tried to be straight with Oliver, but it wasn't easy.

"I know I made a mistake, that I let my emotions cloud my mind, but at the same time, I think I needed some time away from him. I miss him so much it hurts, but I had to learn to be alone by myself. You're going to laugh. Or maybe get mad, I don't know. But you showing up here...it made me feel small. Because I was tempted to go see you in Sydney, and I didn't because I wanted to prove to myself I could handle coming here and not needing someone to hug me right away."

Oliver's forehead creased and he shook his head.

"Don't do that. Don't just go from one extreme to the other. I get what you're saying, and I agree that it's good for you to learn to solve your problems without always relying on other people, but sometimes you do have to rely on other people, Leah. You don't have to do everything alone. I'm your brother, and any time you need me to lend you a hand, I'm there. That's what relationships are, giving and receiving. There's nothing wrong with that."

"Yeah, but it is dangerous."

"Not if you look at it the right way. I mean, I don't need Bega to live, let alone Axel or the Nguyens. I lived without all of them for years, and look at me: I'm still here. I managed to solve my problems on my own, even if I might have liked a little help. But wanting help isn't the same thing as being dependent. I don't need them, but I want them in my life. That's a choice. You didn't need to see me today, but here I am, and I hope you're glad I came."

I hugged him, smiling, and decided to try and enjoy his company for the hours we had left together. I invited him to dinner, telling him I'd pay. I had a little savings left, and I used it, despite how much he complained and flirted with the waitress to try and get her to take his money. When I got my change, he gave me a dirty look.

"Why are you so stubborn?"

"Why are you?"

"It must be our genes."

I laughed. When I picked up the receipt, I saw the waitress had written her name and number on the back. I showed it to him as we walked down the street under a fine rain, and he blew it off, just as I did.

"Looks like you don't have much trouble hooking up."

"It's the years of experience."

"Really I'd just as soon not think about your and Axel's college days here," I said, wrinkling the ticket up and throwing it in the trash.

"Trust me, it's better that way." He started cracking up.

"That's not funny!" I pushed him.

"What do you want me to tell you?" He smiled nostalgically and then turned serious. "We can't change who we've been, but we can decide who we want to be. I remember I told Axel that. When you least expect it, someone shows up and turns your life upside down. I guess I was too focused on myself to realize that it had already happened to him. Come here, pixie."

He wrapped his arm around my shoulders and pulled me into his ribs, and we stayed that way until we reached the door to the dorm. He'd planned on going to a hotel, but I insisted he stay over in my room. We laid out some blankets on the floor and wound up lying there talking about life, our parents, the days we should have treasured more and thought about all the time now.

"Remember that Supertramp song Mom loved so much? What was it called?"

"'The Logical Song.' I bought that record recently."

"You used to dance to it with her in the kitchen."

"I was so little. I barely remember."

"I've forgotten things too." He looked up at the ceiling, which was dark except for the glare of the streetlights. The sound of rain kept us company. "But I do remember that in our house, there was almost always music."

"And color. Lots of color."

"Yeah, color everywhere."

"You need to get up early tomorrow," I reminded him.

"Yeah. We should try and get some sleep."

"Good night, Oliver."

"Good night, pixie."

125

Axel

IT WAS HARD FOR ME to ask Oliver to come to Byron Bay one day, but it was a delicate situation, and even if I didn't need him there for it, I wanted him there.

We decided to have lunch in a little spot facing the sea. After he finished his piña colada and it was starting to get late, I told him what I had in mind for that night. He blinked at first, confused, but when I gave him the details and told him my father and Justin would pitch in, he smiled from ear to ear.

So we did it. We carried on with the plan.

We went to pick them up once it was nighttime. First Dad, then Justin. Oliver laughed when he saw Justin leaving his house dressed entirely in black. He got into the back seat.

"What's so funny?" he asked.

"Nothing. I'm just surprised you took it so seriously."

"All you need is a ski mask to keep from drawing anyone's attention," Oliver added.

"I think your outfit's *sick*, son." Dad smiled.

"You want me to wear fluorescent green?" Justin complained.

"Actually, I'd fucking pay for that." I laughed and he slapped me on the back of the neck. "Hey, I'm driving!" I said. "Dad, say something to him."

"Something," my dad joked.

I smiled, shook my head, and drove through the silent, empty streets. I slowed down when we reached our destination and wheeled around the Joneses' old house to park in the back, behind the wall that faced the woods. When I parked, we noticed how quiet it was, and for a few seconds, none of us moved.

"We should get started, right?" I said.

"Give me a flashlight," Oliver said, stepping out and shutting the door softly behind him.

The rest of us followed. I felt strange as I remembered the night Leah had asked me to go there. I remembered shivering as I held her around the waist to get her over the wall that was now behind us, and how her hand held mine as we walked through the grass, and that intense, warm hug in the middle of that studio full of dust and paint...

I tried not to think of her, but there was no point.

She was beside me every step I took, when we opened the door, when we walked through the living room with the furnishings covered in sheets. She was there when we climbed the steps and looked through every room searching for memories it was now time to recover. Obviously for the new owners, that place meant nothing, they'd turn it to rubble and sweep away those lost moments along with the building dust, but for us, all those old objects and photos were throbbing with life, with joy.

After some struggle, we managed to throw our full backpacks

and the abandoned paintings that had remained too long in darkness over the wall. Justin gave his opinion on each step we took and urged us to be quiet every five minutes. Dad loved the idea that we were doing something illegal and keeping it from Mom. And Oliver could hardly speak as we gathered up those reminders of his family.

For the last trip inside, it was just him and me, while Dad and my brother packed everything into the trunk of the car. We went in one last time to look through all the rooms, our flashlights casting shadows.

"You all right?" I grabbed him by the elbow.

"Yeah. Thanks for this, Axel."

"Don't thank me; this was your sister's idea. She asked me to come here a couple of months ago, just a few weeks before we left for Paris. I... It's strange, I must have just taken it for granted that you all cleared the place out after the accident."

"We couldn't. Leah was so fucked up, we had just rented a small apartment, and all I could get was the really important stuff. It wasn't the best time, you know? I think there was even a part of me that didn't want to take anything, because it still hurt too much. I swear sometimes I can't believe we made it through."

He didn't need to say more. I understood.

Death is like that. It catches you off guard; it shakes you up and leaves you with a pain and emptiness so intense that you can't even think about the people who are gone. It's a shield, a way to keep going from one day to the next, pretending that something didn't happen that made the ground shake beneath your feet. But then time passes, days, months, years. You blink, and you realize that it's been four whole years since everything changed. And on some random afternoon, while you're listening to music, painting, or showering, you get shaken by one of those memories that would have saddened you before and now, all of a sudden, they're just...beautiful.

Yeah, beautiful. Full of light. Of longing.

And your suffering sheds its skin and loses intensity.

And the strong colors give way to softer ones.

"Even if it was Leah's idea, thank you for this."

Oliver gave me a comforting slap on the back.

I looked one last time at the living room where we had spent so much time with Rose and Douglas, with my parents and my brother, and with Leah growing up around me. I had no idea she'd become the love of my life.

Just before stepping outside, I looked at one wall and saw a painting of hers, one of the first she ever did, one that caught the eye of a family friend who invited them all to visit the gallery in Brisbane they were driving to on the day of the accident. I handed Oliver the flashlight.

"Hold this a moment."

I dragged the sofa over to the wall and stood on the back to reach the frame.

"Are you trying to kill yourself?" Oliver asked, waving the light back and forth.

"This is an act of love for your sister. The least you could do is lend me a damn hand."

"Let me give you some advice along with it," he said, climbing up beside me. "Don't try and be romantic. It makes you look pitiful. Just be yourself instead."

"Very funny," I murmured as I grabbed the picture.

Oliver helped me hold it as we lowered it from the nail. We went outside cackling and thinking how happy Douglas would be if he could see us just then. I waited for Oliver to turn around one last time in the weed-ridden yard to say goodbye. Then we tossed the painting to my father and jumped over the wall.

We got into the car. The silence was comforting.

"This was worth it," Oliver said, grinning.

I smiled, too, and stepped on the gas.

126

Leah

THOSE NEXT FEW DAYS, I thought a lot about that conversation with my brother. About the idea of wanting something but not needing it. When I digested that, when I realized that I was doing exactly that by taking things with Axel one step at a time, I enjoyed my solitude more, my walks at evening with my headphones on, listening to music, thinking of Axel, thinking of an *us* that was getting closer and closer.

And the less I needed him...

...the more I wanted him.

I savored his absence. Weighed it. Missed him deep inside.

I learned to feel happy with what I had. I learned to get up every morning in a good mood, hard as that was. I learned to enjoy every breakfast at the café on the corner while I picked apart my strawberry muffin with my fingers and looked out the window at the people passing by on the sidewalk. I learned to enjoy each day I spent in the attic with my brushes and the dust that blew in through the window and shone in the sun in the afternoon. I learned that success and failure go hand in hand and that you can't separate them no matter how hard you try. I learned to go to bed at night without crying, with a tingling feeling in my stomach that reminded me of how I felt when he touched me, when his lips covered mine, when he whispered in my ear with his gravelly voice...him, just him.

And I felt a tingling in my fingers, too, and it told me to paint, to feel again that painting was all I wanted to do, to enjoy the vibration in every brushstroke without thinking of fate or what other people would think of my work.

And a smile started dancing on my lips.

127

Leah

EVERY MORNING I GOT UP and I was closer and closer to Axel. To understanding him. I finally realized that sometimes the distance between holding on to someone and pushing them away is so short it can be hard to find, because we fear what we love: fragility, necessity.

I realized it had been so long since I'd forgiven him that I no longer remembered what it felt like to be angry with him, what I remembered was being angry with myself, but as the days passed, my rage and disappointment faded away, and the few crumbs left of them couldn't touch me, I was walking away from them fast now, surer of myself.

A week before I had to empty out the attic and leave it forever, I found myself walking to a totally different destination. I was listening to music and strolling aimlessly when I arrived in front of a door. I'd been in Brisbane almost a month, but I'd avoided going near it.

I sucked in a big breath and thought. I don't know how long I stayed there, looking at my own reflection in the glass, but when a neighbor came out with a dog on a leash, and I held the door open for him, I didn't let it slam shut. I went inside. I climbed the stairs. I rang the doorbell even though my pulse was racing out of control.

Landon opened up and blinked several times, as if he couldn't believe it.

"Leah..." His voice made me smile.

"I'm sorry I showed up without calling, but..."

"Landon?" A girl called his name.

He turned around and said something I couldn't hear.

"Sorry, I didn't want to bother you..."

"You're not being a bother, come on in." Landon grabbed my arm before I could walk off and took me into the kitchen.

A brown-haired girl with a ponytail gave me a surprised look before putting aside a blender with what looked like juice in it.

"Sarah, this is Leah."

"Nice to meet you." She smiled.

"Same. You need help?"

She looked at the blender and blushed.

"I think I broke it."

"Wow, a blender and a microwave, all in two weeks," Landon said while she frowned at him. "I guess I should rethink that fourth date."

Sarah slapped him on the arm and rolled her eyes.

"Maybe I should come back later," I said, but she shook her head.

"I was on my way out. Especially now, since my breakfast smoothie didn't work out too well." Her smile had something harsh in it that would have been irritating in another person, but I found it tender and infectious.

"I'll call you later," she said. From the corner of my eye, I saw Landon say goodbye to her in the doorway, kissing her quickly on the lips.

"She seems great," I said when he got back.

"She is," he responded with a grin.

"You look good together. Is it serious?"

"For now, anyway. One step at a time."

I didn't tell him sometimes the smallest steps change everything. He already knew that. After a few seconds just looking at each other, he came over and pulled me into his chest. It was a nice hug, full of gentleness and all the good things we'd shared together. And I realized that Landon had been right during that talk we'd had on the phone when I was up on Montmartre. We'd both needed each other. Maybe I'd needed him more and he needed me a little less, but neither of us had been totally free when we were together.

"I'm glad you came," he said.

"Me too."

"I thought about calling you tons of times."

"Why didn't you?"

"Because I knew you were the one who had to do it."

I nodded and hugged him again.

"I want to show you something, Landon."

I told him to grab a light jacket because it was chilly out. We left his building and walked for fifteen or twenty minutes. Landon said nothing, not even when I slid the key into the lock of my attic, my refuge where I'd hidden months ago, thinking I'd grown, not realizing I hadn't.

"Are you sure?" He looked doubtful before he climbed the stairs.

"Yeah." I pulled on his sleeve to encourage him.

Once we were on the top floor, I opened the door for him and encouraged him to go inside. He looked all around with interest, his eyes roving the walls before settling on my more recent pieces and the disaster on the floor where I'd dropped my palette the day before—that little shelter that was all mine.

"I'm really sorry I never let you into my world before. It was my fault. I wanted you... I just wanted it to be right."

"Thanks for this. You didn't have to do it."

"That's not true. You're my friend; you deserved it. So pick one, the one that speaks to you most. I want you to have something of mine. A happy memory." I stood by nervously as he decided.

He landed on one of my favorites. I liked that. Even though he couldn't read my work as well as Axel, that didn't mean it transmitted nothing to him.

When he was done, we spent the rest of the afternoon sitting there leaned against the wood wall with our knees pulled into our chests. Landon talked about his senior project, which he'd just turned in—I would need to start my own pretty soon. He told me about the night he'd met Sarah at a karaoke bar after a dinner with some friends at school and how funny she'd been on their first date. I confessed everything that had happened those past few months: the ups and downs, the slipups, the days I'd cried, the ones when I realized I was still in love.

"So now what?" he asked.

"I think it's time to go back home."

"It's funny," he said, "but even when I sometimes wanted to, I never managed to really hate Axel. I guess it was because he looked at you the way you look at things you want with all your heart but know you can't have."

I felt momentarily numb. It had been so long since I'd talked about him with anyone that even hearing his name made me quiver.

Axel. Four letters that meant everything.

"Promise you won't go this long again without talking to me," he said with gentleness in his eyes.

"I promise." I smiled and leaned my head on his shoulder.

August

—

(WINTER, AUSTRALIA)

128

Leah

I GUESS NOT ALL STORIES proceed in a straight line. Some are full of curves, and you don't know what you'll find around the corner. There are difficult stretches where it's hard to keep going, and you fall apart and have to pick up the pieces of yourself before you keep going. But everything passes. You learn to walk and to file off the sharp edges of the mistakes you've made. You learn to let go of the things that used to work and no longer do. You learn that every scar has a story behind it, and you don't have to cover them up; instead you can be brave and show them off proudly, the wounds that still hurt and the ones that have already healed.

That's what I did that day. Putting one foot in front of the other until I reached that house where we'd lived through so much together, I didn't hide. I walked calmly, focused on my surroundings, on the tree branches leaving shadows on the gravel and the damp grass growing next to the ditch.

When I caught sight of the house, with the wild ivy growing up one side, I felt a tingle in my stomach. I started walking faster. I had to stop myself from running. When I reached the door, I was so nervous I could have vomited. Holding my breath, I rang the doorbell. I wanted a few minutes that felt like forever, increasingly disappointed, until I realized Axel wasn't home.

In the past few days, I'd imagined that moment a million times. And it was always...perfect. The bell rang. He opened up. I threw myself into his arms because the need to touch him was more powerful than anything else. I looked for his lips. I looked for...relief.

But that didn't happen. So I did the same thing I'd done so many times before. I walked around the house, trying not to get caught in the bushes and trees growing flush against the windows. I cursed myself for being so dumb and wearing a dress instead of something more practical, but then I reached the porch, and the memories that overcame me pushed every other thought out of my head.

The magic. The stars. The music.

And then I saw the blue. The red. The violet. And I went weak in the knees. I gulped, felt the blood coursing through my veins, and without realizing it, I brought my hand to my chest. All over the floor were tubes of empty paint. Used, lived, felt.

I entered the house. Or better said, the house entered me.

Because when I opened the door that led out onto the porch and stepped inside, I felt the floor spinning under my feet and the walls full of paint embraced me. I held on to the doorframe to keep from falling and sobbed so hard I could barely breathe.

I was paralyzed as I tried to understand every brushstroke, every image, every line, all of them so full of life. Everything was color. Everything. Axel had painted the walls with his hands, and along with them bits of floor, the legs of chairs, the stools in the kitchen, even the surfboard that was leaning on one wall and the trunk where he kept his records.

He hadn't painted a canvas. He'd painted the objects themselves.

I smiled through my tears as I remembered how he'd told me one time he bought that house because he was in love with the idea of being able to do everything there. And he finally had. Literally. He'd filled it with color, his way, looking for every drab crack and corner, every board, dragging his brush across all of it.

I tried to distinguish the lines and colors crisscrossing the walls and see details of our story within them: that pair of lips in one corner, a soft caress, trembling stars scattered across the night, two bodies interwoven with desire forming the trunk of a tree with pale leaves, the sea, waves swallowing tatters of guilt under a soft light that reminded me of the scent of summer.

I dropped my purse on the floor and walked through the living room feeling the dry paint, the irregular surface of the walls, feeling on my fingertips how he'd painted over those surfaces, feeling... trying to feel him at every step. I ran my fingers over the edge of a wooden frame in what had been my bedroom, where every night I had longed to get up and go to his bed, steal a kiss, show him I was no longer a little girl. There was a gorgeous drawing there, colorful, one that spoke of other worlds.

On the larger wall next to the bed, he had painted a huge yellow submarine. It was beautiful. Special. With round windows in the middle of a blue sea full of starfish, other fish with big eyes, and an octopus with its purple tentacles wrapped around the submarine's tail end. The brushstrokes were soft and delicate, and seemed to glide effortlessly over the walls.

I was still standing there on the threshold when I sensed him behind me. I turned slowly. Very slowly. Trying to stand firm.

Axel was there, in the middle of the room, nude except for wet swim trunks. His chest was rising and falling and his eyes pinned to mine, burning, intense, full...

I wanted to say something. On my way from Brisbane, I had been cooking up a speech, some kind of declaration of intentions, but all those words vanished and I was left empty, trembling and staring.

Axel stepped forward, but then stopped as if he were scared to ruin the moment, break the invisible thread that united us. My mouth was dry. I felt happy, ecstatic really, but also tense. And awkward. Extremely awkward. Maybe that's why I asked the first stupid question that came into my head, because I needed to break the silence.

"Why'd you do this?"

"Because this room is for the children I'm going to have with you."

He said it seriously, but at the same time as if it were obvious, and as if we were wasting time staring at each other with several feet between us. I walked toward him, weeping and grinning, remembering the night he took me to the center of Paris and I came forward without hesitating, recollecting all the good we'd shared, a whole life.

"What would you have done if I didn't come back?"

"No fucking idea," he sighed.

I stopped in front of him, with just a few inches between his mouth and mine, breathing him in, absorbing that scent of the sea that I had missed so much. I couldn't stop crying, but for the first time in ages, they weren't tears of sorrow. They were tears of relief. Of joy. Of the good fortune I now felt. Of my heart, which was beating so hard. Of my yearning to touch him. And kiss him. Kiss him until I couldn't kiss anymore.

His lips were moist. He was so close I could almost feel them, and I remembered what his tongue felt like, his hot breath caressing me. We looked at each other. We looked at each other for an eternity, and the air around us turned electric. Axel slid a hand down to my waist and I looked down at those fingers that seemed to be feeling me to assure themselves that I was real, that he really did have me in front of him, and that our bodies still reacted even to those minor gestures. I looked up and dove into his eyes, blue as the ocean.

"So you're painting again."

It was a lame remark, but Axel grinned.

"So it seems."

"You've got to tell me why."

"Because I was scared to forget all the things I had inside me; there was so much there, too much... And you know I'm not one for words, but look around; what you see here is all we are together. We are the sunrises on the beach, the sound of the sea, starry nights on the porch, the urge to tear off each other's clothes, our songs, the red of sunset, all the brushstrokes I laid down thinking about you. We're these walls surrounding us, all that we've lived. And everything that's still to come."

"Axel..." I was bawling uncontrollably.

"Don't cry, please." He pulled me in tight, and I felt that at last I was home, that everything I wanted was in front of me and I could choose it without needing it, after living, after finding myself, after understanding who I wanted to be.

I pulled back and wiped my eyes.

"I had a speech prepared..."

"Babe, I can't wait anymore."

"...but I need to kiss you instead."

"Thank God." He touched the hem of my dress and pressed his lips into mine, and I melted in his arms in that house full of paint, of stories and scars that Axel had covered over with brilliant colors.

I closed my eyes and smiled as I kissed him slowly.

And then we were new. A blank canvas. But one filled with reflections from the colors that had been there before and those we uncovered and left slowly behind. A white tinted with orange. A bluish white. A yellowish one. A white shaded green.

A white of its own. Unique. Ours.

Epilogue

(A STRETCH OF SEA AT DUSK)

HE'S LYING ON HIS SURFBOARD looking at the sun's soft reflections on the surface of the water just before it disappears over the horizon. All at once, he remembers that day years back when he was in this same stretch of sea asking himself if he was happy and finding a shadow of doubt inside himself, minutes before his best friend asked him for a favor that would change his life forever.

Now he knows that happiness is complicated and fickle.

That it's risk, searching, learning to jump into the void…

And he did jump, a long time ago now. He thinks about that as he leaves the water and walks slowly to the house outlined between two palm trees, with ivy trying to climb over its roof. Then he sees her. He smiles slowly. She looks up.

From inside, he hears the happy chords of "Twist and Shout."

They watch each other as he climbs the steps of the porch. He stops next to her and looks at the complicated lines crossing that canvas full of color, so hers, so his, so chaotic, so measured. He doesn't say anything. He doesn't have to; he just smiles proudly before he goes inside.

She follows his movements with her eyes until he disappears.

Then she closes her paint box and cleans her brushes as the orange light seems to tell the day goodbye. She soon hears Axel in the kitchen making dinner. One time, long ago, she had thought how sad it was to be alone, knowing how special certain moments of life can be, moments now past and warehoused in memory. Now she tries to savor those moments when they happen. She tries to stay in that present he taught her to inhabit. And it's perfect. Beautiful. Even with its bitter parts, the days when the shadows win, the good, the bad. Him. The family you choose. Turning back only to gather strength and remember those no longer there, those who nonetheless stay close to us. But without pain now. With a nostalgic smile it's sometimes impossible to keep inside.

A few hours later, lying together on the hammock, his arms wrapped around her, they recall some of those moments. And they talk about painting, dreams yet to be fulfilled, that unknown future that will take them to who knows where, and magic, which is the one thing you can't do without. The desire for more. The desire for each other. And they become music again. Twinkling stars. Glowing colors. And he smells of the sea, the way she's always remembered him. And her hair is tangled, the way it was when he drew her one random day, just because he felt like it.

They just are. They've let it be.

He sighs and his lips rub against her ears.

"I'm thinking about submarines."

"Our yellow submarine."

ACKNOWLEDGMENTS

There are projects that take time to find their place, and when they finally do, they're surrounded by the care and attention of all the people who added their own grain of sand to them and helped them grow little by little. It's best to start with the home that opened its doors to this book and its predecessor. Thanks to my marketing and communications team, to Raquel and David, and Lola, my editor.

To my agent, Pablo Álvarez, who was the first person to believe in Axel and Leah's story, and who strove to make sure they ended up in the best hands (and they did).

To the readers who helped me improve these novels: Inés (your sincerity is always necessary), Dunia, Lorena, Elena, and my dear Bea.

To Nerea, who didn't hesitate to be part of this project, contributing illustrations and her talent before we even knew where it was going.

To María Martínez, for staying beside me.

To Neïra, Saray, and Abril, thanks for everything.

To Daniel, the best friend I could ever wish for.

To my family. And to my mother, for always reading me.

And to J, whose support made it possible for me to keep writing and lose track of time in front of my keyboard. And because when I look at him, I just keep hearing over and over, "We all live in a yellow submarine."

ABOUT THE AUTHOR

Alice Kellen is an international bestselling author of romantic fiction. She writes of universal crossover themes such as love, friendship, insecurities, losses, and longing for a brighter future, connecting with younger and older readers alike. She lives in Valencia, Spain, with her family.

Website: alicekellen.com

Facebook: 7AliceKellen

Instagram: @alicekellen_

Twitter: @AliceKellen_